Lieutenant Fury

G.S. Beard

W F HOWES LTD

This large print edition published in 2007 by
W F Howes Ltd
Unit 4, Rearsby Business Park, Gaddesby Lane,
Rearsby, Leicester LE7 4YH

1 3 5 7 9 10 8 6 4 2

First published in the United Kingdom in 2007
by Century

Copyright © G.S. Beard, 2007

The right of G.S. Beard to be identified as
the author of this work has been asserted by him
in accordance with the Copyright, Designs and
Patents Act, 1988.

A CIP catalogue record for this book is available
from the British Library

ISBN 978 1 40741 216 0

Typeset by Palimpsest Book Production Limited,
Grangemouth, Stirlingshire
Printed and bound in Great Britain
by Antony Rowe Ltd, Chippenham, Wilts.

CHAPTER 1

MAY 1793, TWELVE LEAGUES WEST OF CAPE ST VINCENT

'Sail ho!'

The hail from the masthead lookout reached Acting Lieutenant Fury as he paced the quarterdeck of His Britannic Majesty's thirty-two-gun frigate *Amazon*, bowling along northwards with a brisk westerly wind. He looked up at the man perched high above at the main-mast head, squinting his eyes from the sun's glare as he did so.

'Where away?' he bellowed back, cupping his hands round his mouth in an attempt to make his voice carry farther.

'Four points off the larboard bow and standing southwards sir!' the man yelled back.

Fury could already sense an air of excitement surrounding the men on deck. The strange sail would pass within speaking distance, and would be the first ship they had seen since leaving Bombay in late December, a little over four months ago. Fury had been expecting the hail for weeks now, ever since they had beat their way round the Cape of Good Hope and turned

1

northwards, following the south-easterly trades up the west coast of Africa towards the Mediterranean. Now, with Cape St Vincent and the coast of Portugal somewhere over to the east, it had finally arrived.

It would be a good opportunity to learn the latest news from Europe. Certainly when they left England over a year ago, events across the Channel had been dominating the newspapers. Many of the French aristocracy who fled when the peasant uprisings began were now living in England. Reports emanating from France in the summer of 1791 stated that King Louis XVI himself had attempted to flee into exile, only to be stopped at the border and sent back to Paris. He had subsequently been merely a puppet controlled by the new French National Assembly.

'What d'you make of her?' he shouted to the lookout.

There was a pause before the reply came back.

'Hard to say sir. I can only see her t'gallants at the moment, but she's ship-rigged for sure. Possibly a frigate sir!'

Fury automatically started pacing again as a number of calculations rushed through his head. In this visibility, with the lookout about one hundred feet above sea level, his observable horizon would be approximately twelve miles. If he could only see her topgallants over the curvature of the earth, the strange sail was liable to be a little farther than that. Still, with both ships

2

heading towards each other, it would not take long to come up with her.

'Well Mr Fury, what have we here?'

The voice startled him, dragging him away from his thoughts as he spun round to see Captain Barber striding across the quarterdeck towards him. The original hail from the lookout had probably drifted through the skylight in the roof of the captain's day cabin, sending him hurrying on deck to investigate. If he had heard the initial shout from the lookout it was logical to assume that he had heard the subsequent hails as well, but regulations demanded that Fury formally make his report.

'A sail to the north sir, four points off the larboard bow and heading south. The lookout can only see her t'gallants at the moment but thinks she may be a frigate sir.'

'Very well,' Barber replied, 'up you go Mr Fury and tell me what you make of her.'

'Aye aye sir!'

Fury was slightly surprised that Barber should choose him to go aloft now he was no longer one of the *Amazon*'s midshipmen. Nevertheless he was grateful for the activity.

He quickly snatched a telescope from the binnacle box drawer and made his way over to the larboard main chains, swinging his legs over the bulwark and perching himself in the channels with the shrouds stretching up above him. Placing his feet on the first of the ratlines and grabbing the vertical shrouds, he began to haul himself up. The fact that

3

the wind was coming from the west and so was pushing Fury on to the shrouds made things easier, but even so he was surprised by how much his heart was thumping as he reached the futtock shrouds leading up and out to the main top.

After he had been made acting lieutenant, discipline demanded that he no longer skylark in the rigging with the rest of the 'young gentlemen', and, thinking back, he was almost certain that this was his first journey aloft since then. The most exercise his duty as lieutenant had demanded of him so far was to walk the quarterdeck during his watches. He had grown out of shape, and as he finally made it to the masthead alongside the lookout, his chest heaving as he sucked in lungfuls of air, he made a mental note to go aloft at least once a day from now on.

He waited for his breathing to subside before hooking one arm through the rigging to steady himself against the ship's roll. Extending the telescope and raising it to his eye, he scanned the horizon with practised ease. The strange sail leapt into focus immediately, already hull up as the two vessels approached each other, probably about eight miles away now.

She was a frigate, and quite a heavy one by the look of her. On their current course, they would probably pass within a couple of cables' lengths of her. Satisfied, he snapped the telescope shut and handed it to the lookout, a painfully thin Welshman named Jones.

'Take this and keep her in sight. Report any changes.'

'Aye aye sir.' The tone of Jones' reply suggested he had just been told the obvious.

Fury started to make his way back down to the deck. As he descended, thankful that it was a lot easier than climbing up, he wondered what nationality the strange sail was. There was every possibility that she was British, but something about her told Fury she wasn't. He could not quite put his finger on what it was; the look of her hull maybe, or perhaps the cut of her sails. Whatever nationality she was, she would have the weather gauge on *Amazon* when they passed. Britain had not been at war with anyone when *Amazon* had left on her journey to India. Had things changed during their long absence? Certainly with events across the Channel escalating, the relationship between Britain and France had been volatile.

He reached the quarterdeck in a matter of seconds and dismissed the thought from his mind – Barber would no doubt take all the necessary precautions. Walking aft to the wheel he saluted and made his report to the captain, who now had Mr Douglas, the first lieutenant, beside him.

'Mmm,' mused Barber, 'so she'll pass two cables to windward of us on her current course eh? Well, we'll never be able to beat up to windward in time before she arrives . . .'

He was silent for a few moments while he considered the implications, no doubt following

5

Fury's own train of thought from a couple of moments ago, before finally making his decision.

'Very well, call the watch below. We'll shorten sail immediately.'

Lieutenant Douglas quickly turned round and started bellowing the orders which would bring the crew on deck, even those down below off watch.

'All hands! All hands to shorten sail!'

The ship came alive as the crew responded to the order, the vibrating thump of feet on planking reverberating around the weather deck as they rushed up from below. The bosun and his mates harried the men until they were all at their stations, petty officers and midshipmen checking their own divisions to ensure all were there. Although Fury still had no timepiece, there could have been no more than two or three minutes before the entire crew was ready and waiting for the captain's orders. Those months of drill had borne fruit.

'We'll shorten down to topsails only if you please, Mr Douglas,' the captain ordered.

'Aye aye sir!' Douglas replied, turning once more to shout his orders to the waiting men.

Fury looked up. The *Amazon* was carrying almost everything she could – courses, topsails, topgallants and royals, along with the fore-and-aft staysails and jib. Able seamen were swarming aloft so they would be ready to dash out on to the yards once the sails were ready, while the less skilled seamen

6

on deck were tailing on to ropes harried by the petty officers.

Slowly the staysails and jib came down as the men on deck hauled on the halliards. More men were hauling at braces to bring the royal and topgallant yards round square, spilling the wind from the sails and making the job of furling much easier for the yardmen high above. Halliards were overhauled, bringing the yards down on to the cap while the clew lines, buntlines and leech lines were hauled on to bring the sail up towards the yards.

The topmen were out on the yards now, feet braced against stirrups as they began fisting the canvas into manageable folds before fastening the gaskets round to secure the sail to the yard. Gradually the sky became more visible as first the royals were furled, then the topgallants, and finally the courses. The men aloft, tasks now completed, slid down backstays as quickly as prudence allowed to regain the deck in the fastest possible time.

Fury could already feel a significant change in the movement of the *Amazon* as her speed through the water gradually slowed, the deck ceasing to cant quite so steeply.

'Sail shortened sir,' reported Lieutenant Douglas, as though the captain had not been standing next to him and watching every move of the men for the last fifteen minutes or so. If Barber was impressed by the men's efficiency, he did not show it.

'Very well, beat to quarters if you please, Mr Douglas, and clear the ship for action, but don't run out the guns just yet.'

'Aye aye sir,' Douglas replied, walking forward shouting yet more orders.

A moment later a small boy of a marine came running up to the top of the companion ladder with his drum, and hastily started banging out a tinny raffle.

Fury made his way to the ladder leading down to the upper deck. Men hurried along in every direction in a highly organised rush, the stamping of hundreds of feet drowning out the sound of his own steps. His new rank of acting lieutenant meant that he was now stationed in command of the larboard-side guns in action, in place of Mr Scott who had been killed almost nine months ago during their fight with two privateers in the Indian Ocean. Not even a year ago! It seemed like another age after everything that had happened since. Cyclones, shipwrecks, cutting-out expeditions and boarding actions – Fury had seen enough fighting in those few months to last a lifetime.

He reached the upper deck where men were busy knocking down the bulkheads aft making up the captain's cabin, while his furniture was being carried below. In a moment the deck would be a continuous line of guns from one end to the other. The wash-deck pump had already been rigged and water was beginning to flow over Fury's boots as he walked further aft, men following with buckets to spread sand along the deck.

Here was Lieutenant Carlisle hurrying along the deck now, on his way to his station in command of the starboard battery of twelve-pounders.

'Good afternoon Mr Fury,' he said cheerfully. He was obviously glad, as most of the men were, to have the possibility of action – remote as it was – looming after four months of monotony during their voyage home. Captain Barber was not a rich man, and could not afford to pay for extra powder so that his men could fire live rounds during drills. He did allow the occasional firing of the guns after drill as a reward for the men's effort, but that was no substitute for real action.

'Good afternoon sir,' Fury replied, breaking into a grin at the sight of Carlisle's beaming face.

'What do you make of her, Mr Fury?'

Carlisle had been down below off watch when the sail was sighted, possibly in his small cabin reading or writing, and so his first indication of action would have been the sound of the bosun and his mates going through the ship rousing out the men below, swiftly followed by the marine drummer hammering on his small drum.

'A frigate sir,' Fury replied. 'She should be passing to windward of us soon, heading south. She was too far away to see her flag when I was aloft.'

'She'll probably turn out to be a Frenchman or a Spaniard,' Carlisle stated. 'It would be good to know if we are at war before we meet one of their ships, don't you think, Mr Fury?'

'Aye sir.'

Fury turned sharply at the sound of a loud clatter, just in time to see a couple of seamen picking up cutlasses and pistols which had obviously fallen from the arms chest placed by the mainmast.

'Handsomely there!' he bellowed, trying to stem the men's excitement.

He looked round at the deck, where all looked ready. Below, the galley fire would be out by now to minimise the risk of fire, while the surgeon would be laying out his tools – all newly sharpened – ready for the first poor victims.

He walked slowly along the larboard side, lit by the sunlight coming down through the open waist of the ship, studying the men standing around the guns with handkerchiefs tied round their heads to block out the noise and stop the sweat running into their eyes. Many were still in the process of removing the tompions from the muzzles of the guns, while the apron – a thin square piece of sheet lead – was taken from over the touch hole.

He could see all the necessary equipment laid next to each gun – sponge, rammer, handspikes and cheeses of wads. Between each gun was a half barrel, with grooves cut round the edge into which smouldering slow matches were placed, lighted ends hanging inwards over the water in the barrel to be used in the event of the gunlocks jamming.

By the side of these were large scuttlebutts of water, placed there for the men's refreshment during battle. Small boys – powder monkeys – were standing with cartridges newly brought up from the gunner down in the magazine, alert and ready to dash back down the hatch to fetch more once those had been used.

As Fury passed the waist, one look above gave him a glimpse of the sky, still a pale blue and dotted with clouds. It looked strange, criss-crossed with the lines of the splinter netting which had been placed over the deck above to prevent falling spars and blocks killing the men stationed below.

Bringing his attention back to the upper deck, he could see that the marines were already stationed at the hatchways to stop seamen going below without good reason, in the event that any man's discretion overcame his valour. Satisfied that the men were ready, he started making his way back aft, wishing that the gun ports could be opened so that he could see something of the situation outside.

Looking over at Carlisle perspiring freely in his full uniform, he was acutely conscious that he was not wearing a sword like the rest of the *Amazon*'s officers. He had not had time to purchase one in Bombay before they had left, and his old midshipman's dirk was not really appropriate for an acting lieutenant, so he made a mental note to remember to grab a cutlass from one of the arms chests in the event of a boarding.

The ship had become strangely quiet again now,

signalling that the *Amazon* was cleared for action with her crew waiting silently at their stations. Fury turned to look along the line of his crews stretching forward down the ship's larboard side. If they were to go into action, it would be his side which would have to fire first.

'Men!' he shouted, 'I want those ports opened and the guns run out like lightning if the order is given, so stay alert!'

He walked over to where Carlisle was standing.

'Larboard battery ready sir.'

'Very good,' Carlisle replied, 'now all we have to do is wait.'

CHAPTER 2

Captain Barber paced casually about the *Amazon*'s quarterdeck with Lieutenant Douglas alongside him. The sail coming down from the north-west was clearly visible from the deck now, even without a glass. He could make out her frigate's lines – the low sweeping hull hiding the menacing line of guns behind those closed ports. She was also under topsails only, like the *Amazon,* and it was obvious that they would pass a little over one cable's length away from each other – ideal gunshot range.

Barber had needed his telescope to see that she was flying the tricolour. Even now, he still had difficulty adjusting to the flag of the new French Republic. He looked up at his masthead for the thousandth time, checking to make sure that the Union flag streaming out to starboard had not vanished.

'Mr Douglas, have the hands on deck stationed ready to tack if I give the word. Station some men on the focsle to raise the jib and haul out the sheet to starboard in the event she looks like missing stays.'

13

Tacking the *Amazon* at that time would be critical, and if she missed stays and fell back, her stern would be vulnerable to being raked. If she looked like she would not turn, then raising the jib and flatting the sheet out to starboard would help push the bow round.

'Aye aye sir,' Douglas replied.

'In the meantime,' Barber continued, 'please station yourself at the quarterdeck rail overlooking the waist to relay my orders down to Mr Carlisle and Mr Fury if necessary.'

'Aye aye sir,' Douglas replied once again, moving away to organise the men before stationing himself at the quarterdeck rail and turning back to watch the captain for his signal.

Captain Barber strode over to the larboard bulwark with glass in hand to look across at the other ship, her cutwater producing a creamy foam as she sliced through the water. He raised the glass to his eye and scanned her deck. There were small figures rushing about, a speck of blue here and there betraying the presence of an officer. One in particular was stationary, possibly her captain, looking over at the *Amazon* and perhaps wondering if Barber was *Amazon*'s captain. He looked down at his blue full dress coat. Once they got closer he would certainly be distinguishable by his uniform. Despite all his precautions he wondered how to play the next few minutes. If they were at peace still, should he give his opposite number a wave as they passed, to signify the friendship of nations? Probably not – it would leave him open to a snub by the French captain.

He looked forward again, the ships now only about a mile from each other. He could feel the tension of the situation weighing down on him. Could they be at war? Even with only topsails set they would pass each other quickly, and so the Frenchman would have to be quick if he intended to unleash a broadside. The first sign Barber would have of that would be the raising of their larboard gun ports as they approached. He would then have to hope that his own crews would be fast enough to open their ports, run out and train the guns, and then fire before the Frenchman passed out of range. After that, her captain could dash down on *Amazon* in an attempt to pass across her stern and rake her, so it would be a case of tacking quickly to keep the *Amazon*'s guns bearing on her and to avoid giving the French ship that chance. With that in mind, the orders he had given were correct.

On and on they came, the figures on the Frenchman's deck becoming clearer as they approached. Barber was staring so hard at her hull, waiting for the slightest movement along her side, that his eyes were now beginning to ache, the sunlight reflecting off the wave caps dazzling him.

They were almost abreast now, the jib boom of the French ship stretching forward and just beginning to overlap the *Amazon*'s own jib boom. A movement from the forward part of her quarterdeck caught his eye, and he looked to see the man he had seen earlier, now clearly wearing a resplendent blue uniform – obviously the captain – waving to him, his hat high in the air as he shouted something which was whipped away by the wind.

What a fool he was! The French captain was merely greeting him as they passed, and there he was, expecting the worst with his ship cleared for action. He began to raise his right arm in the air in response, stopping halfway up as the Frenchman's gun ports suddenly opened.

'Mr Douglas!' he shouted frantically, 'Have the larboard guns run out and fire at will!'

He vaguely heard the first lieutenant acknowledge and shout his order down to Fury on the upper deck, while his own eyes remained glued to the French ship, her guns emerging from her ports like stubby black fingers as her crew hauled on the tackles to run them out.

Their bows were overlapping now and Barber heard the sound of rumbling trucks as their own guns were hauled out, the noise being cut off abruptly a moment later as the side of the French ship erupted in a rippling fire as each gun bore, the deep boom drowning out all other sounds as the muzzles winked with flame before the black smoke belched out, blowing away towards the *Amazon*.

He could not be sure where the broadside went, other than a vague awareness of crashing timber and screaming men down below, the deck heeling slightly with the impact. Almost at once the

Amazon's guns replied as the men quickly trained them and fired, the noise deafening and the deck heeling once more under Barber's feet from the recoil.

The men down below would be choking now as the smoke from the guns was blown back in through the ports by the brisk westerly wind. Nevertheless they had done well, Barber could admit that. Even with the head start from the French ship, the *Amazon*'s broadside had followed closely on the heels of the enemy's.

Lieutenant Douglas was next to him now looking out across the sea at their antagonist, already almost past them 200 yards away. Her name could be clearly seen now emblazoned across her transom. *Thetis*.

'Mr Douglas, I believe we are at war.'

Barber said the words calmly, as if he were merely commenting on the weather. Lieutenant Douglas stared at him for a moment with a wry smile creasing his face.

'Aye sir!'

As they watched, her transom seemed to foreshorten as she began the slow turn to bring her before the wind in an attempt to pass astern of the *Amazon* and rake her.

'We'll tack the ship if you please, Mr Douglas,' Barber said matter-of-factly.

'Aye aye sir,' Douglas replied, walking over to the binnacle to pick up a speaking trumpet to make himself heard.

'Ready about! Stations for stays!'

An unnecessary order considering the men had been ready at their stations for some time.

'Ready! Ready! Ease down the helm!'

The helmsman turned the spokes of the wheel through his fingers to port, the ship's bow gradually coming round towards the direction of the wind.

Barber looked over to where *Thetis* was swooping down on them, *Amazon* still broadside on to her now she was beginning to come up into the wind. Even as he watched, her side lit up once more as she loosed another broadside into *Amazon*'s hull, more screams and crashes from below combined with what sounded like falling blocks from above. He looked up quickly but could see no major damage aloft.

Almost instantaneously *Amazon*'s own broadside thundered out below, the smoke clearing quickly to give him a good view of the scars along the hull of the *Thetis* from *Amazon*'s twelve-pounders. The men were aiming well, he thought.

'Helms alee!'

Douglas was still shouting orders to bring the *Amazon* on to her new tack, stolidly ignoring the hail of shot which had just passed. The wheel was now hard over and the *Amazon*'s bow was approaching the eye of the wind, her way rapidly diminishing. The men stationed at the foretopsail were loosening off the sheets to spill some of the breeze from the sail and allow her to come up easier.

'Haul taut! Main topsail haul!'

The men at the main and mizzen topsail braces began to heave, swinging the yards round the other way, ready for the new tack. She was up in the eye of the wind now, all way lost as she hung there for what seemed like an eternity. Would she make it round? No, no . . . yes!

Her bow began to swing again, falling on to the new tack and saving Barber the task of ordering the men on the focsle to hoist the jib, as he was intending.

'Haul taut! Let go and haul!' Douglas bellowed, sending the men on the foretopsail braces heaving to bring that yard round on to the new tack also.

'Full and bye,' Barber snapped to the helmsman, the man immediately letting the *Amazon* fall off from the wind until she was approximately six points away before steadying her on her course, keeping an eye on the luff of the topsails to ensure he did not get too close.

On this course, and with *Thetis* running before the stiff westerly breeze, there was every chance that they could pass the Frenchman's stern and rake her. Barber looked across at her again but she was already turning to port, the more northerly direction turning her exposed stern away from the *Amazon*'s broadside. This captain was no fool. Barber jumped slightly in shock as the *Amazon*'s guns discharged once more under his feet, followed a second later by another broadside from the *Thetis*.

The smoke from their own broadside was drifting away down on to *Thetis* now, blocking his view, but it was clear that *Amazon*'s rate of fire was slightly superior to her opponents. The smoke began to pass, revealing *Thetis* wearing back round to a more south-easterly heading, bringing the wind on her starboard quarter.

Barber quickly walked over to the binnacle and peered down at the compass card housed within. South-south-west was their current heading. He turned to the helmsman once again.

'Starboard your helm. Bring her round to east-south-east and keep her steady.'

'Aye aye sir,' the man replied, easing the spokes of the wheel through his hand and peering at the compass card to note the course.

The *Amazon*'s bow began to swing round away from the wind, picking up speed slightly as the wind came round on to the starboard quarter. Another succession of crashes sounded as the *Amazon*'s larboard crews fired on *Thetis*, followed by a reply from the French ship after a slight pause.

Looking across at *Thetis*, Barber could see that she had finished her turn and was now about 300 yards away down to leeward, on much the same course as the *Amazon*.

On and on they went, it soon becoming clear that *Thetis* was on a slightly converging course to that of the *Amazon*, so that the staggered broadsides crashing out from each ship as the crews

20

reloaded and fired at their own pace, were progressively closer. It was also clear that the *Amazon*'s gun crews were firing three broadsides to the enemy's two, although Barber grudgingly had to admit he was surprised at the accuracy of the Frenchman's fire.

Another series of crashes rocked the *Amazon* and Barber saw one of the brass six-pounders on the quarterdeck lifted up and flung back off its carriage like a rag doll, its crew disappearing into bloody fragments as the shot swept through them, splinters flying across the deck from the smashed bulwark.

'Men,' he shouted, 'secure that gun!'

The crew of the neighbouring six-pounder abandoned their job for a moment and dashed over to where the gun was lying in the lee scuppers, threatening to slide about the deck. A quick handful of hammocks from the nettings along the bulwark sufficed to shore up the gun against the ship's roll.

Barber turned away from the proceedings and looked across once more to where the distance between the *Amazon* and *Thetis* had now shortened to a little over a hundred yards.

'Mr Douglas,' he said, turning to the first lieutenant who was still at his side, 'I've a mind to run down and cross her stern. Have the men at the braces standing by.'

'Aye aye sir,' Douglas replied, turning to tell off the men stationed at the braces as Barber strode over to the helmsman at the wheel.

21

'Starboard your helm,' he ordered, and once again the wheel spun anticlockwise through the helmsman's fingers, slowly sending her bow further away from the wind. Barber was looking forward along the deck and over to *Thetis* to judge when the *Amazon* had swung round far enough to send her down past the Frenchman's stern. 'Keep her at that,' he ordered the helmsman, just before he judged the course to be ideal.

He watched as the helmsman straightened the wheel, the *Amazon* coming round a trifle further before the rudder steadied her on course. Perfect! He smiled to himself.

The men at the braces were hauling the yards round to catch the wind at the most efficient angle, and the *Amazon* was now surging down upon *Thetis*, who was still drawing ahead on the same course, taken completely by surprise.

'Mr Douglas, inform Mr Carlisle to have the starboard battery standing by, ready to fire as they bear.'

Douglas acknowledged and moved over to the quarterdeck rail overlooking the waist to relay the order. Barber could hear a faint acknowledgement from Carlisle and then thudding feet as the crews dashed over to the other side of the ship to man the starboard battery. Twenty-five yards to go now, with *Thetis* pulling away on *Amazon*'s starboard bow, her stern beginning to show as *Amazon*'s jib boom began to cross her wake.

Barber fancied he could see panic on her quarterdeck as they watched the *Amazon* coming down on them, and they may even have started to turn up into the wind in an attempt to throw her stern away from the *Amazon*'s guns, but it was all too late. They were passing her now and the first gun going off forward confirmed it, followed slowly by each one in turn as they passed.

Even as he watched, her beautiful stern windows disappeared as the balls smashed through, tearing a destructive path along the whole length of her main deck. The lovely gilt transom had also vanished in a hail of splinters, smashed into pulp by more shot. Over the crash and thunder of the great guns Barber could hear the lighter fire of the swivels up in the *Amazon*'s tops under the command of the marines, who were pouring a murderous hail of canister on to the quarterdeck of *Thetis*. It would be interesting to see how long she lasted after that, he mused, the fire now slackening and warning him that they had already passed her stern.

'Quartermaster!' he bellowed, 'Port your helm. Come back round to east-south-east and keep her steady.'

The quartermaster acknowledged and relayed the order to the helmsman, and a moment later, with the aid of the men at the braces, the *Amazon*'s bow began to swing back to her original course, this time some fifty yards to leeward of *Thetis* and on her larboard quarter.

Intermittent firing continued, both from the

Amazon's forward-most guns and *Thetis'* aft-most guns, those being the only ones that would initially bear as the *Amazon* gradually overhauled *Thetis* to come back up alongside her.

Looking across as the smoke passed, it was obvious to Barber that some of the larboard-side guns of the *Thetis* were out of action, numerous empty ports staring back at him like missing teeth to signify the guns were not run out. More ear-splitting thunder from the guns down below showed that the men were firing as quickly as ever and there was a decided gap now until the enemy loosed off a ragged broadside, the crash of that followed instantaneously by the sound of smashing wood and stifled screams.

He began pacing the quarterdeck with Lieutenant Douglas falling in beside him as the two ships glided forward, broadside to broadside. On and on they went, the Frenchman lasting far longer than both Barber and Douglas had anticipated, even if her fire was now slackening considerably. She was probably one of the best ships the French had, with hand-picked crews and experienced officers. Two of her gun ports had been smashed into one jagged hole by numerous shot, and at least three of her larboard guns were now out of action.

Another crash sounded over to the left as another shot hit the bulwark, sending splinters flying across the deck not two feet in front of the pacing officers, both men watching as three men were cut down amid the hail, one clutching his side as it poured blood on to the deck.

A shouted order to those serving another of the quarterdeck six-pounders sent them over to the man, quickly lifting him and carrying him down to the surgeon and his mates.

'Poor bastard,' Barber muttered in a rare show of sympathy.

'Aye sir,' Douglas replied in agreement. He was convinced the man would probably rather bleed to death than be seen to by the surgeon, nothing more than a butcher in disguise.

He spared another glance over at *Thetis* and a movement high above her deck caught his eye, immediately prompting him to turn round and inform Captain Barber, but the captain was no longer at his side . . .

Fury had kept pacing up and down the upper deck all the while, he and his gun crews assisting Carlisle with the starboard battery now that their side had disengaged. He watched as the men, pouring with sweat and blackened from the smoke, reloaded, ran out and fired as fast as they could. His own eyes were stinging from the effects of the black smoke blowing in through the open gun ports, the back of his throat dry and hoarse as he shouted encouragement.

There had been many men killed or wounded. After the casualties suffered in India, Fury wondered how on earth they still had enough manpower to manoeuvre the ship, much less fight. As was customary, he had given the order to throw the bodies over the side like pieces of old rubbish to keep the decks free to work the guns. Perhaps he would feel guilty at the recollection of it afterwards, but now was not the time.

The Frenchman seemed to be firing solely at *Amazon*'s hull, probably in an effort to kill as many as they could before boarding. Nevertheless, their rate of fire was slackening noticeably now, providing further encouragement to the *Amazon*'s men as the long hours of drill took effect.

Another ball crashed into the *Amazon*'s side as he paced, and a moment later a man staggered against him, his face contorted in horror. Fury looked down to the man's arm, the skin raised and swollen, and it took him a moment to realise that lodged underneath his skin was a long sliver of wood, probably about six inches long considering it seemed to stretch the entire length of his forearm. Even as Fury watched, the skin began to turn black as it bruised, and he quickly marched the man over to one of the hatchways leading down below, signalling the marine sentry stationed there to let the man pass.

'Get yourself down below to the surgeon at once!'

The man looked at him blankly for a second, understandably still in shock, before pulling himself together and nodding, turning to go down the hatchway to where the surgeon and his mates would be at work just forward of the wardroom.

Fury walked over to one of the large scuttle-butts of water, trying to put out of his mind the thought of what agonies would await the wretched man once the surgeon began to cut and probe to extract the splinter. With only a mouthful of rum to soften the pain and a leather gag to bite down upon, he would most likely die on that table.

The water, although tepid and stale, was nevertheless refreshing as he thrust his head in and took a mouthful, the back of his throat seeming to burn more as he swallowed it.

He turned round to catch sight of Carlisle, hat in hand, shouting to his men to keep them going as he walked from gun to gun, assisted by the midshipmen running along the guns and jumping up and down in their excitement.

Fury walked over to a spot behind one of the forward guns and crouched down to get a view out of the gun port. There she was, still a hundred yards away and looking severely battered now along her hull and bulwarks, the occasional brief flash and roar followed by an eddy of smoke showing that she at least had some of her guns still in commission.

He was about to straighten up when he caught sight of a movement up high in her rigging. He quickly pushed his way forward through the gun crew who were busy reloading and thrust his head through the open gun port. As he did so he heard cheering on the deck above, and he quickly looked up at *Thetis'* masthead in time to see the battered tricolour of France come slowly fluttering down. They had surrendered!

He turned inboard, the relief surging through him.

'Cease fire! We have him lads!'

The men at the guns, most of whom would not even look out of the ports as they reloaded and fired, realised now that the fight was over. A ragged cheer erupted from the men along the upper deck as they stood up from their guns and congratulated their companions, more for emerging alive than for the actual victory.

Here was Lieutenant Carlisle now, hand outstretched as he approached. Fury shook it.

'Well Mr Fury, that was a hard-fought victory!'

'It certainly was sir. They put up a good fight.'

'That they did,' Carlisle agreed, looking round the deck. 'Well, I'll get these guns secured, you had better get up to the quarterdeck. No doubt there will be much work for us in the next few days.'

'Aye aye sir,' Fury replied, glad to be getting out of the choking atmosphere of the upper deck and hopeful that he may be allowed to go over with the boarding party and take possession of their new prize.

It took him only seconds to reach the top of the companion ladder leading up to the quarterdeck, squinting slightly at the bright sunlight as he looked around for the captain to receive his orders. There was the master, Mr Hoggarth, supervising the swinging out of one of the *Amazon*'s boats held on the booms over the waist, in preparation for going across to the *Thetis*. Lieutenant Douglas was over near the wheel with his back to him, his head bowed looking down at the deck. Fury hurried over to him, Douglas spinning round as he heard his voice.

'Have you any orders for me sir?'

Douglas did not reply, but merely looked at Fury for a moment as though they had just lost the battle, not won it. A quick glance by Douglas behind him drew Fury's gaze down towards the deck, where a pair of legs were sticking out of a bloody mess on the planking. Silk stockings and highly polished shoes with pinchbeck buckles. His family had never been rich – was all that Fury could think of as he looked down at what remained of the captain, his uncle.

CHAPTER 3

Fury woke up in his cot, lying there for a few moments looking round his tiny cabin, the black bulk of his tattered sea chest seemingly filling the whole room. Outside he could hear the sluicing of water as the *Amazon* limped to the south-east, with *Thetis* in company under the temporary command of Lieutenant Carlisle.

He still felt numb over the death of his uncle. He would have thought that his exposure to death over the last year would have steeled him against such grief, but it was not the case. When he had first seen his uncle's body it had been necessary for him to fight back the tears. Barber had always been a hard man, and very aloof, and had almost never shown affection towards him, but he had been more than fair to Fury. He liked to think that, with no wife or family of his own, Barber had always thought of him as a son, and he hoped in the past year he had not proved a disappointment. Certainly, with no father of his own to look to for guidance, Fury had learnt a lot from the man since he had come aboard *Amazon*. Fury's current rank of acting lieutenant was

30

solely down to Barber and the opportunities he had given him. Now he had nobody, and even on a cramped frigate such as *Amazon*, he felt terribly lonely.

It had been another disappointment to him when Douglas, in temporary command of the *Amazon*, had chosen Lieutenant Carlisle to take possession of *Thetis*, leaving Fury to work himself to a standstill helping to get the *Amazon* back into some semblance of order. The prisoners, some 150 of them, had all been transferred over to the *Amazon* and were now under strict guard by armed marines down in the hold. Their original crew of somewhere near 300 showed how terribly they had suffered during the fight, compared to which the *Amazon*'s butcher's bill of twenty-seven killed, including the captain, and thirty-four wounded, seemed relatively light.

Throughout the night and the whole of the next day the men had worked tirelessly plugging shot holes in the hulls of both vessels and repairing damaged rigging, and it was only once that had been completed that they had been able to get under way again. Yesterday had been spent driving south-eastward towards the entrance to the Strait of Gibraltar, where the east-going current had helped them to make a reasonable five knots. They were now no more than half a day away from Gibraltar, their destination, with Tarifa on the southern coast of Spain somewhere to the north-east, and the Barbary Coast of Africa to the south.

Soon the strait would be narrowing down to about eight miles wide, according to the chart Fury had seen.

No doubt it had been the number of prisoners under guard and the state of the two ships which had prompted Lieutenant Douglas to head for Gibraltar instead of continuing their journey home to England. It was obviously the safest bet considering the former captain of *Thetis* had informed them that war had in fact been declared by France on Britain a few months ago, in February, and so there was also a chance of meeting further French ships if they continued north.

Fury was surprised to find that the news of war had not affected him in the slightest. With the loss of Barber, his only patron, there was every chance that he would be demoted back down to midshipman again, losing many months in seniority. Now they were at war, he could at least console himself with the knowledge that his opportunities for advancement would be greater.

'Passing the word for Mr Fury!'

The faint shout reached him as he lay there and he quickly swung his legs out of the cot and jumped to the deck, hurriedly pulling on shirt, breeches, stockings and shoes, along with his old midshipman's jacket, before leaving his flimsy cabin.

With the captain dead and Lieutenant Carlisle on *Thetis*, there could be only one man on board passing the word for him, and the knowledge of

32

that brought with it the realisation that he was presently second in command of the *Amazon*, albeit only temporarily.

He was at the top of the companion ladder on the upper deck now, the guns all housed and secured and looking impotent strapped up against the ship's side. He turned aft to where the captain's cabins were now re-erected, passing the marine sentry who briskly came to attention, slamming his musket butt on the planking and announcing in a voice that would have carried on deck in a gale of wind, 'Mr Fury sir!'

Fury entered, his head instinctively cocked to one side as he stood to prevent it hitting the deck beams above. It was strange to see Lieutenant Douglas sitting behind the captain's desk, working away at the paperwork needed to keep a ship of war afloat. He was looking up now, studying Fury's face intently for a few moments before beckoning him to sit down in one of the chairs opposite. Through the stern windows Fury could see *Thetis* sailing along in their wake, about two cables' lengths away.

'How are you doing Mr Fury?' Douglas asked softly, as if speaking to a child and not an officer in His Britannic Majesty's Navy.

'I am very well, thank you sir,' Fury replied in a matter-of-fact tone. He had long since learned that superior officers had their own ways of approaching subjects, and it was best to let them get on with it until they got to the point.

'I have taken the liberty,' Douglas began, pointing to a number of items laid on the settee beneath the stern windows, 'of getting together some of the captain's personal belongings. As his next of kin you should take these and decide for yourself what to do with them.'

Fury studied the items. It was a paltry enough pile of belongings to represent a man's whole life. A mahogany box which could only contain Captain Barber's quadrant was sat in the middle of the pile. Next to this was a sword in its scabbard, the decoration adorning it identifying it as his dress sword. Barber would have been wearing his other sword when he was cut in two, and so there was no chance of Fury finding that now.

He could also see the plain mahogany box containing two pistols which the captain had always kept in his desk drawer – nothing fancy, but slightly more reliable than the average sea-service pistol, as well as more accurate, no doubt. Along with these was his personal telescope, various books on seamanship from Clark, Falconer and others, two little gold-plated watches, and a small amount of money.

'Thank you sir,' he said, shifting his gaze back from the pile of belongings to Lieutenant Douglas, still sitting there studying him intensely. Fury desperately wanted to ask the man about his own future, but could not bring himself to do it. 'Will that be all sir, only I've got the forenoon watch?' was all he found himself saying.

'Not quite,' Douglas replied, sitting back and seeming to relax slightly, as if he had just finished an unpleasant task and was now moving on to something more enjoyable. 'I have been reading Captain Barber's reports on events since first leaving England.'

A pause now, as if he expected Fury to say something, but Fury remained silent.

'He mentions you very favourably on a number of occasions, as does Lieutenant Carlisle during your time on the *Bedford* and the *Mornington*. For my part, I have drafted my report regarding the capture of *Thetis* and you will also get full credit for your part in that. With this in mind, I am hopeful that the Admiralty will see fit to let you keep your current rank of acting lieutenant until such time arises as you can face a formal examining board.'

'Thank you sir,' he replied, but Douglas held up his hands in protest.

'Do not thank me Mr Fury – a lieutenant is unlikely to hold much sway with Their Lordships at the Admiralty, but I will do my utmost for you. Besides, you are in your current position on merit, not favouritism. If I did not think you were ready for it I would see to it that you remained a midshipman until you were.'

'I understand sir,' Fury said. 'Will that be all now sir?'

'Yes, yes,' Douglas replied, 'you may go – and don't forget to take the captain's belongings to your cabin.'

'Aye aye sir.'

Fury rose from the chair and went over to the settee.

He would have liked to ask Lieutenant Douglas for some assistance in carrying all the things, but he was already bent back down over his paperwork, so Fury resolved to carry it all himself. The sword and scabbard he fastened round his waist, while the watches were small enough to carry in his jacket pocket, along with the few coins there. The rest – pistols, telescope, quadrant and books – he merely had to pile on top of one another and carry carefully out of the cabin, thankful that there was not much of a sea running so he could keep his feet easily on the gently heaving deck as he slowly made his way below.

'Stop!'

The seaman watching the sandglass snapped the order as soon as the last grain of sand had emptied itself into the bottom of the glass. The man next to him holding the log line immediately stopped the knotted line from running out any further and began to haul it in over the taffrail. Once the line was on board the knots were counted, while Fury stood nearby waiting.

'Well?'

The seaman seemed to ignore him for a moment as he finished counting the number of knots which had reeled off the line.

'Seven knots sir,' he reported at last, reeling the log line back in so it could be stowed.

'Very well,' Fury replied, walking over to the binnacle and picking up the slate housed within to record the current speed they were making. A quick check of the compass card revealed they were heading a little south of east until they had weathered Tarifa, the southernmost tip of Spain, at which point they would begin to head approximately east by north for the run up to Gibraltar.

He looked up to check each of the sails were drawing well, more through force of habit than because he expected them to be drawing badly. Each and every man on the *Amazon*, including the quartermaster and helmsmen, were prime seamen, well trained and highly experienced. Not once had he ever had to utter a stern warning due to lack of concentration. Still, it was as well to check, if only to let them know they were still being monitored – it would ensure they kept sharp.

He began pacing the larboard side of the quarterdeck, hoping in time to catch a glimpse of the southern coast of Spain. He was beginning to wish he had left his jacket down in his cabin, for although the sky was filled with cloud and the fresh westerly wind was sweeping along the *Amazon*'s deck, the sun filtering through was quite warm.

'Land ho!'

The shout came down from the foremast lookout.

'Where away?' Fury shouted back instantly.

'Three points on the larboard bow sir!' came the quick reply.

Fury looked around for the midshipman of the watch, finally catching sight of him forward on the focsle.

'Mr Howard!' he shouted to him, still somewhat uncomfortably. Even after five months of holding his rank as acting lieutenant, he still could not shake off the fact that they had all been 'young gentlemen' together. Giving orders to them always felt strange, especially now when he could be back to being a midshipman within the next day. 'Take a glass and aloft with you. You may make your report when you come down.'

'Aye aye sir!' the boy piped, rushing to get a glass before ascending the foremast shrouds to join the lookout at the masthead.

Fury stamped about impatiently on the quarterdeck until at last Howard returned to make his report, just as Lieutenant Douglas arrived on deck.

'Well Mr Howard?' Fury prompted.

'Land sir, now just abaft the beam. At first it just looked like a headland sir, but as it came abeam I saw water separating it from the rest of the coast, so it looks like an island sir!'

'Very good Mr Howard, carry on,' Douglas replied, turning to look at Fury.

'Tarifa Island sir?' Fury ventured.

Douglas nodded his agreement.

'Aye, lay her on a course of east by north a half

north please, Mr Fury. I shall be in my— the captain's cabin, if you need me further.'

'East by north a half north, aye aye sir,' Fury acknowledged as Douglas made his way back down below. 'Quartermaster, lay her on a course of east by north a half north, if you please.'

The quartermaster acknowledged and relayed the order to the man at the wheel. The helmsman let a couple of spokes of the wheel through his fingers as he peered at the compass card. When he finally announced that the course was set, Fury took a look at his watch – his uncle's watch – to see that it was ten o'clock in the morning. Putting the watch back in his pocket he began pacing again, head down and hands behind his back to pass the last two hours of his watch, at which time he would be relieved by the master.

Back and forward he went, seventeen paces to the taffrail, turn, and seventeen paces forward to the foremost quarterdeck six-pounder, the sweat gradually beginning to stick to the shirt under his jacket as he paced, the sound of the ship's bell at half-hour intervals passing unnoticed as he became engrossed in his thoughts, completely losing track of time.

'How are we going Mr Fury?'

The voice startled him and he looked up to see the master, Mr Hoggarth. It took him a moment to drag his mind into the present and give a sensible reply.

'Seven knots by the last heave of the log, Mr

Hoggarth. We sighted Tarifa some time ago and changed course to east by north a half north.'

He could still not get used to talking to the master on equal terms, or at least nearly equal. It was not long ago that Hoggarth had been teaching Midshipman Fury the art of navigation, and it didn't help the fact that he looked old enough to be his grandfather. In fact Fury would not have been surprised if someone had told him the master was old shipmates with Anson or Boscawen, so old did he look.

'This will be your first visit to Gibraltar will it not, Mr Fury?'

'Indeed it will Mr Hoggarth. But not yours I'll warrant!'

If the master was to be believed, then he had visited most places on earth during his career. Hoggarth broke into a broad grin at the jibe, his face wrinkling from years of sun and salt spray.

'What is it like?' Fury asked, eager as always to learn as much as possible.

'Well,' Hoggarth began, 'the first you will see of it is a massive rock jutting out almost to the Mediterranean, nearly 1,400 feet high at its peak. The fortress of Gibraltar stands at its foot, and it is joined to the mainland of Spain by a low isthmus now, although at one time it was most likely an island. It lies at the easternmost tip of Algeciras Bay, or Gibraltar Bay as it is sometimes called, with the town of Algeciras on the western side. Along the western side of the Gibraltar headland reaching out into the Mediterranean there is an extremely dangerous shoal of rocks extending quite far into the bay making a seaward assault virtually impossible. Which is why we've kept it from the French and the Spaniards for years.'

The ship's bell rang out at that moment – eight bells – noon, and the end of Fury's watch at last.

'I have the deck, Mr Fury,' Hoggarth told him, completing the formalities of confirming that he had now taken over as officer of the watch. 'It should not be long now before we sight it,' Hoggarth continued, 'It is an impressive view to behold if you care to wait.'

'Aye, I think I will Mr Hoggarth,' Fury replied, 'I'll take a trip up to the masthead to get a better view.'

It was true that the view aloft would be far better than down on deck, but the main reason was to avoid having to stand on deck in conversation with Hoggarth for a couple of hours or more. In addition, Fury had made his promise to himself that he would get aloft at least once every day to keep himself in shape, and he had not yet done so today.

Quickly ducking down the companion ladder to the upper deck and then down once more to the gun deck, he turned aft and made his way to his flimsy cabin, picking up his uncle's telescope from atop his sea chest and hurrying back up to the focsle. Stuffing the telescope into his waistband he climbed over the bulwark into the channels and began to haul himself up the starboard foremast shrouds.

It was surprising the difference a few days made, he reflected, as he reached the foretop and continued upwards. He was still breathing quite hard due to the exertion but his chest was not nearly as tight and he was no longer struggling for breath. A minute later and he was sitting on the topgallant yard, sweeping the horizon to his left with the telescope, trying to catch a glimpse of the coast of southern Spain.

It was an excellent glass, stronger than the standard ships' telescopes, and the distant coastline showed up as a low grey smudge separating sea and sky. He tried to bring up a mental picture of the *Amazon*'s charts of this area. If his memory served him correctly it would not be long before they entered the narrowest part of the strait. At that point it would be easy enough to see both the Spanish coast to the north and the Barbary Coast to the south on a clear day like today. Not long after that and they would have their first sighting of Gibraltar, so that by nightfall they should be anchored safely. After that, who knows what will happen . . .

CHAPTER 4

Fury could clearly see the jutting tower of rock through his glass, falling down almost vertically to the ground, which stretched forward to end at Europa Point. He scanned to the south-east but could not see the Jebel Musa at Ceuta on the north-eastern tip of Africa. The Jebel Musa and the Rock of Gibraltar together were said to form the mythical Pillars of Hercules.

Giving up, he concentrated on their approach to Gibraltar, sweeping the glass back northward. The *Amazon*, with *Thetis* following astern, was just weathering Cabreta Point and Fury watched as it slowly crept by, hearing the faint orders on the deck below which turned the *Amazon* north-eastward to sweep into the bay along the eastern side, before she would finally be in a position to anchor up at the New Mole.

'Deck there!'

The shout from the nearby foremast lookout startled him.

'Deck here!' came the shout back, from Hoggarth by the sound of it.

'Ships at anchor in the bay sir!' the lookout

43

continued, pausing slightly as he counted. 'Five sir, and all line-of-battle ships by the looks of 'em!'

Fury swung his glass round quickly, the ships leaping into view clearly now that they had weathered the point. Definitely line-of-battle ships, that much was obvious even from this distance with their massive hulls and double row of gun ports. It looked like they were anchored off the New Mole.

He had a sudden apprehension that they were the enemy – maybe Gibraltar had fallen, taken by surprise at the onset of war. He looked carefully but could not quite distinguish flags at this distance, although his fears were quelled somewhat by the look of the ships – they certainly did not look French, even to his inexperienced eye.

The *Amazon* had completed her turn now and was slowly coming into the bay, Douglas having taken in her courses so that they were under topsails only at the moment. A glance back at *Thetis* showed that Carlisle had followed suit. It was not long before Fury could distinguish the flag flying from each of the ships, the Union Jack. One of them – the biggest – a massive three-decker lying with her bow pointing out into the bay, was also flying a red ensign at the fore masthead; the ship was carrying a vice admiral of the Red no less!

Snapping his telescope shut he began to climb down, his legs and buttocks stiff and aching from two hours sat on the yard. It was unlikely that they could see the flag from the deck because one

44

of the other ships was swinging to her anchor in front of the three-decker, blocking their view somewhat. Reaching the focsle, he made his way back along the gangway to the quarterdeck where Douglas and Hoggarth were standing over by the larboard bulwark, telescopes to their eyes.

'The big three-decker is flying a red ensign at her fore masthead sir,' he volunteered.

'Is she indeed!' Douglas exclaimed. 'Mr Turner!' he shouted, turning to the signal midshipman standing by the signal halliards. 'Hoist our number. Mr Fury, please inform the gunner and ask him to kindly make his preparations for the salute.'

'Aye aye sir,' Fury acknowledged, making his way below to inform Mr Tapsell, the gunner.

The man looked flustered when Fury told him, his puffy red cheeks turning even more scarlet as he rushed around to get everything ready, calling for his mates all the while.

By the time Fury reached the deck once again the *Amazon* was well into the bay along the eastern side, a man now standing in the fore chains with a line tied around his chest securing him to the foremast shrouds as he heaved the lead, calling out the depths to Douglas and Hoggarth standing by the wheel.

Midshipman Turner was standing with his glass to his eye, no doubt keeping it trained on the flagship to watch for any signals.

'No signal yet Mr Turner?' Douglas asked impatiently.

'No sir, nothing,' Turner replied, glass still to his eye.

Douglas was nervous, that much was obvious by his question. If there was any signal, Turner would inform him immediately and Douglas knew it. Still, Fury could not blame the man, coming in to anchor under the eye of a strange admiral with no instructions received as to where he should anchor.

A glance forward confirmed that the best bower anchor had been freed from the cat tackle and fish tackle which held it in place against the ship's side, and was now hanging vertically from the cathead by a single rope, the stopper. The cable had been led through a hawse hole and reattached to the anchor some hours ago, while a suitable length was now laying in lines along the upper deck, the inboard end secured to the bitts.

Fury took a quick look around the deck where every man was at his station, ready to furl the sails and drop the anchor as soon as the command was given. One thing was certain: Douglas could not have asked for a better crew with which to come in and anchor, even if it was slightly short-handed. The casualties suffered during the battle with *Thetis*, and then the necessity of sending men aboard as part of the prize crew, had reduced *Amazon*'s number to around 140 men from an initial compliment of 240.

On and on they glided, the sea much smoother now that they had entered the shelter of the bay.

The five battleships were clearly visibly about a mile ahead, and there was still no signal to acknowledge their arrival.

A quick word to the helmsman from Douglas sent the *Amazon* turning slightly to starboard so they could anchor in front of the larger battleships but slightly further inshore, taking advantage of the fact that the *Amazon* would draw only about seventeen feet compared with the larger ships' draught of around thirty-four feet.

'Mr Fury!' Douglas shouted, 'You may begin the salute.'

'Aye aye sir,' Fury acknowledged, bounding down the companion ladder to the upper deck where the gunner was waiting with his crews to begin the *Amazon*'s salute to the unknown admiral. 'Very well Mr Tapsell, you may begin the salute.'

The gunner acknowledged the order, turning round to the first gun.

'Fire one!'

The first gun boomed out as Fury made his way back up to the quarterdeck, the others following at five-second intervals so that after just one minute and five seconds, the thirteen-gun salute had been completed.

Seconds later Fury nearly jumped in surprise as the first deep boom of the flagship's reply resonated around the bay, eleven guns in all. Once that was completed a quick look from Douglas sent Fury calling down to Tapsell to begin the salute to the fort and garrison of Gibraltar.

Those guns, and the fort's reply, largely went unnoticed by Fury as he concentrated on looking forward once more where he could see that only a quarter of a mile separated them now from the first ship, with the big three-decker just behind her. A few moments later and another curt order from Douglas to the helmsman sent the wheel spinning, the *Amazon*'s bow quickly turning to larboard into the wind, her way through the water diminishing as the wind tried to push her back. Finally, her forward momentum all gone, she stopped. The anchor was dropped without incident as the sheets were let fly and the topsails furled.

Fury looked across to starboard where the line of battleships was anchored side on, the nearest about half a cable's length to the north, but further away from the shore. He could make out the names emblazoned across the stern of the first two ships. The first, a two-decker, was the *Agamemnon*, while the large flagship beyond her was the *Victory*. Over to larboard, *Thetis* could be seen slowly coming to her anchor about a cable's length away from the *Amazon*, Carlisle doing a good job with only his small prize crew on board.

He caught sight of Midshipman Turner suddenly lowering his telescope and begin flicking through the pages of his signal book. Fury looked across at *Victory* to see a Union flag breaking out at the mizzen topmast head followed by their own number. He could guess what the signal was right away, his guess confirmed a moment later when Turner made his report to Douglas.

'The flagship's signalling sir. Captain to repair on board.'

'Very well, acknowledge it Mr Turner,' Douglas replied, turning round to Fury. 'Have the launch hoisted out please, Mr Fury.'

'Aye aye sir,' Fury replied, but Douglas was already hurrying down to his cabin below to make himself presentable and to collect his reports.

Fury had just finished supervising the men hoisting out the launch from its booms over the waist, using the yard tackles and fore and main-mast pendant tackles, by the time Douglas returned on deck. The launch's crew were all waiting to go down into her, newly dressed in their best rig.

'Mr Fury, you will be in command until I return,' Douglas said formally as he made his way over to the entry port, a canvas bag under his arm containing all the *Amazon*'s reports for over a year.

'Thank you sir, and good luck.'

Fury waited patiently as Douglas made his descent down the *Amazon*'s side into the waiting boat, using the battens fixed to the outside of the hull. Fury watched him until his head had disappeared below the level of the deck before he turned away to make himself busy, unable to wait quietly to see what news the first lieutenant brought back.

It was nearly two hours before Douglas returned.

Fury heard the shout as the boat approached from below decks as he completed a check of the *Amazon*'s hull with the carpenter, Mr Stubbs. By the time the boat had hooked on, he was back on the quarterdeck, nervously waiting to see what news Douglas would bring. Was his acting rank to be withdrawn? Douglas arrived on deck at last and returned Fury's salute.

'Anything to report, Mr Fury?'

'Mr Stubbs is just finishing his check of the hull, sir. Nothing too serious, but we may need a spell in the dockyard to get to some of the shot holes properly.'

'Very good. No doubt *Amazon*'s new captain will see to that.'

'I see, sir.' Fury had known *Amazon* would be getting a new captain with the death of his uncle, but even so the thought of it was still upsetting to him. He was not looking forward to seeing another man at Barber's desk. 'Everything went well with the admiral I take it, sir?'

'Yes, thank you, Mr Fury. Admiral Lord Hood has requested an interview with you immediately, so you had better make yourself presentable.'

'With me, sir?' Fury was shocked. What on earth could the admiral want with him? Perhaps he wanted to inform Fury himself that he was being reduced back to midshipman. No, Douglas would do that, surely. Most likely he wished to offer his condolences over the death of his uncle. He may even have known Barber personally.

'Yes, with you, Mr Fury. You had better shake a leg, you do not want to keep him waiting.'

'Aye sir.'

'And make sure you have all your certificates and journals with you.'

'Aye aye sir.'

Fury was even more worried now after Douglas' last request, but he resisted the urge to ask why the admiral wished to see his journals with no small effort. He merely saluted and made his way below to get himself ready.

Fury sat stiffly and self-consciously in the stern sheets of the *Amazon*'s launch as they rowed past the stern of the first ship, the *Agamemnon*, curious faces looking down on them from her bulwarks as they passed.

'Put your backs into it,' he growled at the oarsmen, more to relieve his own anxiety than because he was unhappy with their progress.

They were approaching the flagship now, towering above them with Fury deliberately refraining from looking up as they neared, knowing too well that her sides would also probably be full of staring faces.

'Boat ahoy!'

The shout came from above, no doubt from the *Victory*'s quarterdeck. He glanced across at Gibbins, Captain Barber's coxswain, and gave him a slight nod.

'Aye aye!' Gibbins shouted back, signalling that the boat had an officer on board.

51

Fury's attention was diverted as the boat was hooked on to the *Victory*'s side, rising and dropping slightly against her stationary hull. He collected the canvas bag containing his certificates and journals and straightened his sword, making sure it would not trip him as he clambered out of the boat. A small pause while he waited for the right moment, and then he was on the *Victory*'s side, climbing up her tumblehome using the battens provided. He passed closed gun ports on either side of him before he reached the open entry port located in the *Victory*'s side, reaching up with his hands to haul himself in, stepping on to the middle deck and instinctively straightening his sword once more as an officer waited patiently in front of him.

'Acting Lieutenant Fury of His Majesty's frigate *Amazon*, reporting on board sir.'

The officer was wearing the uniform of a captain with more than three years' seniority – probably the flag captain.

'I am Captain Knight. Welcome on board, Mr Fury.'

'Thank you, sir.'

'If you would care to follow me then, Lieutenant, His Lordship will see you immediately.'

Fury followed as Knight led the way aft along the middle deck to a ladder leading to the deck above, Fury glancing aft to where the officers' cabins and wardroom were. Reaching the upper deck, Knight turned aft once more, leading Fury over to larboard, past a saluting sentry and through a doorway. Further aft now and through another doorway which, judging by the carpeted floor and long table contained within, was the admiral's dining cabin stretching the whole width of the ship.

Fury was feeling particularly nervous now, the soft quiet tread of his shoes underfoot on the thick carpet heightening his tension. One more door awaited, Knight this time pausing and knocking before entering and leading Fury through to the admiral's day cabin, the huge sloping stern windows behind overlooking Gibraltar.

Vice Admiral Lord Hood was sat behind his desk as they entered, looking up as Captain Knight introduced him.

'Acting Lieutenant Fury, My Lord, of the *Amazon*.'

'Thank you Captain Knight,' Hood said, transferring his gaze over to Fury.

Knight silently made his way to a chair next to Hood's desk and lowered himself into it. Fury shifted his feet awkwardly at the silence as Hood studied him for a moment. He had only been in the navy a relatively short time, but even Fury was aware of the reputation of the man, one of England's greatest admirals. He fitted his description perfectly; the large beaked nose, the dark bushy eyebrows and the grey hair, combed forward to hide a receding hairline. His mouth was narrow and there were veins showing across the bridge of his nose and his cheeks, perhaps a sign that Hood enjoyed his liquor.

'Please take a seat, Mr Fury,' he said at last, motioning to a chair opposite his desk which Fury sank into gratefully, fearful lest his legs would give way. 'My condolences at the death of Captain Barber,' Hood continued. 'He was a credit to the service.'

'Thank you, My Lord.' Had Hood summoned him to the flagship merely to pass on his commiserations at his uncle's death?

'I have interviewed Lieutenant Douglas this morning,' Hood continued, 'as I am sure you are aware. He has informed me of your excellent conduct during the *Amazon*'s voyage to India. He speaks very highly of you.'

'That is kind of him, sir.'

'Nonsense, it has nothing to do with kindness. Mr Douglas has given a fair appraisal of your abilities based upon what he has seen, no more.'

Fury sat in silence, unsure of what to say. Hood sat studying his face for a few moments more, before glancing down at the package on Fury's lap.

'Those are your certificates and journals, I take it?'

'Yes, My Lord.'

'Excellent. Pass them to me, if you please, Mr Fury.'

'Aye sir, I mean, My Lord.'

His clumsiness over Hood's title was doing

54

nothing to calm his nerves as he half rose out of his chair and passed the canvas bag over the desk to him. Hood took the bag and passed it to Captain Knight, still sitting in silent observation. Knight opened the bag and proceeded to leaf quietly through the paperwork, heightening Fury's curiosity and tension still further.

'Tell me, Mr Fury, how have you found your duties since being made acting lieutenant?'

Fury turned back to Hood. 'I believe I have grown into it over the past months. I flatter myself that Captain Barber's faith in me has not been misplaced.'

'I don't suppose it has. And you have continued with your studies?'

'Yes, My Lord, every day when off watch.'

'Excellent!' There followed another small silence as Hood digested Fury's response. When he finally spoke again his tone was firmer and more businesslike. 'Suppose you are coming into soundings from a long voyage, Mr Fury. How would you prepare for going into port and anchoring?'

Fury looked at Hood for a moment, completely taken aback by the sudden question. He could see out of the corner of his eye that Knight had abandoned his scrutiny of his certificates and journals at Hood's question, and was now looking solemnly at Fury. Hood's eyebrows came together in a frown.

'Well?'

'I, er . . .' Fury tried to clear his brain under the

intense stare of Admiral Hood. The continued silence prompted Hood to open his mouth again to speak, but Fury's memory came back to him at that very moment. 'I would order the anchors got off the bows and the cables to be bent on, sir,' he replied hurriedly. 'Single the stoppers and shank painters, and get the anchor buoys rigged.' Fury paused for a quick breath and a chance to get his racing thoughts into order, before continuing. 'Have the lead lines readied in the fore chains, with breast bands rigged for the leadsmen, and have the tiers cleared out and sufficient cable ranged along the deck.' Fury opened his mouth to continue but Hood's raised hand waved him into silence.

'Thank you, Mr Fury, I think we can be satisfied on that score. Now, suppose you are on a lee shore, and had neither room to veer or stay, nor any anchoring ground. How would you put the ship's head round the other way?'

Fury's brain was sufficiently warmed now after the initial shock of Hood's first question, so that only a short pause for thought was necessary before the answer came to him.

'I would put my helm hard alee. When she comes head to wind, I would have the fore and main tacks raised, make a run with my weather braces and lay all aback at once, then haul forward my lee tacks and bowlines as far as I can, that the ship may fall round on her heel. When the mainsail begins to shiver I would haul it up, fill my

56

headsails and shift the helm hard aweather. Once the wind is on the other quarter, haul aboard the main tack and bring her close to the wind.'

'Very good. Now you are in chase of an enemy's ship of war, upon a wind with all your sails set. She is directly ahead of you. On which side would you engage her?'

'That would depend, My Lord.'

Fury disliked prevaricating in the face of a direct question from a senior admiral, but he felt he had no choice.

'How so?' Hood responded, with not a hint of surprise or irritation.

'It would depend on the weather, My Lord. Ordinarily I would engage her to leeward, so she could not put away before the wind, and in anything of a sea, she may not be able to open her lower tier of gun ports. If in only light breezes and hot weather, however, I would consider attacking from windward, to let them receive the smoke and heat of the fire.'

Hood nodded his head in apparent satisfaction. Again there was no sign from Knight in the corner.

'You are chasing from the wind, and carry away your main topmast. How would you proceed?'

'I would haul up the mainsail, and send hands into the top with a rope or hawser, to clap on that part of the mast which hangs down, then cut the lanyards of the main topmast shrouds and lower away. Once down and the rigging cleared away, unsling the main yard, get the fore tackle on it and bowse forward the yard, and get the spare topmast ready for the crosstrees. Clap the hawser on, and sway it high enough for the rigging.' Fury took a breath to steady himself, and opened his mouth to complete his explanation, but Hood's hand waved him into silence.

'Very well, Mr Fury, I think we have heard enough.' Hood looked across at Knight and received a nod in response. 'Congratulations, Mr Fury, you have just passed your examination for lieutenant.'

Fury thought for a moment that he had misheard. He opened his mouth to speak, but closed it again when nothing came out. Finally he found his tongue.

'Sir?'

'As I said, Lieutenant Douglas spoke highly of your conduct during the past year, and felt confident you were ready for the step up to lieutenant. There was a formal examination held on board the *Agamemnon* this morning, but unfortunately it was too late to have you allocated a place. In view of your late uncle's achievements I decided to examine you myself in company with Captain Knight. I am pleased to say that Lieutenant Douglas' confidence in you was not misplaced. I shall have your name added to the list of passed officers from this morning's examination, and my clerk will draft up your commission upon receipt of your certificates and journals.'

'I – I don't know what to say, My Lord. Thank you.'

'You have nothing to thank me for, Mr Fury. If I had found your seamanship to be lacking, I would have reduced you back to the rank of midshipman immediately. I shall have Captain Knight pass on your certificates and journals to my clerk, so he may write up your commission. You shall be informed in due course of your next appointment, so for the time being return to the *Amazon* and attend to your duties.'

'Aye aye My Lord.'

Fury got to his feet and touched his forehead in salute. Captain Knight led the way through the cabin door and forward through the admiral's suite of cabins, pausing only momentarily to drop off Fury's certificates and journals to Hood's clerk, before escorting Fury towards the ladder leading down to the middle deck and the entry port through which he had arrived. One glance out of the port when they had reached it showed the *Amazon*'s launch still hooked on below.

'Thank you sir.'

'You are welcome, Mr Fury. With any luck you should know of your appointment within the next couple of days.'

'Yes sir.'

Fury saluted and made his way down the battens attached to the *Victory*'s side, scrambled into the bottom of the launch with the ease of long practice, and went to the stern sheets, infinitely more relaxed now than on the outward journey.

'Push off! Give way all!' he ordered, the men at the oars bending their backs as they started the stroke.

Away from the *Victory*'s side, Fury looked up at her black and yellow striped hull, her masts and yards stark against the sky amid the tangled criss-cross of rigging. The sharpness of the grief that he had felt during the last few days since his uncle's death had dulled for the first time at the realisation that he was now made lieutenant. His commission would start from last December when Barber had made him acting lieutenant, meaning he already had nearly six months' seniority. The knowledge of the debt he owed to Barber resurfaced at that thought, so he turned his attention back to the *Amazon* as they approached in an effort to block his uncle from his mind. The journey back to her seemed to take only a fraction of the time, and it hardly seemed two minutes before they were hooking on and making the launch fast with painters.

Fury, his hands now free of certificates and journals, fairly bounded up the side and on to the deck, returning the salute of Hoggarth as he turned to go below to his cabin.

'Mr Douglas requested your company in the great cabin as soon as you returned on board, Mr Fury.'

Fury sighed his disappointment at not being able

to reflect on his promotion in the solitude of his own cabin.

'Very well, Mr Hoggarth.'

He made his way down to the upper deck and hastily returned the salute of the marine sentry as he announced Fury's arrival. Douglas was sitting behind the captain's desk when Fury walked in, and looked up eagerly.

'Well, Mr Fury. How did it go?'

'Very well, thank you, sir. Lord Hood has confirmed my promotion to lieutenant.'

'Excellent! I knew you would not let me down. Do you know of your appointment?'

'Not yet, sir – hopefully in a couple of days.'

'No matter. I am sure we can keep you busy enough until your departure.'

'I understand you spoke well of me, sir. Thank you.'

Douglas waved away his thanks.

'You have deserved it, Mr Fury. And it is what your uncle would have wanted.'

'Aye sir.'

The cabin was engulfed in silence for a few moments at the reminder of Captain Barber. Douglas finally broke it.

'Very well, that will be all.'

'Aye aye sir.'

Fury saluted and swept out of the cabin, feeling only relief. Not because he had actually secured his promotion – although he knew he had been extremely lucky in that respect – but because he would be leaving the *Amazon* soon. With his uncle now dead there was nothing left in the *Amazon* but memories, and he was glad to be free of those, whatever else the future might hold.

CHAPTER 5

'Here we are sir, all done!'
The tailor placed on the table a package containing Fury's new full dress lieutenant's uniform – jacket, white single-breasted waistcoat, breeches, fine silk stockings and new tricorn hat. The hat had cost him a pretty penny and would go straight into his sea chest until needed for special occasions. Laid next to the package was his new undress jacket – a single-breasted blue lined coat with standing collar and nine buttons down the short front, while the back proceeded further down to end in tails. The pockets, round cuffs, lapels and collar had no fancy lace but were piped in white. Fury studied the three gilt buttons on each of the cuffs and pockets, gleaming with the plain fouled anchor design, gloomily deciding that it would not be long before they lost their shine. He pulled off his scruffy midshipman's jacket and laid it on the table, pulling on his new jacket over his waistcoat and buttoning it down the front. The collar felt stiff, but would loosen with wear, no doubt. Other than that, it was an excellent fit. If only he could

have afforded new black Hessian boots, he thought, looking down at the scuffed and worn pair he was wearing.

'Would you like me to dispose of this for you sir?' the tailor said, pointing to his old jacket. No doubt he would be grateful for the extra cloth he could get from it.

'If you would, please,' Fury replied, lifting his second new hat off the table and planting it firmly on his head.

Carefully lodging the package beneath his right arm, he gave his thanks to the tailor and walked out on to the narrow street, the coolness of the shop immediately giving way to the bright sunshine and heat of Gibraltar's early afternoon sun. It had been his intention to take a trip up to the Moorish castle situated on the north-western slope of the rock, but the heat made him think better of it. He had made the mistake a few days ago of climbing the rock in the noonday sun, and the memory of the discomfort was still fresh in his mind. It had almost made him sympathetic to the Barbary apes which lived on the rock, until one of them had picked up a large stone and hurled it at him for venturing too close.

Instead he walked along the cobbled street back towards the harbour, the bustle of people making their way along the narrow road jostling him and increasing his irritation. The buildings were high on either side of the street, but even so they seemed to provide little shade from the sun, the whitewashed exteriors only serving to reflect the glare more intensely.

He turned on to Main Street, glad to be out of the stifling atmosphere of the side streets, and quickly passed the Convent, the official residence of the governor, not even looking up to admire the gardens or the ornate balcony at the front of the building. He was engrossed in his thoughts, mentally going through how much he had spent in the last few days.

All of it had been necessary of course – uniforms for his new rank, a sword to wear next time he went into action so he did not have to rely on a sea-service cutlass, and lodgings while he waited to join his new ship. His uncle's belongings had certainly saved him a large sum of money. He did not need to buy a quadrant, telescope, pistols or a full dress sword, while he also now had all the books on seamanship he would ever need. Still, it was surprising how the money mounted up and he was lucky that his rank of acting lieutenant had been confirmed, so that he had been able to collect six months' back pay. That, along with the small amount which had been in Captain Barber's desk, had been just about enough.

He was due prize money of course, but that would not come through for months; on top of the prizes the *Amazon* had taken in the Indian Ocean, there was now the *Thetis*. She had not yet been condemned by the adjudicator but there should be no problem on that score – she was seaworthy enough. It was ironic that the death of his uncle should result in Fury gaining a much larger share of prize money than he would ordinarily have received. It seemed like even in death, Barber was helping him.

He reached the harbour and a turn left along the front soon brought him to the George Inn where he was staying. Like many sailors when ashore, he had instinctively found somewhere to stay overlooking the sea. He paused before going in to glance out to where the *Amazon* was still swinging gently to her anchor, the *Thetis* a cable to larboard of her.

It had been nearly two weeks now since he had formally left her, a departure made easier by the fact that the crew had been kept so busy with repairs they hardly noticed he was leaving. As for the officers, only Lieutenant Carlisle, Midshipman Turner and Midshipman Howard remained, the new officers assigned by the admiral making his last day seem strangely unreal, almost as if he had been on another ship altogether. He was glad also to get away before the new captain arrived on board – he would no doubt have found it difficult seeing a stranger in his uncle's cabin.

He had received a message from Lieutenant Carlisle only a week ago, telling him that the new captain had arrived on board, and had transferred the entire complement of his old command over to the *Amazon*. The new captain had been given his step up in rank after a marvellous defence of his sloop against a much larger French frigate, escaping only by superlative seamanship and the onset of nightfall. Nevertheless, his sloop was so badly damaged she was condemned by the dockyard back at Gibraltar. As a result, *Amazon* found herself overmanned and distributed a number of Captain Barber's original crew throughout the ships of Hood's Mediterranean fleet. Fury wondered whether he would be reacquainted with any of them on his next ship; it would be good to see some familiar faces at the beginning of his first commission.

He was sweating now. He could feel his thin shirt beginning to stick to him beneath his waistcoat and new jacket, prompting him to dive through the front door of the George Inn into the relative coolness. It seemed remarkably dark after the bright sunshine, and it took a moment for his eyes to become accustomed to it. The tables within were beginning to fill as more patrons sought to avoid the heat of the afternoon sun, most of them naval officers from what Fury could see, with the occasional scarlet tunic betraying the presence of an army officer.

'A glass of wine sir?'

Fury was startled by the appearance of the innkeeper by his side – the man never missed an opportunity to increase his profits slightly.

'No – no thank you,' he replied quickly.

The man's face fell as he attempted to make his feelings clear about naval officers who lodged there but didn't drink, all without saying a word.

Fury walked towards the wooden staircase leading up to the landing. Several men, mostly wearing navy uniforms, glanced at him disinterestedly as he passed, perhaps wondering what ship he was from. The timber stairs creaked in protest as he walked up, reaching the landing at the top which was covered with a thick, dark blue carpet. His tread underfoot was silent as he made his way down the corridor, past rooms on either side with paintings of past naval engagements adorning the walls between each closed door.

Reaching his room, he gratefully flung his jacket on to the bed and stripped off his waistcoat, opening his shirt to let the slightest breeze from the open window cool him. Sitting on the bed, he reached over to the small table next to it and picked up the commission sent to him by Admiral Hood's clerk after his interview, signed at the bottom by Lord Hood himself.

By the Commissioners for executing the Office of Lord High Admiral of Great Britain and Ireland &c and of all His Majesty's Plantations &c.

To Lieut John Thomas Fury, hereby appointed Lieutenant of his Majesty's Ship *Fortitude*.

By Virtue of the Power and Authority to us given We do hereby constitute and appoint you Lieutenant of His Majesty's Ship *Fortitude*, willing and requiring you forthwith to go on board and take upon you the Charge and Command of Lieutenant in her accordingly, Strictly Charging and Commanding all the Officers and Company belonging to the said Ship subordinate to you to behave themselves jointly and severally in their respective Employments with all due Respect and Obedience unto you their said Lieutenant; And you likewise to observe and execute as well the General printed Instructions as what Orders and Directions you shall from time to time receive from your Captain or any other of your superior Officers for His Majesty's service. Hereof nor you nor any of you may fail as you will answer the contrary at your peril And for so doing this shall be your Warrant.

Given under our hands and the Seal of the Office of Admiralty this eighteenth day of May 1793 in the Thirty-Third year of His Majesty's Reign.

At the bottom left was a heading entitled 'Seniority', under which was written '14 December 1792', the date on which he had been promoted by Captain Barber to acting lieutenant. That date determined which lieutenant was more senior on each ship.

Reaching over to the table again he picked up the remaining two folded pieces of paper. The first – his passing certificate – he placed on the bed without looking at it, while the second, the wax seal already broken, he unfolded and read through once more to make sure he had forgotten no detail.

HMS *Fortitude*,
Gibraltar Bay.

Lieutenant Fury,
   Report on board HMS *Fortitude* at eight o'clock on the morning of the 5th. Bring your dunnage and report your arrival to the officer of the watch. We will be weighing on the 6th.
Yr servant,
Wm Young, Captain.

He had been slightly disappointed when he had found out that he was being appointed to a seventy-four, but after some reflection he was gradually coming round to the idea. Certainly his quarters were likely to be much more comfortable than what he was used to in a crowded frigate.
   He slowly refolded the note and lay back on the bed. The 5th was tomorrow, and all he could think about was getting back to sea again, and a chance to repay the French for the death of his uncle . . .

'Aye aye!' the oarsman bellowed in response to the ship's hail, after a quick glance at Fury.

The boat was approaching one of the big two-deckers anchored in Gibraltar Bay, Fury studying her lines as she grew nearer. The gilded writing on her stern had just passed from view, along with the two rows of ornate windows plastered across just above her name – *Fortitude*. Both rows of gun ports were open to let in as much breeze as possible between decks. The boat scraped against her side while the oarsman hooked on.

Fury fumbled in his pocket, pulled out a couple of coins and thrust them into the hand of the nearest man.

'Thankee sir!' he said gratefully, staring down at them in his leathery palm.

'Wait alongside while I organise some men to hoist my chest on board,' Fury ordered, straightening his new coat and pushing his hat further down on to his head as he got up and moved towards the ship's entry ladder.

'Aye sir!' the man replied as Fury leaped, his hands gratefully grasping the rope hanging down on either side of the battens.

Reaching the deck, he looked around him in surprise at how much bigger she was than the *Amazon*. The main difference, though, was the poop deck, a separate smaller deck right aft above the quarterdeck, only present on third rates and above. The captain's quarters were directly underneath the poop, so that on leaving his cabin he would be immediately on the quarterdeck with the wheel in front of him. Much more convenient than a frigate, where his cabin was underneath the quarterdeck on the upper deck.

Looking skywards, Fury could see that his daily trips aloft would be much more demanding here with the extra height of the masts. Dragging his gaze away, he straightened his sword and stepped forward to salute what he assumed to be the officer of the deck, a man in his mid twenties with sandy hair and tanned features.

'Lieutenant Fury, reporting on board as ordered sir,' he said, touching the brim of his hat.

'Welcome aboard Mr Fury. My name's Dullerbury.'

Fury took the proffered hand.

'May I have some men to help hoist my chest on board?'

'Of course,' Dullerbury replied, turning to where a group of seamen were busy reeving some rope. 'Gooseman! Take some men and get the lieutenant's chest up from the boat. Then have it taken down to his cabin.'

'Aye aye sir!' Gooseman replied, at once nudging his companions to follow him.

'So you're the new lieutenant eh?' Dullerbury said, turning back to Fury. 'What's the date of your commission?'

'14 December last year. How about you?' Fury asked.

'16 May '91,' Dullerbury answered. 'You're the junior. Then me, Parker, Oldroyd and Ross, the first.'

'I see,' mused Fury, more to himself than anyone. He hadn't of course expected anything else than to be the junior, this being his first real commission.

A thud behind him told him that his chest had just arrived on board.

'This is your first time on a seventy-four is it, Mr Fury?'

'Yes sir,' Fury replied, turning back to Dullerbury. 'Where will I be berthing?'

'Officers' cabins are in the wardroom on the upper deck. Your cabin is the foremost on the starboard side. Follow these men and they'll take you there. I'll let the captain know you're on board. No doubt he'll call for you when he's ready to see you.'

Fury touched his hat again, the compliment being returned by Dullerbury, before he turned and followed the two seamen who were now carrying his sea chest forward to the hatchway leading below. Penetrating the gloom of the upper deck, Fury looked at the guns as they moved further aft, eighteen-pounders by the looks of them and much larger than those on the *Amazon*. A quick count revealed fourteen ports a side – twenty-eight eighteen-pounders on the upper deck, while down below would be the lower gun deck, carrying the massive thirty-two-pounders.

Looking aft past the upper part of the main capstan he could see the rows of flimsy cabins down each side of the ship stretching away to the stern, where the wide stern windows along with the hanging lanterns cast some light down in the wardroom. A long table stretching down the middle of the rows of cabins was obviously where the officers dined, it being occupied at this moment by a group of men enjoying their breakfast, the babbling of voices becoming louder as they approached. The men carrying his chest walked straight to his empty cabin, leaving the chest within and knuckling their foreheads as they hurriedly left. Fury turned to the table where the conversation had now all but died away.

'You must be our fifth,' came a voice from among the diners.

'I am indeed. My name's Fury – John Fury.'

'Fury eh? With a name like that you must be a fire-eater!' came a retort.

'Take no notice of him,' someone else joined in, rising from the table and proffering an outstretched hand, which Fury took. 'My name's Ross, first lieutenant. Allow me to make the introductions.'

Ross looked around the table, indicating with his hand each man in turn as he presented them. Even after the introductions, the names were still a blur – Fury had never been good with names – only a vague recollection that the men sat there consisted of the second and third lieutenants, a marine captain, the master, the purser, the surgeon and, of course, the first lieutenant.

'Would you care to join us for breakfast?' asked

one man – the marine officer, judging by his uniform.

'No – no thank you. I have already eaten. I think I'll get settled and take a look around her.'

He touched his hat and entered his cabin, the space almost entirely dominated by the large black eighteen-pounder trussed up against the ship's side. A quick struggle to place his sea chest underneath his cot was all the effort needed to settle in, and he left the room barely five minutes after entering, acknowledging the glances of the still-eating officers as he left.

His visit to Lord Hood in the *Victory* aside, this was his first time on board a line-of-battle ship, and he wanted to completely familiarise himself with her as early as possible, deciding to start on the lowest deck and work his way up.

He started on the orlop deck – he did not think it necessary to look into the main hold and cable tiers – passing through the surgeon's and purser's cabins, and the various storerooms down below. Then it was up to the lower gun deck where the men were just finishing their breakfast, removing mess tables and utensils as they hurried back to continue the day's work, giving Fury a chance to inspect some of those great thirty-two-pounders. The lower parts of the jeer capstan and the main capstan were down here also, the upper part being on the deck above allowing more men to operate the capstan at the same time but on different decks.

As he finished inspecting one of the guns, he became aware of a seaman hovering nearby, no doubt waiting for Fury to leave so he could finish clearing away. Fury straightened up and turned to make his way aft, but was interrupted by the seaman.

'Beggin' yer pardon, sir, but welcome aboard.'

'Clark!'

Fury stood looking at him in shock for a moment as the recognition sunk in.

'It's good to see you, sir.'

'And you. How do you come to be on *Fortitude*?'

'I was transferred from the *Amazon* when the new captain brought his own crew over. I was lucky enough to be posted here, and a right fine ship she is, too.'

Since saving Fury's life in the Indian Ocean, he had been an ever-present companion, and Fury wondered for a moment if it was luck or whether Clark had somehow contrived to get posted here deliberately. He dismissed the thought immediately; it would be impossible for a common seaman to have any influence in his posting. Nevertheless it was nice to see a friendly face. The keen sense of loneliness he had felt since the death of his uncle was softened slightly with the knowledge that Clark was aboard.

'She looks a fine ship indeed. Are there any other Amazons aboard?'

'Aye sir. Thomas and Cooke, and Crouder.'

All three of them had taken part in the night-time

cutting out of the *Earl of Mornington*, and Fury's spirits rose further at the news that they were here.

'Excellent! I look forward to seeing them. No doubt you have work to do, Clark, so I'll not detain you any longer.'

'Aye aye sir.'

Clark knuckled his forehead, his face still creased in a huge grin, and moved off. Fury smiled as he watched him go, and then started to make his way aft to the gunroom.

The gunner and all the midshipmen berthed here, and it was much darker than the wardroom above, as expected with no stern windows this far down. A group of four midshipmen were standing in a huddle next to the gunroom table. Fury turned quietly to leave, reluctant to disturb the young men during their leisure time.

'Admit it, Francis. You're nothing but a coward!'

The sentence was delivered with venom, and made Fury pause. He turned towards the voice.

'You're not fit to wear the uniform!'

The speaker was a midshipman of about Fury's height, but probably a little younger. The object of his tirade was another midshipman, much smaller and even younger still.

'How long have you been aboard? Over two years, and you're still a disgrace to your profession. You'll never make a seaman.'

The older midshipman persisted with his insults, and even from where he was standing

Fury could see the younger boy clench his fists down by his side. Fury stepped forward to intervene, still unseen by the group of boys, but he was too late to stop the younger of the protagonists charge at his adversary. He caught him head first round the midriff and they both tumbled to the deck. There was a brief struggle while the larger boy recovered from the surprise of the attack, and then his greater size and strength began to tell. He was already on top of his opponent, raining down a flurry of punches on the smaller boy's face by the time Fury pushed his way through the two startled midshipmen who were watching the fight with glee.

'Avast there!'

There was no mistaking the authority in Fury's voice as he shouted the command, and the fighting stopped immediately, both midshipmen looking up at him, startled.

'On your feet, both of you,' Fury demanded. 'Up!'

They may not have recognised Fury, but they all recognised his lieutenant's uniform. They both got to their feet in silence. The younger boy had blood running freely from his nose.

'We were just playing, sir,' the older boy offered.

'Nonsense!' Fury snapped. 'I heard everything. I do not know what the disagreement is about, and I have no wish to know. You are supposed to be shipmates – whatever differences you have should be put aside. Believe me, you will get more than enough fighting when we meet the French, so I suggest you wait until then.'

'Aye aye sir,' they both replied in unison.

'Good. Now, in the meantime, there is plenty of work to be getting on with.' He pointed at the older boy. 'What is your name?'

'Midshipman Goddard, sir.'

'Very well, Mr Goddard. The purser is down below checking on all the stores. You may go and join him and help him out. I'll be seeing him later mark you, so I'll know if you don't show.'

The boy's face fell at that news, and he nodded resignedly. 'Aye aye sir.'

'Off you go then.'

His smaller opponent, the blood still covering his nose and top lip, grinned surreptitiously at his messmate's punishment, as Goddard saluted and trudged off. Fury turned to him.

'What is your name?'

'Midshipman Francis, sir.'

'Do you require the surgeon, Mr Francis?'

'No sir. It's nothing.'

Francis fingered his nose and top lip gingerly, the flow of blood now stopped. Fury was tempted to ask what the fracas was all about, but resisted – it was none of his business.

'Get yourself cleaned up then. You can give me a tour of the rest of the ship.'

In spite of the fact that Fury was impressed with the young man's spirit in standing up for himself in the face of a much larger opponent, he didn't want him to get off with no punishment. He was satisfied by the look of disappointment on the young boy's face.

'Aye aye sir.'

Fury watched while Francis moved away to clean up his face. The other two midshipmen who had witnessed the fight fidgeted nervously as they stood there, each trying to avoid catching Fury's eye. Francis returned presently, and Fury gestured for him to lead the way.

'I've seen enough down here, Mr Francis, so perhaps you can lead us to the upper deck.'

'Aye aye sir.'

They reached the upper deck, passing quickly forward from the wardroom, past the waist where the rigging showed up black against the sky, on to the galley just abaft the foremast, and then out for a look at the beakhead bulkhead, the enormous bowsprit rising above it. Francis was completely silent as they continued the tour, contenting himself with one- or two-word answers to all of Fury's comments.

Finally they made their way up on to the focsle to catch the morning breeze, moving aft past the galley chimney and the beautifully crafted belfry at the break of the focsle, picking their way through the men scattered about holystoning the deck, polishing brass work or overhauling rigging. They moved in silence along the starboard gangway at the side of the waist and on to the quarterdeck, Fury acknowledging Dullerbury's greeting as he looked aft to the captain's quarters, the wheel and binnacle sitting just in front. Eighteen nine-pounders he had counted up here – twelve on the quarterdeck and six forward on the focsle, completing her armament.

Fury turned to Francis as they stood on the quarterdeck, determined to bring the young man out of himself a little.

'How long have you been in the service, Mr Francis?'

'Two years sir.'

'And you enjoy it?'

There was a small pause before Francis replied, just long enough to suggest that Francis was not being entirely honest.

'Yes sir.'

Have you seen any action?'

'No sir.'

Francis was an extremely shy young man, that much was obvious from his curt responses. Perhaps that was why he was bullied by his messmates. Fury had been lucky enough to get on well with all his messmates on board the *Amazon* as a midshipman, possibly due to their similar ages. If Francis was the youngest of the *Fortitude*'s midshipmen, he would be the natural choice for bullies such as Midshipman Goddard.

'No doubt you will soon enough.'

Fury could detect no hint of fear in Francis' face at that thought. Whatever else he was, he was not a coward.

'Very well, Mr Francis, you may go,' Fury relented, aware that his attempt at opening Francis up a little had been a complete failure.

'Thank you sir.'

Francis saluted with a look of relief on his face and hurried off, while Fury resolved to try again with the boy at a later date. He watched him disappear down the quarterdeck ladder and then turned his attention back to the quarterdeck, with the raised poop deck situated right aft.

He could see no guns up on the poop deck, and had already decided against going up there – he was not sure whether it was reserved just for the captain.

'Passing the word for Lieutenant Fury!'

The deep-throated shout emanating from the captain's quarters reached him at once on the quarterdeck. He hurried aft, glad that he was so close for his first summons from the captain. The sentry announced him as he passed through the sleeping cabin and into the captain's day cabin, where Captain Young was standing with his back to him looking out of the stern windows.

'Lieutenant Fury, reporting as ordered sir,' he said, prompting Young to turn round and study him.

The first thing Fury noticed was his eyes – he could almost feel them boring into him as he stood there. He was slightly shorter than Fury, and was probably in his early forties, judging by the faint lines which marked his face around the eyes and mouth. His black hair was tied back tightly in a queue, tinged with the odd fleck of grey and receding slightly.

'Welcome aboard Mr Fury,' Young began. 'I understand this is only your second ship, and your first ship of the line?'

'Yes sir,' Fury replied – he did not know what else to say to that.

'You will find her different to handle after a frigate I can assure you, but you will see for yourself in due course.'

'Yes sir,' he replied again.

'His Lordship has informed me of your previous service aboard the *Amazon*. Most promising.' He paused, prompting Fury to utter his thanks, before continuing. 'You will no doubt find my methods slightly different to your last captain. Just ensure that when on watch you are attentive to your duty at all times, as are the officers and men under your command, and there will be no problems. If you go and see the first lieutenant, he will provide you with a full copy of my standing orders. He will also provide you with your general quarter, watch and station bill, as well as assigning you a division of the crew whose welfare will be your responsibility. Remember Mr Fury – never neglect the welfare of your men!' His eyes were boring into Fury again now, maybe seeking some sign that Fury understood what he was saying. 'That will be all,' he finished, apparently satisfied.

'Aye aye sir,' Fury replied, leaving the cabin and going in search of the first lieutenant.

The following morning, just after dawn, the *Fortitude*, along with the *Victory*, *Agamemnon*, *Leviathan* and *Ajax*, weighed anchor and sailed out of Gibraltar Bay. They weathered Europa Point in succession before turning to the north-east to join the rest of the Mediterranean fleet blockading Toulon.

For nine days the ships, led by Lord Hood in the *Victory*, battled against contrary winds, some-times backing or veering as much as twelve points in the space of an hour so that the officer of the watch had to be constantly alert against the threat of being taken aback by a sudden shift.

For Fury it was a testing time, being in charge of such a monstrous vessel in difficult conditions, not helped by the fact that the admiral was within full view of any errors. By the second day, however, he was confident that he had familiarised himself with the way she handled. He was in fact pleas-antly surprised by how well she sailed, having to shorten sail on a number of occasions in order to avoid overhauling the *Victory* out ahead.

The weather during this time remained fine, albeit growing gradually cooler as they moved north, so that it was under a baleful sun on the ninth day that the masthead lookout called down that he had sighted a strange sail to the north. The sail then multiplied until the lookout finally

84

reported another sixteen like it, all two-and three-deckers tacking relentlessly back and forth almost as far west as Marseilles, thirty miles away, as they kept a ceaseless watch over the French fleet lying in Toulon harbour.

Fury found himself silently thankful that he had just come off watch before the first sail was sighted, so that the flurry of signals which broke out aboard the *Victory* ordering the ships to their different stations within the fleet, were not his responsibility. He was quite happy to stand on the quarterdeck with his telescope and study each of the ships within the fleet that he could see – four of them three-deckers and the rest two-deckers – and by the time they were in their correct station along with the other ships, darkness had begun to fall.

The next day broke warm and clear – a Sunday. As on every Sunday, the men were piped to breakfast half an hour early, after which they were mustered in divisions on the quarterdeck and focsle, inspected first by their lieutenants and then by the captain. Captain Young then disappeared below to begin his inspection of the entire ship while Fury relaxed on the quarterdeck until his reappearance.

A full hour passed before the captain returned, Fury spending it idly scanning the fleet with his telescope as they slowly beat back and forth in unison, usually tacking at the end of each watch when all hands would be available, as if an invisible line were holding them all together. It was only their first full day on blockade duty and he could already see that it was going to be a tedious business.

He looked up to see the church pendant hoisted to the peak, the men being crowded into the waist while the officers stood on the quarterdeck backed up by the marines in full uniform with muskets loaded and ready, a clear signal to any mutinous seamen.

Fury had fully expected Captain Young to conduct a Sunday service, steeling himself for the boredom while various passages from the Bible were read. To his relief, the captain decided to read the Articles of War instead, which, although Fury had heard them a hundred times before on the *Amazon*, could at least be listened to, digested and abided by, without the need for too much concentration.

The thirty-six articles were read by the captain in a steady voice, the crimes mentioned ranging from mutiny to sodomy, from cowardice to sleeping on watch, with eight out of the thirty-six articles requiring a mandatory punishment of death on conviction, eleven others allowing 'such lesser penalty as the court may decide'.

Fury scanned the faces of the seamen standing down in the waist looking up, as the captain read aloud. Much could be learned from looking at the faces of the crew at times such as this; smiles, passivity, scowls – all told a different story about the current mood throughout the ship. From what he could see the men were happy enough – somewhat surprisingly, since the majority of them had been hastily snatched from their homes and families by the press gangs, or from inbound merchant ships when the initial possibility and subsequent development of war arose.

The captain had reached the thirty-sixth article now, and Fury was glad that it was almost over.

'All other crimes, committed by any person or persons in the fleet, which are not mentioned in this act, or for which no punishment is hereby directed to be inflicted, shall be punished according to the laws and customs in such cases used at sea.'

That last one had always worried Fury somewhat. It gave the captain the opportunity to try anyone with any trumped-up charge he may think of, giving him absolute and total power over the men. Harsh as it may be, he could still see that it was this harshness which maintained discipline on each of the king's ships around the world, and which caused a fleet such as the French Mediterranean fleet in Toulon to sit there impotent, afraid to come out.

The first lieutenant was ordering 'on hats' now, and Fury followed the rest of the officers on the quarterdeck by jamming his hat down on his head. The wind was beginning to increase its strength, whipping at his coat tails and blowing his hair about below his hat. He reached into his pocket and pulled out his watch – nearly noon. The wardroom mess had decided to invite the captain for Sunday dinner today, and Fury was quite glad that he had the afternoon watch and therefore would not be able to join them.

He moved over to where Parker, the second lieutenant, was standing.

'Are you my relief Mr Fury?' Parker asked as he approached and touched the brim of his hat in salute.

'I am Mr Parker.'

He still did not feel sufficiently at home on the *Fortitude* to risk a snub by the use of Christian names.

'Bad luck. I'll be sure to have a glass of wine for you though,' Parker cajoled, alluding to the forthcoming dinner.

'I'm much obliged, and I am sure the knowledge will comfort me during the next four hours!' Fury joked, grinning broadly.

The first of eight bells rang out from the belfry on the focsle at that moment, signalling the end of the forenoon watch and sending Parker and the other officers and men down below to their meals, to be replaced by the men of the next watch, harried to their stations by the bosun's mates.

Here was Mr Francis joining him on the quarterdeck, the midshipman of the watch. Fury took his foot off the slide of the nine-pounder and began his customary walk up and down the weather side of the quarterdeck, bringing forth in his imagination a picture of the wardroom officers down below trying to fight their way through that invisible barrier that existed between captain and crew.

Men were flooding up to the deck now to resume their watch, Fury surprised that half an hour had already passed. The men on watch who had remained on deck through dinner to operate the ship in an emergency, hurried below to get theirs. He picked up the slate kept in the binnacle and studied the speeds and courses noted down there – little more than four knots on average, the courses alternating between easterly and westerly headings as they beat back and forth. A quick glance at the traverse board confirmed what the log told him.

He scanned around for Francis.

'Mr Francis! Have the men take a pull on the weather fore brace there!'

'Aye aye sir!' the lad replied, hurrying away.

There was no particular reason why he had given him the order other than to keep him on his toes. Hoggarth had certainly done the same to him when he had joined the *Amazon* as a young midshipman, and he prided himself that it had done him good. He could see that Francis had potential, but his shyness or lack of confidence was holding him back. If the boy could overcome that, he would make a fine officer one day.

Fury could hear the stamping of feet now as more men came up from below to sit around beneath the waist and on the focsle, some with cloth garments and needles in their hands to mend their clothes, others merely to yarn with each other.

'Sir!'

Francis was demanding his attention once more, although what problems he could have encountered adjusting the weather fore brace Fury was at a loss to know.

'Yes Mr Francis, what is it?' he asked, almost with a sigh.

'Flagship's signalling sir!' Francis replied excitedly.

'Well, what are they signalling?'

Fury tried to keep his patience – it would do the boy no good if he lost his temper with him. Francis snatched up a telescope to read the flags, then grabbed the signal book and began hurriedly flicking through the pages.

'Captain to repair on board sir,' he read off, finally.

'Yes – and the number?'

Another hurried glance from Francis over at the *Victory* and a quick flick through the pages brought him the answer.

'It's ours sir!' he said in surprise.

'So I saw five minutes ago,' Fury retorted. 'Very well, hoist the acknowledgement and then go below and inform the captain.'

Fury turned away, calling to the men on watch.

'Stand by to hoist out the captain's gig!'

A flurry of activity erupted as the men manned

the yard tackles and rigged the main and foremast pendants, ready to hoist the boat out from the booms. By the time it was in the water alongside being dragged along by its painter, the boat's crew were ready to tumble down into it.

Captain Young timed his appearance on deck to perfection, resplendent in full uniform and probably in a foul mood at having his dinner interrupted. The first lieutenant was not far behind to see him off, Young muttering to him as he went down the side.

Ross was coming over to Fury now.

'Any other numbers hoisted Mr Fury?'

'No sir, just ours.'

'I wonder what the admiral wants with us,' Ross muttered, more to himself than to Fury.

'No doubt we shall soon find out,' Fury replied – he had been thinking the same thing himself since the signal had been hoisted with only their number.

'Call me when the captain is on his way back,' Ross ordered. He obviously wanted to be on hand to hear any news first.

'Aye aye sir.'

Fury turned away to continue his pacing of the quarterdeck as Ross made his way below.

Time seemed to drag as Fury walked from the taffrail to the rail overlooking the waist and back, again and again. More than once he paused to look over at the flagship for any sign of activity, but it was a good forty-five minutes before an eagle-eyed Francis reported the captain's gig pushing off from the *Victory*'s side, and a further fifteen minutes before the gig was hooking on to the *Fortitude*, the side boys lined up at the entry port to pipe him back on board. Fury checked his watch. Quarter to four – only fifteen minutes to go before his watch ended.

Ross was back on deck again, Fury having despatched Francis below to fetch him five minutes ago. The two of them stood side by side on the quarterdeck facing the entry port, waiting for the captain to appear. The pipes twittered suddenly as Young's head reached the level of the deck and a second later he was standing in front of Fury and Ross, returning their salutes. The look on his face suggested to Fury that the news was good.

'Good news sir?' Ross asked tentatively – he evidently thought so too.

'Yes indeed!' Young replied, pausing as if trying to decide whether or not to let his subordinates into the secret. 'Lord Hood has ordered us on a cruise along the coast to the west, capturing or destroying anything we can before returning to the fleet, taking a good look at Marseilles on the way back.'

'How long has he given us sir?' Ross asked, his face breaking into a grin at the news.

'Two months – we are to be back by 24 August to rejoin the blockade.'

Ross and Fury stood there stunned for a couple

of seconds, digesting the news and scarcely able to believe that they would shortly be leaving blockade duty, a monotonous and thankless task, if only for a short time.

CHAPTER 6

Fury sat down at the wardroom table, dipped his quill pen in the inkwell, and began to write.

Fortitude, at sea
15 August 1793

Course bearing east, making six knots under all plain sail to the t'gallants, wind steady from the north west. No sail sighted. Ship's position at noon, latitude forty-three degrees six minutes north, longitude three degrees twenty minutes east, French coast bearing north-west by, distant eight miles.

He flicked back through the pages of his personal journal, scarcely able to believe that they had been away from the fleet for almost two months now. His journal told the story – pages of succinct facts regarding courses, weather conditions and landfalls, with not one chance of action. They had sighted plenty of coastal craft on their way, all with a

94

draught small enough to enable them to hug the coastline or seek shelter in coves or inlets, well away from the ponderous bulk of the *Fortitude*. None had been large enough even to warrant a cutting-out raid. Last week they had come across a fishing vessel further off the coast, in the process of hauling in their catch, and the French master had been pleasantly surprised when Captain Young had invited them on board for a drink, before purchasing some fish and sending them on their way. The Royal Navy was not in the habit of waging war on fishermen.

Along to the westward they had gone, all the way round the Gulf of Lion to Perpignan, just above the Spanish border, looking into every cove and bay on the coast for signs of enemy ships of war. In fact the closest they had come to action during that time was when passing a derelict old stone building further along the coast, about fifty yards back from the sea.

Captain Young had ordered the *Fortitude* hove to, and the men had been allowed to have target practice with the guns. First the eighteen-pounders on the upper deck commanded by Lieutenant Parker, then the thirty-two-pounders on the lower gun deck, with Fury and Lieutenant Dullerbury in command. It was the first time Fury had seen those great guns in action, the thunder and recoil eclipsing anything he had experienced with *Amazon*'s little twelve-pounders. Two rounds for each gun the captain had allowed, a great cheer erupting every time the building was hit.

95

When they had finally secured from quarters and continued their course, the building was little more than a wreck.

Fury closed his journal with a snap, aware of someone approaching the wardroom table. He looked up to see Lieutenant Dullerbury sitting down opposite him.

'Good afternoon John,' Dullerbury muttered disconsolately, 'writing up your journal eh?'

'That's right Bill,' Fury replied, 'not that there is much to write about.'

Every lieutenant in the navy was required to keep a journal or personal log, which was mostly just a copy from the ship's official log kept by the master, recording mundane facts about the conditions and courses. That had to be presented to the Admiralty at the end of the commission before they were paid.

'Nearly two months with not a scrap of prize money to our name. Another week and we'll be back on blockade duty with the fleet for the next two years,' Dullerbury continued.

The two of them sat in silence for a while, contemplating what each could do with a couple of hundred pounds in prize money. Fury was eagerly awaiting his, although he did not even know how much it would amount to. There was the *Otter* sloop captured last year – *Bedford* had been wrecked of course, while Captain Barber had reluctantly given the *Mornington* back to the East India Company – and his share of the captured

Thetis, which as far as he was aware had still to be purchased into the service. Until he received it he would have to struggle on as he was. Still, there were a lot of officers out there in a far worse position than he.

'Have you got any family John?' Dullerbury asked suddenly, interrupting Fury's reverie.

'Only my mother and a younger brother, but I haven't seen them in over two years. My uncle commanded the *Amazon*, but he was killed when we took *Thetis*.'

'So I heard. Quite unfortunate, to be struck down at the moment of your greatest triumph.'

'Indeed.' Fury thought it quite unfortunate to be struck down at any moment, but had no wish to get into a conversation with Dullerbury on death and mortality. 'What about your family?' he asked in reply, eager to change the subject.

Dullerbury began telling him about his parents, and then moved on to his brother and three sisters, leaving Fury wishing he had never asked. Fury's had never been much of a family and he had often wondered what it was like to be part of a large one. From what he could gather from Dullerbury, he was the lucky one. He was about to make his excuses and leave when a faint hail from one of the masthead lookouts drifted down to them.

'Deck there! Sail fine on the larboard bow!'

Fury and Dullerbury immediately jumped up from the table, Fury quickly dashing into his cabin to fling his journal on his cot and grab his telescope, before dashing back out and following Dullerbury up on to the quarterdeck.

The sky was overcast as he made the deck although the wind was still warm. Fury could immediately detect a distinct buzz of excitement along the deck at the possibility of action. He quickly moved over to the larboard side, extending his glass and resting it on the top of the hammock nettings as he scanned forward in the direction the lookout had reported.

He could see it almost instantly, which meant that the masthead lookout must have been asleep for the last fifteen minutes. No doubt the captain would see to it that he was punished later.

He dragged his mind from such trivialities and studied the strange sail. She was by far the largest ship they had sighted so far on their cruise, and from what he could see she had only one mast, rigged fore and aft, probably one of the local Mediterranean craft used to sail short distances from port to port along the coast. She now found herself in a great deal of danger with the *Fortitude* bearing down on her, cutting off her escape to seaward and trapping her against the coast.

'Deck there! She looks like a tartane sir!'

Fury looked at her again. He had never actually seen a tartane except in drawings, but he knew it was a very common craft in the Mediterranean, both for merchantmen and even pirates. Now that he looked more closely he could see she had two masts, the fore being raked forward considerably. Each mast had a large lateen sail attached to a curved yard, and she was currently trying desperately to skim along the coast and get far enough ahead to be able to gain sea room. It was obvious however that the *Fortitude*, thrashing along under full sail towards the south coast of France with the wind almost abeam, would easily cut her off.

It was hopeless for her, her commander must see that. Even close into the shore where the *Fortitude* could not go she would still be in range of their guns, one broadside of which would be enough to destroy her completely. The coast was no more than a mile ahead, the tartane with her distinctive curved hull now visible to the naked eye.

'Mr Parker,' Captain Young shouted, 'have the larboard guns on the upper deck loaded and run out!'

Parker acknowledged with a wave, shouting at the men on deck to harry the relevant gun crews to their stations. The fact that Young had not thought it necessary to beat to quarters was an indication of how insignificant the tartane was – the upper deck eighteen-pounders would be quite sufficient. It also allowed Fury to remain on deck and watch the rest of the chase.

'Deck there! There's a bay a mile ahead sir!'

Fury tried to bring up a mental picture of the coastline in this region from his studying of the charts over the past weeks. He could recall only one bay in this area, with the town of Sète on the eastern side covered by a single battery of twenty-four-pounders, which had fired at them on their journey west. The tartane was hurrying for the protection of those twenty-four-pounders now, knowing that was her only chance of survival.

A rumbling of gun trucks transmitted itself through the deck planking as Parker had the guns run out ready, but Fury could see the tartane would make it into the bay before the *Fortitude* was within range.

'Come two points to starboard,' Young muttered to the helmsman, bringing the *Fortitude* round to a course less acute with the shore. 'Shorten sail to topsails only if you please, Mr Ross,' Young continued, prompting the first lieutenant to snatch up a speaking trumpet and bellow the order for all hands.

Within a few minutes the crew were at their stations and the first lieutenant was giving the orders which sent them hauling on sheets, buntlines and clew lines to bring the billowing canvas of the topgallants and the courses up to the yard above, while the topmen quickly laid out along the yard to fasten the sails securely with the gaskets. Another order to the men on the focsle sent them slowly releasing the jib downhaul, the jib gradually coming down to be secured in the netting above the jib boom.

Almost without effort the *Fortitude* was now under topsails only, her speed slowed and the movement of the hull transmitting itself up through Fury's legs as he swayed easily with the pitch and roll.

Looking forward he could see the tartane had reached the bay, easing her helm over and heading for the eastern side under the protection of the battery which Fury could now see standing there, stark and clear against the grey horizon beyond. A flash appeared as he watched, the dull clap reaching his ears a second later swiftly followed by another and then another. Fury could hear no sound of the passing shots, and a quick glance aloft showed that no damage had been sustained. More followed, Fury this time seeing splashes in the sea about fifty yards ahead marking where the shot had landed.

They were just out of range of the battery over there, and Young obviously thought it prudent to keep it that way.

'Port your helm,' he ordered the quartermaster, the order being relayed to the helmsman who began running the spokes of the wheel through his fingers in response.

Fury watched as the *Fortitude* came slowly round until she was running parallel to the shore, running across the mouth of the bay. A muttered command from Young steadied the ship on that course before he moved forward to the quarter-deck rail overlooking the waist.

'Mr Parker!' he shouted down, waiting for Parker's head to appear before continuing. 'You may try the range as we pass.'

'Aye aye sir!' Parker replied.

The tartane had begun to anchor now, over on

the eastern side of the bay and close in with the shore, protected from seaward by the battery. Fury was confused as to why Young wanted to fire at her – they would have to sail in closer to be within range, which would in turn place them within range of the shore battery. Fury doubted very much whether the risk was worth taking.

The first gun banged out below as they began to fire, Fury immediately whipping his telescope to his eye to look for the fall of the shot. He thought he could see a fountain of water shoot up a good 300 yards short of the tartane, but he could not be sure at that distance.

'Well out of range sir,' commented Ross to his captain, both standing there glass to eye as the *Fortitude* finally reached the eastern end of the bay and the last gun below was fired.

'Put the helm down,' Young ordered the helmsman, glass still to his eye towards the shore. 'Have the foreyard braced round if you please, Mr Ross.'

The *Fortitude* slowly began to swing back in towards the shore as Ross barked out the orders which sent the men hauling at the braces to swing the foretopsail yard round the other way.

'Keep her at that,' Young snapped at the helmsman, as the distant coast showed up beyond the *Fortitude*'s jib boom. They were stationary now, just out of range of the shore battery with the backed foretopsail counteracting the forward thrust of the main and mizzen topsails.

'Mr Parker!'

That was the captain hailing down to the upper deck again.

'You may run in and secure the guns! Mr Ross,' he turned to the first lieutenant, 'I would like to see all the lieutenants in my cabin in ten minutes, along with Captain Williams.'

'Aye aye sir,' Ross replied.

Young left the quarterdeck, prompting the men within earshot to begin speculating what the captain was planning. Fury supposed he could only be contemplating a cutting-out attack on the tartane, although he could not quite see why they would need the marine captain, Williams, along. Whatever was planned, he was desperate to be involved. Anything to relieve the monotony of the last few weeks and get the heart pumping again.

Ten minutes later he was standing in the captain's cabin along with the other lieutenants and the marine officer, everyone seated except for Fury and Williams.

'This is what I intend,' the captain began, sitting back in his chair behind the desk and looking round at the faces opposite him. 'We shall get underway again shortly and head south-east. Once we are out of sight of land we shall heave to and wait for dark. We shall then proceed back here where two boats – the launch under Lieutenant Ross and the cutter under Lieutenant Fury – will land with a detachment of marines under Captain

Williams and storm the battery, destroying all the guns and igniting the powder magazine. At the same time Lieutenant Dullerbury will take the gig and cut out the tartane before she can get away. Unfortunately she is too small to be purchased into the service, so there is little point in us taking her; she will have to be destroyed. The crew can be let ashore before she is set ablaze. Any questions?'

He glanced around at the officers but no one said a word. It was all relatively simple. Young was presumably hoping that the sight of the *Fortitude* bearing away would convince the garrison at the battery that they had given up and carried on their journey, making them relaxed and complacent. Whether they would believe the *Fortitude* had given up so easily, Fury was not so sure.

'Very well then,' Young continued, interrupting Fury's thoughts, 'you may each pick your own men and see that they are told off and fully equipped before we arrive back. That is all.' He turned to the first lieutenant. 'Mr Ross, I'll trouble you to get us under way now. Lay in a course of south-east.'

'Aye aye sir,' Ross replied as the officers all left the cabin, Fury's heart already beginning to beat harder at the prospect of action once again.

Lieutenant Ross loomed up out of the darkness in front of Fury as he stood silently on the *Fortitude*'s quarterdeck.

'All ready Mr Fury?' he said softly.

'All ready sir,' Fury replied.

'Very well then, get them down into the cutter.'

'Aye aye sir.'

Fury turned and hissed a quick order to the men standing behind him, all ready with cutlasses and pistols. They immediately began quietly filing down into the waiting cutter below, fastened against the ship's side by the painter attached to the boat's bow.

Fury had made a point of picking all the ex-Amazons on board *Fortitude* – Clark, Thomas, Cooke and Crouder – among his crew. He had fought side by side with these men before, and their presence gave him confidence. The remainder of his cutter's crew was made up by men from his own division, whom he judged to be steady and reliable.

The small number of marines were now making their way down the *Fortitude*'s side, and Fury tried to take a look at his watch while he waited, but could not quite make out the hands in the darkness. It was probably some time after midnight. It had been about four hours since darkness had fallen and the captain had been able to order the *Fortitude* to set a course back for the bay, boats already in the water and towing astern to avoid the necessity of hoisting them out once they arrived – noise would carry on such a still night as this.

A man had been placed at the masthead with a night glass, and on sighting the battery Captain Young had ordered the ship hove to, and the

105

seamen and marines chosen for the task ahead had been assembled and told off.

Fury looked over the side to see that his cutter was now filled with men – seamen at the oars and marines sitting in-between, unloaded muskets pointing upwards. He heard Ross mutter a quick order to his own men which sent them hurrying down into the launch below, leaving only the officers left on deck.

'Remember Mr Fury, absolute silence from now on. Let's go, gentlemen.'

Williams and Fury both acknowledged, Fury slightly annoyed with Ross for reminding him of such an obvious fact like he was some young midshipman on his first action.

Fury went down first, eager to be away from the cloying attentions of the first lieutenant, if only for a short time. It took merely a moment to reach the bottom of the *Fortitude*'s side, and a small leap from there found him in amongst the crew of the cutter, the faces of the ex-Amazons all beaming at him in anticipation. He stifled his own grin and picked his way aft to settle himself in the stern sheets next to the tiller, the feel of the cool solid oak of the tiller bar strangely comforting as he gripped it. He caught sight of Midshipman Francis' face next to him, the boy's nervousness all too apparent. This was to be his first taste of action, and Fury knew that if he came through this unscathed, his self-confidence would soar.

'Shove off!' he ordered, the boat quickly drifting

away from the *Fortitude*'s side as they waited for Ross and Williams to get down into the launch and begin.

'Give way all,' he hissed, once he could see the launch out ahead and surging forward. They crossed the *Fortitude*'s stern as they lay a course for the shore about a mile away from the shore battery.

Hopefully Lieutenant Dullerbury, who had set off half an hour earlier in the gig to get into position, would be ready as soon as they stormed the battery. It had been agreed that they would not rely on a specific time for the attack, but that Dullerbury would merely wait, only attacking the tartane once the fighting on shore became obvious. If he timed it right they should take her before her crew had a chance to weigh anchor and slip out of the bay.

Fury's eyes were hurting now as he peered forward into the darkness to keep the stern of the launch in sight. They were lucky it was a calm night with not much of a sea running so that the men had a relatively easy pull of it. The only noises he could hear were the occasional small splashes of water as the oar blades left and re-entered the swell, the soft grunts of the oarsmen as they pulled, and the low groaning of the muffled oars moving in the rowlocks. Certainly nothing that would carry a mile and alert the garrison.

They must be nearing the shore soon, Fury thought, as he saw what he thought was the darker loom of the coastline up ahead. Fury turned his ear forward, listening intently. Yes! A faint hissing sound. Looking forward beyond the launch ahead he saw a strip of white, and it took him some moments to realise that it was a low beach, the hissing sound of the surf on the sand growing louder as they approached. Five minutes later and the familiar scraping sound told him that the cutter had grounded on the sloping beach, the seamen immediately leaping out to haul the boat sufficiently further in for the marines to disembark safely.

Once emptied, the boats were hauled higher up on to the cold sand and the seamen and marines were quietly assembled. Leaving a seaman each in charge of the two boats, the men set off up the beach, picking their way among scattered rocks as they headed inland before finally coming to grass, with what looked like a wide track running through it, parallel to the coast. It was probably the only road along the coast, used to travel between one village and another and to send supplies to the various garrisons, Fury thought, as the men were stopped and Ross reiterated in a hoarse whisper the need for complete silence, backing it up with the threat of a flogging for any man that made a sound before he gave the order. One more curt command sent them trudging westward along the track, the men travelling two abreast with Fury and Ross at the head of the column. Captain Williams and his sergeant led the column of marines bringing up the rear.

The occasional low curse as an ankle turned on loose stones was all that could be heard as they moved forward steadily, so that in less than half an hour a dark shape out in front, only just discernible against the night sky, heralded their arrival at the battery.

'Pass the word along to stop,' whispered Ross to the seamen behind him, Ross and Fury themselves taking a few more paces forward to ensure no one clattered into them in the darkness.

It was inevitable that there would be some collisions as the men stopped, so Fury was not surprised when the clash of steel on steel drifted forward, betraying at least one clumsy man who had walked into the man in front.

'Wait here,' Ross whispered tersely, before moving forward silently until he was swallowed up in the gloom.

Captain Williams was soon up next to Fury, having left his sergeant in charge of the marines. Together they waited. Five minutes or more must have passed and Fury began to feel uneasy. A noise somewhere ahead in the darkness had his pistol out and his palms sweating. A moment later Ross appeared at last, taking a few moments to catch his breath before he began to tell Fury and Williams what he had seen.

'This path carries on for about another fifty yards, then splits in two. The path to the right probably leads to Sète and any other towns and villages hereabouts. The path to the left leads up to the battery, which is on a slight rise. I could not see any sentries around – they most probably think they're perfectly safe with the thick wooden door bolted shut. God knows how long it'll take our axe men to get through the door, so you, Mr Fury, will lead the seamen round the other side and scale the wall with grapnels as soon as you hear us begin. Understood?'

'Aye sir,' Fury replied.

'Captain Williams, your marines will remain with me at the entrance and enter as soon as the door is down.'

'Yes sir,' replied Williams.

'Very well. Rejoin your men and have them load their muskets now. Then we will begin.'

Williams strode back to his men, Fury and Ross giving him enough time to get back and have his men load their weapons, before ordering them forward once again.

They reached the fork in the road in no time and from there it began to slope up towards the battery, now black and imposing against the starry sky. Either side of the road was low brush and the men were stopped once again by Ross.

'Mr Fury, take all the seamen except for the axe men and approach the battery from the left. I will give you time to get in position before we attack. I will lead the marines over from the right. Carry on.'

'Aye aye sir. Good luck!' Fury replied, moving back through the ranks of seamen whispering the plan and moving them over to the left.

He had sixteen men in all, including Francis, now standing in the brush at the side of the road, leaving two remaining seamen standing behind Ross with axes. He gave a curt order and started to pick his way about thirty yards over to the left, well away from the road so that any sleepy sentry would have little chance of spotting them. Francis was keeping close by Fury on his left, and Fury could sense someone else just on his right shoulder, and knew without looking it would be Clark. He could hear the rest of the men behind him rustling through the brush and no doubt muttering curses to themselves as the bushes tore at their trousers and legs.

He began to lead them forward now towards the battery, standing to their right. It was only a gentle slope but by the time they were halfway there the men were breathing hard – it was difficult to get used to walking on land again after so long at sea. With fifty yards to go he instinctively began to crouch a little as he moved forward, the pistols in his waistband digging into his stomach as he went. Thirty yards left and he was expecting a shout of alarm at any moment, but none came as he reached the flat of the rise and bounded silently over to the wall of the battery, planting his back against the cool stone as he looked up. A quick count revealed that all the men were with him still, standing flat against the wall and waiting for the order to begin.

Fury slowly began to move along the wall,

beckoning the men to follow him. They were walking back towards the sea now and a few seconds later Fury reached one of the corners of the battery, turning right along the wall that faced seaward. He stopped at what he estimated to be about halfway along and looked up, standing back from the wall slightly to get a better view. He could see that the top of the wall had squares cut into it at regular intervals. Those would be the embrasures, through which the guns would be run out to fire seaward. There would doubtless be more embrasures if he led his men round the next corner, along the side of the battery which covered the bay itself, but he judged that this was as good a place as any to attack from. Better in fact, since this wall would be directly behind the French soldiers as they defended Ross' attack from the front.

'Thomas, Cooke, Gooseman,' he whispered softly.

The three seamen, all holding the grapnels that would be used to scale the wall, crowded round him to listen.

'Stand ready with your grapnels. We will begin as soon as we hear Lieutenant Ross attacking from the front, but wait for my order. Is that understood?'

A nod from each man told him it was, and they moved away silently to give themselves more room when the time came to release the grapnels. They could only stand there and wait now, trying to

112

listen intently for any signs of alarm or attack, Fury hoping that his thudding heart would not waken the sleeping garrison.

Francis was still next to him, and Fury thought he could sense the boy trembling a little.

'Mr Francis,' he whispered. 'When we attack, you will wait down here until the last of the men have scaled the wall before ascending. I want to make sure none of the men are tempted to hang back. Is that clear?'

Fury thought he could detect a hint of relief in Francis' reply.

'Aye aye sir.'

It was all nonsense, of course; Fury had no worries whatsoever about the men's courage, or their eagerness to be at the enemy, but he wished to save Francis the ordeal of being one of the first over the top of the wall during his first ever action.

The silence continued, disturbed only by the faint sound of the surf on the rocks below, and the occasional voice or laugh from within the fort. He was not sure how long they all stood there before they heard it: a faint thudding noise, quickly followed by another and then another before a cry rang out, sharp and piercing in the night air.

He looked at the three men holding grapnels all waiting for his order, nodding to them.

'Now's the time lads!'

All three men began swinging the lines with the grapnels attached to the end, trying to get a rhythm going before the throw. All the time,

Fury was conscious of constant thuds as the axe men ploughed their axes into the wooden door at the front, more shouts reverberating from inside the battery as the garrison were awakened.

Gooseman was the first to release his grapnel, Fury watching as it went flying upwards to hit the wall with a clang just below the top. Thomas was now releasing his grapnel and Fury watched as it cleared the top of the wall and disappeared beyond. Several strong tugs on the line confirmed that it was secure.

'Give me that!' snapped Fury, as he saw Thomas about to begin climbing. Thomas passed him the line sheepishly as the noise beyond the walls increased, a volley of shots ringing out, quickly followed by men screaming.

That would be Williams and his marines, Fury thought, as he began hauling himself up the line, walking up with his feet against the wall. He was conscious of a man climbing to his left – obviously Cooke had got his grapnel secured – and he had some recollection of Gooseman having a second attempt as he climbed. He was near the top now, struggling for breath and feeling like his arms would snap as he grabbed the top of the parapet and hauled himself over, wearily rolling on top of the wall and dropping off to the platform just behind. He picked himself up and looked to his left where his other men were coming over, led by Clark.

Along the platform at regular intervals were the

guns, six of them along this wall. He wasted no further time up there, but started running towards the stone steps leading down to the courtyard, drawing his sword as he ran and shouting for his men to follow him. A quick glance as he bounded down the steps was enough to take in the scene below. Dead men were scattered about from the marines' first volley as they burst in through the shattered door. The marines were following their volley with a bayonet charge at the now retreating Frenchmen.

Fury reached the bottom of the steps with Clark to his left and Thomas to his right. The French in front of him were turning in astonishment at the sound of their shouts as they approached, Fury lunging with his sword at the first man in a blue uniform to meet him and sending him writhing to the floor with blood spouting from his stomach. He could sense Clark and Thomas on either side of him, swinging down with their cutlasses, and he could see more Frenchmen go down from the blows. One more wild slash downwards towards another man and it was suddenly all over, the remaining enemy throwing down their swords and pleading for quarter.

The red uniforms of the marines were soon all around him, shepherding the prisoners away and collecting the weapons. Ross was now in front of him, grinning like a child.

'Well done Mr Fury. That was nicely timed.'

'Thank you sir,' Fury replied, grinning back at him.

'Set the men to work spiking the guns if you please,' Ross continued, 'I will see to the magazine.'

'Aye aye sir.'

Fury looked around for Steele, a stocky quarter gunner with rotten teeth who, if his memory served him correctly, was the last man he had seen carrying the tools needed to spike the guns. There he was on the rampart overlooking the bay with bag in hand. Fury made his way up and beckoned Steele to come over. He obliged, knuckling his forehead.

'You know what you have to do?' Fury asked.

'Yes sir,' Steele replied patiently.

Fury could smell his breath and wondered how on earth his messmates could stand it day after day.

'Very well, make a start, but see to it that you hammer the rods down securely before breaking off.'

'Aye aye sir.'

Steele moved over to the first gun and opened the small bag, taking out several metal spikes and a hammer. Picking up a spike, he inserted one end into the touch hole of the first gun and began hammering it down. Satisfied that the spike was down far enough, he then set the hammer to breaking off the remaining end of the spike which was protruding from the touch hole.

Ordinarily it would take a trained gunner a couple of hours with his drill to make the gun serviceable once again, but along with the planned explosion of the magazine downstairs, it was unlikely in this case that they would ever be used again.

Fury moved between two of the guns and peered out into the bay, just able to make out the darker outline of the tartane on the water, helped by the light of the moon. As far as he could recollect he had not heard a sound from her thus far, and he was not able to discern by looking at her whether or not Dullerbury had taken her, but the very fact that she was still there was a positive indication. Certainly her crew of ten or so would be unable to put up much resistance against the *Fortitude*'s boarding party.

He turned round as Francis approached, grinning broadly, whether from relief or satisfaction Fury wasn't sure.

'Are all the men in the fort, Mr Francis?'

'Aye sir. I had a job holding them back.'

'Excellent. Well done. You may make your way below and help with the prisoners.'

'Aye aye sir.'

Francis moved away and Fury watched him, hoping that tonight's experience would help him, even if he hadn't actually had any action. It was enough for now that he had experienced the fear and the adrenalin prior to action, so that next time he would know what to expect and how to control his emotions.

Steele had finished spiking the six guns on this side of the battery and he moved over to those overlooking the sea, Fury walking along and inspecting each gun. He was just rising from inspecting the last of the six when a light caught his eye in the bay.

He looked out, unsure at first as to whether or not his eyes were playing tricks on him. He saw it again, a small orange flicker from within the anchored tartane, growing noticeably as he looked, followed quickly by the appearance of smoke. In minutes her whole deck was ablaze, the flames sweeping up the masts and engulfing yards and sails. He could just make out a boat creeping out to sea like a beetle over the black water. That would be Dullerbury, heading back to the *Fortitude* after setting her ablaze.

'All the guns 'ave been spiked sir.'

The voice startled Fury and he swung round, his night vision all gone after staring at the flames for so long.

'Very well. Get all the men down off the ramparts and mustered at the entrance.'

'Aye aye sir,' Steele acknowledged, hurrying off and beckoning to the two men who had been helping him to follow.

Fury walked over to the side of the battery overlooking the sea to inspect the remaining six guns that Steele had spiked. The job took only a few minutes before he was hurrying down to the courtyard below, seeing a length of match snaking its way out of an open door in the ground as he looked around for Ross. That doorway must lead down to the magazine, he thought, little more than a cellar underneath the floor of the battery. Ross was obviously just finishing the preparations for igniting the magazine as Fury arrived.

'All the guns have been spiked sir,' Fury reported.

'Excellent!'

Ross turned round to where the prisoners were huddled under marine guard, supervised by Francis. He shouted out a torrent of French at them before ordering the guards, in English, to set them free. The men hurriedly ran out of the battery and fled down the road as quickly as they could.

'Mr Fury,' Ross began, turning back to him, 'please make sure all the men are present and have them wait for me down at the fork in the road. I have cut a fuse which will give us ten minutes once it is ignited.'

'Aye aye sir,' Fury replied, moving over to where the men were waiting by the door, which was severely jagged and splintered, and hanging by one hinge.

A quick count confirmed that everyone was present and so he turned to Captain Williams.

'Mr Ross' compliments, and he would be obliged if you would take the men down to where the road forks at the bottom of the slope. When you are there, fire one round and wait for myself and Mr Ross to join you.'

Williams nodded and Fury turned to the men.

'We shall be setting light to the magazine shortly and we will be retreating back to the boats in an orderly manner. Any man who panics and runs will be flogged tomorrow, I guarantee it!'

The marine captain led the way out of the entrance, the men filing out after him so that it was a few minutes before Fury, staring down the slope after them, could no longer see them in the darkness. A short time later a single shot rang out in the distance.

'All the men are in position sir.'

Ross grunted his acknowledgement as he silently sank on to one knee and began struggling with flint and steel, trying to get a satisfactory spark. Fury saw him rise and could already hear the hiss and splutter of the lighted slow match as Ross made his way over to him.

'Come along Mr Fury,' he muttered, as he led the way out of the battery and started to run down the road with Fury following close behind.

The incentive of getting away from an exploding magazine made the journey down much easier, so that it was a matter of moments before they reached the group of men waiting at the bottom. A curt order sent them all marching and stumbling along at a quick pace, Fury wishing there was enough light to see his watch so that he could tell how much time was left.

The chances of one of the French soldiers running back and putting out the fuse crossed his mind, but he quickly dismissed it. They had no idea how long the fuse had been set for, and besides, only a madman would run into a battery that was about to explode.

Ten minutes must have passed by now, he thought, suddenly beginning to experience doubts. What if the fuse had gone out? What if it had been jerked out of the powder at some point?

At that same moment the sky suddenly lit up, and a fraction of a second later an ear-splitting explosion reached them, everyone stopping and turning quickly as the initial flash of light from the explosion faded to reveal earth and stone being flung up high into the air. Luckily they were beyond the blast radius so none of the debris came near. Seconds later all that was left of the battery was a pall of smoke, grey against the black sky.

'Carry on!' Ross shouted.

They reached the beach quickly, clambering into the waiting boats and shoving off, with Fury taking the tiller of the cutter once again as the men bent to their oars to send the boat surging against the weak tide. He could still see the vague outline of the launch up ahead, but it did not matter; it had been agreed that once the battery had been destroyed, *Fortitude* would display stern lights to allow the boats to find her again, and Fury could clearly see those lights ahead, not more than 200 yards now. If no explosion had been seen by four o'clock that morning, it was to be assumed that the attack had failed and the

Fortitude would hoist her lights then, to let the returning boats see her.

In no time they were passing under her stern and hooking on, Fury leaping out and hurrying up the battens which formed the ladder, helped by the ship's tumblehome as he reached the quarterdeck.

'Well done Mr Fury!' Captain Young said as he saluted.

Both Ross and Dullerbury were standing with him, satisfied looks on their faces.

'I think we can call the operation a success,' the captain continued, with a mastery of understatement. He turned to the master, Mr Potter, who was standing aft by the wheel. 'Mr Potter, we'll get underway again now. I think it would be wise to get some sea room. Then you may lay in a course back to Toulon.'

'Aye aye sir.'

'Gentlemen,' the captain continued, turning back to them, 'I think you deserve a little sleep now.'

They all saluted, Fury following Ross and Dullerbury down below. That last order of Young's to the master had dampened his spirits considerably. In a few days – a week at most – they would be back among the fleet, back among the monotony of close blockade.

CHAPTER 7

F ive days later, under a hot and humid mid-afternoon sun, the *Fortitude* found herself once again on blockade duty, this time beating back and forth off Marseilles. Occasionally she would poke her nose in a little too far for the French commander over at the battery on the eastern side of the harbour, prompting him to open fire just in case the *Fortitude*'s captain had misjudged the range and left his ship exposed. On every occasion however, the same result occurred – the shot would fall short, and a curt order by Captain Young would see the *Fortitude* wearing round to gain more sea room, only to beat back again later to repeat the whole process.

Fury was ordered up to the masthead with his uncle's telescope, to take a look into the harbour and see how many ships were anchored there and in what state they were. He was able to see only one frigate without her yards crossed amid the smaller craft, and that was why the British fleet under Hood was largely ignoring Marseilles in favour of Toulon, where the main French Mediterranean fleet were trapped.

As he kept up his watch, he began to wonder why the battery over on the western shore did not open fire on them also. He cursed himself for his curiosity as he prepared to climb down, deciding that the commander of that battery was probably merely trying to save his powder and shot. On regaining the deck he reported his sightings to Captain Young immediately, and Young carefully wrote down his verbal report.

They would be up to the main British fleet by tomorrow, and Young was obviously using this as a chance to gain more intelligence for Lord Hood regarding the harbour and the ships anchored there.

Fury walked away from the captain, his job done, and looked around at the men going about their work. It was amazing to note the change in mood of the crew immediately after the destruction of the French battery and tartane off Sète. Even the men who had not taken part in the attack had found the excitement lifted their spirits. Now, the thought of months of blockade duty ahead was beginning to have its effect once more, not least on Fury himself.

Although he enjoyed his new ship, he could not help wishing he were back in a frigate, away from the apron strings of a fleet. He had already seen how one small action could lift an entire crew, so the thought of blockade duty, wearing down both men and ship with no chance of action, appalled him. Trying to shake his mind free of such depressing thoughts, he stood by the hammock nettings looking out at the sea, the short steep waves turning into a frothy white as the wind whipped at the crests.

The *Fortitude* had just finished tacking, his mind subconsciously registering the orders shouted by Ross which turned the *Fortitude* into the wind, crossing twelve points of the compass, before settling down on to her new tack to beat back closer to the harbour mouth.

Over to the west he could see the sun was now beginning its slow descent towards the horizon, straining his eyes as he stared at it unconsciously for too long.

'Deck there! Fore masthead lookout here!'

Fury looked up, suddenly excited at the possibility of action – perhaps the lookout had spotted a ship to seaward, trying to slip past them into Marseilles harbour.

'Deck here!' Ross bellowed back from the quarterdeck, 'What is it?'

'Sail sir, comin' out of the harbour near the western shore. Looks like a small lugger to me sir!'

Fury immediately walked forward clutching his telescope, steadying himself by the starboard fore chains before resting the glass on the rigging and scanning the harbour. He could see her now, only a small vessel with a handful of crew, just passing underneath the guns of the battery which had not fired a shot. She was hauling her wind and heading

125

out from the shallows of the coastline. Was she mad? On this course she would pass close to the *Fortitude*, but she could not possibly be contemplating that.

Fury stood for a moment and blinked several times to make sure his eyes were not deceiving him, before placing the glass back to his eye. It was no mistake. The strange sail was still coming on towards them, bold as brass, as if they were in a big three-decker instead of a lugger!

He snatched a glance back at the captain on the quarterdeck, gazing over through his own telescope. It was obviously some trick, but for the life of him Fury could not think what it could possibly be. Ross was saying something to the captain now and pointing over towards her, Fury quickly looking back through his glass to see what the first lieutenant had seen. Nothing. No – wait! A flag was breaking out at her masthead now, Fury having to blink once again to confirm his vision. A white flag – yes, there were definitely no other markings or colours on it – it could only be a flag of truce. What on earth would the French over in Marseilles want to speak to the captain of a British ship of the line for?

'Maybe they want to surrender!'

Fury looked round at Lieutenant Parker who was standing next to him, unnoticed and obviously following Fury's own train of thought.

'Probably,' he replied, grinning broadly at the joke.

The lugger was much closer now, visible without the aid of a glass, and Fury could just discern a huddle of three men on deck, apparently taking no part in the sailing of the vessel.

A quick order to the helmsman and the *Fortitude* was eased off the wind, another string of shouts from Lieutenant Ross sending men to the braces, the foreyards swinging round until the sails were backed. They were hove to now, awaiting the arrival of the lugger.

Judging by the short length of time it took the lugger to reach them, she was a fine sailor with a quartering wind. Fury had hardly had time to take his glass below and return to the deck before she bumped alongside and hooked on. He hurried over to the side and looked down to where three men were arguing, perhaps as to who would go first. Only one man wore a uniform – the man who was eventually persuaded to climb aboard first. The others wore civilian dress, one with a plain blue coat and one wearing a green coat with a distinctive yellow waistcoat underneath.

Fury stepped back as the first man appeared on deck, hesitating slightly before catching sight of the captain waiting nearby. A few moments passed before his two companions arrived, all looking thoroughly nervous and unsure of themselves.

'You are the *capitaine* sir?' asked the man wearing uniform in what could only loosely be described as English.

'I am sir. Captain Young.'

Young's curt reply was accompanied by a sharp nod – he was not going to make life easy for them.

'*Parlez-vous français?*' the man continued, having exhausted his English and deciding to resort back to French.

Captain Young shook his head, turning to Ross. 'Ask him what he wants.'

Ross turned to the trio and spoke quickly and fluently in French. The man in the uniform replied, Ross turning back to Captain Young and translating.

'This is Captain Dommartin, of the navy sir. Behind him is Monsieur Dupont and Monsieur Baptiste. He says they wish to see the admiral commanding the British fleet sir.'

'They do, do they?' Young replied dryly. 'Ask them what business they have with Lord Hood.'

Ross turned round again and, following another rapid exchange, translated for Young.

'He won't say what they want. He says they can only discuss it with Lord Hood sir.'

'Do they realise how much work goes into running a fleet? And they expect me to present them to His Lordship with no indication of their business? Tell them if they do not wish to tell me their business they may return to Marseilles. I will honour the flag of truce.'

Ross translated this and the three Frenchmen began another heated exchange with one another. They were clearly anxious that their mission should not fail. Reaching an agreement at last, their spokesman, Dommartin, turned back to Ross and spoke swiftly for some time.

Fury could see from where he was standing that Ross' face now had a look of shock on it.

'Well?' demanded Young.

'Sir,' began Ross, clearly trying to translate the last statement accurately. 'He says that he and his two associates have been elected by the populace of Marseilles as commissioners. They have been given full powers from the sections of the departments of the Mouths of the Rhone to treat for peace. The people of Marseilles are loyal to the king and they,' indicating the three men, 'have been charged with negotiating with Lord Hood for the city's surrender, under His Lordship's protection, until a monarchical government in France has been re-established.'

Ross, along with every other man on deck who had heard the report, stood staring at Young waiting for his response.

'Good God!'

The exclamation from Young was forced from him as he digested the import of the news, and it served to jerk Fury out of his own shock.

'Is it some kind of trick?' Young asked, at once suspicious of French motives.

'It may be sir, but I don't see what they can hope to achieve from it if it is,' Ross replied, turning to Dommartin once again as he started talking.

'He says sir,' Ross began, turning back to Young,

'that the people of Toulon feel the same, and they are expecting commissioners from that city, deputed from the sections of the departments of the Var, to meet with Lord Hood for the same purpose.'

Fury's jaw dropped open at that. If the city of Toulon were to surrender then Lord Hood would take possession of the entire French Mediterranean fleet anchored within. Quite apart from the naval effect, he could readily see that the surrender of two of France's main cities to the British, and their subsequent declaration in favour of the monarchy, would be a crushing blow to the new Republic and could well signal the end of the war.

'Mr Ross, kindly order the lugger to sheer off and return to Marseilles – these three gentlemen will be remaining on board as our guests for the time being.'

'Aye aye sir,' Ross replied, leaning over to the bulwark and shouting down in French to the crew of the lugger.

Fury could see the relief pass over the three men still standing there as they heard Ross shouting to the lugger.

'Mr Potter!' Young shouted to the master, 'kindly square away and lay in a course to rejoin the fleet.'

'Aye aye sir.'

'Mr Ross, kindly inform these gentlemen that I shall endeavour to make their stay as comfortable as possible until we have a chance to transfer them to the flagship.'

With that, Young turned aft and headed towards his cabin, no doubt eager for a moment's peace so he could reflect on the implications of recent events.

Rumours had been flying round the fleet faster than any bird could carry messages ever since *Fortitude* had arrived back off Toulon and transferred the three commissioners from Marseilles to Lord Hood in HMS *Victory*.

Fury was standing on the quarterdeck of HMS *Fortitude* as she kept watch outside the harbour with the rest of the fleet, just out of range of the shore batteries there.

Yesterday Lord Hood had called for a meeting on board the flagship with all admirals and captains present, and that had been their first concrete news on the developments since their arrival back with the fleet.

On his return from the meeting, Captain Young had called the senior officers down to his cabin and had relayed the events of the past few days. Fury had stood for nearly an hour as the captain had carefully explained the current position to his officers.

In the absence of the Toulon commissioners as promised by Dommartin, Lord Hood had sent an officer – Lieutenant Edward Cooke, chosen because of his fluency in French – ashore under a flag of truce, to treat with the deputies or bring them off safely to the *Victory*. After two days he returned to the *Victory* with two of the commissioners deputed for Toulon. On 26 August – last Monday – the deputies of all the sections of Toulon agreed with Lord Hood's proposals and signed a declaration investing him provisionally with the harbour and forts of Toulon.

Being satisfied that the people of the city were unanimously for the surrender, Lord Hood then sent Cooke back on shore to find out the position of the French fleet anchored within, a part of which was still loyal to the Republic.

Every man in the British fleet had heard the gunfire the night before last, but it was not until Cooke had returned that it became apparent that the entire broadside from a French frigate had been directed solely at him as he landed ashore and made his way to the city.

The commander of the French fleet, Rear Admiral Comte de Trogoff, was a staunch Royalist and so his second in command, Rear Admiral St-Julien, who was known to be loyal to the Republic, had superseded Trogoff and taken over the command of the fleet himself. St-Julien had then, along with the crews of seven line-of-battle ships, taken over and manned the forts on the western side of the harbour.

In response to this Lord Hood had decided at a council of war that immediate action was needed, and had resolved to land 1,500 men under the command of Captain Elphinstone to occupy Fort La Malgue on the other side of the harbour. Fury had since looked at a chart of Toulon and could see that Fort La Malgue, situated on a spit of land separating the inner and outer roads, was built on high ground and would therefore be able to dominate St-Julien's much lower forts. Once they were in possession of La Malgue they could demand the surrender of St-Julien and his men or open fire on the French fleet anchored in the bay.

Fury swung his telescope to starboard for any sign of Elphinstone and his troops. They had been disembarked during the night as close as possible to Fort La Malgue, meaning that nearly every telescope in the ship was being constantly trained on the fort for the first sign of a signal which would confirm the success of the landing.

It was approaching midday by the time the shout finally came from Midshipman Jessop that the fort was hoisting a flag, Fury immediately whipping his glass to his eye and studying carefully. It was the Union Jack.

'Deck there! Main masthead here!'

The shout drifted down to the deck and reached Fury as he swung easily with the motion of the *Fortitude*, pushing her way through the short waves and heeling over slightly to the breeze.

'Deck here!' yelled back Dullerbury, as officer of the watch.

'Sails in sight to the south-east sir. Plenty of 'em. They look like two-deckers to me sir!'

'Very well, keep an eye on 'em!' Dullerbury shouted back, despatching Midshipman Jessop to inform the captain.

Captain Young had told them yesterday that Lord Hood was expecting the Spanish fleet under Admiral de Langara, based at Minorca, to join them any day now and assist them in occupying Toulon. Fury's first thought at the time had been scepticism at the idea of two traditional enemies – Britain and Spain – combining in a joint operation as allies. He had absolutely no doubt that there would be trouble ahead.

He stood and watched for hours as the Spanish fleet slowly approached and took up a position to seaward of the blockading British fleet. He could see them clearly through his glass, and grudgingly had to admit that the Spanish could build lovely ships. Twenty-one sails of the line in all, a mixture of two- and three-deckers with the red and gold of Spain streaming in the wind. He was less impressed with their seamanship, however, as he watched their manoeuvres and timed how long it took them to shorten sail.

He looked at his watch again – nearly four o'clock now. He hurried below to put his telescope in his cabin and retrieve his hat in time for his watch, the first of the day's two dog-watches. Fury continued his habit of pacing the quarterdeck during his watch, so that it was Midshipman Jessop who brought his attention halfway through the watch to the fact that the flagship was signalling for all captains once again. Fury immediately ordered the gig swung out and sent Jessop below to inform the captain. Soon after, Young hastily went over the side into his gig.

It was two hours before he returned, the sun already well down on the horizon over to the west as he climbed back on board and signalled Ross to gather the officers together and meet him in his cabin in ten minutes.

The meeting was a much briefer affair than the previous evening's, lasting just long enough for Captain Young to inform them all that the fleet would be entering the bay at first light tomorrow. A quick question from Ross about the batteries held by St-Julien on the western side of the harbour revealed that Captain Elphinstone, after sending across a flag of truce to St-Julien demanding that all ships in the outer road retreat into the inner road and land their powder and men without delay, had found that St-Julien had disappeared during the night, taking with him the crews of seven line-of-battle ships who were loyal to the Republic.

St-Julien had probably decided that in this case discretion was the better part of valour. Not knowing the size of the British blockading fleet, feeling outnumbered by the Royalist support within the city, and happy that his own honour had been satisfied by his token resistance, he had decided to retreat and wait for support to arrive.

And so, Fury thought, as he made his way down to his cabin to get some sleep, Toulon was now officially under the control of the British.

CHAPTER 8

The next morning broke clear, Fury standing on the quarterdeck watching the watery sun light up the mountains inland and fill them with colour. Every officer on board *Fortitude* was on deck now, telescopes in hand, eager not to miss the sight as the fleet bore up in response to a signal from the flagship and headed slowly into Toulon harbour, each ship under topsails only.

HMS *Victory* led the way of course, with *Fortitude* towards the rear of the long column so that it seemed an age before the coast grew nearer. Finally they approached the peninsular jutting out from the mainland, covered with mountains and peaks as it ran down towards the sea to end at Cape Cepet – Fury recalled the name from the chart – protecting the outer road from any southerly winds.

He could see the Croix des Signaux at the northern tip of the peninsula as they began their entrance to the harbour. It stood tall and clear upon one of the many heights dominating the landscape, part of a continuous chain of sema- phore stations running up and down the coast to transmit messages or orders faster than any rider could hope to carry them.

They slowly weathered Cape Cepet, the *Fortitude*'s bow swinging to port until she was heading northerly, and then more to the north-west to enter the outer road, or as the French called it, Grande Rade.

Fury could see that the majority of the French fleet had been moved by their crews into the inner road as demanded, leaving – he counted quickly – seven remaining in the outer road, presumably those ships whose crews had left with St-Julien two nights before.

He turned his attention back to Cape Cepet as it slowly slipped past, continuing his scrutiny of the signal tower, now on the *Fortitude*'s larboard quarter, before moving his attention to the batteries stationed along the peninsular to protect the outer road from the south. One . . . two . . . three. That was it, just the three forts situated on the peninsular. One immediately below the signal tower, another slightly to the west and then another next to what must be the hospital, St-Mandrier.

The mile-and-a-half-wide gap between Cape Cepet to the west and Cape Brun to the east, which formed the entrance to the outer harbour, was now passing astern as the wide expanse of water in the outer road opened up beyond the *Fortitude*'s bow.

Fury, swinging his glass forward, could already see that many of the British fleet had begun to anchor in the outer road. Almost ahead of them as they turned more to the north-west, Fury could see two small spits of land, each having a fort standing at the tip. That must be Fort l'Eguillette on the northernmost spit, directly opposite another spit of land coming to meet it from across the other side of the bay with the old semaphore station at its tip, the two together forming the entrance to the inner road, or Petite Rade, as it was named on the French charts.

The fort to the south of l'Eguillette was Fort Balaguier, which together with l'Eguillette completely covered the outer road from the west. Both the forts were on low ground and were well within range of the guns at La Malgue over to the east, which Elphinstone had taken just the day before.

Fury's head was spinning from the effort of recalling the French names from the chart he had studied, so much so that the curt orders from Young to the helmsman, as the *Fortitude* slowly glided in to find a suitable anchorage, largely went unnoticed.

He swung his glass back south, where he could now clearly see the narrow isthmus which connected the peninsular of Cape Cepet with the mainland. Situated on that narrow strip was another fort, presumably Batterie de Sablettes. That made four forts for the peninsular alone.

Fury was glad they had not had to come in fighting. With the crossfire from all these batteries

138

they would have been shot to pieces before they even got halfway into the outer road.

Ross was shouting out the orders which sent the crew to their stations for anchoring, signalling that Young had found a suitable spot among the maze of shipping. The topmen stood ready to go aloft at the signal and furl the topsails, while the men stationed on the focsle unlashed the anchor from the ship's side, awaiting the order to let go.

A quick command from Young to the helmsman sent the wheel spinning, the *Fortitude*'s bow slowly coming up into the wind. A shout from Ross to the men on the focsle sent the bower anchor dropping with an almighty splash into the deep water of the outer road, the anchor sinking quickly and causing the hempen cable to smoke from the friction as it ran out through the hawsehole.

The *Fortitude* made a slow stern board as the wind on the forward part of her sails pushed her back, another quick order from Ross sending the men scrambling aloft to furl those sails.

When sufficient cable had been let out it was secured round the bitts on the upper deck with deck stoppers, attached to keep the cable secured and leaving the *Fortitude* at a standstill, gently snubbing at her anchor cable as she swung to wind and current.

A quick look at his watch revealed that it was nearly midday, and the absence of any breakfast this morning meant Fury was now ravenous. He swung his glass eastward to try and take his mind away from his protesting stomach, but could see little there – his view was blocked by the masts, spars and rigging of a number of the British fleet which were anchored in his line of sight.

Giving up, he looked at his watch again, willing the hands to turn faster. Just five minutes to go now before the noon meal, and so he snapped his telescope shut and started to make his way below. At the top of the companion ladder leading down to the upper deck he paused, sparing a glance at the van of the Spanish fleet – their allies – now weathering Cape Cepet and entering the outer road in the wake of the British fleet. He found it strange that he was feeling uneasy by their presence, not reassured as he surely should be.

The flags of Great Britain and Spain waved promiscuously together as the two fleets swung to their anchors in the outer road of Toulon harbour.

The day after they had entered and taken possession of the city, a reinforcement of 1,000 men disembarked from the Spanish fleet and dispersed among Elphinstone's men to help man the many forts and redoubts surrounding it.

News began circulating throughout the fleet thick and fast during the next day, the 30th, as the officers of *Fortitude* kept their men busy scrubbing, cleaning and repairing as if an admiral were inspecting.

Lord Hood appointed Rear Admiral Goodall as

governor of Toulon and its dependencies, while at the same time news reached the fleet that the Republican General Carteaux had occupied the village of Ollioulle, to the west of Toulon, with part of his army – some 750 men, a force of cavalry, and ten cannon. On his way past Marseilles his troops had supported an uprising from a Republican mob, resulting in the guillotine for thousands of men and women who were deemed to have participated in the Royalist plot to surrender the city. It was a blessing in disguise for Hood, Fury had thought, now having only Toulon to think about.

That night, walking the quarterdeck to get some air, Fury could clearly hear ferocious gunfire to the west. The following day it was explained by Captain Young who, having returned from a visit to the flagship, informed his officers that Captain Elphinstone had marched out to the west at the head of 600 troops, English and Spanish, attacking Carteaux and his men and sending them fleeing from their posts, abandoning four of their cannon and a quantity of supplies.

Nevertheless, the Republican numbers surrounding the city were growing, and Fury knew it was only a matter of time before their defences were tested to the limit.

To ease the burden of occupation, Lord Hood decided that the remaining 5,000 disaffected seamen from the French fleet should be shipped out to prevent them from rising up against their captors, the least serviceable ships amongst the French fleet being selected for their journey.

For days after that, the whole fleet remained at anchor. During this time Fury and the rest of the *Fortitude*'s officers were allowed the chance to go ashore and explore the city as a diversion from the inactivity suffered on board.

The quayside at the dockyard was bustling as Fury stepped ashore. Stores and munitions were being transferred to and from the ships laying in the inner basins, the boats carrying the stores beetling back and forth across the calm waters. Fury turned away and directed his attention to the dockyard itself, swarming with soldiers, sailors and civilians alike. A gang of convicts was over to his left, helping to load crates down into a waiting boat, overseen by a small number of Spanish soldiers.

Fury found it strange being on French soil in what were essentially peaceful surroundings, although he had made a point of wearing his sword. He picked his way through the throng away from the waterside and towards the many dock-yard buildings which were scattered about the rear of the quay. He passed what looked like the rope walk – the building used to make and house the many fathoms of rope needed on a ship under sail – on his right as the crowds of people thinned and he approached the town of Toulon beyond. A number of soldiers were stationed at the gate in the stone archway cut into the wall surrounding the city, and Fury acknowledged their salute as he passed through.

He fingered the hilt of his sword nervously as he passed along the first of the streets, the wide cobbled road flanked on each side by closely knit buildings at least three storeys high. His uniform gave him away instantly as a British naval officer, and he was aware of curious glances in his direction from those inhabitants of the city who were going about their business in the street, some with mild interest, some with scowls. Fury suddenly wished he had brought his pistols with him, and he had a momentary thought to return to the ship to avoid the possibility of a knife in his back from a Republican fanatic, but his stubbornness made him continue.

The uniforms of the various coalition forces had long since disappeared now, and Fury could feel the loneliness and isolation bearing down upon him, but he was determined to see all he could of the city while he had the chance. A woman came out of a shop in front of him and tipped a bucket full of filthy water into the gutter. She glanced sideways at him as he approached, the frown on her brow deepening as she studied his uniform, before spitting in his path. Fury returned her stare with defiance but ignored the insult, merely carrying on down the street in grim silence.

The streets melded into one another in a monotony of cobbles and tall stone buildings as the sun continued its slow rise to its zenith and

Fury proceeded, the worry that he was lost slowly increasing as he went. Another shopkeeper sat perspiring freely in the noon sun outside his store, waiting for the custom to arrive, as Fury approached. He steeled himself for another insult of some kind, and was pleasantly surprised when he received a smile and a polite greeting instead. He returned the man's smile and continued, the smile still lingering on his face as he approached two men standing in conversation at the side of the road. Fury stepped on to the cobbled road to pass them, seeing out of the corner of his eye one of them nudge his companion and point to Fury. He heard some muffled words coming from the men but they were in French, so he had no knowledge of the insult.

He stopped suddenly as something hit him in the back of his leg, and he turned and looked down to see a half-eaten apple laying on the ground. Verbal insults were one thing, but he was not prepared to be physically assaulted by any man. Stooping down, he picked up the apple. He gulped hard as his heart began to beat faster with the adrenalin of possible action, and walked towards the two men, both of whom were now looking at Fury with open hostility. He stopped just in front of them and looked at each of them, holding the apple up. They continued to stare back in defiance.

'Whose is this?'

Fury was unsure whether the men spoke

English, but his nod in the direction of the apple was a sufficient translation. Both men shrugged but neither answered.

'Have you anything you wish to say to my face?' Fury persisted. He was getting nowhere fast and was beginning to wish he had ignored the incident. Again both men stood looking at him in silence, and Fury was about to turn away in exasperation when one of the men opened his mouth.

'You are not wanted here, English pig.'

The words were said in English, but it took Fury a few seconds to understand, so thick was the man's accent.

'Maybe not by you, but our arrival has been welcomed by the majority of the city, by decent people who are sick of the Republican tyranny sweeping your country.' Fury felt like a politician making a speech, but he could see immediately his words had no impact.

'The traitors of this city will soon suffer their punishment for such treason. Once our army has forced you out, they will have no one to protect them.'

'Your army does not have the discipline to retake the city.'

Fury was not nearly so confident on that point as he sounded, but he wanted to prick the man's arrogance.

'Bah! You will see, Rosbif. The city will be awash with the blood of traitors, and with your blood.'

The man was becoming vehement, and Fury

could see it was useless to argue further. He half turned to go, when the man stepped towards him with his fists clenched. Fury's hand went instinctively to the hilt of his sword, and he half drew it out of its scabbard. The rasping sound of the steel as the sword was withdrawn stopped the man in his tracks. He looked down at the half-drawn sword, and then back up to Fury's face. If he had any doubts about Fury's willingness to use it, they evaporated as he looked at the grim set of Fury's mouth, and the cold eyes. He contented himself with a final verbal threat.

'Go back to your ship, pig, before you get a knife in your back.'

Fury was in wholehearted agreement, and began backing away from the men, still facing them. When he was far enough away, he turned and began walking briskly, still able to feel the glare of the two men's eyes on his back. Twenty yards further on was a small side street, and Fury turned into it gratefully, stopping once he was round the corner and waiting for a few seconds while his heartbeat slowed. Ducking down, he peered round the end of the building back down the road, where the two men had recommenced their discussion, apparently satisfied with their verbal abuse. Relieved, Fury hurried down the side street, eager to get back to the dockyard and some friendly faces. He kept his hand on the hilt of his sword as he walked, aware that he was now off the main streets. A right turn at the end of the current road

146

should take him back towards the dockyard, he decided, trying to bring up a mental picture of the city.

'*Aide!*'

The shout pierced the air somewhere up ahead. Fury had no idea what was said, but could sense the terror in the voice, a female voice.

'*Ai*—'

The shout was this time cut off halfway through, and prompted Fury to break into a run towards the source of the scream. Thirty yards further along, a small alleyway ran perpendicular to the side street, and Fury could see three men struggling with a woman who was writhing on the ground in a futile attempt to get away. They were tearing at her dress, evidently in an attempt to strip her, but she was fighting back furiously. Fury drew his sword as he ran towards them, the adrenalin pumping once again and the usual calmness engulfing him as it always did before physical action. The intensity of the struggle was such that none of the men heard him approach until Fury himself shouted out.

'Avast there!'

Each man swung round, startled. Fury was on them before they had a chance to respond, slashing his sword across the arm of the first man he came to. The man screamed as he looked at his blood-soaked arm but Fury was already past him, sending the hilt of his sword into the next man's temple. The third man hesitated in front of

Fury, but a wild slash of his sword towards the man's stomach prompted him to turn and flee down the alleyway. Fury turned quickly with his sword at the ready, but the other two assailants were already running the other way down the alley, one clutching his arm and the other his face. Satisfied, Fury sheathed his sword and turned to look down at the woman, little more than a girl, still lying propped up against one of the buildings and sobbing hysterically. Fury knelt down close to her and held out his hand slowly.

'Are you hurt?'

The girl continued her sobbing, so Fury repeated the question. He could see her make a concerted effort to pull herself together as she dried her eyes and looked at him.

'You are English?'

Fury was surprised at the quality of her English. She looked little more than a peasant girl, with a very poor quality dress which looked worn and faded; it was obvious that anybody attempting to rob her would receive very little for their efforts, and so rape was the only possible explanation. She was perhaps a year or two younger than Fury, and had large brown eyes and brown hair held up in a bunch, but it was the fullness of her lips which struck Fury most. Even in her current state he could see how beautiful she was.

'Yes, Mademoiselle. You are safe now, I assure you. Are you hurt?'

'No sir, I don't think so.'

'Good. Let us get you to your feet.'

Fury gestured with his outstretched hand and she reached out with a trembling hand to grasp it. Fury pulled her up and waited while she straightened her dress and composed herself. She was only a few inches shorter than Fury himself.

'I am Lieutenant John Fury, of the *Fortitude*, anchored in the outer road.'

'Thank you for your assistance, Mr Fury. My name is Sophie Gourrier.'

'Please call me John, Mademoiselle.'

'Thank you John. I cannot believe my own stupidity; I was in such a hurry to get to the market before it closed, I took a short cut through this alley.'

'You cannot blame yourself, Mademoiselle,' Fury attempted to console her.

'Pah! I even walked past my attackers on the street before coming down here,' she continued, ignoring Fury's efforts. 'It did not occur to me that I would be in any danger, even in the city's current state of disorder. Such arrogance!'

'You are too hard on yourself. Everyone errs in judgement from time to time. Now, I think it is time we left, in case they return. Perhaps it would be wise if you allowed me to escort you home?'

'I would be grateful, thank you.'

She gave him a half smile and for the first time Fury could see the fullness of her beauty. He stood looking at her in awe for so long that she diverted her eyes down towards the ground, snapping Fury out of his trance.

'Perhaps you would be so kind as to lead the way?'

She looked up at him shyly and nodded. 'Of course.'

She turned in the direction which the third of her assailants had fled, and Fury fell into quiet step beside her. They walked on in silence, Fury feeling awkward and uncomfortable in her presence. He wondered whether she was opposed to the English occupation of the city, like many of her countrymen, or whether she was a Royalist. They turned left at the end of the alleyway on to what looked to Fury like a residential street, albeit narrow and somewhat run-down. Finally she broke the silence.

'Will your ship be staying in the harbour for long, John?'

'I do not know, Mademoiselle. We are under the command of Admiral Hood, and must follow his orders.'

'I would be pleased if you would call me Sophie. Mademoiselle seems so formal.'

'Thank you Mademoi — Sophie.'

He smiled sideways at her and she looked up at his face, returning his smile and sending Fury's heart racing. He swallowed hard to compose himself.

'I must compliment you on your English, Sophie. It is excellent.'

150

'Thank you. I had a tutor when I was younger, although I have not had much chance to use it recently.'

'A tutor?' Fury was astonished from her appearance that she had been able to afford a private tutor.

'Yes, a tutor,' Sophie replied indignantly, leaving Fury sufficiently ashamed of his startled exclamation. 'My family has not always struggled as we do now,' she continued. 'Before the Revolution, we lived in a chateau, with a moderate estate managed by my father. He was a *comte* back then. Now he is nothing, hiding his identity for fear of the guillotine and scraping by with any menial job he can find.'

'I am sorry to hear it.' It was a pitiful attempt at consolation, and Fury knew it.

They lapsed into silence again for five minutes or so. Fury was not used to female company and was finding it difficult making polite conversation.

'May I ask how far it is to your house, Sophie?'

'We are almost there.'

She pointed up ahead and to the right, where another small alleyway crossed the street. Fury's heart sank at the realisation that they would soon have to part company. They crossed the road and entered the alleyway, Sophie stopping at the first doorway on the left and turning to look up at Fury.

'Thank you, John. I am most grateful for your assistance.'

Rubbish was strewn along the length of the

alleyway, and the doorway which they were standing at looked in serious need of repair.

'I am heartily glad I was passing,' Fury replied in earnest. 'Perhaps you would do me the favour of keeping to the main streets in future if you have to go out alone. The city is not safe at the moment, and it would set my mind at ease.'

She smiled again at his show of concern. 'I shall – you have my word on it.'

They stood looking at each other in silence for a few seconds, Fury unsure of what to say, yet wanting to prolong the moment for as long as possible.

'I'm sorry, I must go. My father will be worried about me.'

She held out her hand, still trembling slightly after her ordeal. Fury took it in his and gave a small bow.

'Perhaps, erm, I could call upon you soon. To make sure you have fully recovered, that is.'

Fury was not sure he would be able to get any more shore leave, even if the *Fortitude* was to remain at anchor, but he was unwilling to go without at least the possibility of seeing her again.

'I would enjoy that very much, John. I can usually be found at home after four o'clock each day, if that would suit.'

'That would suit very well.'

There was another brief silence, Fury realising he was still holding her hand in his. He let go, his self-consciousness getting the better of him.

'Take care, Mademoiselle.'

She smiled a farewell and opened the door, Fury waiting until she had closed it behind her before turning round and making his way out of the alley. He looked up and made a mental note of the name of the street, then set off in the direction he judged the quayside to be, his mind still racing at the thought of her.

He could only hope that the *Fortitude* would be at anchor for a while, so that he could return as soon as possible and see her again.

Fury arrived back on board with no incident later that night, his mind still able to concentrate on nothing other than Sophie. The next day he threw himself into his duty in an attempt to take his mind off her, keeping the men busy in the process in accordance with Ross' orders. In spite of the work, it was easy to see they were restless after remaining at anchor with no shore leave. Many of the other ships in the British fleet had lost as much as one third of their crews to garrison duties on shore, but as yet the *Fortitude* had not been affected. With rumours that Carteaux's army now numbered some 6,000 men to the west, however, along with another 6,000 men under the so-called Army of Italy to the east, Fury did not think it would be long.

For two days he kept the men as busy as possible, scrubbing and cleaning, blacking the cannon, tarring the rigging and checking for any signs of chafe. Francis was by his side for most of that time, and Fury thought he could detect an improvement in the boy's confidence, as though he felt more comfortable with himself and his own abilities. Perhaps Francis had seen enough during the action ashore at Sète to suggest that he could control his fear and still do his duty in the face of the enemy.

'Mr Francis!'

'Sir?'

'I am going to see the captain. Keep the men working, I shall not be long.'

'Aye aye sir.'

Fury turned aft towards the captain's suite of cabins. He had resisted the urge over the past two days to request additional shore leave, but he could stand it no longer; he wanted to see Sophie again. A shout from Midshipman Goddard, the signal midshipman, stopped Fury in his tracks.

'Flagship's signalling sir!'

Fury turned towards him. 'Well?'

Goddard had his telescope to his eye to check the flags, before replying.

'Captain to repair on board sir. It's our number.'

'Very well. Hoist the acknowledgement.'

The marine sentry announced Fury's arrival as he entered Young's cabin and reported the signal.

'Very well, I shall be on deck presently,' Young replied hurriedly, shuffling papers on his desk. Fury paused for a moment, but thought better of making his request for shore leave; he could wait until Young returned from his visit to the flagship. Returning to the quarterdeck, he waited for Young.

The *Fortitude*'s barge had already been hoisted out prior to the signal, so that by the time the crew were filing down into it, Young was on deck in full dress uniform, ready.

'Keep the men busy, Mr Fury.'

'Aye aye sir.'

Fury touched his forehead in salute and watched as Young descended into the waiting barge. He watched as it pulled away from the *Fortitude*'s side on its way to the flagship, before turning back inboard to continue his supervision of the men.

He worked the men relentlessly, leaving no corner of the deck unscrubbed, unpolished or unchecked. He threw himself into the task so completely that it was a surprise to him when Midshipman Goddard announced the return of Captain Young's barge. Fury looked at his watch; Young had been gone for two hours.

'Mr Francis. Report the captain's return to Lieutenant Ross, if you please.'

'Aye aye sir.'

Francis hurried off below and Fury waited by the entry port as the barge approached and hooked on. Ross appeared silently by Fury's side just in time for Young's head to appear above the level of the deck, the twittering of pipes accompanying his arrival.

'I trust your visit to the admiral went well, sir?' Ross asked, as Young returned their salute.

'Yes, thank you, Mr Ross. If I could trouble you to have the officers assembled in my cabin in five minutes, I shall explain.'

Fury glanced at Ross with raised eyebrows as Young walked aft to his cabins.

'Perhaps we are to lose some of our complement for duties ashore,' Ross speculated.

'Perhaps,' Fury replied. He turned to Francis. 'Mr Francis, inform Mr Dullerbury, Mr Parker and Mr Oldroyd that their presence is required in the captain's cabin in five minutes.'

Francis hurried off once again and Fury began pacing the quarterdeck, hoping that any current developments would not interfere with his plans to visit Sophie.

Five minutes later, all the officers were assembled in Young's day cabin, with Young sitting behind his desk. There was an expectant buzz in the room, and Young seemed to revel in it, before he finally began.

'Well gentlemen.' He looked around at them all before continuing. 'Lord Hood is eager for reinforcements. The *Bedford* and *Leviathan* arrived yesterday with 800 Sardinian troops, along with a small Neapolitan squadron carrying 2,000 troops.'

Fury had seen the ships arrive yesterday as he paced the quarterdeck in the early evening, although he had no idea they were carrying troops. Young continued.

'As I am sure you are all aware, the British fleet has been substantially weakened by the need to send large numbers of seamen ashore to defend the various posts. With the increase in Republican numbers day by day, the arrival of these reinforcements are required to augment these men, not replace them. Therefore Lord Hood has judged it expedient to send the *Fortitude* to Malta with all despatch, and request from the Grand Master of Malta 1,500 Maltese seamen to serve in the British fleet, while our presence in the Mediterranean continues.'

There was silence in the room while this news was digested. Fury was staring at the carpeted floor, thinking of Sophie. She would be expecting a visit from him any day soon, and he would have to disappoint her. The thought of it stung him to the core. Would she forgive him when he finally called upon her? Would she understand? He looked up as Young broke the silence.

'I would like to be underway immediately after the men have had their dinner. That will be all, gentlemen.'

They filed out of the cabin, Fury's disappointment tangible. He refused his dinner, his appetite now gone, and merely stayed on the deck looking across at the shore. He heard the shout for 'All hands' as it rang around the ship once the men had finished their meal, and the subsequent stamp of hundreds of feet accompanied the rush to their stations for getting underway.

And so, that afternoon, after weighing anchor and picking their way out of the outer road with a brisk north-easterly wind, the *Fortitude* weathered the headland and stood out to sea, with Fury staring wistfully through his telescope at the city of Toulon, slowly slipping astern.

CHAPTER 9

Fury reached the maintop and continued upwards, the shrouds narrowing as he reached the topgallant yard and sat there for a few moments to catch his breath.

He had been fastidious about continuing his exercise each day with at least one journey aloft as fast as he could go, even while the *Fortitude* had been at anchor in the outer road at Toulon. It was a habit made slightly easier by the boredom of sitting there with no sight of action. He was now satisfied that he had regained his old speed and nimbleness aloft.

He gave a wry smile as he thought back to the terror and hardship of his first visits aloft, not long after he had joined the *Amazon* at Portsmouth: clutching on to the rigging for dear life, unwilling and sometimes unable to let go and carry on. One look down was enough to freeze his limbs back then so that a handspike could not have prized his fingers off the rope.

That was over two years ago now, but it seemed like another lifetime when he looked back on it. Eventually through repetition, and perhaps also due to the number of times he had been mast-headed by the captain as punishment for some misdemeanour, he had gained more confidence aloft, until finally he was almost able to forget where he was. Now it was one of the only places in the ship where he could find some solitude.

'Excuse me sir.'

The voice startled him, something in his sub-conscious mind telling him it had come from higher up. He looked up to see the mainmast lookout staring down at him from his perch.

'What is it?' he demanded, annoyed that his peaceful reverie had been interrupted.

'A fleck of white sir, on the horizon. It looks too permanent to be a wave cap sir, but I can't be sure.'

The white froth of a wave cap would disappear as the wave moved on, so the most likely explan-ation would be a ship's sail in the distance, hull down over the horizon.

'Where away?' Fury asked, his tone softening at the thought of some possible excitement.

'Over to larboard sir. About five – no, six points off the larboard bow.'

Fury grabbed the telescope which he had in his pocket – he always carried it aloft with him so he could spend time studying the surrounding sea, too often finding it empty, as though they were alone in the world.

He quickly scanned over to his left, seeing nothing initially and so slowing down his search until he saw it, two patches of white on the horizon almost merging into one, but with one slightly lower than the other. The lookout certainly had good eyes, he thought, as he studied it in his glass. It could only be another ship riding along under topgallants, and judging by the two masts was possibly a brig of some kind.

'Sail ho!' He shouted the report down to the deck, and a moment later the bellowed reply of 'Where away?' reached him. 'Six points off the larboard bow!' Fury glanced back up to the masthead lookout. 'Very well, keep an eye on her and report any changes in position,' he ordered, folding his telescope again and preparing to make his way down below.

'Aye aye sir.'

Fury transferred himself on to the shrouds and scampered down as quickly as he could. By the time he reached the quarterdeck he was considerably warmer, quickly crossing to the starboard side where Ross was pacing up and down, no doubt waiting for his report.

'What do you make of her?'

'She's still hull down over the horizon, about six points off the larboard bow. She looked like a brig to me sir, but it's hard to tell at this distance.'

'Why didn't the lookout report?' Ross demanded, probably thinking the lookout had not seen it and was neglecting his duty.

'The lookout reported it to me sir,' Fury explained. 'He wasn't sure whether it was a ship or not at first without a telescope.'

'Very well,' Ross replied, apparently satisfied. 'Please inform the captain.'

'Aye aye sir.'

Fury made his way aft past the men at the wheel and towards the captain's quarters.

'Lieutenant Fury sir!' the marine sentry bellowed as he walked past, knocking on the door of the day cabin before entering.

'Ah, Mr Fury! What can I do for you?' the captain asked, looking up from his desk.

'Mr Ross's compliments sir, and we have sighted a strange sail six points off the larboard bow.'

'Very well,' Young replied, 'My respects to Mr Ross and I will be on deck in a moment.'

Fury acknowledged and left the cabin, a faint shout from the masthead lookout reaching him as he passed through the captain's dining cabin on his way back to the quarterdeck.

'Lookout's just reported,' Ross told him, after Fury had relayed the captain's response. 'She's nearly hull up now. Two masts, square-rigged but with a fore and aft main course. All sail set to the t'gallants and he thinks she's heading north-west.'

With a rig like that it was almost certain she was a brig. Fury took a quick look at the compass card housed in the binnacle. *Fortitude* was currently heading almost south, with the coast of Sardinia somewhere over to larboard. A quick look up at the set of the sails, along with the feel of the breeze on his face, told him the wind was somewhere between south-west and west.

He rubbed his hands excitedly at the realisation that they may stand a chance of catching the strange sail – assuming she was an enemy of course – the longer the brig held on to her present course. As soon as she sighted *Fortitude* and realised who she was, the sensible thing for her captain to do would be to put his ship about and run before the wind, trusting to her faster speed to outrun *Fortitude*. With the wind from the west, however, and the *Fortitude* to windward of her, with any luck the brig would find itself caught on a lee shore. The longer she went before spotting the *Fortitude*, the tighter the net would become.

Another scan by Fury with his telescope brought the brig into view, now hull up even from deck level such was the speed with which they were approaching each other. The fact that they had not spotted the *Fortitude* yet – a big two-decker – suggested that she was a merchant ship, as any warship would be carrying lookouts and would surely have seen them by now.

'Mr Ross, I'll have the royals and weather studdingsails set, if you please.'

Fury turned round to see Captain Young studying the brig with his glass as he gave the order, Ross acknowledging as he picked up a speaking trumpet from its becket and began bellowing orders about the deck.

'Come up four points to port,' Young muttered to the quartermaster.

A quick turn of the wheel brought the *Fortitude*'s

bow round to port, heading in towards the invisible coast and more directly towards the strange sail.

Ah! They had seen them at last. Fury could see the brig in the distance changing shape now – her hull foreshortening as she turned, briefly exposing her stern to Fury's glass before her starboard side came round and she began to head away from them, south-eastward.

The *Fortitude* was now heading directly towards them, still astern by a good mile and a half but now on her best point of sailing, with the wind abeam. Fury turned his attention aloft, watching as the men scrambled up the rigging to loose the royals, followed by the hauling of sheets and clew lines to secure the lower corners of the sails to the yard below, before the halliards were hauled on to send the royal yards up to their working height at the top of the masts, the canvas filling out as it was raised. One more shouted order from Ross sent the men to the braces to swing the royal yards round to achieve the best angle for the wind to catch the sail.

Once that job was finished, more shouted orders immediately followed to get the studdingsails – the large extensions at the side of each sail – set. Men moved swiftly back out along the yards to slide out the studdingsail booms, which were kept secured on top of the yards themselves. The studdingsails and their small spars were scattered along the deck as men finished reeving the ropes through

164

them. That job done, they were hoisted aloft by the halliards and secured, the sails flapping down to the corners of the booms below as men hauled on the tacks.

Immediately the studdingsails began to draw, and the *Fortitude* surged forward as the extra canvas increased her speed, like a majestic swan suddenly spreading its wings.

One more look forward to the brig showed that she too had set more sail in a desperate bid to escape. It was difficult to see if they were gaining on them, but Fury was doubtful. Certainly they did not look as if they had lost any ground, Fury being thankful that the *Fortitude* was probably one of the sweetest sailing seventy-fours in the Navy List. It was also lucky that this chase was not taking them too far off their original course to Malta. Young was no doubt conscious of the urgency with which Lord Hood needed the reinforcements from Malta, and he would not take kindly to any time wasted chasing a small brig.

The only question now was how far ahead the coast of Sardinia was, and whether they would reach it by nightfall. If not, the brig could easily pass them unseen during the night and be out of sight by daybreak.

Fury's attention was caught by two seamen coming down to the quarterdeck from the poop deck above, walking over towards Ross with the log line.

'Eight knots sir,' one of the men reported.

Ross turned round and strode over to the captain to report. 'We're making eight knots sir.'

'Very good,' Young replied in a dull monotone. If he was pleased he did not show it.

Fury reached into his coat pocket and fumbled about for his watch. Half-past four. The sky overhead was predominantly clear, so they probably had another four hours or so before the night began to draw in.

He walked along the gangway to the focsle, passing the belfry just as seven bells was being struck. Looking forward through his glass again, he fancied they had narrowed the distance since he had last checked, although with the difference being so small he could not be sure. He considered rushing below and bringing his quadrant up – the measurement of the angles from the height of the brig's mast would provide a means of calculating their distance from it. He dismissed the idea almost immediately. In this sea it would be difficult to get an accurate measurement and therefore his calculation would be meaningless, even if he did have the patience to sit performing calculations as they thrashed along in pursuit of an enemy.

It took them two hours before Fury estimated that they had closed the gap to only a mile. During that time the captain had ordered the fire pumps rigged, and the men had been employed wetting the sails so that they caught and held the wind more. Fury was sure Young

had ordered it merely to keep the men busy –
he himself did not believe that the trick would
make any difference to the speed of a ship
weighing 2,000 tons.

Fury had stood on the focsle the whole time,
telescope to his eye staring forward until his eye
ached. Even from his advanced position he could
sense the mood of excitement throughout the ship,
not necessarily at the thought of action – it was
becoming more apparent that it was unlikely they
would catch the brig before nightfall – but from
the efforts of gaining the last fraction of a knot
out of the ship.

Numerous times Fury had looked back to see
Young or Ross ordering a slight alteration of trim
as they looked up to see how the sails were
drawing, or snap out a fierce warning to the
helmsman as a momentary lapse of concentration
or a fluke of wind caused the *Fortitude*'s head to
fall off or come up slightly.

'Deck there! Foremast lookout here!'

The shout came from high above Fury's head,
and a moment later Ross' bellowed response
carried forward to where he was standing on the
focsle.

'Deck here! What is it?'

'Looks like land sir!' the lookout reported. 'Dead
ahead – ahead of the sail!'

My God! Fury looked at his watch and noted
the position of the sun, now beginning to lower
itself towards the western horizon. They still had

a chance to catch the brig before darkness came to save them.

The deck erupted into activity as topmen rushed aloft, Fury watching as the studdingsails were lowered down to the deck as men eased off on the lifts and halliards, obviously in response to an order from the captain, although Fury had not heard it. He could sense a small difference in the ship's motion immediately as her speed diminished slightly.

One look forward showed that they were now no more than half a mile astern of the brig, which was still ploughing on. Obviously they had not yet sighted the land ahead.

Ah! Now they must have, because their course was altering to starboard, hoping no doubt to run down the coast until sunset.

Fury looked back as a marine drummer began his familiar beat, in response to which 600 men went rushing to their stations for battle. Fury made his way quickly below to the lower gun deck, where men were already busy wetting down the decks with the wash-deck pumps before sprinkling sand over it. A silent acknowledgement to Lieutenant Dullerbury as he approached, and then he turned his attention to the men rushing to the guns.

It took no more than five minutes for the breechings to be cast off the guns and all the equipment necessary to be laid along the deck – rammers, sponges, wads, buckets of water, and arms chests flung open next to the masts. Powder monkeys were standing patiently behind the guns with ready-made cartridges for the gun captains, while the heavy thirty-two-pound cannonballs lay around the deck in shot garlands ready to be used.

'Larboard side ready sir,' he reported, as Dullerbury approached him.

One word from Dullerbury to the small midshipman who was stationed down there to act as messenger sent him scurrying up on deck to the captain, to report the lower gun deck ready for action.

Fury began to pace now to ease his frustration at not being able to see what was going on up on deck. It took some moments before the small midshipman, Harvey, was back again to report to Dullerbury.

'Captain's compliments sir, and would you open the larboard side gun ports and run out, but don't fire until he gives the order!'

Fury did not wait for a response from Dullerbury, but swung round to his crews.

'Larboard-side crews, stand to your guns. Open ports!'

The ports along the left side slowly raised on their hinges until they were fastened to the hull, letting in shafts of dull light from the early evening sun outside.

'Run out!'

The men threw their weight on to the slide tackles to haul the massive guns forward until their thick black muzzles were sticking menacingly outside the open ports.

It did not take long once this was done for Dullerbury's and Fury's curiosity to overcome them, sending them over to the nearest open port to thrust their heads outside and look forward in an effort to see what was going on.

The brig was now no more than three cables' lengths away on the larboard bow, clear against the low grey smudge beyond, which was the coast of Sardinia. She had changed course to south and was now running along the coast with the *Fortitude* sailing towards her at an angle, trying to cut her off.

At that moment a large sheet of spray hit Fury full in the face, stinging his eyes and sending him back to his post.

'Well, what do you think?' Dullerbury asked, as Fury rubbed his eyes briskly.

'We've got her!' Fury replied confidently.

'It certainly looks that way,' Dullerbury agreed, 'but at some point as we approach her we'll have to yaw off to bring her within range of our guns. If we don't damage her rigging with that one broadside then we'll lose so much distance that she'll get away in the dark.'

Fury nodded his head, realising that Dullerbury was right. They had no choice though – she was obviously not going to surrender until she had to, even if one single broadside from the *Fortitude* could destroy her completely. If they did have to fire a broadside it would be a thin line between merely damaging her rigging and destroying her altogether.

He began to pace up and down behind the guns along the larboard side, the crews standing round each gun, fidgeting restlessly during the wait.

He did not know how much time had passed when a shouted order from above for all sail handlers reached them, the members of the gun crews who were allocated as sail handlers immediately quitting their guns and rushing up on deck. Fury glanced at Dullerbury quizzically before striding over to the nearest port once again and staring out. The brig was now a cable ahead in the ever decreasing light and had come up into the wind to heave to, a white flag now clearly flying from her masthead.

The *Fortitude* was coming round slightly until she was parallel with the coast beyond, her guns now pointing directly at the little brig. From the shouted orders above it was clear that the men were rapidly reducing sail, probably down to topsails only before heaving to and sending across a boat to take possession.

Fury glanced up at her masthead once again, suddenly realising he did not even know what nationality she was. With the wind blowing directly away from them he could not quite make out the flag.

It was some minutes before the movement of the hull under his feet told him they had heaved to, and a moment later the order to run in and secure from quarters was brought down. Fury eagerly harried the crews as they hauled once again on the tackles to bring the guns rumbling in, before closing the ports and making it almost pitch black along the deck.

It took what seemed to Fury an eternity for the men to clear away the equipment and wash down the planking before he could finally make his way to the quarterdeck with all the haste his dignity would allow. As he reached the quarterdeck he could see that the men had just finished hoisting out the launch and cutter, and Ross was standing in front of Young deep in conversation.

'Ah, Mr Fury. Just the man,' said Young, as he caught sight of Fury approaching.

'Sir?' Fury enquired, with rising excitement.

'You will accompany Mr Ross over to our new capture.' Young waved his hand in the direction of the brig, still stationary and wallowing on the swell waves a cable under their lee. 'Mr Ross will take the launch and you will have the cutter. Her crew will be transferred over here while Mr Ross and yourself collect all of her papers. You will then take command of her when Mr Ross leaves and you will lay in a course for Toulon. We will rejoin you once we have finished our business in Malta. Any questions?'

'No sir,' Fury replied simply. He was well aware by now of Young's dislike for explaining anything more than once.

'Very well then. I'll give you five minutes to collect all the things you may need, after which the master will provide you with our current position. Mr Ross has already picked out a prize crew of twenty men and one midshipman, Mr Francis, so off you go.'

'Aye aye sir.'

Fury moved to touch his hat in salute before realising he was not wearing one. His excitement was beginning to overcome him and he made an effort to keep it in check, blocking out of his mind the thought of being in command of his own ship once again.

He reached the upper gun deck quickly, just as the men were finishing re-establishing the bulkheads which formed their different cabins. The chests of belongings had already been brought up from below and were strewn about the deck waiting to be packed back into the respective cabins.

Fury recognised his immediately by its battered appearance; it had been brand new when he had first joined the navy, but it had received some rough treatment during his short service, most notably during his time in the Indian Ocean. Now the leather was worn and faded, with the occasional scratch or tear where it had been damaged during the hurried process of stowing down below when the ship went into action. He strode over to it and flung open the lid to see what he would need. There was an empty canvas sack with a drawstring neck laid on the top of his belongings, which he removed and placed on the deck. He was wearing his undress uniform along with his black Hessian boots, so the only other items of clothing he would need were his hat, and a couple of extra shirts and breeches. He gathered them up and stuffed them down into the canvas sack. Fumbling about in his pocket, he grabbed his telescope, thrusting it back into the chest – he would take one of the *Fortitude*'s own telescopes, so there was no chance of him losing his.

A final hasty inspection of the rest of the contents revealed that the only other items which he would need were the two pistols – his uncle's pair – that were packed neatly down the side in their case. He quickly picked the case up, emptied it of the two pistols and stuffed them into his waistband, replacing the empty case and closing the lid of his chest before making his way back up to the quarterdeck with the sack.

There was an open arms chest on the quarter-deck when he arrived back, half empty now that the boarding parties had taken their choice. Fury reached down and pulled out a cutlass and belt, throwing the belt over his shoulder and slipping the cutlass into the frog down by his left hip. He walked over to the binnacle box and took one of the tele-scopes hanging within, placing it on top of his clothes and pulling the drawstring tightly closed.

'Here is our position, Mr Fury.'

He glanced up to see the master, Mr Potter, holding out a scrap of paper which he accepted with thanks and thrust into his coat pocket.

'All set Mr Fury?'

He spun round to see Captain Young and Lieutenant Ross standing in front of him.

'Yes sir.'

'Very well then, good luck. Carry on gentlemen.'

'Aye aye sir.'

Fury and Ross both touched their hats and turned to make their way towards the entry port. Ross descended into the launch first, settling himself down into the stern sheets before giving the order to shove off, which allowed the cutter to be brought into position.

Fury quickly made his way down the *Fortitude*'s side and scrambled into the crowded boat, thankful there was not a heavy sea running as he made his way to the stern sheets past the silent men clutching cutlasses and fingering pistols. He sank down next to the tiller which had already been shipped and, with a curt 'Shove off, give way all', thrust the tiller bar over to port to send the cutter clear of the Fortitude's side and on its way over to the brig in the wake of the launch.

It was a matter of minutes before they reached the brig, Fury laying the cutter alongside her while the seaman in the bow hooked on. Hurrying up and straightening his jacket and cutlass, he made his way past the oarsmen towards the brig's entry ladder. The sound of voices drifted down as he made his way up the brig's side, surprisingly low compared to the *Fortitude*'s towering hull, so that it was only a moment before he found himself standing on her deck.

Ross was busy talking to a scruffy-looking man, short and stout, with a stained shirt and a large bald head. The rest of the launch's men were standing with pistols in hand covering the brig's crew, all standing sullenly over by the mainmast. Fury hastened over to Ross as the rest of his cutter's crew made their way on board.

His quick scan of the deck revealed enough dirt to infuriate even the most slack first lieutenant, and he even caught sight of some empty bottles rolling around in the scuppers. Ross turned as he approached and beckoned to the scruffy man in front of him.

'This is the captain, Mr Fury. And this . . .' he spread his arms around the deck in an extravagant gesture, '. . . is *Renard*. The captain has kindly offered to escort us below to his cabin so we may collect the ship's papers.'

'Aye sir,' Fury replied, looking at the man as he stood there swaying slightly – he was obviously drunk.

'Mr Francis!' Ross bellowed over Fury's shoulder, in response to which the midshipman hurried over. 'We are going below. Kindly begin to transfer the prisoners over to the *Fortitude*.'

'Aye aye sir,' Francis replied, scurrying off piping out orders as he went.

A quick gesture from Ross sent *Renard*'s captain waddling down towards his cabin below, closely followed by Ross and Fury.

His cabin was no cleaner than the rest of the brig, a number of empty bottles strewn about the deck being a further indication of what he had been doing while he waited for the boarding parties to arrive.

Ross strode quickly over to the desk, took a pull at the top drawer and quickly demanded the keys from the captain, who gave them up quietly. The contents of all three drawers were promptly emptied out on to the desk by Ross, who then started to sift through them quickly, sorting them out into two piles as Fury watched.

'You come from Ragusa eh?' Ross asked the man, looking up. A grunted assent was the only reply he received.

Ragusa was a fortified seaport city on the coast of southern Dalmatia, in the Adriatic Sea.

'We're not going to get any more sense out of him for a while.' Ross used his hand to indicate the captain, who was now merely staring down at the deck as if concentrating fiercely on trying to stay on his feet. 'I've got all her papers here,' he continued, resting his hand on the larger of the two piles on the desk, 'the rest of the papers contain the captain's charts of the whole region, from the western Mediterranean to Egypt and the

Levant, so they may come in handy for you. There are also separate charts here for the Adriatic and the Aegean Sea.'

'Yes sir,' Fury acknowledged. 'What's she carrying?'

'I was just coming to that,' Ross started. 'She's on her way from Smyrna to Marseilles with a cargo of timber. As you are no doubt aware from the state of the captain here, there is also liquor on board. Mark me, Mr Fury, on no account are you to let the men near it. Once a seaman gets his hands on ardent spirits then you can kiss goodbye to discipline.'

'Yes sir.'

'It is locked away currently in the hold, so you should be safe enough. Here is the key.'

He handed Fury the key and turned away, placing the papers in a waterproof bag and leading the way out of the cabin. Fury dumped his own sack of belongings on the floor of the cabin and followed, literally dragging *Renard*'s captain along with him by the arm. By the time they reached the upper deck the light had faded perceptibly, so that the occasional star could be seen in the deeper blue of the sky.

The deck was now clear of the brig's original crew and Fury could see the launch returning after what must have been the final leg transferring the prisoners over to the *Fortitude*. The cutter was still secured to *Fortitude*'s side, waiting to be hoisted back on board. Once the launch had arrived back at *Renard*'s side the boarding party scrambled down into it, roughly dragging the brig's captain down with them.

Ross turned briefly to wish Fury good luck and then he too was gone from view, reappearing moments later in the stern sheets of the launch as the boat was cast off from the brig's side to make her final trip back to the *Fortitude*.

Fury glanced briefly aloft to see the British flag now flying above the ship's own colours, before turning round to look at the twenty men who constituted his prize crew, all standing along the deck in the gathering gloom. The towering presence of Clark was there, along with the other ex-Amazons – Thomas, Cooke and Crouder – their presence reassuring. Some of the other men he recognised from his own division on the *Fortitude* – Gooseman, Perrin and Haycock – but the rest of the faces were still anonymous. No doubt he would know them all soon enough. Young Midshipman Francis was by the mainmast, waiting for his first orders.

Fury had been a midshipman in the *Amazon* the last time he had commanded his own ship, and the sensation felt strangely new to him as he tried to drag his mind back to what orders he would need to give. One look over to larboard, where the low smudge of the coast of Sardinia was now rapidly fading in the dwindling light, made his first task obvious. Even hove to as she currently was, the brig was drifting down towards that coast and so it was imperative that he gain as much sea room as possible, especially with night approaching.

He took a quick glance aloft to where the fore-topsail was backed against the mast, with the main topsail drawing to balance it out.

'Mr Francis!'

'Aye sir?'

'We'll get under way now. Split the men into two groups if you please. One will be responsible for the foremast, the other group for the mainmast.'

'Aye aye sir!' Francis replied, quickly splitting the men into two groups of ten and herding them into position by their respective masts.

Fury stood there, quietly thanking Captain Young for giving him able seamen so that he need only give an order and it would be carried out with no confusion or delay. He was thankful too that the wind had backed three points to westerly so that they had a chance of weathering the south-western tip of Sardinia without having to tack. He had no wish to throw her in irons on a lee shore and with his captain watching.

He walked over to the tiller, looking forward to satisfy himself that the men were ready before beginning his orders.

'Brace the foreyard round there!' he bellowed, the men stationed by the foremast immediately tailing on to the braces and hauling the yard round until the foretopsail began to fill again and *Renard* slowly started to gather way.

One look ahead gave him a faint glimpse of the rocks at the south-western corner of Sardinia, which had effectively trapped the brig between the *Fortitude* and the coast. She had steerage way on her now and he eased the tiller over himself, bringing her bow round until she was heading – he took a quick glance at the compass – south-west by south, close hauled on the starboard tack. The large bulk of the *Fortitude* slowly dropped astern to starboard as they passed between her and the rocky coast over to the left.

A sharp flutter overhead told him he had gone too close to the wind and he eased her off slightly, watching over to larboard as the coast, now nothing more than a black hump against the dark horizon beyond, slowly slipped past. He waited tensely for the sudden jerk or tearing sound which would tell him that they had not weathered the rocks, but none came, and half an hour later he was confident that they had passed the southern end of Sardinia and gained sufficient sea room.

It was now completely dark, with *Fortitude* long ago out of sight. Fury took out from his pocket the scrap of paper on which the master had scribbled down their position. He could only just make out the master's scrawly handwriting with the aid of the dim light from the binnacle lantern – latitude thirty-nine degrees seventeen minutes north, longitude eight degrees forty-one minutes east. The course they were currently steering was taking them away from Toulon and so his next task, now that he had sea room, was to tack and begin heading north.

He decided to do so immediately, as it was not necessary at the moment to look at the chart and plot an accurate heading – a rough knowledge of the area would do for now until they could take their own noon sight tomorrow.

'Mr Francis.' He beckoned to the young midshipman, who had been standing silently nearby ever since they had got underway. 'I am going to tack the ship now.'

He saw a look of relief on Francis' face as the boy realised Fury had no intention of leaving such a manoeuvre in his inexperienced hands.

'Ready about! Stations for stays!'

The shout escaped from his mouth before he realised the men had no stations, but it seemed to get their attention. He could see them standing ready, darker shapes around the two masts, jostling for position as Clark and Thomas took responsibility and tried to arrange them into some sort of order, quietly allocating duties to different men for the forthcoming manoeuvre.

He slowly started to ease the tiller over, *Renard*'s bow coming up into the wind until the tiller was as far over as it would go.

'Helms alee!' he shouted, the men at the foremast starting to slacken off the sheets of the foretopsail to lessen the effect of the forward sail.

Her head was in the eye of the wind now and

the momentum that she had carried into the turn, combined with the pressure of the backed fore-topsail, was helping to push her head off the wind the other way, completing the turn surprisingly easily as Fury quickly centred the tiller to right the rudder.

'Mainsail haul!' he bellowed, sending the men stationed at the mainmast hauling quickly on the braces to bring the main topsail yard creaking round on to the other tack, the wind soon filling the sail once again.

'Haul taut! Let go and haul!'

The foretopsail yard was now swung round on to the new tack, the sail flapping as it passed through the eye of the wind before numerous sharp slapping sounds told him it was filling and sending them forward on the larboard tack, the wind on the larboard beam. One glance at the compass, lit by the dim light in the binnacle, told him they were heading north, and, happy with that heading for the night, he called over the nearest seaman he could recognise in the darkness, the sandy-haired cockney called Perrin.

'Take over the helm, Perrin. Keep her at north.'

'North sir. Aye aye sir,' Perrin repeated as he grasped the tiller from Fury.

Fury stooped once again over the light in the binnacle, taking out his watch and holding it open to the light. Almost eight o'clock. Good timing, he thought, as he walked over to the larboard bulwark where young Francis was still standing.

'Mr Francis, I want the men split into two watches. One watch can go below and get some rest until called. It's almost eight o'clock so we can start a new watch immediately. Make sure we have four lookouts posted round the deck tonight – one on each bow and one on each quarter. We will remain under topsails only tonight and continue on our heading of north. You can take the first watch while I go below and look over the charts. If you need me during the next four hours then call me. Understood?'

'Aye sir,' Francis replied, as he tried to memorise everything Fury had just said.

'Very well then. You have the deck.'

Fury made his way below to the shouts of Francis dividing the men up into their two watches and organising the four lookouts. The master's cabin was in blackness, and it took a quick grope around to reveal the location of a lantern. Some moments of fumbling and cursing with flint and steel swiftly followed, until at last it was lit, throwing just enough light to cover the desk and the remaining papers on it.

He sat and started to leaf through them, and it was not long before he could hear half the men on deck coming below to find somewhere to sleep for the next few hours. Francis had obviously completed the first of his tasks, Fury thought. The boy was doing well, and being part of *Renard*'s prize crew would only help him further. Strange to think that he was not much older than Francis

184

himself; if Fury had been on the *Fortitude* a year ago, they would have been messmates, skylarking around together. Now they were separated by the invisible barrier of discipline. He took out his watch again. Twenty minutes of poring over the charts and he would take another look on deck to ensure the boy hadn't forgotten anything, he decided.

CHAPTER 10

The night passed smoothly, the wind remaining fresh and steady from the westward. *Renard* thrashed along to the north with a beam wind during the entire night, with Fury and Francis keeping the deck alternately, four hours on and four hours off.

The following morning Fury woke up automatically, through two years of routine, to find that the cabin was still quite dark. It took him a few moments to realise where he was before his befogged brain cleared and he remembered he was on board a prize. As he swung himself out of the cot, he could just make out the needle on the telltale compass fixed to the deck head above him in the poor light, noting they were still making good their course of north. He made his way over to the bowl which he had found the previous night, filled it with water and plunged his face into it. The cold water gave him a shock but he was grateful for its stimulating effect, helping to clear his mind further as he threw off the last effects of sleep.

As he sat down and began to pull his boots

on, he tried to sort the myriad thoughts in his head into some kind of coherent order. He stood up and put on his uniform jacket, buttoning it all the way up to the collar, before reaching for his hat and pressing it down firmly on his head as he made his way out of the cabin and up to the deck.

Dawn was slowly beginning to approach, cold and grey, as he reached the upper deck trying to shake off the depression which always seemed to engulf him at this time of the morning.

The men were all on deck now, some on hands and knees busily scrubbing with holystones to get rid of the dirt on the planking, while others rubbed the ship's brass work with brick dust to bring out the shine. A quick glance at his watch as he walked over to Francis showed it was just before half-past six.

'Good morning sir,' said Francis cheerfully.

'Morning,' Fury replied curtly, deliberately leaving out the 'good'. 'Anything to report?'

'No sir,' Francis replied, 'course at north still and I've just sent the lookouts aloft. I took the liberty of ordering the galley fire lit sir, and breakfast should be along in an hour. Oatmeal gruel, ship's biscuit and we found a little cheese too sir.' Francis was grinning eagerly and rubbing his hands together.

'Very good,' Fury grunted begrudgingly, slightly nettled that the youngster had taken it upon himself to order the men's breakfast. 'Carry on,' he continued, moving over to the weather side of the deck, eager to walk off his depression.

Head down he walked, subconsciously picking his way among the men cleaning the decks; short-handed though they were, Fury's attention to duty still could not tolerate the state *Renard*'s deck had been left in. The sight of the men gave him a sudden thought, and he turned to find Francis.

'Mr Francis!'

'Sir?'

'Set the rest of the men to going throughout the ship cleaning and scrubbing, including my cabin. Any clutter lying about which is not needed for the direct running of the ship should be stowed below out of the way. We may not be aboard for very long, but we may as well make it habitable.'

'Aye aye sir.'

Francis hurried away shouting orders. It was true that they would probably not be aboard *Renard* for more than a week or two, but Fury was secretly proud of his temporary command, and he wanted to feel at home aboard her. He continued his pacing with dozens of thoughts and ideas milling through his head demanding his attention, so much so that he did not notice the wind pick up slightly, carrying with it a slight drizzle from the overcast sky.

Midshipman Francis had the good sense to keep out of his way and leave him alone among his thoughts, so that by the time breakfast was

188

reported ready just over an hour later, his mood had lifted perceptibly.

He had just finished breakfast in his newly cleaned cabin and returned on deck when eight bells sounded, the men below hurrying up to take over the watch as Fury relieved Francis of his duty. The drizzle had thickened slightly in the last half an hour, leaving visibility shortened. He stood there, gently swaying to the motion of the ship, looking forward.

The upper deck on which he was stood ran the whole length of the ship, with no raised quarter-deck or focsle as on larger ships. He took a look at the guns lining the sides, ten in all – small six-pounders by the looks of them. Pop guns, he thought, carried merely to deter the smaller privateers. He would definitely be in trouble if he ran across anything on his way back to Toulon, especially with a crew of only twenty men. He shook off the thought – with the British controlling the Mediterranean only the odd privateer would likely be found at sea, and the chances of meeting one so close to Toulon were tiny.

He glanced aloft to where the two masts stood sharp against the sky, all square-rigged apart from the main course which was a gaff-headed fore-and-aft mainsail, extended by a boom at the foot and a crossjack rather than a main yard. He could see that the topsails were bellying nicely, yards braced up to catch the beam wind at the most efficient angle. The sight of it brought him to the sudden decision to clap on more sail, his impatience getting the better of him.

A quick glance further aloft revealed the topgallant yards down on the cap with no other yards beyond them, not surprising considering merchant captains were notoriously reluctant to increase sail even to topgallants, let alone royals, because of their relatively small crews and their miserly desire to conserve canvas.

He transferred his gaze back to the deck, where those men of the watch whose duties allowed it were huddled round the deck below the bulwark, yarning amongst themselves. Walking over to the binnacle box drawer, he picked up a speaking trumpet.

'All hands! All hands to make sail!' he bellowed, feeling slightly absurd at shouting for all hands when he only had a crew of twenty.

Nevertheless the ten men constituting the watch below, having just finished their breakfast, came streaming up eagerly enough and ran to their stations. Fury paused for a moment to make sure everybody was ready before he began.

'Lay aloft and loose the fore course!' he shouted, knowing that it was the only order he need give for the time being. Experienced seamen like these would work better on their own than with Fury bellowing orders step by step.

Already the men were flying up the shrouds to the lower yard before laying out along it using the stirrups underneath. It took them only a minute or two to undo the gaskets which were keeping the sail tightly bundled against the yard, and the great folds of canvas came flapping down.

The men on deck quickly clapped on to the sheets and hauled taut to bring the corners of the sail down, the lee sheet being secured aft with the weather tack down forward so that the canvas soon began to belly with the pressure of the wind, the patches of lighter and darker cloth on the canvas betraying where previous repairs had been made. A slight adjustment by the men at the braces brought the yard round to the right angle as the rest of the men stood by ready for his next order.

Already he could sense a difference in movement as *Renard* picked up speed and the bow lifted slightly from the effect of the fore course.

'Set the mainsail!'

The men at the mainmast sprang into life now, some swarming up to release the brails which were holding the fore-and-aft sail up to the gaff and mast, while the men on deck hauled on the sheet to bring the lower corner extending out to the foot of the boom below. Another quick adjustment to the tackles attached to the boom, which acted as sheets, had the sail at the right angle, blocking out much of the grey sky from Fury's sight.

He moved forward along the deck so that he could get a clearer view of the bow. He had already decided against setting the topgallants. With only a small crew he did not want to be taken unawares by a sudden change in wind or weather, as was very likely in the Mediterranean.

'Set the jib!'

The men stationed at the foremast moved forward towards the bowsprit, some stationing themselves at the outhaul, some at the halliards, and some at the sheets. The men were pulling on the outhaul now which was attached to the tack of the jib, sending it running out along the jib boom. Once there, the men began hauling on the halliards to send it rising up along the foretop-mast stay, while the men tended the sheets to secure the inner corner of the sail aft along the bowsprit.

A quick nod by Fury as the men secured every-thing and moved back to the foremast told them that it had all been done to his satisfaction, and a word to Mr Francis as he arrived back near the tiller had the watch below stood down once again.

Happy that he had done as much as he could for now, Fury spent the rest of his watch pacing, pausing occasionally to look up at the set of the sails. At midday he had time to rush down and collect the sextant he had found in the master's cabin, before coming back on deck to perform the ritual of the noon sight, a task made somewhat more difficult today with the horizon obscured by the drizzle which was still coming down.

He had searched the master's cabin the previous evening for a chronometer, but had not been able to find one. Upon later reflection he had come to the conclusion that this was unsurprising due to the fact that the brig was unlikely to venture any farther than the Mediterranean, and so navigation would have been possible by a combination of latitude calculations and landfalls.

And so it was that Fury found himself sitting behind the desk in the master's cabin with only a latitude figure calculated, of forty-one degrees forty-five minutes north. The position seemed reasonable looking at the charts, and there was little else he could do now but to keep her on the current heading until they sighted the French or Italian coast ahead.

Later that day the wind strengthened somewhat, obliging Fury to order a reef to be taken in the topsails. They carried on throughout that night and all the following day, the wind maintaining a steady strength so that the one reef in the topsails proved to be sufficient.

It was not until just after three bells in the first dogwatch, the sun now well down towards the horizon over in the west, that a hail from the fore masthead lookout warned of the sight of land ahead. It loomed up through the darkening haze half an hour later, leaving Fury eminently relieved that it had still been light when they had approached.

He immediately ordered sail to be reduced to topsails and jib only, and gave the order to the helmsman to come up to the wind and keep her close hauled until it was time to tack, bringing the wind on to the brig's starboard side.

The rest of the night was spent standing off and on, beating up to the west close hauled towards where he hoped Toulon would be. His common sense told him that he had done everything right, and his calculations and the charts all told him that he was on the correct course to reach the British fleet, but no amount of calculation could erase the nagging doubts which plagued him.

He was on deck several times during the night as a result of his standing orders to young Francis to call him whenever the ship needed tacking once more. Each time he would take a walk around the deck, quietly asking the lookouts stationed around the ship if they had seen anything yet, causing Francis to send several anxious glances in his direction. Each time he would dive back down below exasperated, to attempt sleep again.

By the time the sun peered over the eastern horizon, showing the coastline about two miles distant off their starboard bow, Fury was quite exhausted. He tried to shake off his tiredness with a brisk run up to the fore masthead later in the morning while Francis had the watch, giving him the opportunity to study the coastline through his glass. The patchy grass, intermingled with the harsh grey of the rocky ground beneath, was backed by a string of mountainous peaks and winding valleys beyond, stretching away inland. It was so much like the landscape he had seen surrounding Toulon that by the time he had regained the deck his worries about their position had subsided to a slight doubt.

The rest of that day and throughout the night they continued beating up close hauled against the westerly wind, so that it felt like it would be weeks before they finally reached their destination.

The following day broke grey, each man aboard thoroughly exhausted from the slow beat to windward. It was not until nearly seven bells in the afternoon watch that the fore masthead lookout hailed the deck to report the sight of several batteries dotted on the coast ahead and inland. Fury, busy pacing the deck at the time trying to pass the last half hour of his watch quickly, felt a sudden surge of confidence that they had at last reached Toulon.

Two hours later, after another series of tacks against the wind, the harbour of Toulon opened up to starboard, Fury's glass picking out the crowded anchorage of the outer road.

He snapped his glass shut and turned to the man standing at the tiller.

'Ease her off two points.'

They were already on the larboard tack heading in towards the coast, so it only needed a slight alteration of course to bring her further off until the wind was abeam and they were heading directly into the harbour mouth itself.

Fury walked up the heeling deck to the larboard bulwark and watched as Cape Cepet, jutting out from the opposite shore, slowly slid past with the tall semaphore tower at its tip standing stark and clear.

'Clear away the anchor there!' he shouted forward to the men stationed round the foremast.

The anchor was unlashed from the brig's side and the men hauled it up to the cathead before securing it, ready to drop when Fury gave the order.

The huge bulks of the two-and three-deck line-of-battle ships anchored at the eastern end of the outer road were looming up ahead now, the Spanish or British flags streaming out in the wind. The western side of the road was still slightly blocked from view by the last of Cape Cepet, as Fury scanned forward anxiously with his telescope to find the best place to anchor.

The western side of the road slowly opened up as they weathered Cape Cepet and Fury could see that it was not quite as crowded on that side.

'Bring her up full and bye!' he ordered the helmsman.

'Full and bye sir. Aye aye sir,' the man replied, easing over the tiller to bring her further into the wind.

Fury heard the leech of the topsails begin to flutter as she came up too far into the wind before the helmsman eased her off a trifle.

'Full and bye sir,' he reported.

'Very good.'

Fury was looking ahead, finally deciding that he

would take *Renard* between the big line-of-battle ships and the shore, where there was plenty of room due to the fact that the ships were all anchored in the deep water towards the middle of the bay.

Two more tacks and they should be in position, he thought. It sounded simple, but those two tacks were going to be performed in full view of two fleets, and Vice Admiral Lord Hood.

A big three-decker flying a Spanish flag slipped slowly past about two cables' lengths off to starboard, and then they were beyond her into a relatively clear area.

'Stations for stays!' he shouted, followed by a low growl to the helmsman, 'Ease down your helm.'

Renard came round slowly into the wind, the men on deck easing off the jib sheets to help her round, before those at fore and main hauled to swing the yards round to fill on the starboard tack.

Fury glanced at the compass to see they were now heading south by west, a look ahead showing the northern shore of the Cape Cepet peninsular approaching, with the hospital of St-Mandrier clearly visible.

They had picked up sufficient speed now and the shore was getting ever closer, Fury waiting for as long as he dared before giving the order to tack once again, to ensure that they would be able to reach their anchorage on the next tack. A look over the starboard quarter where he was planning to anchor told him that now was the time. Another shout to the men, another growl at the helmsman to put the helm down, and they were swinging once more, hanging for a terrifying moment in the eye of the wind so that Fury thought she was going to be caught in irons, before finally completing her turn and gathering way on the new tack as the men braced the yards round.

They were now heading north-west with the Balaguier battery atop the small spit of land jutting out into the bay, approaching off the larboard bow.

Fury hastily scanned the anchorage for sign of HMS *Victory*. Ah, there she was, about half a mile further into the outer road, beyond three other ships but clearly visible with her ensign hanging lazily at the fore masthead denoting the presence on board of a Vice Admiral of the Red. No doubt Lord Hood had been informed of the arrival of the captured brig some time ago and was waiting impatiently for the commanding officer to report on board to him.

A sudden breath of wind blew out the ensign at her masthead, the sight of it prompting his memory with a shock. He had not yet offered the salute due to a vice admiral! He turned and hurriedly instructed Francis to have the larboard guns cast loose and loaded with blank charges ready for the salute of thirteen guns.

Francis had the task completed with commendable speed, but even so it was not quick enough for Fury as he stood on the deck of *Renard*, shuffling his feet uncomfortably.

Finally the first gun barked out, and as it did so Fury's confidence began to wane. Had he remembered the passage correctly? It would not go well on an officer who made a hash of the Royal Navy's precious ceremonials.

The last gun of the thirteen due had just sounded, and a moment later HMS *Victory*, as if satisfied, began her reply. By the time that had been completed, they had the battery of Balaguier abeam, her guns looking black and menacing through the embrasures.

Fury, the relief coursing through him, tore his gaze away from Balaguier and looked at the water ahead, all worries over salutes pushed aside as he decided now that the time was right to anchor.

'Hard astarboard!' he snapped to the man at the tiller.

The brig's bow immediately began to swing into the wind, losing way rapidly until finally coming to a brief standstill.

'Let go the anchor!'

The men forward released the anchor, the sound of a huge splash quickly followed by the steady humming as the cable roared out of the hawsehole.

They were making sternway now as the wind pushed them backwards, helping the anchor on the seabed to dig in.

'Lay aloft and furl!'

Men went streaming aloft, while those on deck

eased off the halliards to bring the topsail yards down to the cap before the men scrambled out along them. More hauling of the clew lines and buntlines by the men on deck brought the lower corners and foot of the topsails up to the yard, where the men were waiting to fist the canvas into submission before securing it to the yard with the gaskets.

With the sail now furled the sternway diminished, until finally the last of the anchor cable ranged out on deck was reached and she came to a standstill, swinging slightly to the light current within the outer road.

CHAPTER 11

The relief that he had managed to bring *Renard* in safely in front of Lord Hood and the remainder of the two fleets surged through Fury. His hands were still trembling slightly with the release of tension as he looked across to the shore where he could clearly see Fort Balaguier staring at them, the British flag flying proudly in place of the French tricolour. That was as much time as he dared spare for the shore at that moment.

'Mr Francis!' he bellowed, turning round startled as Francis replied just behind him. 'Please be so kind as to have the boat cleared away so that I may make my call upon the admiral. I will be down below in the master's cabin.'

'Aye aye sir,' Francis replied, as Fury descended down the hatchway and made his way aft to the master's cabin.

A quick search of the sleeping cabin revealed the boat cloak which he had seen when he first came aboard with Lieutenant Ross, and he placed it on his cot. One look in the grubby mirror hanging in the cabin confirmed his worst fears.

His face looked exhausted and dirty, with growths of stubble here and there. A glance down at his clothes showed his white breeches were also dirty and his jacket was creased.

Fury quickly changed into a new pair of breeches and hastily plunged his hands into the bowl of water sitting on the sideboard, vigorously rubbing his face. By the time he arrived back on deck in his clumsily straightened jacket and stock with the boat cloak folded under his right arm, Francis had finished having the boat hoisted out and was standing waiting for him.

Fury picked the nearest ten seamen and ordered them down into the boat, before turning back to Francis.

'You will take command until I return, Mr Francis.'

'Aye aye sir,' Francis replied formally, saluting and following Fury as he walked over to *Renard*'s side.

One look down showed the men were already in the boat waiting for him, five oars a side. He pulled the boat cloak over him and made the short journey down into her, moving aft and settling himself in the stern sheets at the tiller.

'Shove off. Give way all,' he growled, taking his apprehension out on his men.

He steered a course which would take them between two large three-deckers and past the stern of another two-decker before arriving at the one-hundred-gun *Victory*.

The wind was whipping up spray all around as the small boat ploughed through the waves, Fury glad that he had at least had the foresight to look for the boat cloak. Nevertheless his eyes were stinging from the salt spray as he looked forward, licking his lips occasionally to prevent the salt from drying them out.

He could see curious eyes above the bulwarks of the huge ships as they passed, all looking down at the boat and no doubt wondering who he was and how the brig was captured.

'Come on lads, put your backs into it!' he encouraged, as the men struggled at the oars.

They were past the last two-decker now and there was the *Victory* ahead. Luckily her starboard side – the side used by officers – was nearest to them, so they would not have to row round to the other side to hook on.

As soon as they were within earshot, a figure by her quarterdeck rail high above leaned over the netting with a speaking trumpet to his mouth.

'Boat ahoy!'

The shout came drifting down to Fury carried by the wind. There was no coxswain in the boat so Fury took a deep breath before shouting his reply.

'Aye aye!'

He pushed aside his boat cloak so that his uniform could be seen from her deck. The man above disappeared and Fury was left to concentrate on laying the boat alongside her properly, a quick turn of the tiller to port sending the boat sliding alongside her massive bulk, the men raising and stowing their oars without the need for orders while a man in the bow stood ready with the boat hook to fasten on.

Fury shrugged off the boat cloak fully, straightened his jacket and walked towards the familiar entry ladder stretching away above. He paused for a moment as the boat rose on a wave before leaping for the ladder, grasping the ropes hanging down the side of the battens, held out by the side boys.

It did not take him long to reach the entry port located about halfway up the *Victory*'s side, pulling himself in and coming face to face with Captain Knight, whom he recognised from his previous visit to the *Victory* on passing for lieutenant.

'Lieutenant Fury sir, of HMS *Fortitude*, reporting on board,' he said, straightening himself up and touching his hat.

He had the impression that Knight was looking him up and down, no doubt noting his slightly ragged appearance.

'Lord Hood will see you shortly Mr Fury. If you will follow me I will show you the way.'

The words betrayed no hint of disapproval at Fury's appearance, which helped to settle his nerves as he followed quietly behind the *Victory*'s captain. He was led to a cabin aft which contained a table and a number of chairs, one of which he gratefully sank into as Knight made his excuses and left the room.

It was a full fifteen minutes before the appearance of a man in a sparkling lieutenant's uniform interrupted his thoughts.

'Good afternoon, I am Lord Hood's flag lieutenant. His Lordship will see you now.'

Fury followed him, cursing his luck that he should be ushered in to see Lord Hood by a man wearing one of the most sparkling and well-cut uniforms he had ever seen, in comparison to his own well used and slightly grubby undress uniform.

Lord Hood looked up from his desk as they entered the admiral's day cabin, his bulbous red nose pointing at them as he beckoned the two officers in further.

'Lieutenant Fury, My Lord, of HMS *Fortitude*,' the flag lieutenant announced formally.

Fury touched his hat self-consciously and muttered, 'My Lord.'

'Very well Hodge, you can leave us now,' the admiral said with a wave of his hand at the flag lieutenant. Hodge slipped out and Hood turned his attention to Fury. 'Well Mr Fury. How is it going aboard the *Fortitude*?'

'Very well thank you, My Lord.'

'Excellent. Pray take a seat and give me a verbal report of how you come to be here without your ship.'

Fury sat down in one of the chairs opposite the admiral's desk, placed his hat on his knee, and paused while he mentally arranged his report.

'Four days out from Toulon My Lord, en route to Malta as ordered, we encountered a Ragusan brig, the *Renard*, on her way from Smyrna to Marseilles with a cargo of timber. There is also a quantity of liquor on board. After chasing her for over four hours she finally surrendered without a shot and I was placed in command by Captain Young. I was given orders to sail back to Toulon and await his return.'

'How does she sail?'

'Very well My Lord. She seems weatherly enough.'

'Hmm,' Hood mused, 'I will have someone take a look at her with a view to purchasing her into the service. We're always in need of runners to deliver reports and the like.'

A small smile crept across Fury's face as he mentally began spending his share of the prize money.

'Now,' Hood continued, 'on to more pressing matters – how many men have you got with you?'

'Twenty able seamen and one midshipman, My Lord,' Fury replied, dragging his mind back to the present.

'Excellent. I may need to avail myself of the services of you and your men, Mr Fury, while you wait for Captain Young and the *Fortitude* to return.'

'I am at your service, My Lord,' Fury replied. He couldn't very well say much else.

'Excellent!' Hood repeated, rising slowly from his chair to signal that the brief interview was at an end. 'You and your crew may stay on board *Renard*. You will no doubt receive your orders shortly, once we have assessed where the next Republican threat will come from.'

'Aye aye sir. What about the cargo and liquor, My Lord?'

Fury did not particularly like the idea of sitting idly at anchor when ardent spirits were to be had on board.

'Ah yes, the liquor. Uncomfortable with those spirits on board eh?' Hood didn't wait for an answer. He knew as well as anyone the capacity of the ordinary seaman to get at drink when given half an opportunity. 'Very well, I shall make arrangements to have them both unloaded tomorrow.'

'Thank you My Lord. And resupply, sir?'

'I shall have *Renard* added on to the fleet list. You will get reprovisioned from the hoys along with the rest of the fleet.'

'Thank you, My Lord.'

'Oh yes, and there will be a vessel leaving for England in two or three days. I shall be instructing a boat to visit each ship and collect any letters, so if you have any, you had better make sure they are bagged and ready.'

'Yes, My Lord.'

Fury touched the brim of his hat in salute and left the cabin. Five minutes later he was sitting in the stern sheets of the boat once again, as the crew shoved off from the *Victory*'s side and began the pull back to *Renard*.

Fury waited patiently as the men tugged at the oars to send the boat slowly bobbing through the choppy waters towards the brig, snubbing quietly at her anchor cable.

Finally they were hooked on and Fury, eager to get aboard and rest his weary limbs, clambered swiftly up her low side and on to the deck. Francis was in front of him with a worried look on his face.

'What is it Mr Francis?'

The boy was shaking his head. Had the brig sprung a leak?

'You're not going to like it sir,' he stammered.

'Out with it, for God's sake!' Fury snapped, his tiredness fraying at his temper.

'It's some of the men sir.' Francis paused, but the sudden look of thunder on Fury's brow prompted a hasty continuance. 'They got at the liquor sir, while you were visiting the flagship.'

'God damn and blast it!'

Francis was looking terrified now, but Fury was in no mood to calm him, even if he did think the boy innocent of any wrongdoing. He blamed himself and no one else. He should have taken more precautions once they had reached Toulon. It had been easy to keep the men away from the stuff when they had been beating back against that westerly wind – the men were so exhausted then that once off watch, the only thought had been sleep. Now, though, with time on their hands, they had contrived to get at it.

The words of Ross, words he had considered

patronising at the time, returned to haunt him. Would he never learn? The sounds of laughter drifted up from below as if to mock him further.

'How many Mr Francis?'

It took a large effort to bring his temper under control and ask the question calmly, but the shame at his previous outburst spurred him on.

'Only six sir. The men not on anchor watch.'

Once safely in harbour, the majority of a ship's crew were stood down from duties, a skeleton 'anchor watch' being the only watch needed. Naturally it had been the idle men, allowed peace and quiet down below, who had transgressed.

'Where are they now?' Fury demanded.

The shuffling of feet behind him told him that the boat's crew were now all up on deck, listening to the exchange with curiosity.

'Still down below sir. We only have four men sober sir, and I didn't want a confrontation.'

That may be so, Fury thought, but with his boat's crew back, he now had plenty of men to deal with them.

'Wait here.'

He hurried to the master's cabin and unlocked the desk drawer, taking out his pistols. They were still loaded, so it took only moments before he was back on deck, suddenly wishing he had some marines on board to back him up. He would have to rely on the loyalty of the men on deck. He knew Clark and the other ex-Amazons would stand by him, but what about the others? Would they back

209

him up if the men below decided to fight? Probably so, he thought. They would be in no hurry to let their shipmates continue drinking when they were stone-cold sober.

'Mr Francis, you will remain on deck with the anchor watch.'

Francis merely nodded. He had been looking even more worried since he had seen Fury return on deck with two pistols in his hands.

Fury turned to his assembled boat's crew.

'Follow me lads!'

He tried to sound confident but his stomach was churning and his palms were beginning to sweat. He had no wish to fire on a British seaman, one of his own crew.

They followed him below to the berth deck, where a hanging lantern forward cast its orange glow over the small group of men, sitting on the bare planking with empty bottles strewn about them.

Fury strode towards them, his stomach tightening still more as he went. One of the men saw him and stumbled to his feet, swaying slightly as his comrades followed suit. Fury stopped. He could see frightened eyes glancing from his face, down to the pistol in each hand.

'Who's in charge here?' he demanded.

No one spoke.

'Who gave you permission to take that liquor?'

Still silence.

'By God!' Fury continued in a rising voice,

sensing that he had the upper hand, 'I could have you all flogged for this! I could have the skin hanging from your backs!'

He paused to let the image sink in.

'We worn't doin' no harm sir, just a little lubricating.'

Fury recognised the speaker from his own division on the *Fortitude*, the short stocky foretopman called Gooseman. He felt let down.

'Put those bottles down at once!'

One of the men at the back of the group was foolish enough to take a sly swig, and Fury saw it. His calmness evaporated in an instant.

'Down, I tell you!'

The men hesitated and Fury raised his hands, pointing the pistols at them. The sight of those pistols proved a powerful persuader, even if Fury hadn't yet decided if he had the courage to use them.

Bottles smashed on the deck planking as reluctant hands released their grip.

'Now up on deck, all of you.'

The men began to reach for their jackets, but stopped short as Fury thrust the pistols at them again.

'Leave the jackets! Move!'

He stepped aside to let the men trudge past, each wearing only shirt and trousers. They reached the deck where darkness was beginning to fall, the temperature dropping as the heat of the sun was lost.

'Mr Francis!'

'Sir?'

'These men will supplement the anchor watch for the next four hours. After that they can retire below for some sleep. Two hours to be precise, then I want them back on duty, in jackets if they wish.'

Fury could see grins from the men around as they heard his orders, the small huddle of men in front of him looking miserable and already shivering slightly in the wind.

'Take these.' Fury handed Francis his two pistols. 'You have my permission to shoot any man who attempts to leave the deck before the four hours are up. Is that understood?'

'Yes sir.'

Fury turned to go below and supervise the securing of the rest of the liquor. It would be unloaded tomorrow if Hood was as good as his word, but Fury wanted to take no more chances until then. He would be hard pushed to come up with a satisfactory explanation to the admiral should half the cargo go missing.

He stopped at the hatchway leading down to the deck below, remembering a small point and half turning to seek out Francis once again.

'Oh and Mr Francis.'

'Sir?'

'There will be a boat coming round the fleet in a day or two to collect mail for England. Inform the men they'd better have any letters ready by then.'

'Aye aye sir.'

Satisfied, he made his way down below to see to the liquor. Half an hour later saw him laid in his cot in the master's cabin, his weary limbs finally enjoying some rest after a long, hard day.

Fury was up before dawn the next day, eager to make the preparations for the removal of *Renard*'s cargo as soon as the lighters arrived.

Hood was as good as his word, the lighters beetling out to them across the bay in the first light of morning. Fury immediately set the men to work rigging tackles and blocks with which the cargo could be swung up and out of the hold, so that by the time the lighters pulled alongside, they were ready.

Those men who had got to the liquor the previous day were obviously suffering from the after-effects of their binge, which raised a smile from Fury as he watched them sweating and grumbling.

It took all morning before the last of the liquor and timber was hauled up and lowered down on to the deck of the last lighter left alongside. It was just after midday, the men sitting about the deck eating hard biscuit and rancid cheese, when the first sounds of gunfire reached them. It came from the shore to the north-west, overlooking the inner road where many of the fleet were now anchored.

An hour later and the cannonade continued

unabated, Fury seeing the sails of the warships in the inner road as they glided slowly to the east to get themselves out of range of the enemy's guns.

Fury stood on the deck with his telescope, training it forward past the village of La Seyne and on to the heights covering the horizon, trying to catch a glimpse of where the Republicans had erected their battery. He saw nothing, save for the occasional drift of smoke which may or may not betray the location of the guns.

His eye was aching by the time the familiar sound of a twelve-pounder reached his ears nearer at hand, swiftly followed by another and then another as the allies finally responded to the new threat. He could see the masts and yards of the ship which was firing, presumably a frigate, stationed to the west of the inner road and bombarding the heights in an attempt to silence the enemy battery. He would recognise the sound of a twelve-pounder anywhere after his service on board the *Amazon*, and the memories of it came flooding back.

For over three hours the firing continued, long enough for the ears and mind to become accustomed to it, so that when it finally stopped just after four bells in the afternoon watch, the anchorage was eerily quiet.

Fury, now perched as near to the truck of the mainmast as he could get, scanned the bay in the fading light. A boat pulled out from the lee of the ninety-eight-gun *Royal George*, anchored just within the inner road. Fury watched it slowly pull across the current heading for the outer road, presumably to deliver despatches of some sort. His curiosity increased as the boat turned to the west and pulled directly for *Renard*.

'Boat coming sir!' shouted Francis from the deck, but Fury was already scrambling down the rigging.

He reached the deck, half expecting the boat to have changed course by now and be approaching one of the other anchored ships nearby, but she was still pulling for *Renard* and was not far off now. It was too early for it to be the boat collecting mail, surely.

Fury began pacing in an effort to calm his racing thoughts, so that he was oblivious to the exchange of shouts as the boat approached and hooked on. He stopped short as a midshipman scurried through the brig's entry port and addressed himself to Francis, who led him over to where Fury was standing and introduced him.

'Midshipman Gregory sir, from the *Royal George*.'

'Yes, Mr Gregory. And what may we do for you?'

For a midshipman he was remarkably old, probably in his late thirties, so that Fury felt slightly uncomfortable addressing him as a subordinate.

'Orders from the admiral sir.'

Gregory held out a sealed paper.

'Admiral?' Fury enquired, taking the package. He knew very well that Rear Admiral Gell had his flag hoisted on the *Royal George*, but it was as well to make sure.

'Rear Admiral Gell sir,' Gregory confirmed. 'I am to await your confirmation.'

Fury nodded and walked over to the larboard side to gain some privacy, quickly tearing the seal as he walked. The first page was brief.

Lieutenant Fury, HMS *Fortitude*
18 September 1793

The Republicans have opened up two masked batteries to the west of the inner road. We have, this afternoon, prepared two floating batteries with which to counter this threat. In accordance with the recommendation of Lord Hood, I am placing you in command of one of these, the *Tempest*. She is lying ready to the east of the inner road, with forty men on board, currently under a midshipman, along with a gunnery expert to operate the mortars. You are to make sure you are on board by dawn tomorrow so that you can be towed into a position to engage the enemy. Your official orders are overleaf.

Your servant,
Rear Admiral Gell

Fury turned to the second page where his official orders were written, brief and formal, beginning with the increasingly familiar 'You are hereby requested and required'. He turned to Gregory, waiting patiently with Francis alongside.

'Very well. You may inform the admiral I shall be in position by dawn tomorrow as ordered.'

Francis looked confused, but Fury didn't have time to explain. He saw Gregory over the side and hurried down to his cabin, aware that he had a letter to write to his mother before he left. He may be dead tomorrow.

CHAPTER 12

F ury sat in the stern sheets of the boat and
looked forward through the maze of shipping to his new command, albeit temporary.
A brisk wind whipped at the sheltered waters of
the inner road, sending the spray in great swathes
over those huddled in the boat as they gradually
neared their objective.

He blinked to try and relieve the discomfort
caused by the salt in his eyes. His vision cleared
somewhat and he studied her closely, registering
the distant thuds of cannon over to the left.

She must once have been an imposing two-
decker, built to stand in the line of battle and
assert the will of her masters. Through age and
use, however, she was now nothing more than a
hulk, a floating battery whose only task was to aid
in the destruction of the masked batteries of the
Republicans over to the west, which were causing
havoc to the shipping in the inner road.

Fury fumbled in his brain for the right term,
finally plucking it from his memory as another
sheet of spray soaked him through. Razee. The
once proud line-of-battle ship had been cut down

to facilitate her current use from one of the unseaworthy two-deckers in the French fleet, found in
the harbour when the British had entered. Her poop
and quarterdeck were long gone, so too her focsle.
Her upper deck had been removed and her sides
cut down, except for forward and aft where it had
seemingly been untouched, probably to provide
shelter for the men forward, and a magazine for
her powder aft. Her mainmast was missing entirely,
while those of the fore and main were cut off at
the junction of the topmasts. Each had a scrap of
sail loosely hanging from a yard, presumably to
aid her in manoeuvring into position. Doubtless
there would be sweeps aboard too – a ship of that
size, cut down or not, would not make much
headway with that measly canvas.

They were nearly there now, the vast bulk of the
ninety-eight-gun *Royal George* nearby, waiting
patiently to take her under tow. Rear Admiral Gell
in command of her would probably be fuming at
the delay, thought Fury, but he had a clear
conscience. He had only received his orders last
night, and had set off from *Renard* this morning
before the weak sun was even peering over the
eastern horizon.

If he had been given sufficient men, she would
not have needed to be towed. A combination of
sail and sweeps would have been sufficient to
get her over to the required position in order to
help the prize frigate *Aurora*, the *Royal George*,
and the other gunboat currently engaged with

the Republican batteries. But of course Lord Hood was already desperately short of men trying to defend the fifteen-mile perimeter of Toulon and its environs from the enemy, and so Fury had to make do with a little over forty men, hardly enough to man her armament, much less move her ponderous bulk.

Finally reaching her, Fury put the tiller over to send the boat gliding alongside, the men unshipping their oars while the bowman forward hooked on. Fury stood up and made his way to the battens leading up the short side of his new command. He jumped through the improvised entry port on to what used to be the lower deck.

Four twenty-four-pounders were ranged at intervals along the starboard side, currently bowsed taut and impotent. At a number of the old gun ports large thole pins had been erected for use with the sweeps. These sweeps were now laid silently along the larboard side, lashed firmly in place until needed. The forward and aft-most sections of the deck, under cover of what used to be the upper deck, were both sectioned off with hanging canvas screens, so that he could not see what lay beyond.

One glance amidships showed immediately why the mainmast had been removed. Two large brass mortars had been installed in the centre of the hull, where the mainmast used to be. Fury was glad there was a gunnery expert on board to operate them. Using mortars was a specialist business, requiring knowledge of trajectories, fuse lengths and charges. The only thing he knew about them was that they were housed within a solid carriage of timber, called the bed, and bolted securely so that no movement was possible when fired.

There was a young midshipman shuffling his feet before him now, trying to get his attention.

'Midshipman Vansittart sir, from the *Victory*. Welcome aboard the *Tempest*.'

'Thank you Mr Vansittart. Is the tiller manned?'

'Yes sir.'

'And is the tow rope ready?'

'Yes sir. It was passed over from the *Royal George* more than an hour ago. They are waiting for our signal to begin.'

Fury could almost picture Rear Admiral Gell stomping around the quarterdeck of the *Royal George*, fuming at the delay.

'Then perhaps you had better hoist it so we can get underway.'

'Aye aye sir,' Vansittart replied, hurrying over to a man standing near what was left of the foremast.

Strong arms clapped on to the halliards, and a moment later a flag rose jerkily upwards, breaking out at the top of the foremast and telling the *Royal George* they were ready to begin.

'Man the capstan!' Fury yelled.

The *Tempest* was riding to her bower anchor, the thick hempen cable coming in at the hawsehole and leading down to the tiers below. Lightened of stores and armament and cut down greatly, they should have sufficient men at the capstan to break the anchor loose of the seabed.

It took only a moment for the men to assemble at the capstan bars and begin, slowly walking round as the cable slithered aboard. He could tell when the anchor was free of the seabed by the ease with which the men suddenly walked round the capstan barrel. He could also see from the shore that they had begun to drift with the current now that the anchor was atrip, and he made his way over to the side to look forward at the *Royal George*. She had just sheeted home topsails and was beginning to fill slowly away, the large hempen tow rope connecting the two vessels rising up out of the water as the strain came on it. He could feel the bow swing as the tow rope reached its full length and she started to come round in response to the *Royal George*.

'Mr Vansittart!'

'Sir?'

The lad came running across to stand at his side.

'Have that scrap of canvas set on fore and mizzen if you please. We may as well help the admiral as much as we can.'

'Aye aye sir,' Vansittart piped.

As large as the *Royal George* was, and as light as they were, it was no easy task towing a ship through a seaway, so any small scrap of canvas they could set would have a tremendous effect.

It only took a few of the men hauling on sheets and halliards to send the damp, yellow canvas rising pathetically to the makeshift yards. A little pull on the braces had them trimmed identically to the *Royal George*, so that the two of them increased speed perceptibly as they moved westward.

Glad to be underway, and feeling slightly powerless at not being fully in control of her movements, Fury turned inboard once again to continue his scan of the deck.

His attention was diverted by the approach of a man wearing just shirt and breeches and sweating profusely as he warmly held out his hand to Fury.

'My name's Watson sir, formerly a lieutenant in His Majesty's Artillery, now seconded to this old tub.'

'I am Lieutenant Fury, of the *Fortitude*. You have knowledge of mortars then?'

'Yes sir. All on land of course, but then what's the difference eh?'

Fury couldn't bring himself to dampen the man's spirit by pointing out that a ship did not provide a steady platform for gunnery, nor was it easy to hide a ship from the enemy. The Republicans had a distinct advantage in this small battle, and Fury knew it.

'Perhaps you could take me quickly through your preparations.'

Watson nodded his head eagerly, as if glad to have a willing audience to listen to his expertise.

'Of course Mr Fury. If you'll follow me back here, I'll show you how it works.'

He pointed aft to where the canvas screen blocked off Fury's view. Fury followed him, Watson staggering occasionally as the *Tempest* shifted her bulk in deference to wind and wave. Thrusting aside the canvas screen, Fury stepped beyond to see a makeshift magazine, just as he had expected. Buckets of water were everywhere and it was obvious the deck beneath him had recently been sluiced down to avoid any stray grains of powder igniting.

'This is the filling room. As you can see we keep it well watered. The hanging magazine down on the orlop deck is used to make up the cartridges for the propellant powder.'

Fury nodded his approval. Watson held up a metallic ball for his inspection.

'Your typical thirteen-inch shell.'

Fury shook it gingerly and realised it was empty.

'Hollow,' Watson confirmed. 'We don't fill 'em with powder until they're needed. Usually that's done in the boat appointed to carry 'em but, not having our own tender, we have to run the risk of doing it here.'

'And the fuse?' Fury asked.

'Inserted by me – fixing, we call it – but first cut to the required length depending on how far the enemy is. Cut it too long and they'll have time to extinguish it when it lands, too short and it'll explode harmlessly mid flight.'

'I see.' Fury was beginning to appreciate the many different complexities of using them accurately. 'And the loading?'

'That's simple enough. The fixed shells are taken as needed to the mortars. The powder used to propel the mortar is put into the chamber first, followed by a wad, rammed down. The shell is placed on this wad, fuse hole uppermost, followed by a final wad to keep the shell firmly in position. After that it's simply a case of lighting the fuse of the shell and then lighting the mortar itself.'

'I see. And what if we cannot see the enemy batteries?'

'We'll be able to calculate their position by studying the smoke trails from their shells. Then we'll drop our own shells right on top of them.'

'You have enough men?'

'Not quite, but we'll make do. It's not as if His Lordship can spare the men, is it?'

Fury was cut off from responding by Mr Vansittart, vying for his attention.

'Please sir, the *Royal George* has just signalled to cast off the tow. We're just about in position now.'

'Very well Mr Vansittart, have the men at the bows cast it loose. We'll furl those scraps of sail once we find a suitable anchorage.'

Fury left the magazine in Vansittart's wake and looked forward to the *Royal George*. The tow rope had been cast off and lay in the water, trailing astern of the big second rate. He could see the fort of Malbousquet over to starboard, with Missiessi further to the east. They were at the north-western end of the inner road, with the heights of La Petite-Garenne presumably hiding the Republican mortar batteries situated just below the crest on the other side of the heights.

The landscape looked barren and bleak, course scrub vegetation scattered across the many hills and valleys. Perhaps it would look more appealing during the springtime when the rainfall would provide some more colour, Fury thought magnanimously, giving the place the benefit of the doubt.

A distant bang followed by a curious whistling sound reached his ears, and he turned with a look of confusion on his face. A second later a small explosion tore at the air, the black smoke billowing out over to larboard close by the French prize frigate *Aurora*, which was just coming to her anchor.

It was the first shell of the day, Fury realised, coming from one of the Republican's hidden batteries, and it had luckily just missed its target.

'Ready away the anchor there!' he bellowed, anxious to be at the French.

They were the farthest right of a staggered line of vessels consisting of the *Aurora*, another floating battery similar to themselves, the *Royal George* and then the *Tempest*.

The first shots were already beginning to erupt from the sides of the *Aurora* and the *Royal George* as Fury gave the commands which saw the anchor dropped and the small scrap of sail at fore and mizzen furled.

A hawser was laid out of the aft-most gun port and attached to the anchor cable forward so that by hauling on it, the *Tempest* could be shifted round to bring her small battery of twenty-four-pounders to bear. Those twenty-four-pounders, at a signal from Fury, had already been loaded and were now ready to reply.

He scanned the heights with his telescope but could see no sign of the enemy batteries. The bombardment continued as Fury peered through the glass, making a mental note of where the smoke trails from the shells were originating. He was about to turn away to give his first order, when something caught his eye: a bright glint of light from up on the heights, caused by the sun reflecting off glass, perhaps. Was that the French spotters, up on the heights with telescopes directing the fire of their own shells? Probably, Fury thought, snapping his glass shut and turning inboard.

'Maximum elevation!'

The gun captains ensured the guns were aiming as high as they could, before standing back, ready for the word. Fury was doubtful whether any of the shot would be able to reach the enemy batteries on the other side of the heights, but their firing might provide nuisance value while Watson's mortars did the real damage.

'Fire!'

Fury gave the word and they bellowed out, joining in the cacophony of noise nearby as the four vessels bombarded the estimated positions of the enemy.

He caught glimpses of Watson going to and from the magazine as he brought out fixed shells, the sharper bark of the mortars adding their weight to the din.

Fury felt a sudden urge to see these remarkable weapons in action and left the twenty-four-pounders for a few moments. Watson was busy handing the first of the filled shells over to his assistant, while he cut a length of fuse and inserted it into the cylindrical body, lighting it before placing it into the barrel. The same was done with the second. Satisfied, they stood back and his assistant touched the slow match to the touch-holes.

The mortar barked out and the sharp whistling sound as the cylindrical ball soared upwards gradually diminished. The smoke from the protruding fuses marked a helpful trail through the air as the shells arced up and over the hills and dropped beyond, the explosions drifting to them across the water a moment later.

'At least the fuses were the right length,' Watson observed, apparently happy with his work.

His curiosity satisfied, Fury grunted and left him to it, preferring to supervise the more familiar twenty-four-pound cannon. Those cannons were crashing out at commendably short intervals, much to Fury's satisfaction. The smoke generated at each discharge drifted back over the crews, choking and stinging the eyes so that Fury marvelled at their endurance.

The men reloaded and fired like automata, the noise and smoke invading the senses as Fury kept his telescope trained on the distant heights until his arm ached with the effort. In spite of their fire, the enemy shells rained down unabated, albeit largely ineffectively. Fury lowered his telescope and looked at his watch to see that it was only ten o'clock. They had been going almost three hours and he had not the slightest idea whether they had hit anything.

More whistling sounds told him of further shells raining down on their positions. He looked across at the *Aurora* to see an explosion on her focsle, the black smoke hanging thick over her bow. He could see men rushing towards it with water buckets to put out any smouldering fragments of iron. Fury forced his mind to ignore what kind of carnage an exploding shell would do to those around it.

His attention was diverted by a deeper boom over to his right, not far from Malbousquet. A splash was thrown up in the inner road near the *Tempest*'s bow and Fury wondered for a moment where it had originated. Malbousquet was not firing at them, was it?

The sound of another cannon reached his ears, and then another, but he was looking at Malbousquet and none of her guns had fired. A crash nearby told him that at least one of them had struck. The Republicans must have opened up another battery, this one of cannon, and by the sound of it, twenty-four-pounders too. He whipped the telescope back to his eye and studied the land-scape to the west of Malbousquet. A minute later they fired again, and Fury saw the smoke from their discharge. He waited until the smoke cleared, and fancied he could distinguish the black muzzles of the enemy cannon looking back at him. The rest of the battery he could not see, evidently camou-flaged by the Republicans.

'Take a turn on the spring there!' he shouted, unwilling to sit and be fired at without the chance of reply.

Men ran from their guns and hauled on the spring to bring the *Tempest*'s broadside slowly round until her guns would bear. By the time the crews were back at their pieces and ready to fire, more balls were coming down from the masked battery of enemy cannon, two hitting them near the bow. He had counted four discharges with that salvo. Looking down at the side he could see the holes where the balls had struck.

'Fire!'

Their own cannon roared out at maximum elevation and the crews flung themselves into the process of reloading without even bothering to look at where their shot had fallen. Fury had his glass to his eye, studying the landscape intently, and even he could not see where they fell.

More whistling sounds came overhead, Fury shuffling his feet with unease as the sound grew louder. A loud thud sounded from forward and a second later an explosion ripped through the foremast rigging, iron fragments scything in every direction as the shell casing burst apart. He could hear loud screams from at least one man who had been caught in the blast.

Grabbing the nearest water bucket, he rushed forward and flung it up at the sail to stop the red hot iron fragments smouldering. He put the bucket down on the deck, only then seeing the man writhing on the planking not ten feet away. His body was a bloody mess, fragments of iron protruding everywhere, the smoke still pouring from them as they burned his flesh.

Still he was alive, in the most agonising pain imaginable, his screams now little more than whimpers as his last grains of strength left him. He was dead by the time Fury reached him, thankfully, so there was nothing left for him to do but drag the body to the side of the deck and return to his position. He could feel the bile rising in his throat, and he tried to push the sight of the wretched man from his mind.

He looked across at the other vessels, each showing visible signs of damage. Even as he watched a cannonball plummeted into the side of the *Royal George*, smashing timbers and sending up showers of splinters. A moment later another crashed into their own hull near the low bulwark, the splinters being thrown across the deck and slicing open a seaman along the way. Fury saw the blood on the planking gradually spread as the man stood there dumbstruck looking down at his midriff.

Two of his comrades were quickly at his side, carrying him forward to the screened-off section under the upper deck. The sight of it made Fury realise they had no surgeon on board, and he wondered what they would do with him. Here was Watson coming over to him, that smile of his still on his face. Was the man mad?

'How are we doing Mr Fury?'

'Not too well. I can't even see their batteries so I have no idea if we're hitting anything. We can't take too much of this ourselves.'

'We'll be hitting them,' Watson declared confidently, 'I've studied the smoke trails of their shells and I've calculated their points of origin. Just a little over 2,000 yards, twenty-two-second flight time with a nine-pound powder charge.'

Fury was impressed by the man's expertise and could only hope his confidence was not misplaced. He spared a further glance at his watch, hoping for the day to end quickly. His heart sank when he saw it was barely half-past eleven. He was not sure how much more of this his nerves could take.

More crashes further forward told him of at least two balls ploughing into their hull from the masked battery over near Malbousquet. A quick glance at the men around the twenty-four-pounders heartened him a little, the speed with which they reloaded reminding him how professional they were. Those guns thundered out once again as he watched, the smoke blowing back on board to wreath the crews in a choking, sulphurous mass.

Whistling noises betrayed the approach of yet more enemy mortar shells. An explosion over to the left near the *Royal George* was followed quickly by another, much closer, sending the hull of the *Tempest* shuddering from the force. Fury rushed to the side and looked down. Part of the hull near the waterline was charred black, jagged splinters protruding from the surface, the smoke still rising from the burning shell fragments. Fury hurriedly grabbed another water bucket and slung it over the side, beckoning a couple of men to do the same.

'Sir!'

That was Vansittart, rushing towards him.

'What is it Mr Vansittart?' Fury asked, thinking he had enough on his plate already without more distractions.

'*Royal George* has just signalled sir. We are to withdraw out of range until further orders.'

'Very well,' Fury replied, his mind racing too quickly to register any relief. 'Secure the guns!' he bellowed.

Rear Admiral Gell had presumably seen the punishment they had been taking and had come to the correct decision. The sight of their withdrawal would no doubt give the Republicans a huge boost.

'Man the capstan!'

The guns were all secure now and the men raced to the capstan to begin the process of weighing anchor, obviously eager to get out of range as quickly as possible. The clank, clank of the capstan pawls could soon be heard as the heavy cable was brought in, Fury having the scraps of canvas set on fore and mizzen as soon as the anchor was free.

He could see the other floating battery withdrawing as well, leaving just the *Royal George* and the *Aurora* to continue the fight. They glided slowly to the east – too slowly it seemed to Fury – with cannon splashing around them all the time as they went.

Eventually the cannonade ceased, the enemy battery judging them to be out of range and turning their attention to the *Royal George* and the *Aurora*. It wasn't until they brought the fort of Missiessi up on the larboard beam that Fury had the *Tempest* brought to anchor once again, satisfied that they were quite safe.

He let the men rest for over an hour while chewing on their measly rations. They had worked hard all morning, and there would be much more work still to do before they could rejoin the fight tomorrow.

CHAPTER 13

Fury and his small crew spent all afternoon and long into the night effecting repairs to the damaged hull of the *Tempest*. The inner and outer hull was completely checked to ensure she was not shipping any water, while the battered bulwarks and deck were patched up as well as could be expected.

While the repair work was underway, the wounded were transferred over to the *Royal George* so they could be properly tended to by a surgeon, and able-bodied replacements were provided so as not to diminish Fury's meagre crew.

The men, Fury included, were exhausted by the time they finally got to sleep, lying on the bare deck beyond the canvas screen forward of the foremast. In a little over four hours they were up again, beckoned by the approach of dawn.

The whole morning swept by in a blur of exhaustion and fatigue, the shells and cannon continuing to rain down in an almost relentless bombardment. Fury could remember nothing much apart from the need to have the *Tempest* moved every couple of hours to avoid the masked batteries of the

Republicans to the west of Malbousquet getting their range.

Still, as he lay down that night to catch up on some much needed sleep, he could honestly count the day a success. They had managed to last the whole day in action, along with the other floating batteries, the *Aurora* and the *Royal George*.

Perhaps it was the constant shift of anchorage. Whatever it was, the *Tempest* had been hit remarkably few times and all by cannonballs into the hull, not a single mortar shell coming close. With any luck, tomorrow would be more of the same, he thought, as he closed his weary eyes and let sleep overtake him.

It was still dark when Fury awoke the next morning, the 21st. He had slept only fitfully, cold and uncomfortable on deck with the snores of his men a constant distraction. He had become used to sleeping in the privacy of his own cabin, undisturbed by the noise of others.

He got gingerly to his feet, his limbs stiff and sore and doing nothing to lighten his mood.

'Rouse up men!' he shouted, jealous of their slumber and deciding they had slept enough.

The first stirrings sounded in the pre-dawn darkness as the men clung on to the last vestiges of sleep.

'Come on! Shake a leg there!'

He walked amongst them, prodding his boot into stationary bodies to encourage them. They were all awake now, groans and moans emanating from the darkness telling him what they thought to his early call.

'I want to be in position by first light, so get yourself some hard tack and take your stations.'

Hard tack was all they had, of course. No chance of lighting a galley fire on a floating battery with makeshift magazines, powder and mortar shells nearby. Fury got himself a piece of biscuit, struggling with its solidity as he made his way aft towards the magazine. Watson loomed up alongside him in the gloom, still irritatingly cheerful in spite of the hour.

'Ready to go again Mr Fury?'

'Of course,' Fury lied, the tiredness still tugging at him. 'Have we sufficient shells?'

'We have plenty. As soon as we are in position, I shall have one of my men begin filling them.'

'Excellent. I hope to be in position within an hour or so, so you may begin your preparations.'

Fury looked at his watch, the first hint of dawn just starting to creep over the eastern horizon providing sufficient light. It would be daylight by half-past six, so they did not have long to get into position.

'Hands to the capstan!' he bawled, unconcerned by whether the men had finished their measly breakfast yet.

The sound of stamping feet reverberated along the deck as the men ran to the capstan wheel, slotting home the bars and standing ready. Fury could see that those men whose job it would be to raise the small scrap of sail once they were at the mercy of wind and current, were already at fore and mizzen masts, awaiting the order.

Satisfied, Fury set the men heaving at the capstan to bring the anchor up from the shallow waters of the inner road. Once free of the bottom, the mildewed sails were set and the *Tempest* began making slow steerage way through the water. The anchor, now free of the water altogether, was catted temporarily but not fished. It would be dropped again within the next thirty minutes, once they were within range of the masked batteries of the Republicans.

Fury looked over to starboard, the recent activity of getting underway having stripped him of his tiredness. The fort of Malbousquet overlooking the inner road stood high and proud, slowly slipping astern as they passed.

The sun was almost up, the dark purple of the sky now a lighter blue with hardly a cloud to be seen. Turning his attention to the task at hand, Fury looked forward to the north-west shore of the inner road, where yesterday the two masked batteries had been. They were well within range of them now.

'Let go the anchor!' he shouted.

The bower anchor, still hanging from the cathead, was released, and dropped swiftly into the steely grey water. The sails were quickly furled and at another command from Fury, men got to work passing a hawser out of one of the aft gun ports and leading it forward to attach to the anchor cable for use as a spring.

The sun was up fully now, already beginning to warm his back and promising a fine day. He could see *Aurora*, *Royal George* and the other gun battery slowly gliding to their positions, and he felt a little surge of satisfaction that the *Tempest* had been the first in position.

Pulling his telescope from his jacket pocket, his turned his attention back to the shore, studying every inch of terrain for any sign of Republican activity which would betray the presence of a battery. Nothing. Nothing to disturb the monotony of that harsh, grey landscape. Surely it wouldn't be long now before they began the bombardment.

'Stand to your guns!' he shouted, wanting to be ready to reply as soon as the first shots came.

The men crowded round their pieces and made sure everything was ready.

'You may load, ready,' he ordered the men at the twenty-four-pounders. The men at the mortars would have to wait until they had some idea of where the enemy lay, so that the correct powder charge and fuse length could be estimated.

He continued his scan of the shore, Watson soon joining him with his own telescope.

'Perhaps they've given up,' he suggested, hopefully.

'I doubt it.'

Nevertheless the sun had been up for nearly an

hour now, and there was no sign of any batteries ashore. Had they given up?

Fury's slowly rising hope was whipped away from him in a flash as a bang followed by a faint whistling sound reached his ears, gradually getting louder. He looked up quickly to try and catch a glimpse of the shell, the sky seemingly exploding a hundred feet from the ground over to their left, thick black smoke drifting away on the breeze.

'Fuse cut too short,' Watson commented matter-of-factly.

Fury nodded. He was staring back at the shore now, trying to detect the first signs of smoke which would give away the position of the masked battery. Was that a faint trace of smoke, up in the hills behind La Petite-Garenne? Watson was pointing to the same position now.

'Is that it?'

'It must be,' Fury decided.

As if to confirm their thoughts, the sound of more mortars could be heard whistling through the air, the arc of the burning fuses definitely emanating from where they were looking.

'Two batteries still,' Watson declared. 'They could never have reloaded that quickly.'

Fury was of the same opinion. They still had the two batteries of mortars, just as they had yesterday. The disappointment welled within him. Their slow start to the day had given Fury a glimmer of hope that they had at least forced one battery to retire from the fight.

Watson studied the position for a few more moments, mentally judging trajectories and distances, before hurrying off to the magazine to have the mortars filled with powder ready for their reply. As he went, a deeper boom rent the air, over to the left of Malbousquet, quickly followed by three more as the enemy resumed their fire. A splash rose up in the sea thirty yards short of their position, and then another nearby. Fury could not see where the other two balls went.

'Man the spring!' he shouted.

By hauling on the hawser laid out of the aft gun port and attached to the anchor cable, the *Tempest* was turned in the water so that she was broadside on to the position Fury judged the latest shots to have come from.

He was vaguely conscious of loud crashes nearby as *Royal George*, *Aurora*, and the other floating battery, opened fire themselves. The men operating the four twenty-four-pounders were standing ready, the guns already loaded some time ago and set to maximum elevation.

'Fire!' he called, the guns going off in succession to lessen the stress on the hull from the recoils.

Fury thought he could see the line of the balls going up over the heights, but had no idea how close they fell to the enemy. The men were already reloading as Watson and another man came hurrying amidships, carefully carrying a shell apiece for the mortars.

The shells and shot continued to pour down on the inner road where the *Tempest* and her three consorts lay, returning like for like. Fury spent the time standing with telescope to his eye searching the hills in vain for any sign of the enemy. He ordered the *Tempest* shifted once before lunch to throw off the aim of the enemy gunners, even if it did necessitate Watson and his mortar crews changing their own range and trajectory.

It had been almost two and a half hours since they had last moved, and he contemplated giving the order again as he stared through his glass. The shells had been getting continuously closer during the past half-hour, and he did not wish to risk staying in their current position much longer.

He lowered his glass and half turned, sucking the air into his lungs so that he could bellow the necessary orders. The distant bangs of the enemy's mortar battery reached him, signalling another avalanche. He delayed his shout, preferring to wait until this new bombardment had passed to ensure he had every man's full attention.

The whistling of the airborne shells was already evident as they started to descend. Fury could hear the noise gradually get louder, shifting his feet uneasily as he realised at least one of the incoming shells was going to be a lot closer than any of the previous ones. He looked up in a vain attempt to catch a glimpse of it but could see nothing. A second later he heard a thud some-where behind him and he swung round.

The men stationed round the two brass mortars housed amidships were looking down at the deck in terror, and it took Fury a moment to see why. The shell had landed amidst the mortar crews, miraculously missing every man but now rolling around the deck with its fuse sputtering menacingly. Fury instinctively threw himself to the deck.

'Throw it overbo—'

His shout was too late, the explosion cutting off his words and the shell casing scything out in all directions, cutting down the mortar crews who were packed around it. Fury, sprawled head first on the deck planking, could feel the rush of wind over him as the shock of the blast spread outwards. He got to his feet in shock, his ears ringing from the explosion. The ringing sensation was not enough to drown out the sound of men screaming in agony, terrible agony, as Fury looked around. The deck was tilting beneath him, but the smoke was blocking his vision.

He moved forward towards the blast, picking his way past the badly charred remains of two men as he approached. One of the two brass mortars was sitting sideways, the timber beneath, housing its carriage, having been blown away. Fury could see now that the shell, dropping beneath the mortar's carriage, had ripped a hole in the keel, fracturing the spine of the *Tempest* and causing her deck to cant as the water poured in.

The crews of the two mortars, what was left of them, were all dead, Fury recognising Watson's artillery uniform on one of the burnt bodies lying on the deck.

'We have to abandon ship!' he bellowed. 'Get the wounded overboard!'

Fury was glad he had not forgotten about the wounded, housed forward behind the canvas screen. Depending on how bad they were, they would not stand much of a chance overboard, but it was a better fate than being left on the *Tempest* when she finally went under.

The men at the twenty-four-pounders threw down their tools and men came bursting from the closed off section aft, leaving the magazine in a rush. The deck was canting more steeply by the minute as the hull of the *Tempest* began to collapse.

'Throw anything that'll float into the water!'

It was likely that most of the men could not swim, so they would need to cling on to anything they could until the rescue boats arrived to pick them up. Crowbars and handspikes began hacking into the bulwarks and deck planking as the men set to work finding anything that would float. Fury could see the gun carriages of the twenty-four-pounders slewing round on the canting deck, the breeching ropes straining to keep them. They did not have long, he thought. Once the guns broke loose and plummeted down the deck, the *Tempest* would sink like a stone.

The sea nearby was now littered with wreckage as the men flung broken planking, hatch gratings or bulwarks into the water, some jumping in hurriedly after them. Fury spared a glance over at the *Royal George*, thankful that a boat was already in the water and beginning to pull towards them. It should not be long before they were picked up.

Men emerged from behind the canvas screen with the five men who were wounded, some being carried, some dragged. The groans of pain and discomfort added to the din. The two mildly wounded men were gently lowered overboard, making sure sufficient wreckage was nearby for them to cling on to. The three more seriously wounded were attached to a line and lowered down on to floating hatch gratings by men standing at the bulwarks, while all the time more shot and shells from the Republican batteries continued to rain down around them. The French spotters must be able to see that they were now defenceless, and yet still they directed the fire of their mortar batteries on to the *Tempest*. Fury cursed them fiercely under his breath for their lack of common humanity.

Finally the wounded were all off successfully.

'Everyone over!' he bellowed, nervously looking at the precarious guns, still making every effort to break through their lashings. He was determined to be the last man to leave.

The rest of the men climbed over the low bulwark and launched themselves into the sea. Fury hesitated in order to glance around at the broken deck, unwilling to jump until he could be sure he was the last man on board. He could see no one else alive.

Satisfied, he stood up on top of the bulwark, still wearing boots and with his telescope stuffed firmly into the pocket of his jacket. He hesitated a moment, slightly unsure of himself. Although he could swim fairly well he was fully clothed and it was quite a drop, even though the *Tempest* was now lying very low in the water. Swallowing hard and steeling himself, he launched himself forward, dropping quickly.

The coldness of the water thrust the breath from his body so that by the time he had struggled back to the surface, he was gasping for air. His boots and clothes were weighing heavy on him and he looked around for a buoyancy aid.

There was a thick section of deck planking nearby and four hurried strokes brought him to it, the feel of the wet timber reassuring. He lay half across it amidst the rest of his floating crew, watching as the *Tempest* slowly crumpled in on herself, the four heavy crashes as the guns broke free and careered down the deck coming not five minutes after he had jumped. The end came quickly after that, the *Tempest*'s stern being the last visible section as it rose up almost vertical before sliding gracefully beneath the surface.

The boat from the *Royal George* was among them by now, picking up the first of the crew. Fury could see another boat not far behind it. It was only five minutes before that boat pulled alongside Fury, two of the oarsmen reaching over and pulling him into the bottom. He lay there among some of his former crew, all dripping and shivering despite the early afternoon sun. The officer sat in the stern sheets holding the tiller spied his uniform and introduced himself.

'Lieutenant Miller, of the *Royal George*. We'll be alongside her in a moment and you can get out of those wet clothes.'

'Thank you,' replied Fury through chattering teeth, 'I'm Lieutenant Fury, formerly commanding the *Tempest*, gunboat.'

'Bad luck Mr Fury, bad luck,' was all Lieutenant Miller said, leaving Fury sat with only his thoughts as they made their way back to Rear Admiral Gell's flagship.

It was Fury's first real independent command in the face of the enemy, and he had lost it. That thought plagued him during the whole of the journey to the *Royal George*, eating away at him and enveloping him in a black depression. He did not like to fail, and he was damned if it was going to happen again.

CHAPTER 14

Fury took a deep breath to compose himself and knocked on the door in the centre of Toulon. He had been there nearly three weeks before, his last sight of Sophie, and he was nervous. A few minutes' silence ensued, broken only by the sound of shouting from somewhere within, but no one answered.

Three days had passed since the destruction of the *Tempest*, and Fury had spent them wondering whether Sophie would agree to see him again after such a long absence with no word. Finally he had plucked up the courage to make the visit and, leaving Francis in command of *Renard*, had taken a boat to the quayside. He had been surprised, walking through the streets, of how things seemed to have degenerated since his last visit. He felt even more vulnerable than during his first visit in his British uniform; desperation and disorder seemed to hover over every citizen and every street. Now here he was in front of her door, fervently hoping she would not be too angry.

He clenched his fist and knocked again, this time so hard that the door shook. After a small wait he heard footsteps within, and the sound of a key scraping in the lock. The door swung open and Fury forced a smile to the short, thickset man standing in front of him, his hair completely grey and his clothes little more than rags. The man frowned as he studied Fury in his uniform jacket.

'*Parlez-vous anglais?*' Fury asked, hesitantly.

'I speak English, Capitaine.'

'It's, erm, lieutenant, sir,' Fury corrected him. 'Lieutenant Fury, of HMS *Fortitude*. I have come to enquire about Sophie Gourrier. Is she at home?'

The man nodded, his frown deepening. 'She is. What is it you want with her?'

'I would like to ensure she has recovered from her ordeal the other week.'

The man's features softened immediately. 'Ah, so you are the gentleman who rescued her? My apologies, sir, she did not tell me you were an English naval officer.' He offered his hand and Fury shook it. 'I am her father, François Gourrier, the Comte de Chabeuil, although I have found it prudent not to use my title for the last four years. You have my gratitude, sir, for coming to her assistance. God forbid what would have happened if you had not been passing.'

'I am glad I could be of some service, sir. May I see her?'

'Of course, Lieutenant. Come in, please.'

He beckoned Fury inside the doorway and closed the door after him. The hallway was tiny, barely large enough for the two of them, and the light within was dull. Immediately to the right was a steep staircase leading up, the timber stairs bare and worn.

'Follow me, please, Lieutenant,' Gourrier said, leading the way up the stairs. 'You catch us at the height of our misfortune, so that I feel compelled to apologise for the condition of our lodgings. There was a time when a gentleman calling upon my daughter would have needed to travel across three miles of my land before arriving at her door. Manservants and maids would have made him welcome and provided refreshments while he waited, but alas now I can offer you nothing.' There was no hint of bitterness in his voice, just wistful reminiscence with perhaps a touch of regret.

They came to the top, still with bare floorboards, and Gourrier turned left down the small landing to a door on the right, stopping before it and knocking. Fury heard a female voice from within and in response Gourrier said something in rapid French. There was a small pause and then the door opened, Fury catching his breath as he saw Sophie standing in the doorway still fixing her hair. She looked even more beautiful than he had remembered.

'I hope I do not intrude, Mademoiselle,' he asked over her father's shoulder.

She smiled at him. 'Of course not, John. I am glad to see you.' She turned to her father again and muttered something in French, in response to which her father nodded his head. She turned back to Fury. 'Shall we go for a walk?'

'With pleasure,' Fury replied, relieved that he would not be spending his visit making nervous small talk with her father.

She disappeared into the room momentarily and returned carrying a thin shawl, which she placed around her shoulders over her dress – the same dress, Fury noted, as the one she had been wearing when they had first met. He led the way down the stairs and out into the alley. He turned to her.

'May I offer you my arm, Sophie?'

'Thank you, John.'

She smiled and hooked her arm through his, resting her hand on his forearm. Every time she smiled at him, Fury's heart seemed to freeze for an instant. She led the way out of the alley and on to the street, where they walked in silence for a short time, Fury acutely conscious of the feel of her body next to his.

'I must apologise for the length of time it has taken me to visit you. My ship was ordered away, and upon my return I was ordered to take charge of a gunboat defending the harbour. This is the first chance I have had to see you.'

'You need not apologise. You have your duty to perform.'

'You are very understanding.'

Another short silence ensued, before Sophie spoke again.

'Are you still in command of the gunboat, John?'

'Unfortunately not. It was destroyed by the Republicans three days ago.'

Fury felt her hand flinch as it rested on his forearm, and instantly regretted his frankness. The look of alarm on her face as she looked up at him tugged at his heart strings.

'Destroyed? So you could have been killed?'

Fury swallowed hard at the recollection of those last moments on board *Tempest*, with the horrible mutilated bodies of his crew all around. He tensed his arm in an attempt to stop it trembling, lest Sophie detect it. 'No, not at all,' he replied quickly, trying to reassure her. 'It was a lucky shot, nothing more.'

She looked only slightly less worried at his feeble attempt to comfort her, and Fury decided immediately that he would not worry her with details of how the Republican batteries had eventually forced the *Royal George*, *Aurora* and the second gunboat to retire, effectively ceding the western end of the inner harbour to enemy control. He tried instead to change the subject.

'I trust you have been good to your word, and steered clear of alleyways?'

'Yes, you have no need to worry. I have learnt my lesson.'

'Good.' He paused. 'I am glad you agreed to see me again, Sophie.'

She looked up at him. 'Why wouldn't I?'

'I am an English officer. It cannot be easy seeing the English in charge of your city.'

'It is preferable to the Republican fanatics who murder and pillage. Anyway, it is not our city. We only moved here four years ago when we lost our chateau. Now we barely have enough to eat. My father has vast experience of managing estates and tenants, but what use is that here? He has no other skills so he struggles to find enough work to support us.'

Fury reached over and squeezed her hand, still resting on top of his forearm. 'I am sorry to hear it. Hopefully this war will be over soon, so that we may all return to normality.'

'And where is your home, John?'

'I grew up in a small village called Swampton, about forty miles from the south coast of England. As far as I know my mother and brother still live there. I haven't seen them in nearly two years.'

'It must be difficult, leaving your home at such a young age and being away from your family for so long.'

'You get used to it, in the end,' he assured her, catching sight of what looked like a coffee house up ahead on the other side of the street. There were two empty tables placed outside on the pavement, directly in front of the shop's large bay window, the glass reaching down almost to the ground. The stone front of the shop looked cleaner than those of the buildings either side, perhaps an indication of the owner's pride in his establishment, and the sign above the doorway looked freshly painted. Even from here Fury could see through the window, where several patrons were sitting at the tables inside. 'Could I buy you a cup of coffee?' he asked, turning to Sophie.

She hesitated, as though unwilling to accept any kind of charity. 'Very well then,' she relented. 'But I shall return the favour some time in the future.'

'Of course,' Fury replied, beaming now at this hint that they would be seeing each other again after this.

They entered and ignored the stares of the several patrons who were inside, some glancing at them in mere curiosity, some with more hostility. Fury led Sophie over to a table near the window and ordered them both a coffee. She plied him incessantly with questions about his childhood, his family and his home, and about his service in India with the *Amazon*. He told her of the village of Swampton where he grew up, of his mother and his brother, and of his departure to join the *Amazon*. He gave her a brief outline of his experiences in India, but spared her the horrors of the details, about the men he had seen killed next to him, about the blood and thunder of battle, of comrades lost.

The coffee came and went, and Sophie told him about her childhood at her father's chateau near Chabeuil, of her love for horses, and of their eventual flight.

Her mother had died when Sophie was in her infancy, so it had just been her and her father for as long as she could remember. They had come to Toulon to start afresh, hoping to disappear among the populace of such a large city. Sophie tried to find work to help her father, who had quickly become frustrated at his lack of opportunity. Waiting on tables, laundress, shop assistant – she had tried it all, and Fury realised how difficult it must have been for a girl who had been brought up in comfort on a country estate, with every need catered for.

Fury's heart went out to her as she told him her story, and his hand moved across the small table to hers without him even realising it. She made no attempt to withdraw it, and when she had finished her story they sat in silence for a while, looking at each other. A sharp cough sounded from somewhere within the shop, startling Fury out of his trance and bringing his self-consciousness flooding back. He withdrew his hand with a shy smile.

The shopkeeper was standing hovering nearby, and Fury noticed that the rest of the shop was now empty. He glanced outside and was surprised to see that darkness was already beginning to fall.

'I think he wants to close up,' Sophie explained, with a guilty smile on her face at the realisation of how long they had been talking.

'Yes, I had better be getting you back. Your father will be getting worried.'

They got up and left the shop, walking down the street arm in arm with Fury fingering the hilt of his sword nervously, conscious that with the darkness the danger increased, especially to a man wearing the King's uniform. They walked in silence, but it was comfortable with no hint of awkwardness between them. Presently they reached the alley where she lived and they stopped outside her door, Sophie extricating her arm and turning to face him.

'I have had a lovely time, John, thank you. It is a shame it could not last longer.'

'There will hopefully be other times in the near future.'

'I shall look forward to it.'

She held out her hand and Fury took it, his confidence sufficient to risk a snub by stooping to kiss it. He straightened up to find her smiling still, and he held on to her hand slightly longer than was customary.

'Goodbye, John, and take care.'

'Goodbye.'

He finally released her hand and she turned to open the door, Fury waiting until it had been closed again before setting off through the darkening streets back to the quayside, and his duty.

'Signal from the flagship sir!'

Francis didn't like interrupting Fury when he was pacing the deck, especially when he was still brooding over his failure with the gunboat just over a week ago, but he had no choice.

Fury looked up, his mind only barely registering the report.

'Eh? What's that?'

'Flagship's signalling sir,' Francis repeated.

'Well, what is it?' Fury demanded testily.

'Captain to repair on board sir. It's the *Fortitude*'s number.'

'The *Fortitude*?' Fury asked incredulously. The *Fortitude* was still not back from Malta as far as he was aware, and Lord Hood knew it. 'Very well. Have the boat's crew made ready.'

With the *Fortitude* absent, there was only one ship which the *Victory* could be intending her signal for, and that was *Renard*.

Fury hurried down to the master's cabin and put on his uniform, newly washed. Planting his hat on his head, he made his way back up on deck. *Renard*'s longboat, which had been fastened by a painter to the brig's stern, had been brought round to the side and secured, so that the crew were already filing down into it by the time Fury said his farewell to Francis.

Fury went down last into the waiting boat and settled himself in the stern sheets, grunting out the orders which sent the boat on its way.

He was already wondering what Admiral Hood wanted with him now, and was hoping that whatever it was would not interfere with rejoining *Fortitude* once they had returned. That would be any day now, hopefully with suitable reinforcements.

'Boat ahoy!'

The shout drifted down from the deck of HMS *Victory*, now looming large above them.

'Aye aye!' Fury shouted back, readying himself.

The boat swung round and glided nicely to the *Victory*'s side as Fury put the tiller over and the oarsmen raised their oars simultaneously. Once the bowman had hooked on, Fury reached for the side ropes and hauled himself up, a moment later appearing through the entry port.

The flag captain, Captain Knight, was there once again to greet him. Knight must be sick of the sight of him by now, Fury thought, as he was led aft towards the admiral's quarters.

'Lieutenant Fury, My Lord,' Knight announced, as he ushered Fury into the by now familiar surroundings of Lord Hood's day cabin. Hood was, as ever, seated at his desk behind a mound of paperwork.

'Sit down Mr Fury, sit down.'

'Thank you My Lord.'

Fury sank gratefully into the chair opposite, while Hood finished his paragraph.

'A nasty business, with those Republican batteries,' Hood said at last, placing his pen on the desk and leaning back in his chair to study Fury.

'Indeed sir.'

Was this a reprimand for losing the *Tempest*?

'You did well, Lieutenant. A little unlucky perhaps, to suffer a direct hit.'

Fury remained silent, waiting for Hood to get to the point.

'You escaped unscathed I take it?'

'Yes My Lord,' Fury replied, thinking it better not to mention the damage suffered to his pride.

'Good. Then you are ready for more active duty?'

'Yes My Lord.' There was nothing else he could say to that.

'Good,' Hood repeated. 'As you are no doubt aware, Mr Fury, I am desperately short of men to defend the perimeter of the city against the Republicans. Every day new reports come in telling of reinforcements to their numbers while not a day goes by when they don't try some mischief against our positions.'

Fury sat listening and nodding, wondering what on earth this could be leading to. Lord Hood continued.

'I have recently lost one of my lieutenants at Fort Pomet, during one such incident; he was shot while defending the valley from a small number of Republican skirmishers. I therefore need someone to take command of the garrison there.'

Fury nodded again, his heart sinking as he began to realise what the admiral had in mind.

'I am placing you in command of the garrison at Fort Pomet, Mr Fury, and you may take with you as many of your prize crew as you see fit, to increase the numbers. Your midshipman can remain in command of *Renard* at anchor with the remaining men until Captain Young returns. Any questions?'

Fury knew that it was unwise to raise objections

to any senior officer, let alone an admiral, a peer and commander-in-chief all in one, but the thought of leaving his ship and fighting in the rough terrain of southern France appalled him.

'What will happen when Captain Young returns with the *Fortitude*, My Lord? He is due back any day now and he will be expecting me.'

The argument was a weak one and Fury knew it, but it was the only objection he dared raise.

'I'm sorry Mr Fury, but I need you ashore at the moment. I'm sure your ship can manage without you and your men for a short time. I shall be sure to apprise Captain Young of the invaluable service you are providing when he returns. That shall perhaps soften the blow of losing such an able officer.'

Fury could not be sure whether Hood was being sarcastic. The old admiral's face was expressionless.

'Now, if you would be so kind as to wait in my clerk's office while I have him draft up some orders for you and your midshipman.'

'Aye aye My Lord,' Fury replied, trying to keep the dejection out of his voice as he rose from his chair and saluted before leaving the cabin.

An hour later Fury finally left the *Victory*, descending into the waiting boat with a small package under his arm wrapped in canvas which contained both his own orders and those for Mr Francis. He sat in the stern sheets at the tiller thoroughly depressed by this new development.

On top of his dejection over the loss of *Tempest*, he was now being sent into more danger, an unfamiliar danger in strange surroundings. He had already seen enough within the city of Toulon to suggest that ashore was not the safest place to be; he would be further away from *Fortitude* and, more importantly, from Sophie.

When they reached *Renard* he scrambled aboard with a brow like thunder, discouraging Francis to make any comment other than the routine 'Welcome aboard sir', before he dived below to his cabin.

Once there he quickly opened the canvas bag, pulled out the two sets of sealed orders and sliced open the set addressed to him. He was surprised at how brief it was:

Lieutenant Fury, HMS *Fortitude*.

By virtue of the power and authority to me given, I do hereby appoint you Commander of Fort Pomet, requiring and directing you forthwith to take upon you the responsibility of commander of her accordingly, strictly charging and commanding all officers and men employed in the garrison of the said Fort subordinate to you to behave themselves jointly and severally in their respective employments with all due respect and obedience to you their said Commander. You are hereby ordered to hold the said Fort at all costs from the advances

261

of the enemy until such time as you may receive orders to the contrary. In addition you will, at such time as may be required and on the receipt of further orders, further aid in the defence of the city of Toulon by reinforcing the garrisons of the surrounding batteries and redoubts in the event of sustained attacks by the enemy. In such cases you will first ensure that Fort Pomet itself is sufficiently manned and defended at all times.

Given under my hand this first day of October, 1793.
Vice-Admiral of the Red
Lord Hood

He re-read it twice to ensure he had not missed anything before folding it and sitting back deep in thought. While he had waited for his orders to be drafted up on board the *Victory*, he had used the opportunity to study a copy of a map of Toulon and its surrounding area to see exactly where Fort Pomet was located. He had been disappointed when he had finally found it, the furthest flung of any of the outposts around the city, approximately three miles inland to the north-west as the crow flies. It defended the main valley running between the mountains to the city and the bay, and the main road leading to the north. It was more likely that the Republicans would attack from the east and west, so the road from the north should be relatively clear, but their objectives were undoubtedly to take the heights surrounding the city, and Pomet was one of a chain of forts protecting one approach to those heights.

It had looked remarkably isolated to Fury on the small chart because of its forward position and the high ground all around. He could only hope that the posts nearby occupying that high ground, such as the redoubts of de l'Andre, St-Antoine le Grand, and le Petit, held firm. If the enemy managed to overrun them, or indeed forts Missiessi or Malbousquet overlooking the inner road, then Fury and his men could find themselves easily cut off.

He tried to push the gloomy thoughts from his head. Suddenly remembering the other set of orders he had brought back, he walked over to open the cabin door.

'Pass the word for Mr Francis!' he shouted, hearing the faint echo as other men on deck repeated the call. Fury was sitting back at the desk when Francis arrived, accepting the only other chair at Fury's invitation.

'I have some orders here for you from Lord Hood, Mr Francis,' he began, watching Francis' face as it creased up in surprise, and then worry.

'For me sir? From the admiral?'

His sudden alarm set Fury grinning for the first time that day.

'You have nothing to worry about Mr Francis.

I have been ordered ashore to take command of one of the outposts, Fort Pomet, taking some of the men and leaving you in command here. Those are merely confirmation of your orders.'

He thrust the sealed orders across the desk to him, which Francis picked up, broke the seal and began to read, his face relaxing as he saw that his task was merely to stay on board in command of the remainder of the prize crew until he received further orders.

'I understand sir,' Francis said, folding up his orders. 'When do you leave sir?'

'At dawn tomorrow. Have the men mustered aft at the next change of watch. I will pick the men to accompany me and make sure they are fully equipped. That is all Mr Francis.'

'Aye aye sir,' the boy piped, leaving the cabin.

Fury sat back in his chair and closed his eyes, trying his hardest not to let the fresh wave of despair sweep over him.

The brig's longboat gave one last surge as the last stroke of the men's oars sliced through the water. Fury swung the tiller over to send the boat alongside the quay in front of the new arsenal basin as the men stowed their oars.

The steely grey light of dawn was only just apparent as Fury leapt from the bow on to the stone quay, glad of the exercise at last after the thirty-minute pull from the brig in the cold October air.

He slung the cutlass belt over his shoulder,

sliding the cutlass into the frog by his left hip. The two sea-service pistols sticking in his waistband had been brought along instead of his uncle's expensive pair; Fury was too afraid of losing them to risk taking them off *Renard*.

'Out you get lads!' he said, trying to sound as cheerful as he could as the seven men he had picked, amidst groans and curses, filed on to the quay.

They had been unhappy last night when he had mustered the crew and informed them of his orders, especially when they found out they would be joining him. The ex-Amazons – Clark, Thomas, Cooke and Crouder – could not have been surprised to be selected by him, all having served with him before, but the others – Gooseman, McSherry and Perrin – could count themselves unfortunate. He had chosen them at random from the rest of *Renard*'s small prize crew, and they had done nothing but moan ever since. He could sympathise with them of course – they were sailors, used to living and fighting on board a ship, not in the mud and dirt of southern France. Nevertheless the iron discipline of the navy ensured that, despite the moaning and cursing, they would follow Fury and obey any order that he gave them.

He turned round on the quay and looked to his left where Fort Missiessi stood, a black bulk against the lightening sky beyond, with the fort of Malbousquet similarly placed further along to the west. Over to his right, beyond the buildings of the dockyard, he could see the high walls which surrounded the city of Toulon itself.

'Right lads, follow me and keep in line!'

He growled the order, unwilling to show too much sympathy lest they take advantage of it. The seamen, now looking around with cutlasses slung over their shoulders and pistols in their belts, groaned once more. He set off at a brisk pace, eager to work some warmth into his stiff limbs and those of his men following close behind.

He led them along the quay, past the gun wharf and the general magazine where dockyard workers and red-coated soldiers cast them mildly curious glances. Fury exchanged salutes with the officer in charge of the small detachment of troops guarding the Royal Gate and led his men through into the countryside beyond. He followed the road north towards the hospital, and at a crossroads he paused, bringing up a picture of the chart in his mind's eye. Turning left he led his men silently along the road back to the west, over a small bridge crossing the meagre Le Las river, before finally coming to the road leading off inland, to the north.

A thin drizzle began to fall from the overcast sky, soon increasing as the wind picked up, flicking up coat-tails and tugging at Fury's hat. The road was badly rutted and the rain was causing frequent large puddles, doing nothing to raise Fury's mood as he dwelt on the knowledge that every step was taking him further from safety, and from Sophie.

He could hear the men behind him cursing as ankles were overturned on the loose stones scattered along the road. Up ahead a large column of troops were marching toward him, the familiar scarlet tunics of regular British infantry stark against the grey landscape all around.

'Make way there,' Fury growled to his men, stepping on to the side of the road to let the troops pass.

Small scrub brush lined the countryside, and Fury and his men stood shin deep in it while the troops marched by. Curious looks darted at them from within the ranks. One of the officers on horseback at the rear of the column reigned in beside them.

'I am Lieutenant Fleming, of the 31st Foot.'

'Lieutenant Fury, of His Britannic Majesty's Navy. I am to take command of the garrison at Fort Pomet.'

'You have my sympathy, Lieutenant.'

Fury smiled grimly. 'Is it far?'

Fleming twisted in his saddle and pointed to the north-west. 'Fort Pomet lies over there, on low ground in a valley separating the western end of the Faron ridge from its neighbouring height, Le Croupatier. It can't be more than four miles distant.'

'What is it like?'

'Exposed. The valley is wide, but is constricted

at its northern end by a series of spurs. These spurs overlook a road which passes through the village of Les Moulins. Pomet is about a mile from the village, located at the southernmost spur.'

'Many thanks for the information, Lieutenant.'

Fleming smiled, said his farewells, and wheeled his horse after the marching troops. Fury muttered a curt command to his men, led them back on to the road, and continued in silence.

It took them almost an hour to draw abreast of the first of the peaks, about a mile inland and away to their right. They continued on, and after another thirty minutes the road wound to the right, running along the river Neuve and avoiding a flat peak which was directly in their path. As they rounded it another smaller peak came into view across the river, with a battery standing high at the top and pointing inland. Fury guessed that it could only be the redoubt of l'Andre. They were nearly there.

Leaving the road, Fury led them across the shallow river and into the valley proper, winding their way round the left of the smaller peak and bringing them into view of Fort Pomet, situated on the low ground a little further down the valley.

As they approached Fury could see that there was a ditch surrounding the fort to prevent attackers from getting close. From the bottom of the ditch he estimated the height of the walls to be at least twenty feet, so that tall ladders would be needed in any attempt to get over. The main entrance was reached via a small bridge across the ditch, and Fury could see the heads of two men patrolling the ramparts. One of the sentries shouted a challenge as Fury arrived at the small bridge crossing the ditch, and at Fury's response and the sight of his uniform jacket, the doors swung open.

The first thing Fury saw as they entered was a group of horses tethered together, presumably for delivering messages, next to what must be the officers' quarters. He looked up to the ramparts where he could see the black breeches of the field cannon poking out of the embrasures, but any further scrutiny was ended by the approach of an army subaltern.

'Sergeant Hawkins sir, of the King's 69th Regiment. I am in temporary command of this detachment.'

'Good morning Sergeant. My name is Lieutenant Fury of His Majesty's Navy. I have been ordered to take command here.'

Fury handed him his orders and waited while the sergeant read them, or at least made the appearance of reading them – by the look of him Fury doubted whether he could read at all.

'Yes sir, we've been expecting you,' Hawkins replied, handing his orders back. 'I've taken the liberty of arranging quarters for yourself sir. There is room in the barracks for your men.'

He glanced over Fury's shoulder with a look of disdain at the rabble of seamen standing behind Fury.

'Thank you Sergeant. Please be so kind as to lead the way.'

Hawkins nodded and turned to lead the way over to a large building on the right which housed the men of the garrison. Fury conducted a quick inspection of the beds allocated to his men – weak-looking bed frames with paper-thin mattresses and one blanket each, but all relatively clean. He granted his grudging approval, leaving his men to settle in. He could hear from the men's voices as he left that they were beginning to think this job was not such a bad one after all; after the constant work needed in keeping a ship seaworthy and presentable, they evidently thought that garrison duty ashore would not involve much hardship, and would provide uninterrupted sleep in a proper bed each night.

As he followed Hawkins over to the officers' quarters, passing the restless horses on the way, Fury doubted whether the Republicans would be so courteous as to leave them undisturbed every night.

Fury paced the ramparts later that evening feeling thoroughly inadequate to the task given him. The sun had just dipped below the western horizon and the temperature was now dropping as dusk settled in. As well as Sergeant Hawkins, he had eighty-three men under his command, the majority of whom were soldiers of the 69th Regiment and therefore men whose drills, procedures or skills he knew nothing about.

They had been lucky recently, Hawkins had told him, in that the Republicans had concentrated most of their efforts over to the east upon the batteries at Faron, and over to the west upon the batteries commanding the western side of the outer road.

The walls of the valley on either side of the fort were too precipitous to be used for descent, so the only way the Republicans would be able to attack would be from the north, straight down the valley floor in the face of Pomet's guns. Fury could see nothing much in that direction as the raised spurs crossing the valley floor obstructed views further north. Those spurs would provide cover for any enemy troops advancing, until the valley floor flattened out and they would be fully exposed for the final 300 yards to the fort. Fury made a mental note to post advance guards at those spurs in the morning, to provide more advanced warning of any attack.

If they were overwhelmed, they would have a long retreat back to Toulon and the dockside. Fury could only hope that if the time did come, they would be able to make it back before getting cut off by enemy advances from elsewhere.

The sound of cannon fire could still be heard in the distance. It was difficult to pinpoint its location but probably from both the east and west,

Fury mused. It was so constant now throughout most of the day that the mind tended not to register the sound after a while.

He nodded in greeting to one of the sentries posted along the ramparts to act as lookouts during the night in case of a surprise Republican assault. Down the stone steps and he was in the courtyard again, heading towards the faint glimmer of light visible from one of the windows in the officers' quarters. A moment later he was lying on his bed under the single blanket, concentrating hard on trying to get some sleep.

It was some time before sleep crept up on him, finally shutting out the distant thunder of cannon fire that continued throughout the night.

The following morning Fury was up before dawn, a new sense of purpose coursing through him. He had made the decision to treat his current command just like any other, a decision which had come to him, strangely, while still asleep. The look of the men in front of him, standing in the pre-dawn darkness in the courtyard, suggested that many of them were still asleep.

'All those not on sentry duty shall muster here each morning at six o'clock for inspection, in full kit.'

A groan arose from the soldiers. At least they were awake now.

'Any man late for muster shall be given extra duties.'

Fury looked at them all, trying to detect any

sullen faces which might speak of something more sinister than mere lethargy. He found none.

'We shall start today by cleaning this fort from top to bottom.'

More groans at that, although none from his own seamen, Fury noted – they were used to continual cleaning on board ship.

'Very well Sergeant Hawkins, you may dismiss the men. Once they have had their breakfast I want five men sent north to keep lookout at intervals among the spurs. Any man who spots the enemy advancing is to fire his musket as a warning and they are all to retreat immediately to the fort.'

'Yes sir.'

'The rest of the troops can begin the clean-up.'

Hawkins saluted, not looking particularly pleased himself, and dismissed the men to breakfast. Fury did not care what Hawkins thought, nor any of them. He knew as well as anyone that idleness bred trouble, and he was determined to prevent that here, more so now than ever after his recent experience on *Renard*.

He gave the men a good hour to enjoy their breakfast. By the time the advance lookouts had departed and the first of the men began to trudge reluctantly out of the barracks to begin the clean-up, it was light.

It took nearly the whole day to complete the task, the echo of cannon fire the only accompaniment to the sound of scrubbing and scraping. As the sun went down that evening, Fury inspected the guns along the ramparts, all now considerably cleaner than before.

Satisfied for the first time in days, he went down to his quarters and was asleep in minutes.

CHAPTER 15

He was as good as his word during the course of the next week, parading the men each morning at six o'clock despite the frequent bouts of heavy rain which teemed down and seemed to seep into every part of the body.

After breakfast, Fury would have the men vigorously training with the great guns, staring mutely out of the embrasures down the empty valley. There was no chance of firing off the guns, of course – with the Republican army all around he had no wish to draw their attention – but the loading, reloading and pointing were all worked at incessantly until it became almost second nature.

Most of the afternoons were spent in the courtyard at small-arms drill, practising with musket and bayonet, so that by the time the sun began to sink over to the west, the men were thoroughly exhausted and in no condition to contemplate mischief.

With nothing else to think about, Fury found his mind increasingly wandering to his ship, the *Fortitude*, wishing he was still on board in familiar surroundings. It was not helped by the fact that after five days a message arrived at the fort for him from Captain Young, telling him that the *Fortitude* had arrived back at Toulon, but had been ordered by Lord Hood to Corsica to aid in the capture of all French possessions, and he had therefore had Fury's belongings transferred to Midshipman Francis in *Renard* until such time as Fury could return. When would he be able to rejoin her? He longed to be back at sea, even if it did mean he would be taken further away from Sophie.

His worry at that turn of events was short-lived, his mind soon diverted by matters closer to hand. It was becoming clear that merely keeping the men busy was not enough. He had to provide some variety to keep them happy and avoid the petty squabbles which would soon begin breaking out.

He was pacing the courtyard debating this very problem when a shout from the sentry at the gate broke his concentration.

'Rider approaching from the south sir!'

Fury looked up eagerly, wondering if this could be the answer to the very question he had just been pondering. He walked towards the entrance, still a blur in the pre-dawn darkness.

A fog was beginning to settle, reducing visibility still further and making him marvel that the sentry had managed to see a thing. A few moments later the large thick double doors at the main entrance were swung slowly open with a loud creak, and the rider trotted in with head bowed to avoid any possibility of hitting the frame of the doorway. He dismounted with graceful ease and secured his horse outside the window of Fury's quarters.

The light from the window allowed Fury to have a good look at him. The man glanced around the courtyard, unsure as to where he should go now. He was a young man, perhaps mid twenties, with a small amount of black hair showing beneath the large hat that was planted firmly on his head. Fury did not immediately recognise the red uniform he was wearing – similar to that of the marines – along with the white breeches and black boots.

He had obviously spotted Fury because he was now walking over to him, holding the hilt of the large sword by his side to keep the blade away from his legs.

'Lieutenant Fury sir?' he asked.

'I am Lieutenant Fury,' Fury replied, impressed that the man had recognised the uniform of a naval lieutenant.

'Good morning sir. My name is Lieutenant Carter, of the King's 30th Regiment, and I bring you orders from Lord Mulgrave.'

Lord Mulgrave was the man whom Lord Hood had appointed governor of Toulon to replace Rear Admiral Goodall, and was therefore currently in command of the forces occupying the city. What he could possibly want with Fury was a mystery.

'Yes?' Fury prompted.

'Late last night sir, the enemy attacked our posts

277

on the heights of Faron, over to the east.' He indicated the direction with a stab of his hand. 'They
drove off the Spaniards and captured the battery.
His Lordship intends to retake it as soon as
possible and requires you to supply as many men
as you can spare to join him.'

Fury stood in silence for a moment as he tried
to decide how many men he could sensibly spare
while still providing sufficient men to defend Fort
Pomet.

'Very well,' he said, making his mind up at last.
'I can spare His Lordship forty men.'

That was almost half the garrison he had at his
disposal and would leave them short-handed here,
especially if the Republicans should choose this
moment to attack.

'If you follow the road back towards the bay sir,'
Carter continued, 'and then turn left along the
foot of the hills, you will reach Lord Mulgrave
and his men.'

Fury nodded. He had studied the charts of the
surrounding area enough to know where the
heights of Faron were.

'I must take my leave now sir, to round up more
men from the other outposts.'

Fury acknowledged his salute and Carter
hurried back to his horse, quickly mounting with
the speed and ease of someone who had spent a
lifetime around the beasts, before trotting out of
the fort and galloping down the valley in the direction of the harbour.

Beyond the open door, Fury could see the fog thickening out in the valley, so much so that it swallowed up Lieutenant Carter in a matter of seconds. Would that help or hinder their attack, he wondered?

'Sergeant Hawkins!' he bellowed, unnecessarily given the fact that Hawkins, like every off-duty man in the fort, was standing at the open door of the barrack room in order to overhear what was being said.

'Sir?' Hawkins said as he hurried over to Fury almost immediately, skidding to a stop in front of him and offering a hasty salute.

'You will take forty men to assist Lord Mulgrave in retaking the heights of Faron. I will remain here in command of the fort in your absence. I expect you to leave in twenty minutes.'

It was still a good half-hour before the men were due for their morning parade so this was an even earlier start than usual, but Fury doubted whether any of them would mind now that the chance of action was imminent. Fury was desperately tempted to lead the attack himself, but knew that his place was here, in command of the fort.

'Yes sir,' Hawkins replied, grinning at this unexpected excitement.

Hawkins hurried away shouting orders at his corporal while Fury resumed pacing. It could have been no more than fifteen minutes before Hawkins reported his men ready. Fury returned his salute, wished him luck, and watched as Hawkins led the men out of the fort and down the valley, envious of their chance of action while he had to remain behind and wait.

Fury went back to his quarters and lay on the thin mattress, trying to get some rest until Hawkins and his men returned. Ten minutes of fidgeting was enough to drive him back on to his feet and outside, where those men on sentry duty paced at the main door and up on the ramparts. Corporal Jackson was drilling the remainder of the 69th at loading their muskets in the middle of the courtyard, and Fury left him to it and tried to occupy his mind elsewhere. He was surprised at how difficult it was to sit idle when other men – his men – were fighting for their lives not so very far away.

The sound of laughter drifted across to him as he passed the men's barracks, and Fury could not resist the temptation to investigate. The door was ajar as he approached, and he could now make out voices from within, loud but good-natured. He could distinguish Perrin's broad cockney accent, followed quickly by Gooseman's thick Yorkshire tongue. Fury had always tried to remain aloof from the men, as he thought an officer ought to, and as his uncle, Captain Barber, had done with his offi-cers, but his inactivity was getting the better of his usual reserve. He pushed the door open fully and walked in, seeing his seven Fortitudes sitting in a rough circle in the middle of the room, some on the floor and others on the edge of nearby beds.

They looked up as the door creaked open and began to rise at the sight of him, but Fury waved them back down.

'As you are, lads. As you are. I just came to see how you were doing.'

He stepped forward towards them and glanced at the faces around the group; tough, practical men with a remarkably cheerful outlook on life, in spite of all their hardships. He suddenly felt proud to be in command of such men.

'Very well, thankee sir,' Clark responded, sitting on the end of a bed to Fury's right.

'Good. So you are coping with the inactivity?'

'We struggle on, sir,' Gooseman replied.

'How's that ship coming along Perrin?' Fury asked, looking at the brash cockney. For hours while off watch on the *Fortitude*, Fury had seen him carving furiously into a block of wood, trying to fashion a replica of their ship. His skill with a knife was impressive.

'Right well, thank you sir,' Perrin replied with a grin. 'The hull's all done, just need to step the masts and set up her standing and running rigging.'

The rest of the men were grinning along with Perrin, all seemingly pleased at Fury remembering such a trivial thing about one of their group. Fury looked down at the ground in the middle of the men, where two dice were sitting. The men saw the direction of his glance and their grinning faces turned to looks of apprehension. Gambling was forbidden by the Articles of War; the sight of those two dice was enough to have each and every man flogged, and they knew it.

Fury turned back to Perrin. 'Perhaps when you have finished, if you are of a mind to sell her, I could have first refusal.'

The look of relief spreading across the men's faces was obvious, and almost prompted Fury to break into a grin. He stifled it with an effort.

'Aye sir, of course,' Perrin replied.

'Excellent! In the meantime, to help you cope with your inactivity,' Fury flashed a wry glance at Gooseman, 'perhaps you will all join me in the courtyard for some sword drills. The 69th are there as we speak practising with muskets, and it would be a shame to give them the impression that His Majesty's sailors enjoyed an easier life than theirs.'

The men got slowly to their feet with barely concealed reluctance, McSherry surreptitiously sweeping up the two dice from the floor and stuffing them in his pocket. They picked up their cutlasses and Fury led them out of the barracks and into the courtyard, where the fog lay low on the ground like a blanket. Fury partnered McSherry, who was as tall as Clark and nearly as wide. The remaining six Fortitudes paired up and began circling each other, weapons ready.

Soon the clash of steel on steel could be heard along with the clicking and scraping of the musket drills from the 69th. It was an interesting problem for Fury, tackling an opponent with a much longer reach than his own; he had to rely on his own speed and nimbleness to dart in and out of his opponent's guard at the right moments, while not allowing himself to get too close and hence give McSherry a chance to use his greater body strength.

They were all panting and sweating by the time Fury was satisfied with their efforts, calling time on the drill and allowing the men to return to their barracks for some well-deserved rest. The 69th had long since finished their musket drills, so the only men remaining were the sentries on duty. Fury looked at his watch; they had been at it for nearly two hours, with barely a pause. His chest was tight and his arm was heavy, but it had served to put from his mind all thoughts of Hawkins and his men.

He spent the rest of the day impatiently pacing throughout the fort and on the ramparts, scanning further down the valley to the north for any signs of life. The fog had lifted during the early afternoon so that he could see as far as the first ridge constricting the valley floor. Nothing. Not even a sign of his own advance lookouts.

The sound of distant cannonading could be heard as usual, betraying the continued bombardment from the Republican batteries scattered around the allies defensive perimeter, but no small-arms fire could be heard from the allied attack to retake the heights, which only seemed to intensify the feeling of utter isolation.

The sun had already begun its slow descent over to the west, the light fading fast, by the time the first of the shouts came from the sentry posted at the main door to inform them that Hawkins and his men were returning.

Fury hurried down from the ramparts, pausing only long enough to throw his telescope on to his bed, before making his way to the entrance, the relief pouring through him that the waiting was over. Hawkins was the first through the door, his uniform filthy and torn, with what looked like a dark stain of blood smeared across the front. His men following behind looked little better, all exhausted and perspiring freely. Hawkins came to a standstill in front of Fury and offered him a weary salute.

'Well Mr Hawkins? How went it?'

'Tolerably well, sir. We managed to drive them off and retake the heights.'

'How many men did you lose?'

'Three men killed, sir, and another four injured. They've been taken to the field hospital for treatment.'

'But the heights are secure?'

'For the time being, sir. We just haven't got the men to defend the whole perimeter. The Republicans have got tens of thousands of men available, and numbers are growing all the time. At some point in the future they are going to penetrate our defence again, and we may not be able to respond quite so swiftly next time.'

'I see. Well, you and your men should get some food, Sergeant. I've had some cold meat and biscuit left out for you. After that you can get some rest, you've earned it. Have them ready for parade an hour later tomorrow, at seven.'

'Yes sir.'

Hawkins turned to his men and ordered them to fall out, before making his way over to his barracks, leaving Fury to ponder on what he had been told. The heights of Faron had been retaken, giving the city of Toulon a further reprieve. But for how long?

It was only a week since they had retaken the heights of Faron, and the excitement and adrenalin of action already seemed like a distant memory. Fury persisted with the daily drills, even though they were hardly enough to occupy the men indefinitely. He even began to question their necessity, having seen no evidence of Republican activity nearby. Lookouts were posted with telescopes on the ramparts day and night, keeping a ceaseless watch inland for any sign of the enemy approaching through the spurs which dotted the valley floor in front of the fort to the north-east, but to no avail. From the sound of the cannon fire in the distance, it seemed the Republicans were concentrating their efforts over to the west.

After Hawkins' pessimistic report following the action to retake the heights of Faron, Fury's thoughts had turned more and more to Sophie and her fate should the Republicans succeed in driving out the occupying allied forces. After almost three days of deliberation he finally found a solution to set his mind at ease: he wrote a note to her father instructing them to head for a rendezvous point should the city fall, assuring him that he would pick them up and take them off to safety. He enclosed a map of the bay and the surrounding land, clearly marking the rendezvous, and entrusted both to Clark and Thomas with directions to their lodgings and strict instructions to hand the letter over to him and him alone, and wait for his confirmation.

It was almost six hours before they returned, and Fury was sure that he could smell alcohol on their breath, but as they reported the delivery a success and handed Fury a note from Sophie's father confirming his agreement, Fury had been satisfied. The successful completion of the task had at least enabled him to cease worrying quite so much, and to turn his attention back to his duty.

As the weeks wore on, the days became more and more of a struggle as Fury began to run out of activities with which to keep the men occupied. Small-arms drill and practice with the cannon sat on the ramparts could only take up so much time, while the maintenance of the garrison and its equipment was a simple matter once the initial cleaning had been completed on the first day. He even found himself wishing he had brought the

Articles of War with him so he could read them each morning to the men, just to take up some more of the day and perhaps impress upon them the continued importance of discipline.

They were resupplied after three weeks from wagons escorted by the 14th Foot Regiment. The chance of slightly fresher food at least served the purpose of lifting the men's spirits again, if only for a short time.

The tentative patrols which Fury sent out further down the valley, in an effort to gain some intelligence about the whereabouts of the enemy, came back with nothing. They went as far north as the northernmost lateral ridge crossing the valley floor, but could not see anything. They even passed through the village of Les Moulins on the banks of the river Neuve to the north-east, but still no sign of the enemy. If it wasn't for the continued presence of cannon fire in the distance, Fury would have thought the war was at an end, and he tried his very best to ward off the complacency which inactivity inevitably produced, hoping that when the time came, his men would be ready.

'Rider approaching sir!'

The shout came from one of the patrolling sentries on the ramparts after almost a month had passed. Fury was pacing round the courtyard, more to keep warm in the cold November air and stave off the boredom than anything else. He felt a surge of excitement course through his body as he acknowledged the report and turned towards the entrance, his mind racing with the possible implications of their unknown caller.

The doors were swung open to admit the visitor. He looked to be a messenger, and glanced around the courtyard upon entering. In stark contrast to Lieutenant Carter, their previous messenger, this one looked so ill at ease sitting on his horse, it was almost laughable. Fury had to stifle a chuckle as the man clumsily attempted to climb down from the saddle, his sword getting caught between his legs and sending him tumbling to the ground. One or two of Fury's men nearby were not quite so discreet in their merriment.

'Silence,' growled Fury, stooping to help the man back on his feet.

'Many thanks, many thanks,' their visitor said. 'Bloody horses. I hate the things!'

His red uniform was now thick with dirt and dust from where he had fallen, while the packet which he was holding in his hand was crumpled and torn. He offered the packet to Fury with an apologetic look as he tried to adjust his sword and jacket into some semblance of order.

Fury noticed that the seal had already been broken, and he pulled out a sheet of paper. It was a written order, signed by Lieutenant General O'Hara, stating that the bearer was acting under his authority and must be given whatever assistance he required.

'What is all this about?' Fury demanded, waving the sheet of paper in front of the officer.

'I have been ordered to round up as many men as I can for an attack on one of the Republican batteries over to the west. It has been harassing the flank of Fort Malbousquet since yesterday, and the General wishes to be rid of it.'

Fury thought for a moment about the position of the enemy battery. It must be somewhere near the heights of Le Petite-Garenne, where the batteries which had destroyed his gunboat had been sited. The thought of revenge gave him a fierce pleasure.

'I shall, of course, provide you with whatever you require. I am Lieutenant Fury, commander of the garrison here at Fort Pomet.'

'A pleasure, Mr Fury. I am Lieutenant Carrick, on the staff of Major General Dundas. He will be leading the initial attack.'

Fury baulked slightly at having to follow the orders of an officer who was, technically at least, junior to him, but he bit his tongue and waited for Carrick to explain what he wanted.

'Due to the shortage of men available to defend the perimeter of the city, we shall require sixty men from your garrison to aid in the attack.'

Fury shook his head.

'Out of the question I'm afraid, Lieutenant Carrick. I can spare you forty men at most.'

'You have read my authority?' Carrick asked.

'I have. My orders from Lord Hood, however,

were explicit. I am to ensure that this garrison is able to defend itself at all times.'

Fury stood there staring at him, while Carrick searched his eyes for any signs of weakness.

'Very well,' Carrick relented, 'I shall accept forty, but I shall be obliged to mention this matter in my report.'

The implied threat irked Fury, but he had no wish to let Carrick know it.

'You must do as you see fit, of course, Lieutenant.'

It took all Fury's willpower to answer using his best manners. Carrick sighed at his stubbornness. He had fully expected Fury to accede to his request in the face of a possible disciplinary charge from General Dundas.

'Very well. You may pick your men now, Mr Fury. I wish to be under way within thirty minutes. General Dundas will be wanting to get into position before nightfall.'

Fury nodded and went to seek out Sergeant Hawkins to have him pick the men. He was wondering as he went whether he should let the sergeant lead the men again – Hawkins had led the attack to retake the heights of Faron, and there was nothing in Carrick's orders which stated that Fury himself had to go.

By the time he reached Hawkins he had already decided. He would go himself, and to hell with Hawkins' feelings. The thought of sitting back in ignorance for a second time while his men went into action appalled him.

The face of Hawkins when he broke the news tugged at Fury's conscience, but by the time he left the fort at the head of his forty men a little under half an hour later, with Lieutenant Carrick leading the way, there was only one thing on his mind. Revenge.

The battery, sitting high on the flat top of the hill, could not be seen from where Fury was lying, face down in the dirt and shivering with the bitter cold which seemed to reach everywhere with every breath of wind.

The sky was littered with stars, but the moon had not yet risen. The slope began gently but then got steeper, and even in the dark Fury could see the loose rock and stone scattered everywhere, with only the occasional small scrub brush breaking the monotony of brown and grey.

It was too dark to look at his watch, but Fury knew it could not be much past nine o'clock. Plenty of time for what they had to do. He glanced to his right and then to his left to look along the line of men waiting silently at the bottom of the slope. He thought he could see the uniform of Lieutenant General O'Hara away to his right, but he could not be sure in the darkness. As far as Fury was aware, Major General Dundas was supposed to be leading the initial attack, but his senior, O'Hara, seemed intent on joining them.

Another glance above showed that they had a good 200-yard dash up the slope until they came to the battery, which the Republicans had erected to lay down a continuous fire upon the battery of Malbousquet overlooking the inner road.

The approach to their present position, conducted only after darkness had fallen, had been effected without a single sound. And now, 200 men, mostly soldiers or marines but with a scattering of seamen among them, were waiting for the final charge.

A movement to his right drew Fury's gaze, and he saw the first men begin to rise to their feet, presumably on a signal from General Dundas. Fury himself rose to his feet instinctively, followed shortly by the men to his right and left, so that soon the whole group were standing amid the low sound of swords being drawn.

Starting from the right over where the general was, the men moved forward up the slope like a huge wave. Fury had to make a conscious effort to control himself and not go running ahead like a madman, which would inevitably set off the men around him and lead to chaos.

It was difficult to keep his footing on the slope, the loose rocks giving way under his feet and falling in mini avalanches to hinder the men struggling up behind him. A hundred yards to go now and he was conscious of his legs aching slightly with the climb, a glance above showing a face peering over the hastily constructed works housing the French mortars.

Fury thought initially that the French had seen them long before and were waiting silently at the top to massacre them as they arrived, but a moment later a terrified shout from above told him that the man who had first spotted them was taken completely by surprise.

They were almost there, and the men were shouting and screaming now that the need for secrecy was gone. As they approached the flat of the high ground, a ragged volley of musket shots pierced the air, and a man to Fury's right fell with a shriek, but Fury could spare no more time for him as the low wooden parapet loomed up in front of him and, with cutlass in his right hand, he managed to hurl himself over with the help of the men pushing up behind him.

More musket shots rang out, this time from their own soldiers as they neared the French who were rapidly falling back from the works. Fury whipped one of the pistols out of his waistband and fired it at the man closest to him before flinging it at another and lunging forward with his cutlass. He felt the jar and heard the familiar sound of steel on steel as the man in front parried and quickly countered, Fury only just recovering his balance and deflecting the strike heading towards his side. It took only a slight movement for Fury to adjust his cutlass as his opponent lost his balance and almost fell on to the point of his blade, Fury managing to wrench it free quickly and continue forward.

The French had been thoroughly surprised and were now running away from the works as fast as they could across the flat summit towards the opposite slope. They were followed by the majority of the British soldiers shouting and screaming after them, their impetuosity and ardour overcoming their discipline.

Fierce shouting over to his right attracted Fury's attention and he looked over to see both General O'Hara and one of his aides shouting at the top of their voices for the men to return. It was no good, however – the men were now completely overcome by fighting madness and blood lust. Even if they could hear the shouted orders, Fury doubted whether they would have obeyed.

Looking around, Fury estimated that no more than about twenty men now remained at the works, and the general was bawling orders to them to destroy the mortars as quickly as possible before the Republicans managed to regroup and advance in force.

It took twenty minutes for the men to spike the touchholes and manhandle the mortars off their carriages and throw them down the slope. Fury and his men pulled down the temporary wooden parapet and works, setting light to as much of it as possible after dragging the wicker baskets containing powder cartridges out of harm's way. The flames sprang up readily enough and the heat reminded Fury of how cold he was, at the same time providing sufficient light to see further across the summit.

A large volley of musketry sounded in the distance, warning of a probable counterattack, but even so it was another twenty minutes before the first of the British soldiers arrived back exhausted.

The remainder of the troops came running in complete disorder shortly after, musket shots ringing after them as the French advanced. General O'Hara was standing and shouting frantically at his men in an attempt to rally them, but they carried on in a panic down the slope into the darkness.

All the advantages gained by the surprise attack had now been lost as the rest of the British troops fled back from the advancing French looming up out of the dark. As Fury watched him, the general suddenly spun round on his feet and fell heavily to the ground, and in a few steps Fury was over to him.

O'Hara sat up with Fury's help, and it was clear that he had been hit in the left arm with a musket ball, the blood staining his coat and running down his arm towards his hand. His aide was dead, lying in the mud with one eye missing and a widening pool of blood beneath his head. Fury looked to his left where the French were now no more than a hundred yards away, approaching more cautiously as they neared what was left of their battery.

A smaller volley of shots rang out from the works and Fury looked over to see Clark and the rest of the Fortitudes hastily reloading. He felt a sudden surge of pride that they had stayed to cover his retreat.

For a second he was unsure of what he should do: with the French approaching he needed to retreat as quickly as possible, yet he could not leave the General here as prisoner – Lord Hood would never forgive him for that.

'Can you stand sir?'

The question was more a rhetorical one as Fury physically pulled O'Hara to his feet, looking pale and weak from the loss of blood. A mumbled order from O'Hara to leave him was ignored by Fury as he roughly grabbed him under his armpits and dragged him back over to the edge of the slope which they had climbed up not forty minutes past.

A glance back over his shoulder showed his men firing one more volley, before a shouted order from Fury had them abandoning their position and fleeing down the slope. Behind him Fury could hear the approaching French, and it crossed his mind to fling O'Hara down the slope, reasoning that it was the quickest way of getting him down and was infinitely preferable to being taken prisoner by the Republicans. The risk of serious injury from the fall was too great, however, so he dismissed it.

Clark and Thomas came bounding across to him, evidently having disobeyed his order to retreat.

'Do you need a hand, sir?' Clark asked breathlessly.

Fury nodded. 'We need to get him down the slope, and quickly.'

Clark picked the general up and slung him across his shoulder like a rag doll.

'Can you manage him?' Fury demanded.

'Aye sir, I think so.'

Fury nodded again. 'Off you go, then.'

Clark began to pick his way down the slope with Thomas attempting to steady him. A musket shot sounded, quickly followed by another and another, the ground nearby kicking up dirt. Part of the wooden parapet was still alight to his left and Fury had a sudden idea. If the French decided to pursue them down the slope, they would easily catch Clark and Thomas, burdened as they were with General O'Hara. Fury needed to dissuade them, and fast. There was a tub still containing cartridges for the mortars which had been moved aside when the works had been set alight, and Fury grabbed a handful, aware of the sound of stamping feet on the ground behind him. He dared not look in that direction as he ran towards the edge of the slope and began slipping and stumbling down it, with more musket balls flying overhead.

He managed to stop himself about fifty feet down the slope and turned to look up. The first of the Republicans could be seen peering down at him and some made a move forward in pursuit. Fury took one of the cartridges in his right hand and hurled it back up the slope, missing the burning works by inches. He took another and tried again, the explosion as the cartridge landed amongst the flames flinging the men closest to it to the ground. Taking his last cartridge, Fury flung it back up the slope and continued his descent, only just registering the second explosion as he scrambled down.

He was near the bottom by the time he reached Clark and Thomas with O'Hara. Only now did Fury take the chance to look back up the slope, but he could see no further signs of pursuit, only the distant flames against the dark sky. Clark was breathing heavily by the time they reached flat ground, lowering O'Hara down with ill-concealed relief.

Fury could hear some of their exhausted men over to the left as they were rounded up by the officers. He quickly bent over O'Hara and gave him a shake. O'Hara began to come to his senses as Fury helped him to his feet, and he and Thomas half dragged him over to where he estimated the remaining British troops to be, with Clark bringing up the rear.

They were not long in finding stragglers of weary men in bloody, torn uniforms. Even those who had not been wounded directly by enemy fire had suffered some kind of injury as they had flung themselves down the slope to avoid the charge of the Republicans.

Looking round, Fury felt lucky to be among the few who seemed genuinely unscathed by the attack. Still propping up the heavy frame of General O'Hara with Thomas, he staggered forward amidst the scattering of men, finally catching sight of a couple of officers on horseback.

'I have Lieutenant General O'Hara here!'

The horsemen turned towards him and, seeing the uniform of the man he was holding, galloped across.

'We thought he was taken!' exclaimed the first, as he fairly jumped from the saddle and knelt down beside O'Hara, now lying on the ground and groaning slightly as he began regaining full consciousness.

'He very nearly was,' Fury replied, remembering how close it had been. 'His arm is shot through. He needs a surgeon quickly before he loses too much blood.'

One of the officers produced a rag and tied a rough tourniquet round the top of O'Hara's arm to stem the flow of blood. A canteen was removed from the saddlebags of one of the horses and he was given water, the combination of pain and fluid helping to bring him round more quickly.

'What happened?'

The question was asked in little more than a whisper.

'We thought you'd been taken sir. This officer,' the cavalryman pointed to Fury, 'somehow brought you off.'

O'Hara turned his gaze on Fury and offered a weak smile.

'Yes, I think I remember a little. Name and rank sir?'

'Lieutenant Fury sir, of HMS *Fortitude*, now commanding the garrison of Fort Pomet.'

'You have my sincere thanks Mr Fury, indeed you do.'

'It is my men, sir,' Fury protested, indicating Clark and Thomas, 'who deserve your thanks. It was they who brought you off.'

O'Hara smiled weakly at them as Clark and Thomas shuffled their feet uncomfortably.

'If you will excuse me sir,' Fury interrupted. 'I must attend to the rest of my men.'

O'Hara gave a small nod of approval and Fury turned away in search of them. They were not far away, largely unscathed and still together after having come down the slope in relatively good order. They seemed relieved to see Fury, but the compliment was lost on him in his current state of exhaustion.

'How many have we lost?'

'One dead sir,' Gooseman replied, 'another six injured. They've been taken to the field hospital.'

'Any Fortitudes?'

'No sir. We are all safe and sound.'

Fury supposed that they had been quite lucky considering the mayhem up there.

'Very well. We shall begin heading back to the fort now. The men can have tomorrow off; I think they've earned it.'

Fury led the way back to Fort Pomet, the

memory of his men standing firm to give him cover in the face of that Republican onslaught bringing a small smile of satisfaction to his face as he walked, so that the long journey back did not seem quite so tiresome.

CHAPTER 16

Fury awoke with a start to find a man standing over him gently shaking his shoulder. He was one of the men whom Fury had inherited upon taking over the fort, and his stale breath invaded Fury's nostrils.

'Eh? What is it?' he growled, vaguely aware that he had only laid down for a second to take the weight off his feet – he must have dozed off.

'Beggin' yer pardon sir, but there's a messenger arrived for you.'

Fury struggled to his feet, shaking off the drowsiness which still hung over him like a blanket.

'Very well. I shall be out presently.'

The man left and Fury took a little time to straighten his uniform and put on his hat.

It had been three weeks since the attack on the Republican mortar battery, and because of his refusal to supply the requested number of men to Lieutenant Carrick, he had been expecting a rebuke of some sort ever since. He had hoped that his rescue of Lieutenant General O'Hara would protect him from anything more serious, but perhaps he was wrong.

Satisfied with his appearance, he strode out into the courtyard to hear the worst. The messenger stood there tightly holding the reins of his horse as it nuzzled his shoulder, its breath clearly visible in the bitterly cold air.

'Lieutenant Fury?' he enquired, as Fury approached.

'Yes?'

'Orders sir, from the admiral.'

He reached into the half-open breast of his jacket and pulled out a folded sheet of paper with a thin wax seal holding it together, which he handed over. Fury turned and slowly walked away to get some privacy as he opened the orders, the relief flooding over him now he knew the messenger had not come from General Dundas.

The orders were dated 16 December 1793, and must have been completed the night before. Fury's eyes widened perceptibly as he read them with an increasing sense of alarm. He hurriedly refolded the orders and walked back to the messenger.

'Very well. We shall begin at once.'

The messenger hastily saluted and climbed back on his horse, wheeling it away and trotting out of the entrance.

'Mr Hawkins!' Fury bellowed, anger welling up inside him at the lateness of the order, combined with a nagging uneasiness at being so far away from Toulon with the Republican French advancing. The idea of getting cut off from his ship did not appeal to him.

303

'Sir?' enquired the sergeant as he hurried up, breathless.

'We have been ordered to withdraw at once. The French have taken possession of the heights of Faron and have captured Fort Balaguier.'

'I see sir.'

Hawkins' reply was so calm and was uttered with such matter-of-factness that Fury warmed to the man, not for the first time. He glanced around to confirm the presence of the horses which were kept at the fort to deliver messages quickly. They were still tethered near the officers' quarters, busily chewing on a large pile of hay. Fury turned back to Hawkins.

'Who is your best rider?'

'Rider sir?' Hawkins repeated, slightly surprised at the question considering his men were infantry soldiers, not cavalrymen. 'Well, sir – I suppose that would be Fisk.'

'Have him report to me at once. In the meantime, have your men stationed at the guns. I want them loaded and ready to fire.'

Hawkins hurried off shouting orders to his corporal while Fury made his way quickly to the small barracks which had been his quarters for the past couple of months. A musket shot rang out in the distance, presumably from one of the advance lookouts which Fury had posted to the north. They did not have long before the Republicans would arrive.

It took only a moment to throw the cutlass belt

over his shoulder and thrust the two loaded pistols into his waistband before diving back out into the courtyard to see Sergeant Hawkins coming towards him with a private in company.

'Private Fisk sir.'

'You can ride?' Fury demanded, dispensing with the pleasantries.

'Yes sir. Me father wer an ostler in Yorkshire when a werra lad.'

A shout from one of the men on the ramparts above interrupted him.

'Lookouts returning, sir!'

A few moments later the entrance doors swung inwards and the five advance lookouts ran into the courtyard, exhausted. Fury turned back to Fisk, aware that time was running out.

'Very good. I want you to take that horse and ride to the harbour. There is a small brig anchored in the outer road called *Renard*. I want you to get a message to her commander, Mr Francis – I don't care how – tell him to have a boat waiting at the quay in front of the general magazine, ready to take the Fortitudes off when we arrive.' The general magazine overlooked the inner basin in front of the new arsenal, and was the closest place Fury could think of to the Royal Gate, by which they would hopefully enter the city walls. Fury looked at his watch. 'We shall be there by nine. Have you got that?'

Private Fisk nodded and repeated his orders at Fury's request.

'Cut along now then. You may remain with the boats till we arrive.'

Fisk saluted and any apprehensions Fury may have had regarding his horsemanship were quickly dispelled when he expertly jumped into the saddle and rode out of the fort.

'All men present and ready sir!' Hawkins reported, bringing Fury back to the task at hand.

Fury looked up at the ramparts and could see the men standing ready next to each cannon. Those men not required to work the great guns were keeping lookout with muskets ready.

Fury bounded up the stone steps to the ramparts to get an idea of how much time he had. As he arrived on the ramparts the first of Hawkins' men began to fire muskets down the valley. Fury could immediately see scatterings of Republican troops – skirmishers, most likely – darting from cover to cover as they advanced through the series of lateral ridges dominating the valley floor. The sound of musket balls ricocheting off stonework betrayed the fact that they were returning fire.

It was clear to Fury that this was merely the advance force making their way down towards them, and he was sure the main body of the enemy – far too numerous for his small garrison to defend against – would not be far behind. What should he do? Should he put up a fight or order his men to retreat immediately, before they got cut off altogether?

'Pick your targets! Don't waste balls and

cartridge!' he snapped, aware that some of the firing from the troops was erratic and hasty. 'Sergeant Hawkins!'

'Sir?'

'Have the men open fire with the cannon once you judge there to be sufficient troops to aim at.'

'Yes sir!'

The sight of those cannon sitting impotently on the ramparts had made his decision for him – he would not order the retreat until they had at least fired them once, and given the enemy a bloody nose. Besides, the Royal Navy did not train its officers to run at the first sign of trouble, nor to gift their guns and supplies to the enemy. He would do his duty, no matter what the consequences.

He hurried back down to the courtyard and rushed into his quarters. He knew the chest in the corner would contain all he needed for the task at hand. The lid lifted with a creak and he rummaged inside, finally pulling out two reels, one of slow match and one of quick match, along with a knife and a waterproof packet containing flint and steel. Carrying his small bundle back out into the courtyard, he hastened over to the two horizontal wooden doors which were located in the far left of the fort, as far away as possible from the barracks.

He had not looked in here since he had taken over command of the garrison, but Sergeant Hawkins had assured him that the magazine contained barrels of gunpowder. It would hopefully make an explosion sufficient to destroy the fort if he could complete the preparations in time.

One pull at the right-hand door and it opened to reveal the gloominess within. The stone staircase leading downwards was swallowed up in the darkness after only five or six steps. He placed the waterproof packet on the floor along with the reel of slow match, only keeping hold of the quick match as he opened the other door in an effort to let in more light before cautiously descending the steps.

The first cannon on the ramparts bellowed out, followed by the rest in quick succession. Republican numbers down the valley were obviously increasing, placing even more pressure on Fury to complete his task quickly.

He reached the bottom, feeling in front with his feet to confirm it was indeed the bottom before slowly moving forward, the gritty feeling underneath his boots telling him there were at least some loose grains of gunpowder scattered on the stone floor. The knowledge that one small spark could set the whole place off did nothing to calm his nerves or bolster his confidence. Constant blinking and no small amount of concentration had their reward, however, as his eyes became accustomed to the gloom and he perceived the darker shapes of barrels all around, stacked up wherever there was space. His face broke into a fierce grin as he thought of the destruction it would cause, so much the better if the advancing Republicans were caught up in the blast.

He moved over to the nearest dark shape on the floor only three paces in front of him and stooped down to feel with his hands. It was not long before he had found the bunghole in the barrel, placed upwards to allow easy access to the powder within when the gunner was making up his cartridges. He managed to prize the bung out with his knife, which he hesitantly thrust within, feeling the soft resistance of the powder which confirmed the barrel was full. He carefully tied the end of the quick match round the handle of the knife, before inserting it once more into the barrel.

Satisfied, he got slowly to his feet and backed away towards the steps, gently unreeling the quick match as he went. He moved steadily up the stairs towards the light, finally arriving back in the courtyard, shocked to hear the fierceness of the musketry from without and within the fort.

Now safely out of the magazine he could move more hurriedly across the courtyard to the entrance, stooping just inside the doors to lay down the quick match before running back to the magazine entrance to pick up slow match and combustibles.

On reaching the main doors to the fort once again, he stooped and reached for his knife before realising it was no longer with him. He unsheathed his cutlass instead, and cut a length off the slow match, which by his estimate would give them about five minutes to get as far away from the fort as possible before the flame reached the quick match. After that it would take only a second to reach the magazine.

It was a difficult decision to make – how much time to give his men to escape, knowing that every extra second increased the chances of the enemy discovering the match and extinguishing it before it could reach the magazine. Five minutes would barely give them time to get beyond the radius of falling debris.

After having made sure the two lengths of match were securely fastened together, Fury got to his feet and sheathed his cutlass. An idea occurred to him and he got back to his knees and started scraping up as much dirt from the ground as he could carry. He then went along the length of match running to the magazine entrance, scattering the loose earth over it to cover it from enemy eyes should they arrive in time to discover it.

That done, he rushed back up the steps to join the men on the ramparts. Peering over the top he could clearly see many more men within fifty yards of the fort, sheltering behind anything they could to avoid being hit by the ragged volley fire, before firing their own weapons and moving forward in skirmish order.

Now, looking beyond them, Fury could discern the main body of the troops further back, breasting the last of the spurs crossing the valley floor.

These men were walking calmly forward in a great mass, making no attempt to run or find shelter. They were marching four abreast in a long column, all wearing the blue jackets of Republican infantry with the distinctive red piping at the cuffs and collars, and white cross belts. Fury estimated there to be at least 600 of them, probably comprising one battalion. The faint sound of singing reached his ears a moment later, carried by the wind from the approaching troops as they lustily recited Republican songs while they marched.

'Sergeant Hawkins!' he shouted, making himself heard above the myriad of other noises.

'Sir?' Hawkins replied, moving out of the line of men where he had been firing.

'You will take half your men and all the seamen and quit the fort, taking up a defensive position a hundred yards down the valley to provide covering fire as the rest of the troops evacuate. Is that understood?'

'Yes sir,' Hawkins shouted back, turning away to address orders to his corporal.

After only a moment, half the troops of the 69th began filing hurriedly down the steps led by Hawkins, followed also by the seamen. Fury and forty or so others were now left to defend the fort.

Fury picked up a musket which was leaning against the wall, quickly aimed down the ravine and fired. The soldiers left behind under the command of the corporal were firing briskly and with an efficiency which impressed Fury, understandable considering the amount of drill they had been through recently. He gave Hawkins and his men as much time as he dared to get into position down the valley. Finally, prompted by the fact that he had no other musket to fire, and unwilling to use the two pistols stuck in his belt at this stage – they would be nearly useless at this range – he decided that he could put off their final retreat no longer.

'You will remain here and keep up your fire until I tell you to retreat.'

The corporal nodded and Fury rushed down the steps towards the entrance. Looking out of the doors he could see Hawkins and the rest of the men still hurrying down the valley to find favourable positions from which to provide cover.

Giving them no more notice, he stooped over the end of the slow match and began fumbling with flint and steel. He got a spark quickly and within seconds the match was spluttering away, Fury waiting to make sure it was fully ignited before turning his attention to the ramparts.

'Corporal Jackson!' he shouted. The musket fire drowned out his shout and it took another bellow to attract the attention of Jackson. 'Come off now!' he shouted, beckoning with his arm lest his voice could not be fully heard.

Jackson nodded, and a moment later the remainder of the men were scrambling down the steps.

Fury remained by the entrance, ushering them out of the fort and down the valley as they passed him, before taking one last look at the ground to ensure the slow match was adequately hidden by the scattered earth.

Satisfied there was nothing more he could do, he set out at a run after the others, happily throwing aside any pretence of a dignified, controlled retreat as he thought of the coming explosion.

He was three quarters of the way to his own troops before he became conscious of the first sounds of musket fire behind him, the whistling of the balls through the air and the occasional flick up of dirt showing how close they were. A moment later the sound of louder musketry – from in front of him this time – told of Hawkins and his men providing covering fire.

He reached them, finally, out of breath, looking round for the first time to see the advance party of Republicans at the fort's entrance, kneeling and firing down the valley at them.

'Sergeant Hawkins – you will take your men a further hundred yards down the valley while the corporal and his men cover you. When you are prepared, we will then retreat in your wake.'

Hawkins gathered together his portion of men and they set off hurriedly while Corporal Jackson and the remainder of the men took shelter and began firing.

It looked for a while like the Republicans were of a mind to keep following them, to harry their retreat or possibly attack them before they could get within the relative safety of the city walls. Two well-trained volleys from Jackson and his men, however, which accounted for eight or nine of the enemy from what Fury could see, changed their mind. They seemed content to consolidate their position at the fort, the sound of singing springing up again as they celebrated their victory.

How long had it been since he had set the charges? The question nagged at him while he waited for Hawkins and his men to get in position.

'That is sufficient Corporal, lets make our retreat at the double.'

Fury led the men at the run down towards where he could see the rest of the 69th dug in, muskets at the ready.

'We'll stay here for a few moments, Sergeant,' he said as he reached them, slightly out of breath. 'Take some shelter lads!' he shouted to the men around him.

Finding a perch behind a large rock with the steep slope of the ravine wall to his left, he stared down the valley at the fort, over 200 yards away. Many of the Republicans were there now, swarming about the entrance and in the courtyard, while the remonstrations of one of the officers sent a body of men down towards them.

He began to feel uncomfortable now – surely five minutes had passed. If they had discovered it then Fury and his men were waiting here for nothing, while every second the Republican troops came nearer. The anxiety within his breast grew alarmingly, and he half turned to give the order to recommence the retreat when a loud explosion erupted, the earth trembling beneath them at the force.

The sound, even from this distance, was ear-piercing. Fury turned in time to see a huge flash of white, followed by a small pause, before the fort was blown apart by the force of the blast, masonry and debris shooting up into the air as black smoke began appearing. A moment of apparent calm proceeded before the debris – some pieces as large as a house – came raining down. A piece nearly as large as a twelve-pounder gun landed with a thud ten yards in front of where Fury was crouched, swiftly followed by small stone-sized fragments raining down all around them, landing on heads and bodies but causing no serious injury among his men.

As for the Republicans, there could be no chance for those within the fort or nearby, while those who had been advancing towards them suffered terribly from the downfall of debris. Many dead bodies covered the ground and others screamed in terrible agony. Those lucky enough to have survived unscathed were retreating back to what was left of the fort, unwilling to carry on fighting after what they had just witnessed.

As for the fort, its position was hidden by a large pall of black smoke and Fury was certain it was completely destroyed, so much so that he rose and gave the order to Sergeant Hawkins to set the men off at the march without waiting for the smoke to clear to see the results of his work.

He led the way in silence as quickly as his legs would take him without breaking into a disordered run, which he knew would be disastrous. Once the thudding in his head had subsided, his ears began ringing, probably from the sound of the blast, and he contrived to ignore the sensation by studying their surroundings.

They had reached the end of the valley now and Fury could see the river Neuve through the gathering dusk. He led his men across it and on to the road beyond, turning them south until the mountainous peaks on either side dropped away to the flat expanses of land running east and west.

It was almost completely dark now, making navigation difficult, but Fury's memory told him that he need only follow the road as it swung eastward and he would eventually reach the crossroads, where a right turn would take them directly into the walled defences of Toulon.

He held his hand up as a signal to silence the chatter of the Fortitudes behind him. Something had caught his attention over the sound of the men's voices, carried by the wind. He craned his head forward as though that would help him hear better, but it proved unnecessary as the sound grew louder. Republican singing. He recognised it immediately, having only just heard it back at the fort, but it took him a moment to pinpoint its westerly origin. It got steadily louder as he listened, and by the sound of it was from a large body of troops, certainly more than he had at his disposal. Was that a light to the west, bobbing up and down and moving towards them?

'Lads! We'll start out at the trot. Follow me and keep in your ranks!'

He waited while word was passed to those troops at the rear of the column, before setting off down the road to the east at a brisk jog, the clash and jangle of equipment behind telling him that his troops were following closely. Somewhere over to the right, unseen in the darkness, was the marshy ground leading to the water of the inner road. Had Sophie and her father managed to escape the city and get to the rendezvous point amongst that marshland? He would find out within the next hour. Until then he could only hope.

It took another thirty minutes to reach the cross-roads where the hospital was situated. The sounds of Republican singing had long since faded, but nevertheless Fury's anxiety had been increasing constantly as they made their way along the road without seeing any other retreating troops. Were they the last to leave? Had they already been cut off by the attacking Republicans? It was about

500 yards from the hospital to the Royal Gate through which they would enter Toulon, and in the darkness he could only just make out the time from his pocket watch – a little before eight o'clock in the evening.

As he placed his watch back in his pocket a cannonading started from over on the right in the direction of the batteries of Malbousquet and Missiessi, overlooking the inner road. He could hear the flight of the balls through the air and, even at this distance, the crashes as they landed on the town and the dockyard. The realisation that the Republicans had taken those batteries came as somewhat of a shock. The implications dawned on him: they would not only be able to fire upon the town and dockyard, but also upon the ships in the inner road and basins. The knowledge that they had already fired upon the town suggested that it was still held by the British, so they had time.

Amongst the sound of cannonading, Fury could now hear the distinctive noise of small-arms fire. Over to the west he saw flashes in the darkness as muskets were fired. Were those the same troops they had narrowly avoided on their way back from Fort Pomet? Presumably the Republicans were attempting to breach the defensive wall adjacent to the dockyard. That made it even more imperative that Fury get his men to the Royal Gate as quickly as possible, so he set out on the last stretch of the journey at a brisk pace.

The high wall surrounding Toulon loomed up out of the darkness in front of them, the Royal Gate firmly closed. Fury fought against the panic which threatened to overwhelm him.

A musket shot sounded from close at hand, Fury taking a moment to realise it had come from above, behind the wall surrounding the city.

'Identify yourself!'

The shout pierced the night air and Fury, looking up, fancied he could see a face peering over the top of the wall.

'I am Lieutenant Fury, commander of the garrison at Fort Pomet. I was ordered to evacuate immediately and return to the city!'

The relief was coursing through Fury now that he knew that the Royal Gate was still being manned.

'Very well, I'll have the guards let you in, but be damned quick about it. Half the Republican army is advancing on our position.'

Fury heard shouted orders from behind the wall, swiftly followed by the creaking of timber as the heavy doors of the Royal Gate swung slowly open. Fury stood at the side of the road, ushering his men across the small bridge which spanned the moat surrounding the city.

When all his men were past, Fury ran across the bridge and through the doors, the raised muskets of the guard within proving that they were taking no chances. The same officer who had challenged them from the wall approached.

'You may make your way across the city to the Italian Gate in the north-eastern quarter,' he suggested. 'The fleet has boats waiting off Fort La Malgue to embark the troops.'

Fury turned to Sergeant Hawkins. 'Very well, Sergeant. You may lead your men to Fort La Malgue for embarkation.'

'Yes sir.' Hawkins paused. 'And you sir?'

'I have made my own arrangements for escape. I will be sure to return Private Fisk to you as soon as the opportunity arises.'

Hawkins saluted and began bellowing orders to his troops. Fury turned to his own men.

'Follow me lads. Stay close together and keep your muskets ready.'

Fury struck out to the west through the dockyard and towards the inner basin, following the wall to ensure he did not lose his way. The sound of cannon fire was a constant companion, occasionally accompanied by a loud crash as the ball landed within earshot among the dockyard.

Men were moving about in every direction, more so as they approached the general magazine overlooking the quayside in front of the new arsenal. Many were obviously sailors, with the occasional officer's uniform interspersed, but there were also soldiers rushing to and fro to defend different parts of the wall from attack.

Fury eyed them all suspiciously and made sure of

keeping his men in good order, but no one bothered them. The cannon fire was growing louder now, intermingled with the smaller popping of musket fire, but nevertheless Fury could feel his confidence returning as they neared the quayside, and hopefully Sophie.

To his men's obvious surprise, Fury did not stop at the quayside, but continued on past the gun wharf and out along the stone jetty comprising the western side of the inner basin of the new arsenal. Four French ships of the line were secured bow first against the jetty to their left, but Fury was uninterested in them. The narrow tidal moat surrounding the city and the dockyard had now reached the juncture of the moat and inner harbour itself, and there was a fifty-yard expanse of that water now separating them from the mainland, which began as marsh. Fury could see from the water that the tide was on the ebb, but the moat would still be deep.

Quickly they reached the corner of the jetty, where the coast jutted out slightly to within twenty yards of the stone quay they were on. Fury stopped and stared into the darkness towards the shore. Nothing.

'Sophie! Sophie!'

His heart began to sink as his shouts were greeted with silence. He tried again, but still nothing. He peered anxiously into the darkness at the shore, hoping to see something, anything. His men were shuffling their feet nervously behind him, and Fury knew he could not risk their safety any further because of his own selfish needs.

'Come on,' he growled, beginning to make his way back to the quayside, frequently staring back at the shore in the hope of catching a glimpse of some movement. Was she merely late, or had something happened to her in the confusion?

Fury led them to the water's edge, immediately in front of the general magazine, almost exactly where he had disembarked over two months previously with his Fortitudes. He looked at his watch to see that it was still only half-past eight. They still had half an hour before Francis was due to meet him with the boat. Did he have time to look around for Sophie? He couldn't just leave her at the mercy of the Republicans, but what were the chances of him finding her now?

A voice startled him from the stygian gloom of some stone steps leading down to the water, prompting several of the men to bring their muskets to bear. Private Fisk hurriedly made himself known to them.

'The boat is over 'ere sir,' he whispered.

'Well done Fisk,' Fury said quietly, going down to the water's edge. A sharp whistle from Fisk – obviously a prearranged signal – brought the boat gliding out of the darkness to the quayside, a man at the bow manning the swivel in case they were the enemy.

'Welcome back sir,' hissed Midshipman Francis as he jumped on to the stone steps next to Fury.

'Thank you, Mr Francis,' Fury replied, taking the proffered hand. 'Where is *Renard*?'

'I was obliged to anchor her over to the east in the outer road sir, under the guns of Fort La Malgue which is still in our hands. The Neapolitans broke and ran at the first sign of attack, leaving the Republicans Malbousquet and Missiessi with which to sweep the inner road.'

'I see. And what about the *Fortitude*?'

'She was badly damaged off Corsica sir, during an engagement with a Mortello tower. Lord Hood ordered her to Gibraltar for a full refit.'

Fury groaned, wondering if he would ever get to rejoin his ship. He turned to Clark.

'Very well Clark, get them aboard.'

Clark saluted and Fury, eager for more news, turned back to Francis.

'Do you know what the situation is elsewhere?'

'Not really sir, I haven't had much communication from the shore or the fleet recently. The ships in the outer road have been taking refugees on board as far as I can make out sir, but what with me only having a few men, I decided against it for the time being. There was a lot of fighting over there' – pointing behind him – 'near Balaguier and l'Eguillette, but I don't know any more than that. We were not fired upon by them as we entered the inner road at any events, although it may have been just too dark for them to see us.'

'All ready sir,' hissed Clark from the bows, a subtle

reminder to them that this was not the place to stand talking.

Fury looked at the boat, ready at the quayside with the men now all on board, and he knew he could not go. He would never be able to forgive himself if he left now without any attempt to find her.

'Get them back to *Renard*, Mr Francis. I have something to take care of, so I shall make my own way back.'

'Sir?'

'I have business in the town.'

'But sir, entering the town now on your own in a British uniform would not be safe.'

'Let me worry about that, Mr Francis,' Fury snapped. 'You have your orders.' He caught sight of Clark clambering out of the boat back on to the quayside, followed by Thomas. 'What d'you think you're doing?'

'Coming with you sir, beggin' yer pardon.'

Fury opened his mouth to argue, but changed his mind. He would feel safer with a couple of his men along, and they were unlikely to be bothered if there were three of them, all armed. Besides, he knew Clark too well to think that he would give up easily.

'Oh, very well. But stay close by me.'

'But how will you get back to *Renard*, sir?' Francis persisted.

Fury had not thought that far ahead, but was reluctant to let Francis know. 'It's all in hand. Just concentrate on getting the men back to *Renard*.'

Francis acknowledged reluctantly and clambered back into the boat, while Fury turned to Clark and Thomas, standing silently waiting.

'Come on.'

He led them, half running, past the mast house and towards the timber storehouse at the edge of the dockyard. The number of soldiers increased as they neared the entrance to the city. The massive gates were closed and locked to keep out the citizens of Toulon, and Fury had to argue fiercely with the soldier commanding to get him to open them. Fury led Clark and Thomas through as the soldiers struggled to shut them again amidst the press of people.

They pushed their way through the throng, Fury only subconsciously registering the shouts and screams emanating from the crowd as they passed through and into the darkened streets beyond, with people in near panic everywhere. Intermittent loud crashes sounded as several cannonballs from the Republicans over at Fort Missiessi landed on buildings.

'Come on,' he growled over his shoulder, encouraging Clark and Thomas to keep up with him. He was gasping for air just as much as they were, but his anxiousness for the welfare of Sophie took precedence over any physical discomfort.

He reached the end of the street and paused on the corner, looking left and right in an attempt to get his bearings. The lack of any lighting was making it difficult for him to find his way, and he could only hope that soon he would come across a familiar street.

A small group of men caught sight of his uniform and started to approach, shouting at him aggressively. Fury turned towards them and raised both his pistols, causing the men to pause in their tracks. Clark and Thomas placed themselves on either side of Fury and stood ready with cutlasses and pistols, and the sight of them made the group think better of it. They turned away with a final shouted insult, or so Fury assumed it to be.

'This way!'

He turned left and broke into a run, his instinct telling him that he was heading in the right direction. He increased his speed without even looking over his shoulder to check if Clark and Thomas were still with him. He could feel the anxiety welling up within him at the thought of Sophie being unprotected amid such mayhem and lawlessness.

People were emerging on to the streets from buildings carrying armfuls of clothing or other belongings, some even with furniture, all with as much as they could manage. Fury was unsure whether the people were trying to save their possessions, or whether they were looters, using the current panic to pillage and plunder.

He became aware of a whistling sound overhead, and a moment later the front of the building immediately to his right erupted into a shower of stone and glass. A shout of pain behind him caused him to stop, and he turned around to find Thomas bent over the crouching figure of Clark. Fury rushed over to them.

'Are you hurt, Clark?'

'It's nothing sir, just a flesh wound,' he said through gritted teeth.

Fury helped him gingerly to his feet, and could see the blood soaking through the shoulder of Clark's jacket.

'Are you sure? Can you move your arm?'

Clark moved it in a circular motion, the grimace on his face betraying the pain of the wound.

'See, sir? It's fine.'

A child's crying penetrated the din of the continuing bombardment overhead. The front of the building next to them had been destroyed, presumably by one of the Republican cannonballs, and Fury could see wreckage within.

'Wait here.'

Fury moved over to the building, the sound of the crying increasing as he neared. Stuffing his pistols in his belt, he used his hands to clamber over the rubble and into the room. Dust was everywhere, along with broken furniture and shards of glass. A woman lay in the corner, her body broken and twisted at a sickening angle. A toddler was bent over her, a girl of no more than three years old, crying hysterically as she tried to prod her mother back to life. Her hair was plastered with blood and her dress was torn and caked with dust.

Fury went over to her and picked her up, prying her fingers off her dead mother's dress and resisting her frenzied kicks as he took a final look around the room to ensure no one else lay alive. There was nobody. Picking his way carefully over the rubble with the girl still crying and kicking frantically, he arrived back on to the street.

An old woman came towards him crying and holding out her arms, and Fury passed the child to her in silence, the tears beginning to sting his own eyes. He blinked them away and turned to Clark and Thomas.

'There's nothing more we can do here. Let's go.'

He set off at a run again, his worries over Sophie intensifying after witnessing the destruction caused by the Republican batteries at first hand. His chest was tight and heaving by the time they reached the coffee shop where he and Sophie had talked together. He stopped momentarily to get his bearings.

'What is it sir?'

That was Thomas asking the question, in between sucking in lungfuls of air. Fury ignored him and crossed the street, knowing that they were nearly there.

'We're not far off now,' he explained, keeping his pace to a brisk walk as he hurried down the street. They came to a crossroads and he turned left, breaking into another jog without looking over his shoulder to check that Clark and Thomas were still with him. Another hundred yards and they came to the alleyway on the left, running perpendicular to the street.

The door to Sophie's apartment was off its hinges and lying in the alley. Fury pulled his pistols out of his belt and plunged into the darkness of the lower hall, fumbling his way up the stairs. He could hear the grunts and curses of Clark and Thomas behind him as they struggled in the near pitch black.

'Sophie!'

His shout pierced the darkness but there was no response, Fury's anxiety increasing yet further as it became clear the premises were deserted. He reached the top of the stairs and poked his head into the first room, which had a window on the far side allowing Fury to see a little better. Broken furniture was strewn about the floor, but, thankfully, there was no sign of any bodies. He bumped into Clark as he turned to check Sophie's room.

'Beggin' yer pardon, sir,' Clark muttered.

'No matter,' Fury replied, pushing past him down the hall. The door to Sophie's room was half closed when he reached it, and he steeled himself before entering, attempting to prepare for the worst. He pushed the door open and went inside. There was no window in this room and he stood still for a few nervous moments, struggling to see as his eyes adjusted to the blackness within.

It was much as the first room had been, the furniture broken and scattered about the floor, and signs of other belongings intermingled with it. Fury let out an imperceptible sigh of relief that there was no body there either.

'There's nothing here,' he stated. 'We'll have to be getting back to the quayside before the city is overrun with Republicans.'

They filed out of the building and back into the dark alleyway. Fury's initial relief at not finding a body was now waning as he realised that he had lost her. Wherever she was, safe or not, he would never find her now. With their two countries at war there was every chance he would never see her again, and the knowledge of it tugged fiercely at his heart.

They set off at a brisk walk, much to the relief of Thomas and Clark. The bombardment continued overhead but Fury paid no heed to it, in fact hardly even heard it as his mind raced with thoughts of Sophie – her eyes and lips, the touch of her skin, and the way her face lit up when she smiled.

They arrived at the gate separating the city from the dockyard, the crowd of frantic people still desperate to gain entry. Fury began trying to push his way through, but there were too many of them. He pulled one of the pistols from his belt, cocked it and aimed it high into the air.

The sharp crack as it went off startled the whole crowd, and as Fury pushed through they began to separate. He reached the gate and the soldiers parted for him when they recognised his uniform.

It took only minutes to reach the waterside over-looking the inner basin of the new arsenal. Fury desperately wanted to check the agreed rendezvous point with Sophie one last time to see if she had made it, but he knew that time was running out.

He began to lead Clark and Thomas over to the stone jetty when a shout from the darkness of the water stopped him in his tracks.

'Here sir!'

A boat came gliding out of the gloom to the dockside, with Francis half standing at the bow.

'Mr Francis!' Fury exclaimed in shock. 'What are you doing here? I thought I ordered you back to *Renard*.'

Francis looked slightly guilty, but Fury saw a flicker of defiance cross his face. 'Sorry sir, but I couldn't leave without you. We were safe enough away from the shore sir.'

Fury opened his mouth to admonish him, but then closed it; now was not the time.

Francis jumped on to the quay next to Fury. 'All ready sir?'

Again Fury thought about the rendezvous with Sophie, his heart pleading with him to check it one last time. He gritted his teeth; he would not risk his men's lives over his own feelings any longer, no matter how strong they were.

'Clark, Thomas. In you get.' Fury gestured to the waiting boat and the two men climbed aboard, Clark still nursing his wounded shoulder. 'After you, Mr Francis.'

Fury waited for Francis to clamber on board

331

before following. The boat was overcrowded, so it was some struggle to get to the stern sheets and uproot the man currently holding the tiller.

'Shove off. Give way all!'

The boat drifted away from the quayside and, when enough distance had been gained, the oars came down into the water and began gliding back and forth as the men bent to them. Fury swung the tiller over to send the boat in the direction of the narrow entrance which would take them through to the inner road, with the outer road and relative safety beyond.

CHAPTER 17

The going was understandably slow due to the overcrowding, exacerbated by the rising wind blowing across their path from west to east and reminding Fury for the first time today of how bitterly cold it was, now he was sitting inactive.

Shadows loomed surprisingly close on their right, and he could just make out the outlines of the four huge ships of war which they had passed on the jetty, lying at anchor about half a cable away and secured to the wharf. They would be the remnants of the French fleet which was in the harbour when the British fleet had arrived and which Lord Hood had ordered to be removed into the inner basin and stripped of all men, powder and stores.

Faint sounds from up ahead drew his attention – the splashing of oars preceding another looming shape, darker against the black of the night sky.

'Easy all!' he hissed, the men ceasing their pull at the oars while Fury anxiously peered forward, waiting to see what the ship was. She was definitely moving, that much he could be sure of. Was she being towed?

As she crept closer the sound of splashes grew louder and the smaller outline of boats in front of her came into view, confirming Fury's suspicion. They would cross their path soon, heading straight for the group of line-of-battle ships which Fury had been studying moments previously. There could only be one answer and Fury was quick to identify it. The boats were towing a fire ship in to destroy the remnants of the French fleet lying in the inner basin.

'Sir?'

Francis was looking at him, confused by the sudden stop.

'A fire ship, Mr Francis, being towed in to destroy the French ships there.' He pointed to where the ships were moored up against the quay. 'We will hold position here until they have passed.'

'Aye aye sir,' Francis replied.

The fire ship was crossing their path now, her lighter sails clear against the dark sky, hanging down from her yards but not sheeted home to ensure the fire caught quickly. Even in the darkness Fury could see that she was a frigate, her single row of gun ports open to let in as much air as possible below decks with which to feed the hungry flames. Presumably she was one of the French frigates which had been found to be too unseaworthy to be attached to the British fleet.

Fury heard the order from the officer in one of her boats to cast off the towline, obviously satisfied that the ship was in position to drift down upon her targets and wreak her havoc.

He watched as she continued to drift slowly down towards the four ships, and after a moment he became aware of a small orange glow from within her hull where the officer on board must have just set light to her. The glow became slowly bigger as the flames spread, followed shortly afterwards by her fore course erupting in flames, lighting up a small area of the inner basin.

Even as he watched, his seaman's instinct, honed sufficiently even after a relatively short time at sea, became aware of a shift in the wind. The effect of it on the hull of the fire ship was noticeable, changing her course slightly so that she was now slowly drifting down towards the last in the line of French ships which were grouped together. Fury wondered whether she would miss them altogether.

The officer on deck must still be at the wheel, turning it to bring her back on course for her target. He watched anxiously for some small sign that she was still under helm control, but saw nothing, forcing him into making a decision which he knew to be both dangerous and foolhardy. At least the activity would take his mind off Sophie, he thought.

'Mr Francis!' He raised his voice to make sure he was heard over the crackling of the flames. 'I am going on board that fire ship, for if I do not she will miss her intended target. You will lead the boat back to *Renard* to embark the men.'

'But—'

Francis began to protest but Fury cut him short.

'No arguments, Mr Francis. You have your orders.'

Francis reluctantly acknowledged and Fury turned back to his crew, giving the orders which sent the boat surging forward after the fire ship. To the men's credit, in spite of the number in the boat, they gave their all in pulling as fast as they could so that by the time they were approaching the larboard quarter of the flaming ship, there was still time.

Looking up, Fury could see the rigging and sails were a mass of flames, but there was no sign yet of the flames within her hull spreading out of her open gun ports. The boat's crew pulled him alongside the drifting ship and held her there below the battens leading up to the entry port above. Fury hurriedly pushed his way amidships and jumped without hesitation.

He grasped the side ropes gratefully and found his feet on one of the battens before hauling himself up and through the entry port on to the deck. The heat from the flames as he gained the deck was tangible, like a wall in front of him stopping him going further. After the initial shock he braced himself and ran aft to where the wheel was, sheltering his face with his arm as he went.

The wheel itself was spinning aimlessly. A loose rope attached to one of the spokes and dangling on the deck told him that the wheel had been secured, but the flames had burnt through the rope. Grasping the spokes he stopped the wheel turning and, using his best judgement as to which was the correct direction to steer, kept it steady.

His eye caught sight of a bulk on the deck over near the larboard scuppers, and he was surprised to see from the epaulettes on the jacket that it was the body of an officer. He made a mental note to check it before leaving and turned forward again to concentrate on the task at hand.

Although no flames were actually upon him, he could feel his face and hands burning from the fire all about the deck, while forward he could see flames rising from out of the waist.

Looking to his side at the lights on shore in the distance, he could discern the ship slowly changing direction as the bite of the rudder took hold. It was possible, by staring intently forward, to see the shape of the French ships ahead through the smoke, but even so it was a while before he felt the first soft jar of contact as they came alongside one of them.

He heard the sound of scraping wood as the fireship continued her momentum down the entire length of the French ship, until a lurch of the hull told Fury she had come to an abrupt standstill.

It was a miraculous stroke of good fortune that he had managed to run alongside rather than hit one of them head on, and it was even more miraculous that the yards overhead should manage to lock with those of the French ship on his right.

One glance above showed that the fire in the rigging had already started to spread.

Satisfied that there was no more he could do, and anxious to get away before being burnt to death, he left the wheel and started to make his way towards the unconscious officer. One of the other French ships was anchored about ten yards from the larboard side, so he must have managed to drift the fire ship between the last ship in the line and her neighbour.

Unhappy with the thought of just the one ship destroyed, he fumbled about the deck looking for some combustible material. Finding several charred sections of rope, he picked up two.

The flames were beginning to come up through parts of the deck now and he knew he didn't have long. He thrust both bits of rope among the flames until they were well alight, before hurrying over to the larboard bulwark. The first he threw on the deck of the neighbouring ship, seeing it disappear behind the bulwark. He did the same with the second, but aimed higher in an attempt to catch furled sails or heavily tarred rigging.

Disappointed at missing, he turned away and rushed over to where the officer was lying. His coat was that of a naval lieutenant, the same as Fury, and his hair was thickly matted with blood. There was a block next to him on the deck, with the remnants of some burnt rope through it; presumably it had fallen from aloft and hit the man on the head, knocking him senseless. The skin on his face was beginning to blister from exposure to the heat, but it appeared from his pulse that he was alive so Fury tried to shake him awake, receiving an encouraging groan in response. Two sharp slaps across the face was enough to bring him round at least to semi-consciousness.

There was no time to help him recover further and so Fury began to half drag, half carry him to the side, suddenly realising for the first time that he had not spared any thought whatsoever as to how he would escape.

The fire ship had been stopped in her tracks before reaching the stone quay, and the French ship alongside was a seventy-four. There was no chance of climbing on to her higher deck, even if she hadn't been well ablaze. The only option seemed to be to jump overboard. Once in the water, however, he would have no way of climbing up on to the quay, as there were no steps on this side of the inner basin. His only hope then, would be to try swimming back to where Francis had picked him up, where the stone steps rose out of the water to the quayside in front of the dockyard.

At that moment a loud crash erupted below, giving Fury an almighty shock. It was one of the guns on the main deck going off as the flames reached the priming. A moment later numerous other guns discharged, the deck heaving slightly at each one as Fury looked up in time to see the side of the French vessel opposite erupt into splinters at the impact.

He was also vaguely aware of smoke rising from the deck of the French ship to larboard, but there was no more time to think about that as he dragged his companion to the taffrail, deciding that jumping from the stern was preferable to jumping over the side now that he knew all the guns had been shotted. A quick look at the water beneath told him that the drop was about twelve feet. Without pausing for reflection, he pushed the officer over the side and quickly followed into the oily black water below.

The icy coldness of the water as he hit it was enough to shock the breath from his body, so that it was a frantic few seconds before he finally resurfaced, gasping for air. He became conscious that it was very difficult to swim with his boots on, not to mention the excess weight of the two sea-service pistols which were still stuck in his waistband, now useless. The latter problem was quickly resolved by two quick tugs, the pistols sinking rapidly once free of his body.

The other officer was nearby, evidently brought sharply back to consciousness by his sudden immersion. In the distance Fury could see the lights of the dockyard and town beyond, while overhead the cannonading from Malbousquet and Missiessi continued.

He pointed towards the lights in an effort to make the other officer understand, trying to keep

340

the water out of his mouth as the wind flicked up the waves in the inner basin. The man gave a weak nod in comprehension and Fury struck out towards it with his slow breaststroke, knowing instantly that they would never make it.

He had not gone more than ten strokes when he became aware of splashing over to his right, and a moment later a boat loomed up out of the darkness.

'Lieutenant Gore!'

The voice rang out as the men at the oars ceased their exertions.

'Here!' gasped out Fury's companion, not more than five yards behind him.

Another dip of the oars from the crew brought the boat gliding alongside, where ready hands were waiting to haul the lieutenant on board.

'Over here!' Fury cried out quickly, worried that the boat's crew may not have seen him.

Lusty strokes brought the boat rapidly alongside, much to Fury's relief, and a moment later he too was sitting in the bottom, dripping and shivering uncontrollably.

'Who are you, and where the devil did you spring from?'

Fury recognised the uniform of a post captain upon the man who had asked the question, although the single epaulette on his right shoulder denoted he had less than three years' seniority.

'I am Lieutenant Fury sir, of the *Fortitude*. I was in the process of transferring the late garrison of

Fort Pomet to the fleet, when I saw your fire ship drifting off course. I took the liberty of having myself put on board to take the wheel sir.'

'And a damn good thing you did, or else I'd be burnt to a cinder right now,' interrupted his shivering companion. 'I am Lieutenant Gore, and I am much obliged to you sir.'

Fury shook his outstretched hand.

'And I,' the captain continued, 'am Captain Hare, commanding this small party. We are indeed obliged to you Mr Fury. The *Fortitude* did you say? But she is refitting at Gibraltar is she not?'

'She is sir. I was placed in command of the garrison of Fort Pomet by Lord Hood. We received the order to retreat this afternoon.'

'I see,' replied Hare, 'I regret I cannot guarantee you safe return to your ship. We are currently pulling for the new arsenal to assist Sir Sydney Smith and his men in their endeavours to destroy all they can.'

'I was not aware Captain Smith was a member of the Mediterranean fleet, sir.'

'He is not, technically. When he heard of the onset of war, he purchased a trim little cutter, the *Swallow*, and brought her here as a private vessel. He volunteered for this madness!'

Fury nodded and settled down in silence, bitterly cold and wet, as they pulled towards the dockyard.

They passed a number of gunboats just off from the quay as they approached, all busily firing their swivels in addition to the sole cannon mounted at the bows, to suppress the advance of the Republicans, some of whom Fury could see attempting to get round the wall enclosing the dockyard and city.

Fury and his companion Lieutenant Gore were both shivering hard by the time the boat pulled up to the stone quay in front of the new arsenal. Fury leaped out behind Captain Hare, grateful for the chance to work some life into his frozen limbs. Lieutenant Gore had to be helped out – he was now in some pain from the burns he had suffered along with his head wound.

A quick glance around showed the position clearly enough. Despite the fire from the gunboats the Republicans were still attempting to cross the moat which separated the western end of the new arsenal from the mainland. Numerous soldiers positioned on the quay were firing muskets in an effort to discourage them as the various fire parties from within the arsenal withdrew, presumably after laying down their charges and setting the place alight.

Moments later, flames leapt up into the night sky with amazing suddenness, so that in a matter of minutes many of the buildings of the dockyard were thoroughly alight.

Almost immediately the cannonading from Malbousquet and Missiessi increased, the shot falling all around the arsenal and the quay as they stood there. The light from the flames rising up within the dockyard was providing the Republican

343

gunners across the bay with a better sight of what they were firing at.

Captain Hare was addressing another man wearing the uniform of a post captain, the epaulettes signifying that the wearer had held his rank for more than three years, both men impervious to the fall of shot around them. The man had an aristocratic face, with high cheekbones and a sharp, pointed nose.

'This is Lieutenant Fury sir,' Captain Hare was saying to him. 'He boarded the fire ship and held her on course before bringing Gore off.'

'Much obliged to you Mr Fury,' the officer said, turning to Fury. 'I am Captain Smith. Glad to have you with us.'

'Thank you sir.'

'Your appearance here is a blessing,' Smith continued. 'Poor Mr Gore is too badly injured to be much more use to me tonight, while I believe Lieutenant Pater has been much burnt in setting light to the rope walk, so that I find myself in desperate need of officers.'

At that moment a tremendous blast was heard behind them out in the inner road, everyone turning round instantly to see the water lit up with white as one of the ships lying at anchor exploded, burning timber and spars falling all around the area. Even from the quay the force of the blast could be felt, albeit largely diminished by the distance.

Fury looked on in mute horror as a large piece of burning wreckage – a lower mast perhaps – landed squarely on top of one of the gunboats employed in keeping the Republicans pinned down. The boat itself was holed and sank almost immediately. Its two consorts pulled towards it with commendable rapidity in an attempt to pick up what survivors they could.

'Blasted Spaniards!' raged Smith, once he had recovered from the shock. 'The powder ships were supposed to be scuttled and sank, not set alight!'

Suddenly Fury understood – the ship had been one of those used to store all the powder taken from the other ships of the French fleet, hence the size of the blast.

By now there was quite a gathering on the quay in front of the arsenal; all those who had been tasked with setting the place alight had now returned. There was also a noticeable slackening of fire from the Republicans, so shocked had they been by the explosion.

'Captain Hare, please make preparations to abandon our positions,' Smith ordered. 'You shall make your way out through the east of the city and over to Fort La Malgue where our boats will take you off.'

Captain Hare walked briskly off. The bombardment of their positions now being resumed after the shock of the explosion. Splashes not far off from the quay, combined with what sounded like Spanish invectives, induced Fury to turn around sharply, instinctively reaching for his pistols as two boats came into view.

'Our Spanish allies,' Smith announced sarcastic-ally, as Fury discovered his waistband empty of pistols.

A Spanish officer, resplendent in gold lace, clam-bered awkwardly from the boat on to the quay and proffered a measly salute to Captain Smith. What was said Fury could not tell, the conversa-tion being in Spanish, but he could tell by the look of thunder growing on Smith's face that the news was not good. Nevertheless Smith kept his temper, maintaining an air of icy formality. Finally, in response to a gesture from Smith, the Spaniard shrugged and, turning to bark an order to the men behind him, led them towards the town.

'Incompetence! Sheer incompetence!'

Smith was fuming.

'Sir?' Fury enquired hesitantly.

'The Dagoes, Mr Fury, have betrayed us. They were ordered to scuttle the two powder ships, and then set light to as many of the remaining ships in the basin as possible before retiring. Instead, this rabble have set alight one of the powder ships while managing to destroy none of the other French ships, which will now likely fall back into the hands of the Republicans!'

Fury was thankfully saved from replying by the arrival back of Hare to report the men ready to begin the retreat.

'Very well,' Smith replied, 'you will take command of the retreat, Captain Hare. I shall take our two remaining gunboats, along with my *Swallow*, and attempt to set fire to the remaining ships in the basin of the old arsenal.' Captain Smith took a moment to look around him at the small group of officers. 'Mr Fury, you will command one of the boats, Mr Brisbane will command the other.'

Fury nodded along with the other lieutenant chosen, a thickset man with unruly blond hair. The crowd dispersed to begin preparing for the retreat, leaving Fury, Smith and Brisbane alone.

'Lads!' shouted Smith to the gunboats, 'Come and take us off!'

The men sent the two boats surging in towards the quay while Smith turned to address Fury and Brisbane.

'Now gentlemen, these gunboats should still have their supply of fuses and matches stored in the lockers which we can use. I shall lead in the *Swallow*. Lieutenant Brisbane, you will oblige me by carrying me off to her.'

The soldiers lately employed keeping the attacking Republicans at bay across the moat and opposite the bakehouse were now hurriedly retreating past the still-burning new arsenal towards the old arsenal with the town of Toulon behind. There was a rearguard still firing ragged volleys at the Republicans as they swept forward in a surge across the shallow moat. The rearguard fell back another twenty paces and closed up their ranks for the men who had fallen from the last enemy volley. With the Republicans now in the dockyard the firing intensified, the balls flicking up chips of stone nearby. Fury shuffled his feet uncomfortably, fighting down the urge to take cover. He tried to focus his concentration on Captain Smith, who seemed completely oblivious to the danger.

The grinding of wood on concrete followed by muttered oaths caused Fury to turn round, to see that the two gunboats had reached the quay and were waiting for them to embark. Fury descended the steps in relief and leaped down into the nearest boat, glad to be on water again. Moving past the men at the oars he sat gratefully down in the stern sheets and grasped the tiller. Captain Smith followed Lieutenant Brisbane down into the other boat and Fury allowed them to shove off first before giving the order to follow. The men pushed off from the side and then dipped their oars in pursuit.

Looking down into the dark water, Fury shuddered, amazed that it was not more than thirty minutes ago that he had been in it, desperately swimming for the shore.

CHAPTER 18

The fires throughout the dockyard, subsiding somewhat now, were nevertheless sufficient to provide light enough by which to see their intended victims. The masts and yards could be seen against the dark night sky, their hulls hidden by the stone quay separating the two basins.

The men at the oars paused while Smith transferred himself to his own little vessel, the *Swallow*, before leading them towards their target. For a few anxious moments as they crept across the basin Fury was fearful lest the forts should open fire on them, but it was clear that even with the light from the flames, they would have no way of telling whether they were friend or foe.

They were not more than forty yards from the narrow gut linking the two basins now. He could see Captain Smith's small ship ahead slewing round slightly, and a moment later Brisbane's boat, the next in line, did the same a little to the right of the *Swallow*.

Not sure what was happening, Fury eased the tiller over to send them towards the left of Smith's position, where he could see men leaning over the side struggling with something. What it was became apparent to Fury a moment later when his own boat hit something solid which caused it to slow rapidly before slewing round like the others.

'Boom!' Smith hissed across at him. 'See if you can get through it.'

For some inexplicable reason there was a boom blocking the entrance to the inner basin in front of the old arsenal. Instructing one of the men to keep hold of his legs, Fury swung his upper body over the side and down towards the sea. The freezing water was another reminder of his recent swim, but this time laying just beneath the surface his hands found a large wooden log.

Moving along it towards the stern of the boat he found the end, plunging down deeper to grasp the chain which kept the log secured to the next in line. A curt command to the men in the boat saw one of them pass him a cutlass, Fury reaching back to grasp it before plunging it into the water.

Even as he frantically hacked at the joint of log and chain with the cutlass, he knew it was useless. The chain was so large and well secured that he doubted if he could make any impression on it even if he had an axe. A splash nearby caught his eye and a moment later several more appeared, Fury's mind only latterly registering the sound of musket fire which accompanied them. He hauled himself back inboard.

'It's no use sir,' he shouted across to Smith, 'it won't part.'

Fury could hear the whine of balls through the air as the musketry rained down on them from men standing on the wall of the Batterie Royale, and it was becoming more intense as others joined them. The men in the three boats manned the swivels and pointed them into the darkness in the direction of the enemy, jerking the lanyards and sending a murderous hail of musket balls towards the Republicans, but still the fire was returned unabated.

One of the men in Fury's boat let out a scream as a musket ball hit him in the thigh, two of his comrades springing into action to tie their scarves round his leg as a tourniquet. Further thuds sounded as balls smashed into the hull and planking of the boat, and a moment later Captain Smith's voice rose above the noise.

'Belay there! Pull back out of range!'

Not before time, Fury thought, as he settled himself back in the stern sheets while making an effort to appear calm and unworried by the hail of musketry raining down on them. The men at the larboard oars needed no second invitation to prize the boat away from the boom, and soon they were out of range and out of danger.

'We'll head out into the inner road and make for the vessels anchored offshore, to see what other mischief we can cause,' Smith ordered as they sat at their oars.

Again the two gunboats followed Smith in the *Swallow* as they pulled on, Fury looking in envy at the activity of the men at the oars in comparison to his own inactivity, which was slowly causing him to shiver again as the wind pierced his damp clothing.

The fires in the dockyard were beginning to wane as the boats moved steadily across the basin in front of the new arsenal. Shouts and screams drifted across the water, and Fury looked over to the shore to see hundreds of people emerging from the town and the dockyard on to the quay.

The soldiers manning the gate to the dockyard must have begun their retreat to Fort Le Malgue through the city, leaving the gate open for the citizens to enter.

The cannon of Malbousquet and Missiessi, both high atop hills on the north shore of the inner road, were now silent, presumably reluctant to fire lest they should hit their own troops who were now pouring into the dockyard and town after the British and their allies had made their retreat.

The occasional orange glow within the town told of fires being started as, even now, the first wave of revenge attacks by staunch Republicans began. Peering back, Fury could see the quay in front of the town was a mass of confusion and panic. The lucky ones had procured boats which they were hurriedly pushing off from the quay, horribly over-crowded, in an attempt to escape from the wrath of the advancing Republicans.

The sound of musketry was very close. Some people, terrified and unable to obtain a boat, were actually rushing into the freezing water and attempting to swim to safety.

They were not more than twenty yards from the quay in front of the dockyard when Smith's voice carried over the noises of screams and shot.

'We will lay down covering fire for those boats!'

The two boats and the *Swallow* split up to find an advantageous position from which they could train their swivels on the enemy. Fury took his boat over to the left towards the western side of the quay and ordered his men to hold their position. He scrambled forward to the bow of the boat to see to the swivel himself.

Approximately thirty boats were now in the water, slowly increasing their distance from the shore, the oarsmen struggling to make headway in the crowded craft.

The Republicans were flooding on to the quay now from across the moat, firing at the boats and at the struggling swimmers in the water. Those who were unfortunate enough to be on the quay as the Republicans approached were shot without mercy, or bayoneted as the troops passed. Women and children were among the people cut down indiscriminately, some clutching their meagre belongings. Please God Sophie was not among them, Fury thought. He saw a young mother in a worn and dirty dress holding a sobbing child to her bosom. She stopped in panic as a Republican soldier ran towards her screaming. Fury was convinced that the soldier would ignore her, but he levelled his musket with bayonet fixed, and thrust it through the exposed back of the child and into the chest of the mother. Fury gagged at the sight and thought for a moment he was going to vomit. He was certain he could still hear the last dying screams of the child as the woman fell back on to the stone with the half-dead toddler still clutched to her. Fury instinctively grabbed the swivel gun as the rage began to well inside him.

One jerk of the lanyard was enough to send the tightly packed bag of musket balls hurtling into the crowd of men on the quay, cutting them down in swathes and sending back screams and cries of agony from those who had been unfortunate enough to survive.

Another shot from over to their right and more screams ashore told him that at least one of the other gunboats was pouring in canister, and Fury felt a surge of satisfaction at the sight.

He quickly reached down into the locker and took out cartridge, wads and another bag of musket balls. He hurriedly thrust these into the barrel and poured some gunpowder into the touch hole before swinging it round again towards the shore.

The Republicans were beating a hasty retreat from the quay as more canister poured in from the other gunboats, and Fury had only time for a quick aim before pulling the lanyard and sending the second hail of shot in. The Republican troops who had survived this final onslaught now took cover. For the moment there was no firing towards the escaping boats.

Fury turned his attention back to the quay itself, which was littered with the dead and dying. Many of these were Republican troops caught in the deadly fire from the swivel guns, but littered amongst these could be seen civilians – including more women and children – lying dead after they had been butchered by the troops. He glanced back at the body of the woman, with the lifeless bloodied body of her small child lying on top of her. His nausea returned and so he looked away quickly.

Several splashes in the water showed where those civilians who had not yet drowned were still struggling, and Fury hurried back to his place at the tiller and gave the order which set the boat surging closer in towards them.

Isolated potshots were aimed at them from the Republicans still sheltering on the quay, but Fury was not aware of any coming close to them. The first man they approached disappeared below the water before they could haul him on board, utterly exhausted from his exertions. Thankfully the others in the water nearby managed to last until they had been dragged shivering into the bottom of the boat. Six in all, two of them women, and a small enough return on the twenty or more who Fury was certain he had seen jump into the bay.

When he was sure there were no more left alive, he put the tiller over and the men bent to their oars to send them surging back to where Captain Smith was waiting with the *Swallow* tender and the other gunboat, both with swivels still trained on the quay lest the Republicans should decide to become a nuisance.

'How many Mr Fury?' Smith shouted to him.

'Six sir,' Fury replied, aware that it sounded a pitifully small number.

'Very well. You may transfer them to the *Swallow*.'

Fury sent the boat alongside the *Swallow* with Smith looking down, and numerous hands above helped haul the wretches on board.

The majority of the boats which had escaped from the town had taken the chance to cease their efforts and rest, and so a fairly large expanse of water was now covered by them. Fury could see numerous Neapolitan uniforms among those men in the boats and a surge of anger rose within him at the thought of their cowardice in running from their posts at Malbousquet and Missiessi, leaving the French the opportunity of pouring in fire upon the retreating allies.

As if to heighten the irony of the occasion, at that moment the first shot from either Malbousquet of Missiessi was fired towards them. Sharp eyes had probably been monitoring events closely through their night glasses, and had deduced that the boats had successfully escaped.

Smith took a speaking trumpet from the deck of the *Swallow* and began shouting instructions to the crowded boats in fluent French, gesticulating and pointing with his arm to ensure he was understood. The boats slowly turned and headed away towards the inner road. Women and children cried as falling shot churned up the water all around them. The *Swallow* and the two other boats shadowed them out of the basin and into the inner road to ensure they were safely on their way, before Smith ordered the boats to lay on their oars.

'Sir!'

Smith looked across at him through the darkness. 'Yes, Mr Fury, what is it?'

'There is something I must do first, before we leave. I will rejoin you in fifteen minutes.'

Fury was half expecting Smith to refuse, and he was quite prepared to disobey him if he did. He was not technically under Smith's command, and therefore was confident that he would not be too severely punished.

'Very well, Mr Fury.'

Fury swung the tiller over with relief and the boat surged towards the north shore of the inner road. He could see very little through the darkness save for the marshland backing away inland. The inner basin was to their right and he could distinguish the small river Nez as it flowed into the bay from its source up on the heights.

'Easy all,' he growled, when he judged them to

be twenty yards or so from the shore. The men ceased their efforts and the boat continued to drift in towards the land as the momentum gradually diminished. Malbousquet was continuing its bombardment of the town and the dockyard, but they were safe enough here.

'Sophie!'

He shouted the name into the darkness, unaware of the curious glances of his boat's crew as he strained forward to listen. Nothing. He could feel the desperation rising within his breast and he tried to control the feelings of utter helplessness which seemed to cling to him.

'Sophie!'

He desperately wished to stay, to scour the shoreline for any sign of her so that in the future he would at least have the comfort of knowing he had done all he could, but he knew that it was hopeless.

'Give way al—'

'John!'

The shout came from somewhere among the marshland, unmistakeably female, and Fury's heart skipped a beat.

'Sophie?'

'Over here John!'

Fury thought he could discern a movement of white down by the water's edge, and the sounds of splashing drifted over. He pointed forward with his arm for the benefit of the oarsmen.

'Over there lads, quickly.'

The men bent to their oars and the boat surged forward. He could see Sophie now, only her head above water as she set off towards them, further splashes behind her betraying the presence of someone else, presumably her father.

'Easy all!'

The men ceased their efforts and the boat drifted down to her. She swam in between the static oars and clung on to the side of the boat, turning back to the shore to check on the progress of her father. Fury rushed to the side of the boat, pushing his way between the oarsmen, and reached down to grab her by the arm.

'Lend a hand here, lads.'

More hands grabbed her and she was hauled quickly up into the boat, a little more roughly than she would have liked, perhaps, but at least she was safe. Fury took off his jacket, still damp, and wrapped it around her shoulders as she began to shiver. They exchanged a glance – only briefly – but that one glance conveyed their relief more than any words could.

Her father had reached the side of the boat by now, and lusty hands were hauling him aboard, so Fury moved Sophie towards the stern sheets and settled her down on the thwart next to the tiller. He sat next to her and one look forward told him that Sophie's father was now safely on board.

'Give way all.'

The men bent to their oars again and Fury

swung the tiller over to turn the boat around and send it back towards the entrance to the outer road, in the wake of Smith and the other gunboat.

He felt a slight pressure on his hand as it rested on the tiller, and he looked down to see Sophie's hand on top of his. He smiled across at her but said nothing, feeling suddenly self-conscious with the boat's crew all sitting nearby.

Smith's boats could be seen ahead now, stationary in the water near two frigates which were anchored side by side.

'Ah! Mr Fury, just in time, sir!'

That was Smith calling across to him from the *Swallow* as they approached.

'Sir?'

'There is a crew on board the nearest frigate, *Themistocles*, and they have agreed to let us ferry them ashore. They have assured me they will be no trouble, but as a precaution I would be obliged if you could keep your swivels on them at all time. Once they are out of our hair, we can burn these ships. Then we shall have to call it a night.'

Smith looked slightly disappointed as he made the last statement, and Fury realised that the mission would probably be regarded as a failure because of the lack of shipping destroyed. Only those who had been here, who had seen not only the advances of the enemy, but also the incompetence and treachery of their allies, would understand. The man had done as much as anyone could by causing as much damage as he had.

'Yes sir.'

Smith then turned to address the Frenchman on board the *Themistocles*.

'This officer here' – he pointed over to Fury – 'will have a swivel gun loaded with canister trained on you and your men at all times while you are being ferried ashore. If you show any sign of trouble, he is under orders to open fire at once. Do you understand?'

The man uttered a resigned '*Oui*' and Smith gave the order which sent his boat surging forward towards the side of the ship, quickly followed by Lieutenant Brisbane in the second boat.

'You two forrard,' Fury called. It was unfortunate that he did not know the names of any of the men in his boat. 'Ship your oars and take hold of that swivel gun at the bow. See that it is loaded and ready for firing, but don't point it at the other boats unless I give the order.'

The last thing Fury wanted was for a nervous hand to pour a tempest of canister into their own boats accidentally.

By the time the two men had stowed their oars on board and taken up the swivel gun, men were already pouring down the side of *Themistocles* and into Smith's boat.

All in all it took three journeys before they had transferred the last of the men from the ship, dropping them on the north shore well away from the arsenal and the town. Fury's boat had shadowed them carefully on each journey, but the Frenchmen showed no signs of trouble at all. They had so far been unmolested by the batteries of Malbousquet and Missiessi too. Perhaps they had realised that the boats were full of French sailors.

Now, the transfer complete, all three boats approached the two empty ships swinging lazily at their anchors.

'Mr Fury! I shall give you the task of burning the second ship. See to it at once, if you please,' Smith called to him.

'Aye aye sir.'

A quick order sent their boat gliding across the stern of the first ship, *Themistocles*, and under the counter of the second ship. Fury looked up and saw the name *Hero* emblazoned across her stern. He turned to Sophie and her father.

'Please forgive me, I must leave you for a short time. You will be perfectly safe here until I return, then we shall make our way back to my ship.'

They both nodded, although Fury could see they were frightened. He tried to give them a reassuring smile, before passing control of the tiller to one of the seamen and moving forward to retrieve the packet of combustibles from the locker underneath the bow.

They were alongside the *Hero* by the time he was ready, making one final check that the packet was tightly closed with the string fastenings. Satisfied he had forgotten nothing, he moved into position and, clamping down firmly with his teeth on the string of the handle, reached up for the battens on the ship's side and clambered swiftly up to the entry port.

At that moment either Malbousquet or Missiessi – Fury was not sure which – opened fire and a crash forward told where one of the balls struck. He became aware of splashes in the water all around, and he hurriedly shot a glance down to the boat to reassure himself that it was safe. Sophie was looking up at him with a look of terror on her face, and Fury resolved to complete his mission as quickly as possible so he could get back and take her out of danger. He turned back inboard, concentrating again on the task at hand.

It was a strange feeling, being on the deck of a deserted ship while thousands of Republican troops were massed not far away. He hurried forward through the darkness and found the rail overlooking the waist, moving along it until he came to the ladder leading to the deck below. Once on the upper deck he stood still for a short while so that his eyes became accustomed to the dark, before going along each side and hauling on the tackles to open several of the gun ports.

With more light now infiltrating, he could see that although the guns were still lashed securely, the deck was nevertheless in a poor state. There was thick dirt and rubbish everywhere, while most of the mess tables were slung down over the guns from the deck head above, as if her former crew had left abruptly. The whole effect was so eerie, Fury shuddered to himself as he walked along.

More distant thunder sounded, followed a second later by another crashing and splintering. The deck head to starboard disintegrated in a shower of splinters as one ball pierced the deck above and wedged itself in the timbers of the upper deck. Fury wiped his forehead with his sleeve and tried to put out of his mind just how close it had been.

He peered through the gloom, soon finding what he was looking for: lanterns sat on mess tables or hung from the beams above, all now extinguished but holding what Fury hoped would be sufficient combustible oil to get a good fire going. He put his packet down on the deck and collected as many of the lanterns as he could find, about eight of them all told, putting them down in the middle of the deck. Opening the packet, he pulled out its contents. Flint and steel he put to one side along with the lengths of slow and quick match, leaving the small bundle of rags, each one soaked in tar and wax.

He gulped hard as he heard another salvo unleashed by the Republicans, pausing in his work and bracing himself for the impact. Nothing. The sound of splashes all around reached him, raising a panic within his breast at the thought of Sophie being exposed as she was. Fumbling hurriedly with each lantern in turn, he opened up the bottom which contained the oil and poured it upon the bundle of rags, being careful to avoid any spills on his own clothing. This task done, he fumbled about with flint and steel until he at last got a spark, igniting the rags instantly.

The speed with which the fire shot up startled him, so that he fell back on to the deck to avoid being singed by the flames. Recovering himself, and being satisfied that the fire had taken sufficient hold, he grabbed a length of slow match and stuck it into the flames at arm's length until it caught light.

Even as he made his way to the ladder leading back up to the quarterdeck he could feel the heat from the flames behind him quickly spreading, crackling furiously. Once on the quarterdeck he ran to the nearest shrouds, those providing lateral support to the mainmast, and set them alight using the lighted slow match he was still carrying. He watched as the flames slowly moved up the rigging, hungrily fed by the thick coating of tar on each rope.

Lastly he went aft past the mizzen mast, to where the spanker boom extended out over the taffrail. The sail itself was not set but was loosely furled against the gaff above, ready to be raised the moment men hauled on sheets and halliards. With match still in hand he managed to heave himself up the mizzen mast using the rope around it for footholds. He did not ascend far, just enough to enable him to reach that part of the sail which was secured down against the mast, thrusting his lighted match against it long enough for it to catch light. Jumping back down to the deck he abandoned the lighted match and hurried over to the entry port.

Fury heard another cannonade as he reached the bulwark. It was quickly accompanied by a splintering sound from above, and he looked up to see the mainmast sagging sideways above the topmast cap. It hung there a moment, suspended by its stays, before they finally parted and it dropped, Fury flinging himself to the deck between two of the quarterdeck carronades. He heard the crash and clatter as it hit the deck along with its parted stays and blocks, including a loud thud nearby. He tentatively raised his head and looked around; there was a block sitting on the deck six inches from his head, presumably thrown there as the mast finally snapped. Part of the splintered main yard was laid at an angle, propped up on the carronade to Fury's right which had stopped it from snapping his back like a twig. He took a relieved intake of breath and crawled out from beneath the tangled spars and rigging, standing up and dusting himself off.

The smoke was now billowing up from the waist, blotting out the few stars which were overhead. The occasional tongue of flame could also be seen rising up from the deck below, while the rigging above was well alight.

Reaching the entry port Fury looked down for his boat, momentarily freezing in panic as he saw

366

it was not there, before realising that they were merely waiting a short distance from the ship's side to avoid the flames which were now protruding from her open gun ports. At the sight of him they pulled a few swift strokes to cover the short distance, so that by the time he had descended the battens they were ready and waiting beneath him.

'Has everything been completed?' Sophie's father asked hopefully, as Fury made his way to the stern of the boat.

'Yes it has,' Fury replied. 'We can be on our way now.'

Sophie placed a trembling hand on his as Fury settled himself next to the tiller. He took her hand for a moment and gave a soft squeeze of reassurance, before withdrawing it and grasping the tiller bar.

The whole of the ship was a mass of flame by the time Fury had taken their boat out of danger, the men resting on their oars to watch the sight as Smith and Brisbane approached in their boats. Beyond the flames Fury could just discern the *Themistocles* well alight, so that it looked very much like their work was completed.

'Well done Mr Fury!' shouted Smith as they approached. 'I think it prudent that we effect our own retreat now before our luck runs out.'

Fury could not agree more. 'Aye aye sir!'

The *Swallow* turned away to lead them towards the entrance to the outer road, with Brisbane in the second boat following and Fury in the last boat close behind.

He had no idea what the time was, or even whether *Renard* would still be there when they reached the remnants of the fleet taking off the last of the men. Looking forward beyond the *Swallow* he could see the small peninsular of land with the old semaphore tower upon it. That peninsular marked the border between the outer and inner road. Beyond it, further over to the right, he could see a vague outline of the heights of de Grasse with all its batteries, while down below, almost at the water's edge, were the two forts, Balaguier and l'Eguillette. If the Republicans had possession of them – which was more than likely, having seen the Neapolitans and Spanish in action – then they would have to undergo their fire on the way out to the outer road.

As Fury peered forward intently, trying to distinguish the two forts against the darker background of hills and peaks, a thunderous explosion rent the air, the second that night. It took him some time to locate the source of the blast, somewhere over to the left not far from where the first powder ship had blown up. If anything, this blast seemed to be more violent than the first, and Fury was nearly blinded by the brilliant white which momentarily lit up the bay.

He looked up at the sky, which appeared as if it were on fire as the burning wreckage and timber shot up and outwards before finally starting to fall.

The boat was rocking more now as the shock waves sent a heavier swell spreading out, and the water swiftly turned into a boiling mass as the burning debris landed in the sea all around the two boats and the *Swallow*. There was nothing they could do but wait and hope. Everyone instinctively ducked their heads slightly as if to provide some protection from the deluge. And then it was all over, Fury looking up to see no more splashes and their consorts apparently unharmed.

He was shaking slightly, well aware of how fortunate they had all been to escape serious injury or death, especially after witnessing the sinking of one of their gunboats earlier in the evening from a similar blast.

'Those damnable Spaniards have done it again! We would fare better in this war if they joined the French!'

The enraged voice of Captain Smith on board the *Swallow* drifted across to them. Fury sat silently for a few seconds to let his beating heart slow before giving the order which would hopefully see them soon safely back with the fleet. He was sick of this night. It seemed to be dragging on interminably and he just wanted it to end.

'Give way,' he growled, the oarsmen resuming their stroke in pursuit of the other boats which were now carrying on towards the entrance.

It was a further ten minutes before they reached the quarter-mile-wide entrance to the outer road, the semaphore tower to the left clearly visible and slowly moving astern as the oarsmen struggled against the waves which became increasingly choppy as they entered the more exposed anchorage. No sign of life over in the forts to Fury's right buoyed his confidence that they might pass unscathed.

Suddenly a deep boom rang out from that direction, followed by another and then another, as the batteries of Balaguier and l'Eguillette opened fire. Fury noticed the white spray as one of the balls threw up a splash half a cable to their right, but he couldn't distinguish any other sign of the shot.

'Put your backs into it,' he growled to the men straining at the oars.

For twenty minutes they pulled hard, while the two forts kept up a constant if slightly erratic bombardment. Fury eased the tiller over as they rounded the peninsular on the left and turned away towards Fort La Malgue and the remnants of the British fleet, looking over his shoulder in an attempt to ascertain when they would be out of range.

They must be at the limit of their range already, he judged, his pulse slowing as his tension diminished. He looked to his right and gave Sophie a small smile of reassurance, which she returned with an effort. Another cannonade sounded from one of the forts, probably their last effort, and Fury saw a splash thrown up about twenty yards behind him and to the right. He looked forward, startled, as a loud crash was quickly followed by screams of anguish. The second gunboat, immediately ahead, was in pieces and already sinking fast as the few survivors struggled to cling on to what remained of their craft. The last cannonball must have ricocheted off the water and ploughed straight into them.

'Pull for them!' Fury shouted as the last of the boat disappeared below the surface and – he counted – the four men left alive struggled to stay afloat in the water.

They were among them in an instant, the men at the oars leaning over the side to pull in two of the survivors. Smith in the *Swallow* picked up one man, unable to get to the fourth before he slipped below the waves. Fury could hear Sophie sobbing quietly as the bodies of some of the boat's crew drifted face down nearby. Even in the darkness Fury thought he could see blood on the surface of the water, but he could not be sure.

'Give way all!' he snapped, sending the boat in the wake of the *Swallow*.

It was still a further twenty minutes before the outline of ships at anchor and boats passing to and from the shore became visible. Fury breathed a sigh of relief as he distinguished the outline of a small brig lying not far from the large two-deckers. Although unable to make out her identity in the darkness from this range, she looked very much like *Renard*, and the chances of another such brig

371

being anchored here were so slim as to drive all doubt from his mind.

A short time later and the *Swallow* heaved to, awaiting the arrival of Fury's boat.

'Can I take it that is your ship Mr Fury?' Smith asked when within earshot.

'I believe it is sir,' Fury replied.

'Very well then, I think it's about time you joined her. I am much obliged sir, for your able assistance. I shall make a full report of it to the admiral.'

'Thank you sir.'

'You may keep those men with you and return them to their ships when you rendezvous with the fleet.'

Fury touched his hat and shouted the order which sent the men rowing again, hopefully for the last time.

The sudden realisation that he was not at all sure of what the rendezvous was, sent his hand anxiously reaching inside his pocket to confirm his orders were still there. He could feel that they were still damp from his previous immersion in the waters of the inner basin, but they should still be legible. Satisfied, he allowed himself to relax as they approached *Renard* and hooked on.

He looked up to see the surprised face of Midshipman Francis peering down at them.

'You made it sir!' Francis exclaimed, his face lighting up as Fury made his way on to the low deck of the brig.

A feeling of relief swept through Fury as he gained the deck, almost like a homecoming after a long absence. He had survived, along with his men, and they were back among familiar surroundings at last. He could feel tears welling up inside him, perhaps as a result of the release of all the pent-up tension from the continued mortal peril he had been in recently. He fought them back, cursing his own stupid weaknesses, and turned his concentration elsewhere to get himself under control.

The deck was a mess as Fury looked around him, with belongings scattered everywhere and small huddles of frightened people.

'Refugees sir,' Francis explained. 'We've taken as many as we can.'

Fury stood in silence for a while as he studied the pitiful groups, lucky though they were at having escaped at all. The memory of that mother and child lying dead sprang into his mind and he quickly turned to try and shake it away. Sophie was just being helped on to the deck, still wearing his coat, and Fury held her by the arm to steady her.

'Very well Mr Francis. Have them taken below and then prepare to weigh anchor. There are some extra hands down in the boat for you. Call me when everything is ready.'

He strode aft without waiting for Francis to acknowledge, leading Sophie and her father down to his cabin. They entered the day cabin and Fury helped Sophie into a chair.

'You can stay in the cabins just forward of this one. I am sorry it will not be more comfortable.'

'It is more than enough, Lieutenant,' Sophie's father reassured him. 'We owe you our lives.'

Fury waved away his thanks in sudden embarrassment.

'We do not mind sleeping with the other refugees,' Sophie interrupted, darting her father an admonishing glance. Fury looked at her, amazed at her beauty even with her wet hair a mess and after everything she had endured.

'I am sure you do not, but the cabins are empty.' She opened her mouth to protest further but Fury placed his hand gently on her shoulder. 'Please do not protest. The captain's orders are final.' He smiled. 'I have no wish to place you under arrest for disobedience.'

She smiled back at him, in spite of his poor attempt at humour.

'Very well, John. Thank you.'

'If you will excuse me, I must change before I return on deck to supervise the preparations for getting underway.'

He bowed stiffly and opened the door to the sleeping cabin, relieved to see his chest still wedged in the corner. He was grateful for the chance to change into new shirt and breeches, along with his second uniform jacket, creased but dry. Sitting on the edge of his cot he paused to compose himself. The memory of that mother and child returned to him, and the sound of Sophie's voice through the bulkhead reminded him of what he had very nearly lost.

He put his head down and felt tears on his hand, and with the first drops the floodgates opened in an outpouring of emotions which had been locked up for months. He dried his eyes in embarrassment afterwards, and got up with a large sigh, straightening his uniform and preparing himself for the work ahead. There would be much to do.

CHAPTER 19

Renard thrashed her way along eastward under the dark grey cloud dominating the sky. Fury stood on deck staring landward through the thin drizzle which had persistently fallen since they had cleared the outer road of Toulon some four hours before. Looking at the bleak landscape did nothing to lighten his mood.

According to the chart, the rendezvous of Hierres Bay which Lord Hood had chosen for the British fleet lay some twenty miles ahead, and Fury was hopeful that once there he would be able to unload the passengers who seemed to occupy every corner of the ship from stem to stern. Those on deck tried their best to shelter from the bitterly cold north-westerly wind, which drove *Renard* along the coast at six knots with everything but the royals and topgallants set.

Fury caught occasional glimpses of one face or another as he glanced around, each one looking thoroughly miserable and seasick as they huddled together with loved ones or friends. They had lost everything, and Fury had every sympathy for them. He could only admire the way they carried

376

on, with little or no complaints. He had not even seen Sophie cry since she had come on board, and her strength only served to intensify his feelings for her. Still, they were the lucky ones. He was reasonably sure that those Royalists left behind would soon be meeting Madame Guillotine in their hundreds, if not thousands, as the Republicans seeked reprisals amongst the populace.

He started forward as a light shove in his back sent him momentarily off balance.

'*Pardonez-moi Monsieur*,' muttered a small bald-headed man – green from seasickness – as he lurched along the deck looking for a suitable space along the bulwarks into which he could squeeze.

As much sympathy as Fury had for them, their presence about his deck was proving an irritation to him, when all he wanted was to pace up and down in solitude and let his mind run free. He wished to analyse events during the last few months at Toulon, to ascertain what had gone wrong. He was well aware that it would be seen as a defeat, and he wished to satisfy himself that he had done everything he could. He did not like to lose, and the thought of it was causing a foul mood to descend upon him.

'Mr Francis!' he shouted.

'Sir?'

'I am going down to my cabin to get a little sleep. Please call me as soon as we come up with the fleet.'

If he could not pace his own deck in freedom, he would go below.

'Aye aye sir,' Francis replied.

Now that the thought of sleep had crossed his mind, Fury realised how tired he was after having had no sleep since the night before last. It was a vast effort to drag himself over to the main hatchway and make his way below, passing more sullen refugees before reaching the cabin aft. Quickly pulling off his boots, he swung himself into the cot and was fast asleep in an instant.

When he awoke, he lay for some time staring at the deck beams above, trying to work up the effort required to get up and go on deck. A quick glance at his watch told him it was a little before eleven in the morning and so he could not have been asleep for more than two hours.

'Deck there! Sails in sight on the larboard bow!'

The faint shout coming down from the mast-head lookout stripped Fury's drowsiness away in a flash. By the time the expected knock on his cabin door came to report the sighting, he had struggled into his boots and was ready.

He nodded to Midshipman Francis as he gained the deck, turning his face skyward.

'How many?' he shouted.

There was a slight pause before the reply came while the lookout made a quick count.

''Bout twenty or more sir. Looks like the fleet!'

Fury had guessed that as soon as the initial sighting had been made. With the Spanish under

Admiral de Langara back at Minorca, the only large body of ships in this vicinity was the Mediterranean fleet under Lord Hood.

With the wind on her quarter *Renard* was still making a good six knots through the choppy water, so that the numerous mastheads which the lookout had reported were already visible through the thin veil of drizzle. The ships themselves were hidden by the spit of land which formed the western end of the bay, but would soon reveal themselves as the entrance opened up.

Fury realised with a start that the whole side of the brig was lined with refugees staring forward, pointing and chattering wildly amongst themselves.

'Mr Francis!'

'Sir?'

'We shall soon be anchoring amongst the fleet. Get these people below and out of the way immediately.' With a wave of his hand Fury indicated the multitude of French littering the deck. 'I don't care if you have to shove 'em into casks and stow 'em all in the hold.'

'Aye aye sir!' Francis replied, trying to stifle the grin which that last remark had triggered.

While Francis walked off bellowing at the passengers, attempting to make himself understood, and ordering the Fortitudes to begin herding them all down below like sheep, Fury turned his attention back to the bay which was now approaching.

It took nearly an hour before they reached it, Fury giving the orders which saw *Renard* shorten down to topsails alone and haul her wind to make good her entrance into the bay.

He stood by the larboard main channel watching as they slowly glided in, the man forward with the lead calling out the depths to ensure they did not go aground. The chart that Fury had been given showed ten fathoms almost up to the shore, but it was as well to be cautious, especially under the eyes of the entire fleet.

He could see HMS *Victory*, Hood's flagship, among the lofty two- and three-deckers swinging restlessly at anchor.

'Mr Francis, prepare to salute the admiral's flag at my order. Thirteen guns if you please.'

Fury waited patiently while Francis made the arrangements, unusually content that he had everything under control. The anchor had been unfished and brought up to the cathead ready for dropping long before, with thirty fathom of cable ranged out on deck.

'Begin the salute,' he ordered Francis, who was waiting for the word.

Francis turned to give the order to the man standing by the first gun, but he had already heard and the gun barked out a moment later. The whole of *Renard*'s larboard battery fired slowly in succession, most of the guns being quickly readied for another shot so that the whole thirteen could be completed.

A quick thought crossed Fury's mind for the terrified French below decks, Sophie amongst them, startled by the sound of gunfire and wondering whether they were all about to die. It was too late to do anything now.

The salute was finished and the men were securing the guns while the flagship returned the salute, with two guns less as the regulations demanded. Fury paused to let the men get back to their stations after securing the guns before giving his next sequence of orders to bring *Renard* to anchor. Once they were ready he began, and the meagre crew performed the task much to Fury's satisfaction. He turned to Francis, standing by the man at the tiller.

'Very well Mr Francis,' he muttered, 'those passengers who wish to regain the deck may do so now.'

He had no doubt that the cramped, musty atmosphere down below would be exacerbating their seasickness. The brisk December weather would do them good, he thought, as he began to make his way below, knowing that all the pleasure he derived from being on deck would soon evaporate once they were up there.

'Inform me immediately the flagship signals,' was all he said as he passed Francis on the way to the hatchway leading to the cabin below.

It was in the day cabin, sitting at the desk finishing off his report to the admiral, that he first became aware of a commotion outside the door. Some moments later there was a tap on the door and in response to Fury's curt 'Enter!', an apologetic-looking seaman came in followed by one of the French passengers, slightly hidden by the bulk of the seaman who was a good six feet and bent sharply to avoid hitting his head on the deck beams.

'Beggin' yer pardon sir,' the seaman began, knuckling his forehead, 'but this gennelman here insisted on seein' yer. I tried ter tell 'im you was busy sir, but he wouldn't take no fer an answer. Says it's most important. Just say the word sir, an I'll truss 'im up nice an tight and stick 'im in the hold.'

Fury shook his head.

'That won't be necessary.'

It briefly crossed his mind that the man might be intending some mischief, but with over twenty of his men aboard and his uncle's two pistols sitting in front of him on the desk, he dismissed the thought.

'Very well Johnson, you may go.'

The seaman knuckled his forehead once more and left the cabin, but not before shooting a fierce glance at the Frenchman that would have terrified most men. The man looked completely oblivious to Johnson's hostility as he stepped further forward into the cabin to present Fury with his first full view of him.

He was about fifty, with a look and an air about him, now that Fury had time to study him closely, of someone who was used to getting his own way. Judging by the fact that he needed only to bend his head, and not his back, to avoid the deck beams, he could not have been more than five feet five inches tall, his once black hair now mostly grey and tied back tightly in a queue. His face was grave, understandable after recent events, but the deep brown eyes still looked sharp and attentive like a hawk's, a comparison which was made all the more fitting by his high cheekbones and thin jutting nose.

'I am sorry to interrupt your work, Capitaine.'

The man spoke such perfect English that Fury thought at first he must be an Englishman. Fury held out his arm towards the chair opposite his desk.

'Pray take a seat sir,' he offered.

The man accepted with a small bow and settled himself comfortably in the chair before Fury continued.

'Whom have I the pleasure of addressing sir?'

'My name is Antoine Gaspart de Lissey.'

'A pleasure, Monsieur de Lissey,' Fury said, 'and I am Lieutenant Fury, in temporary command of *Renard*. How may I be of service to you sir?'

'I wish to arrange an interview with your admiral,' de Lissey replied. He said it so quietly and matter-of-factly that it took Fury a moment to register what he wanted.

'Do you indeed!'

'I do sir,' de Lissey replied calmly, as if he had every expectation of being obeyed.

'I must inform you sir,' Fury began, 'that Admiral Hood is an extremely busy man. He does not have time to see every French refugee who desires it.'

He sat back, fully expecting this to be the end of the argument.

'But I insist sir,' de Lissey replied calmly.

'You insist sir?' Fury repeated incredulously. 'I will have you know sir, that there is only one man on board this ship who can insist on anything, and he insists that you mention no more about this nonsense!'

'Does my name mean nothing to you sir?' de Lissey asked, going off on another tack completely.

Fury paused for a moment, muttering the name to himself in case it was familiar.

'I regret sir, that it does not,' he replied at length. 'Should it?'

'Perhaps not. I have been using it for months now, since to use my proper title would have certainly caused my own death and that of my family.'

Fury waited for him to continue but he did not, prompting him to encourage him further.

'And your title is?'

'I am the Duc d'Avigne.'

Fury had still not heard of the man, even if he was telling the truth.

'May I ask then sir,' Fury began, 'why you wish to see the admiral?'

He was not sure how to address a French duke

– if he was indeed genuine – but the simple 'sir' seemed to suffice.

'I wish to claim the protection of His Britannic Majesty King George,' de Lissey explained. 'The admiral will no doubt be able to arrange immediate passage to, and refuge in, England, for myself and my family.'

'I see,' Fury replied. 'Your family are on board sir?'

'They are. We were fortunate enough to find anonymity after my estates were seized. We had been living in Toulon for some time when your fleet arrived, and we were among the fortunate few to escape when the city was evacuated. We have made ourselves as comfortable as possible at the front of the ship.'

'Very well,' Fury relented. 'If the admiral desires my presence on board the flagship then you may accompany me. In the meantime I will speak to one of my men and have you and your family moved into one of the other cabins aft, for more comfort and privacy. That is as much as I can do for the moment sir.'

'Very well,' de Lissey agreed, standing up to take his leave. 'I thank you Lieutenant, for your courtesy.'

With a stiff bow he turned and left the cabin. Fury paused only long enough to ensure the desk was locked, with the pistols inside, before following him out and making his way up the main hatchway to the deck above.

Midshipman Francis was standing over by the starboard fore chains with some of the men, checking the lanyards securing the lower shrouds to the channels for any signs of chafe.

'Mr Francis, a word if you please.'

Francis touched his hat and followed him over to the larboard side of the deck.

'It would seem,' Fury began, 'that among our guests on board we have the Duc d'Avigne and his family.'

Fury could see from the boy's raised eyebrows that the title had its effect.

'Please be so kind,' he continued, 'as to move the gentleman in question, and his family, into the cabins on the starboard side, and have the men help with their belongings.'

'Aye aye sir,' Francis replied.

'Mark you Mr Francis, this information is between you and I. I would like to keep it that way for the time being.'

'I understand sir.'

'Very well then. The gentleman in question is down below just forrard of the foremast, with white breeches and a thick green velvet jacket. You will address him as Monsieur de Lissey in front of the other passengers to avoid any embarrassment.'

Francis touched his hat once more and walked aft towards the main hatchway, shouting to a number of the men to join him as he went.

Fury looked over at the rest of the fleet, sitting

there at anchor in the grey choppy waters of the bay wondering how long it would be before Admiral Hood made up his mind what his next move would be.

CHAPTER 20

Fury looked up as a knock on the cabin door heralded the arrival of Midshipman Francis.

'The flagship's signalling sir. All captains to repair on board.'

'Very well Mr Francis. Hoist the acknowledgement and have the boat's crew ready.'

'Aye aye sir,' Francis replied, turning to slip out of the cabin.

'And Mr Francis!' Fury called after him.

The small head craned back round the rim of the door.

'Sir?'

'Please be so kind as to inform our friend Monsieur de Lissey and have him meet me on deck immediately.'

'Aye aye sir.'

The door closed after him and Fury reached into the desk drawer, pulling out his full written report of events since Hood placed him in command of Fort Pomet. He quickly rose from behind the desk, walked over to the settee, and picked up his hat and sword. He took a moment to check his appearance in the small mirror hanging on the bulkhead. Satisfied, he left the small cabin.

By the time he had reached the deck, his sword was clipped on and his hat was firmly shoved atop his head. Francis was there on deck, nervously making conversation with de Lissey. One look over the side confirmed that the men were already down in the boat alongside, waiting.

'You have the deck Mr Francis,' Fury said formally, turning to the young midshipman and returning his salute. 'Monsieur de Lissey – after you sir.'

He beckoned the Frenchman towards the entry port but the man stood fast.

'No Capitaine, after you.'

Fury realised de Lissey was attempting to be polite in letting him go first, unaware that it was the custom of the navy for the captain to be last down the side.

'I must go last sir,' he insisted.

'Very well,' de Lissey replied, beginning to make his way down the little brig's side.

Fury watched him go with a wry smile on his face – de Lissey was lucky there was barely seven feet to climb down, he thought, the way he was struggling.

He had made it now, falling into the boat in somewhat of a heap. Fury followed him down, waited for the boat to rise on the choppy sea, and jumped in, making his way to the stern sheets to take the tiller.

The painter and stern fast were cast off and a gruff order of 'Shove off! Out oars! Give way all!' sent the boat dancing away from the brig as the men gave a lusty pull. A little port helm brought the bow round to point at the bulk of HMS *Victory*, massive even at a distance of two cables' lengths. Other boats could be seen pulling for the flagship as their captains tried to outdo each other in promptness.

It took fifteen minutes of heavy rowing against the waves before they were up to her, the men gaining a small pause for rest as they waited for another gig – fresh from delivering her captain aboard – to cast off so they could come alongside.

Fury managed to scramble out of the boat and up the *Victory*'s side before de Lissey had even managed to stand up. Fury watched him again from the *Victory*'s entry port as he tentatively moved to the battens, holding on to the oarsmen's shoulders for balance, before heaving himself up and scrambling aboard with a surprising nimbleness considering his descent down the side of *Renard*.

Fury turned inboard once the man was safely next to him, and found the now familiar face of the flag captain, Knight, in front of him.

'Lieutenant Fury sir, in command of HMS *Fortitude*'s prize, the *Renard*.'

'Welcome aboard Mr Fury,' Knight replied, turning slightly to de Lissey. 'And who is this gentleman?'

Fury hastily made the introductions, introducing de Lissey as the Duc d'Avigne.

'The gentleman made himself known to me yesterday,' Fury explained, 'and expressed a wish to see His Lordship.'

Knight seemed satisfied by the explanation and turned to lead them towards the admiral's quarters.

'It would perhaps be best,' Captain Knight explained, 'If His Grace were to wait in the admiral's dining compartment until His Lordship has completed his briefing.'

De Lissey bowed slightly and followed Knight into the room, from which the flag captain returned after a brief period and closed the door. Fury then followed him into the admiral's day cabin, now bustling with an array of lofty post captains from throughout the fleet. He recognised some of them, in spite of his relatively short time in the Mediterranean; Captain Nelson of the *Agamemnon*, Foley of the *St George* and Linzee of the *Alcide*. Fury promptly found himself the most inconspicuous corner of the room and stayed there so as not to attract too much attention.

Presently Lord Hood entered, whereupon the buzz of conversation died down as he took his usual seat behind his desk, the light through the great stern windows behind him casting him in shadow.

'Gentlemen,' he began, 'after the recent unfortunate events at Toulon I have decided to occupy the fleet in the reduction of Corsica. There is absolutely no value in continuing the blockade of Toulon. Those ships of the French fleet which we did not take or destroy are in no fit condition to take the sea, even if there were seamen enough in Toulon to man them. Corsica has numerous fine ports and would make an excellent base of operations for the fleet.'

There was a short murmur of conversation as the officers in the room digested this information, before Hood continued.

'We shall begin with Calvi and then proceed to Bastia. I shall brief you all further when we arrive at our destination. I have no doubt of our success in these operations.'

Hood was interrupted at this point by Captain Nelson.

'What about the refugees within the fleet, My Lord?'

'I was coming to that presently,' Hood replied. 'All the refugees taken by the fleet will be transferred to every transport we have available and will be taken to Gibraltar immediately. A number of the frigates among the French fleet which were found seaworthy enough were brought out for that purpose. Are there any further questions?'

He looked round the room as if to dare anyone to raise a question. No one took up the challenge.

'Very well then. We shall weigh at dawn tomorrow. Could Captain Keene and lieutenants Stephenson, Lycett, Allan, Cousins, Wood and

Fury please remain behind. The rest of you gentlemen are dismissed.'

There was a general scraping of chairs as the captains of the fleet took their leave. With the last of them gone, the room was quiet once more, and Fury looked around at his companions. They were all lieutenants from the various ships of the fleet who had been commandeered to command prizes and transports, like himself. The only exception wore the uniform of a captain, the one epaulette on his left shoulder showing he was a captain with less than three years' seniority. He must be Captain Keene, mused Fury, looking at his huge bulk and flame-red hair.

Lord Hood broke the silence at last.

'Gentlemen, you will weigh anchor tomorrow immediately after the fleet, and set course for Gibraltar. Captain Keene will be your escort in the *Lowestoft*. My clerk will be in shortly. Please supply him with details of how many refugees you can take in addition to your current number. I will then arrange for those others throughout the fleet to be distributed to you accordingly before nightfall. You will be reprovisioned for the short journey tomorrow morning. Are there any questions gentlemen?'

Again there was silence.

'Very well then, I shall send my clerk in presently.'

With that, he swept round the desk and out of the cabin door, prompting the room to explode into conversation. A short time later the admiral's clerk entered, a small balding man with spectacles on the end of his nose who reminded Fury of a weasel.

It did not take long for each officer to go through which ship they commanded and how many more refugees they could take on board. Fury was the last of these, and he reluctantly accepted another ten passengers.

He got up to leave, resolving that he would first have to seek out de Lissey – he could not very well leave him behind with his family on board *Renard*. He was saved from the task by the entrance of Captain Knight.

'Ah Mr Fury! His Lordship would like a word with you in the dining cabin. Follow me please.'

Fury followed him through into the dining cabin, where seated at the table were Lord Hood and de Lissey, deep in conversation.

'Lieutenant Fury sir,' Knight announced as they entered.

'Come in Mr Fury – take a seat.'

Fury took the proffered chair as Knight quietly slipped out of the room.

'His Grace, the Duc d'Avigne, has been telling me how well he and his family have been treated on board the *Renard*, Fury.'

After his first meeting with de Lissey yesterday, Fury found this hard to believe.

'Indeed sir?' he replied non-committally, trying to detect any trace of sarcasm in Hood's voice.

The old admiral merely returned his stare with not the slightest hint of either humour or admonishment.

'As you are probably aware Mr Fury, His Grace is eager to travel to England with his family, to live until such a time as he may safely return to his home and estates.'

'So I understood,' Fury responded cautiously, beginning to wonder why His Lordship should feel the need to tell him all this.

'Unfortunately, the *Lowestoft* is only going as far as Gibraltar, and I cannot currently spare any other frigates from the fleet for His Grace and his family to take passage in. He has, however, expressed a willingness to travel home in *Renard*, in spite of the potential dangers of capture.'

'I am flattered, My Lord,' Fury mumbled, his heart sinking at the thought of being a babysitter to a nobleman and his family.

'Excellent, then that is settled,' Hood continued. 'You will also carry my despatches home, which you will personally deliver to Their Lordships at the Admiralty immediately upon your arrival. I have agreed to furnish His Grace with letters of introduction which will enable him to settle in England as quickly as possible. I will send across written orders this afternoon in confirmation, along with the despatches you are to take. Do you have any questions?'

'We are extremely short-handed, My Lord. Only

about thirty men, mostly the prize crew from the *Fortitude* when we captured her. If it came to a fight . . .'

Fury was hoping that the knowledge of how short-handed they were would persuade Lord Hood to choose another ship for the task. He was disappointed.

'Very well, when you reach Gibraltar I shall make sure you get another twenty seaman to complete your complement,' Hood offered. 'They can be taken from the transports. I shall have orders drafted up for Captain Keene to that effect. Anything else, Lieutenant?'

'My ship sir, the *Fortitude*. How am I to rejoin her?'

Judging by the length of time it took Hood to answer, it was a question which he had not previously considered. He spoke at last.

'She is currently refitting at Gibraltar, as you know. I shall write to Captain Young to inform him that I am discharging you from her complement. Upon your arrival at the Admiralty you will have to apply for another appointment.'

Fury's bottom jaw dropped at that news – not only did he have to take this man and his aristocratic family back to England, but he was also to lose his employment in the process. He glanced up to see Lord Hood looking at him in anticipation, having presumably just asked a question.

'You have your dunnage with you?' Hood repeated.

'Yes, My Lord,' Fury stammered.

'Good, then I will send orders to Captain Young informing him. Captain Keene can deliver these once the convoy has safely arrived in Gibraltar.'

'Yes, My Lord.'

'Very well then, I think that concludes our business.'

Fury rose out of his chair, quickly followed by both Hood and de Lissey.

CHAPTER 21

The next morning broke crisp and clear, with a thin layer of frost covering *Renard*'s rigging and decks. The breeze was light but icy cold and seemed to blow right through the men whose duty kept them upon the deck.

Fury stood on deck and watched as the fleet weighed anchor and stood out of the bay led by the *Victory*, surprisingly graceful for a vessel her size. Progress was slow as he watched the column of vessels – under full sail to try and catch as much of the breeze as possible – tack in succession to the eastward as soon as they had gained enough sea room.

At first light this morning they had hoisted sufficient provisions on board to feed their passengers for the short journey to Gibraltar. Fury looked at his watch as the last of the ships cleared the mouth of the bay and was surprised to find it was nearly eleven o'clock now. One more quick glance around the bay showed the only vessels remaining were the transports, now packed full with all the refugees from Toulon whom the fleet had been able to rescue, along with the escorting frigate, HMS *Lowestoft*, under Captain Keene. The prearranged signal for weighing anchor was now flying from her mast, and Fury watched her topsails unfold as the gaskets were untied and the men on deck hauled on the sheets.

'Mr Francis!' he shouted, waiting until the young midshipman had bounded across the deck to him before continuing. 'Prepare to weigh anchor.'

Francis acknowledged and repeated the instructions to the men, waiting at their stations around the deck.

As soon as the *Lowestoft* had glided past them on her way out, Fury had the anchor hove up, the men on the focsle busy with the cat and fish tackle as the topsails were loosed and sheeted home, sending *Renard* gliding forward in the *Lowestoft*'s wake.

By one o'clock all the transports had cleared the bay and had all plain sail set to keep up with the *Lowestoft* out ahead. Once dinner was finished, Fury reluctantly consented to allow those passengers who wished to go up on deck for fresh air after having been kept down below all day as *Renard* sailed.

As the first of the passengers were coming up the main hatchway, Fury made his way below to the relative peace of his cabin, telling Francis on the way to keep a sharp lookout for any signals from the *Lowestoft*.

He was barely settled behind the desk when

there was a knock on the door. In response to his shout the door opened and Sophie poked her head round the frame.

'Come in,' Fury beckoned. 'Please, take a seat.'

Sophie settled herself in the chair opposite Fury's desk with a smile. 'I haven't had a chance to thank you properly for rescuing us. My father and I owe you our lives.'

Fury waved away her thanks in embarrassment, and tried to make light of his efforts.

'It was the only way I could think of getting to see you again.'

She smiled again at that. 'My father worries constantly about the future and about me. At least we can now look forward without fear for our lives. I don't know how we can repay you.'

'Seeing you safe is repayment enough. I know the future is uncertain for you, but I can assure you I will see that you are taken care of. I would consider it an honour.'

Another knock on the door interrupted Fury and saved him from saying too much. Perrin half entered with an apologetic look on his face.

'Sorry to bother you sir, but Mr Francis sends his compliments, and the *Lowestoft* is signalling.'

'Very well, I shall be up presently.'

Perrin nodded and quietly slipped out, while Fury turned back to Sophie.

'I am sorry. I have my duty to attend to.'

'Of course. I should be getting back to my father, to make sure he is not getting up to any mischief.'

Fury escorted her out and hurried up on deck, where *Lowestoft* was flying the signal for all transports to make all sail they could carry. *Renard* was a sufficiently swift sailer to keep up with the other transports without the need to increase her current spread of canvas, so after half an hour Fury returned below to his cabin, hoping fervently that Captain Keene in the *Lowestoft* was not the kind of captain who felt it necessary to make signals every ten minutes.

As luck would have it, very few signals were made by the *Lowestoft* during the whole of the passage south-westward to Gibraltar. Not another vessel was sighted until Europa Point was spied fine on the starboard bow, four bells in the forenoon watch on the sixth day out. The precipitous rock could very soon be seen from the deck with the naked eye as the convoy of transports approached, so that the whole of the starboard side of *Renard* was filled with the craning necks of Royalist refugees, eager to catch a first glimpse of the landmark which towered high above the town where many of them would no doubt make their home.

An exasperated Fury paced the larboard side from the tiller to the mainmast and back, trying to keep as far away from them as possible while ignoring the incessant chatter and conversation in garbled French which the sighting had provoked.

'Mr Francis!' he shouted, his patience exhausted at last. 'Have our passengers escorted below. They are not to be allowed back on deck until we are swinging at our anchor in Gibraltar Bay. Is that understood?'

Francis acknowledged hastily. He knew Fury's moods well enough by now to recognise the need for caution when those dark brown eyebrows came together in a frown.

Fury watched the refugees shepherded below, his mood temporarily lifted by the knowledge that his passengers would not have the pleasure of seeing the Rock of Gibraltar in all its beauty as *Renard* rounded Europa Point and stood north into the magnificent bay.

Fury himself could spare little enough time for the view, concentrating his efforts on their approach to the bay in the wake of their escort. They followed the *Lowestoft* right up to the New Mole along with the rest of the makeshift squadron, the salutes ringing out around the bay as they glided in.

Fury kept a careful eye on the *Lowestoft* up ahead, watching for the first sign of her head coming up into the wind. He saw it at last, quickly turning to the helmsman and ordering the tiller put over so that by the time the topsails had been furled and the bower anchor dropped, *Renard* was making a slow stern board a little under two cables from her.

'Have the boats lowered away!' he shouted, anxious to be rid of his passengers as quickly as possible.

The boats were lowered alongside in no time, ready to ship the first of the refugees ashore. Fury could already see the boats from the other transports beginning the slow pull to the quayside. As the first of his own passengers began their awkward descent down the low side of *Renard* into the waiting boats, Fury felt his mood lift for the first time in days.

'Two boats shoving off from the jetty sir,' Perrin reported, as Fury paced the deck of *Renard* the following morning under a weak wintry sun.

A quick pause to glance over to starboard confirmed that it would be another fifteen minutes before the boats reached them, and so Fury continued his pacing, anxious lest one small pause might give de Lissey and his family the opportunity of inviting him over to where they stood by the fore chains.

The transfer of his other passengers had been completed late yesterday evening, and this morning had been taken up with reprovisioning the ship from the hoys for their journey home. Only de Lissey and family, along with Sophie and her father, remained. Fury had not gained official permission to transport Sophie and her father all the way to England, but he did not wish to abandon them in Gibraltar. He was confident that Gourrier's title of Comte de Chabeuil would save him from any official admonishment should the authorities become aware of it.

'Boats approaching sir,' Perrin repeated ten minutes later, interrupting Fury's thoughts. He walked over to the starboard bulwark to peer down into the approaching boats.

As he had been expecting, the boats were full of men taken from the other transports, promised to him now that they had reached Gibraltar. They would be very useful for the voyage back to England, more to man the guns and beat off a boarding attempt by any privateers than to help handle *Renard*. Hood obviously attached some importance to de Lissey and his family.

The first boat hooked on and a callow-faced youth appeared on deck in an ill-fitting midshipman's coat, dirk at his hip. It only took him a moment to spy out Fury's uniform and make his way across to him.

'Midshipman Fleck sir, from the *Lowestoft*. Captain Keene sent me across with the men you were promised. Twenty of 'em sir.'

'Get 'em up on deck then,' Fury replied impatiently.

Fleck shouted down to the first boat, and they boarded *Renard* with their dunnage slung over their shoulders.

Some moments passed while the second boat hooked on and the rest of the men came on deck.

'Please convey my thanks to Captain Keene, and inform him I will be sailing immediately,' Fury said to Midshipman Fleck, walking him over to the entry port.

'Aye aye sir,' Fleck replied, making his way down the brig's side into the waiting boat. The first boat had already begun the pull back to the jetty.

Fury stood there for a moment watching until the second boat unhooked from the side and began to row away, then turned inboard to face the large group of seamen who were standing waiting.

He could see de Lissey, with his wife and two sons, looking aft from the forechains with mild curiosity on their faces, and he was aware that everyone was expecting him to make some kind of speech to welcome the new men on board. Every new captain reading himself in on board a new ship with a new crew was expected to say at least a few words to the men, but this was not his ship and these were not his men.

'Mr Francis!' he barked. 'Take the men below and have 'em sling their hammocks. Divide the new men into two watches and assign them duties. Then set 'em to work. I want every yard of rigging checked, blocks greased, decks scrubbed and sails inspected before we sail.'

'Aye aye sir!' Francis piped, as Fury strode to the main hatchway to go below.

'Oh and Mr Francis,' he called, hovering with one foot over the companion ladder. 'I'll expect a list of each watch and every man's station by four bells.'

'Aye aye sir.'

Francis looked slightly crestfallen at the thought

of having to sit down and draw up a watch and station bill for the new men, but Fury was unsympathetic. It would do him good, Fury thought, as he entered his cabin and made for the desk, throwing his coat on to the settee.

He sat and wrote up his journal, the stuffiness in the cabin oppressive, even in the winter. Mr Francis' arrival with the newly drawn-up watch bill deprived him of the chance to dive up on deck into the fresh air, and so it was nearly half-past one in the afternoon when he finally rose.

'The decks have been scrubbed sir,' Francis reported as he reached the deck, 'the blocks have been greased, and the men are still checking over the sails and rigging.'

'Very well Mr Francis,' Fury replied. 'The men can finish that once we are under way. If you would be so kind as to call the men to their stations, we will weigh anchor.'

'Aye aye sir.'

Francis turned round and bellowed to the men around the decks, sending them rushing about in apparent confusion. Fury watched as the bars were rigged to the capstan, and the messenger cable was brought up and taken round the capstan barrel before being led forward and attached to the thick anchor cable.

'Heave away!' called Francis, after a nod from Fury.

The men threw their weight on to the capstan bars and began walking slowly round, causing *Renard* to be pulled in against her cable.

Fury suddenly noticed de Lissey and his family forward by the cathead watching the events in fascination, and he cursed himself for forgetting to send them below.

'At short stay sir,' called the man forward near de Lissey, peering over the bow to where the cable dropped away into the murky depths of Gibraltar Bay.

A few minutes later and the call of 'Up and down' resonated from the same man, *Renard* now being directly over her anchor.

'Keep at it lads!' Fury called, as the men's progress slowed momentarily as they fought to release the anchor flukes from the seabed.

Finally the call of 'Anchors aweigh' came from the man forward and the men were able to heave much easier as the anchor came rising up to the surface.

'Let fall the topsails!' Fury bellowed, as soon as the anchor was free.

The men rushed aloft and scampered out along the topsail yards, untying the gaskets and sending the canvas flapping down as the men on deck hauled on sheets.

'Steady at the braces there. Handsomely now!' he bellowed, as the yards swung slowly round.

A loud clapping overhead from the fore and main topsails told that the yards had passed the eye of the wind, and seconds later they began to fill, sending *Renard* surging forward through the sheltered waters of the bay.

The anchor was catted and fished while they

glided out of the bay, finally meeting the choppier waters of the Mediterranean as they entered the strait and turned westward, with the wind steady at north by east.

Fury stood by the starboard main chains, watching as the coast of southern Spain slipped lazily past. He was finally going home, to England. After more than two long years he would see his homeland again, and the thought of it brought a smile to his weather-beaten face. He wondered what his mother would make of him when he finally arrived back. He was barely the same person now. The transformation he had undergone surprised even him when he took the time to contemplate it.

He shuddered at the memory of some of the sights he had seen during that time, sights which would have hardened the toughest children. And now there was Sophie too. How would she and her father settle in England? Would they be accepted without discrimination, or would they feel trapped and persecuted? Fury was not even sure if his lieutenant's pay would be enough to sustain them until they could get on their feet. It would have to be, he decided; Sophie was his responsibility now, no matter what society thought. His smile was long gone as he stared at the bare hills of the Spanish mainland as they passed, acutely aware that he had much to think about.

CHAPTER 22

'Sail ho!'

The shout came down from the lookout perched high up at the fore topmast head as *Renard* made her way north with a brisk westerly wind. Fury was attempting to get a clear noon sight with his sextant, de Lissey standing next to him having expressed an interest in the art of navigation.

Fury looked up, glad of the distraction – he had been struggling to get an accurate sight amid the distant haze clouding the horizon, with the grey overcast sky frequently hiding the sun.

'Where away?'

'About five points off the larboard bow sir, heading eastward!'

'Keep an eye on her and let me know how she steers!' Fury shot back, turning to de Lissey to make his apologies.

'There will no doubt be another opportunity for you to observe the noon sight, Your Grace,' Fury told him. 'Now if you will excuse me sir, I must attend to my duties.'

He touched his hat and hurried to the main

hatchway leading to the deck below and his cabin. Throwing his sextant on the settee without another thought, he clipped on his sword, grabbed his telescope and made his way back up on deck.

He was surprised to find de Lissey's wife and two sons now standing with de Lissey by the nettings, having heard the shouted report from the lookout, but Fury could afford to spare them little more than a glance as he stared aloft once again to address the lookout.

'How does she bear now?' he shouted, cupping his hands to his mouth to help his voice carry.

'Still five points off the larboard bow sir – wait – she's altered course sir – towards us!'

Fury tried to betray no emotion at the news, and thought hard for a moment. Whoever she was, she had obviously just spotted *Renard* and had moved to intercept her. That suggested she was a vessel of war, or at least of some force. Normally he would be confident that she was a British frigate or sloop cruising the area, but the fact that the vessel had originally been heading east, towards the Bay of Biscay, suggested she was a Frenchman.

Certainly any British ship with no specific business there would try to avoid getting caught in the Bay of Biscay, where a strong westerly wind often meant being caught on a dangerous lee shore. If he was right, then the chances are she was probably a privateer on a short cruise, hoping to snap up a prize or two before dashing back to the safety of port. In that case she would be heavily manned at least, if not heavily armed too.

He was well aware of his duty in a situation such as this. Carrying the admiral's despatches concerning the fall of Toulon last month, and transporting an important family back to England, his course of action could not be more clear – bear away now into the Bay of Biscay and keep their distance until nightfall would guarantee their safety.

The only problem, however, was the wind. If it remained steady as it was, they might spend days beating back to make the entrance to the English Channel, which would delay the delivery of Hood's despatches to Their Lordships at the Admiralty.

He glanced around, aware that the men on deck were looking at him, waiting for his decision. He noticed Sophie and her father clasping tightly on to the bulwarks, looking at him expectantly. Sophie flashed him a nervous smile and he returned it, making an effort to drag his mind from her and back to the decision at hand.

In the end, his own inherent impatience brought the answer to him. He would risk remaining on this course, unwilling to endure days of delay beating back up to the entrance to the Channel. Besides, the thought of turning tail and running at the first possible sign of danger appalled him.

'Mr Francis!' he called. 'Take a glass up to the man at the masthead – quickly now!'

Francis ran to the binnacle in front of the tiller,

grabbed one of the telescopes held there and dashed up the shrouds to the man at the fore masthead. Fury waited for him to hand the telescope over to the lookout, and gave the man a chance to study the strange sail, before he asked his next question.

'What d'you make of her?'

'She looked ship-rigged when I first saw her sir. She's under full sail now – her hull looks low and she looks to be pretty fast sir!'

'Keep me informed!' Fury shouted back as he paced the deck, feeling much more relaxed now that he had made the decision to remain on their current course.

He was interrupted a moment later by de Lissey next to him, awaiting his attention.

'Is everything well Your Grace?' Fury asked, with as much politeness as he could muster after having his reverie interrupted.

'Is she an enemy?' de Lissey asked, ignoring the question. Typical of a Frenchman to ask a silly question such as that, Fury thought, as he mentally phrased his reply.

'We cannot tell at this distance sir, but we will know soon enough. There is every chance she is a British ship of war cruising this area.'

That was perhaps an exaggeration, but there was no point in alarming the man at this stage. Besides, there was every chance de Lissey might insist they bear away now if he voiced his concerns over her identity.

'As I told my wife and sons!' de Lissey said. 'Perhaps you would be good enough to tell them sir, to put their minds at ease. They would believe it better coming from you.'

'Certainly Your Grace,' Fury replied, following him over to his family, where he made his bow.

'Madame, messieurs,' he began, trying his best to put on a reassuring smile but feeling awkward and fake as he did so. He was not helped by the arrival of Sophie and her father, no doubt also eager to hear the news. 'As I was just saying to His Grace, many British cruisers patrol this area, and there is every chance that this is merely one of them.'

'And if it is not?'

That was Sophie asking the question, Fury feeling momentarily lost as he stared into her deep brown eyes.

'Then, Mademoiselle, we shall bear away at once. *Renard* is a fine sailer and I am confident we would have the legs of her.'

He dared not lie blatantly to this young woman, as he feared she would see right through him with those penetrating dark eyes of hers. She held her stare for a brief moment so that he thought she had not believed him, before the pursed lips broke into a warm smile.

'Thank you Lieutenant, it is a great comfort to us.'

Fury smiled back, holding his own stare for a few seconds before he shook himself out of his trance, straightening up stiffly.

'If you will excuse me, I have my duty to attend to. Your Grace. Madame. Mademoiselle. Messieurs.'

With a curt bow he walked back up the canting deck to the tiller.

'Deck there!'

Fury was not sure how many minutes it had been since he had resumed his pacing and he stopped abruptly at the call.

'Deck here!' he called back quickly. 'What is it?'

'She's about four miles off now sir – definitely a ship-rigged sloop sir – I think I can make out ten ports along her side sir, but I can't be certain from this distance!'

'How is she heading?'

'Still south-east sir, on an intercepting course!'

Fury turned round to spy out Mr Francis, who was standing nearby waiting for the orders which he knew would come.

'Mr Francis!'

'Sir?'

'Have the recognition signal bent on and ready to hoist.'

'Aye aye sir!' Francis replied, hurrying off to prepare the current flag which, if answered correctly by the strange sail, would confirm she was British.

A moment later Francis was back to report the task completed.

'Very good,' Fury replied. 'Have the hammocks brought up and stowed in the nettings, then make sure we have plenty of shot in the garlands in case we have to use the guns. Once that is completed have all the small arms on board brought up and placed ready about the decks please.'

Francis acknowledged and scurried off once more, leaving Fury to question the effectiveness of the small six-pounders which constituted the main armament of the *Renard*. Certainly against a larger opponent, such as the ten guns per side of the strange sail, with twelve-pounders or eighteen-pounder carronades most likely, *Renard* would stand little chance if they got close enough.

He thrust his hands into his coat pockets and his fingers closed around his telescope. Moving quickly over to the larboard bulwark, he placed the glass to his eye and scanned the horizon, finding the ship almost at once about four points off the bow now. She was under full sail and was making good speed judging by the sheet of spray which was thrown up every time she thrust her bow eagerly into the next wave.

He turned round to find Francis supervising the men bringing up the folded hammocks from the deck below, passing them through the standard hoop which would determine whether they were the correct size or not, before placing them in the nettings on top of the bulwarks and covering them to prevent the spray getting to them.

A moment later another small group of men appeared from the main hatchway, struggling with the large chest which contained the pistols and cutlasses.

'Mr Francis!' he called over to him. 'Hoist our colours and the private recognition signal at once, if you please.'

After a few minutes their pennant streamed out in the breeze from the masthead, followed a moment later by the private signal. Fury whipped the glass to his eye once again to study the ship, now only three miles distant.

Agonising seconds passed during which he could detect no change in her appearance, and then at last he saw a flag spring out at her masthead – the British flag.

'Deck there!' the lookout reported. 'She's hoisted British colours sir!'

Fury looked up at the signal flags to make sure they could be seen clearly. The westerly wind was blowing them out to starboard but they should still be visible from the deck of the other ship.

He waited a little longer with his glass to his eye, but no answering signal was made, and he finally made the decision he had been hoping to avoid since noon.

'Put your helm up – bring her before the wind!' he snapped at the helmsman.

The tiller was put over and *Renard*'s bow began to swing to starboard, turning first her quarter and then her stern to the wind, and flying before it.

'Brail up the main course! Furl the fore topsail!'

The orders were greeted by a stamping of feet as men tailed on to clew lines, sheets and braces. The fore and aft main course was brailed up quickly as the men hauled on the halliards, so that the sail was gone by the time the men swarming aloft were out along the fore topsail yard. More hauling by the men on deck brought the clews of the fore topsail up to the yard, enabling the topmen to gather great bundles of the canvas and secure it against the yard with the gaskets.

Renard was now under topgallants, main topsail and fore course, so that as far as possible all sails were drawing well with no sail taking the wind out of another one to deaden their speed.

The de Lisseys and the Gourriers were looking at him with worry on their faces, and he felt suddenly ashamed of not explaining the full facts to them before. There was nothing he could do now, he thought philosophically, except ensure they escaped. In order to achieve that, he thrust them out of his mind and concentrated his efforts on the task in hand.

He strode to the taffrail to join Francis who was staring back at the strange sail, easily visible to the naked eye now and thrashing along on their larboard quarter.

'How far Mr Francis?' he asked.

'About three miles I'd say sir,' Francis guessed.

'More like two miles if I'm any judge,' Fury replied. 'Get your sextant up from below and calculate how far off she actually is by the angle to her mainmast. Then take another measurement after fifteen minutes to see if she is gaining on us or not.'

Francis looked crestfallen as he acknowledged the order and hurried below to find his sextant. Fury raised a smile as he watched him go – he could well understand his reluctance to sit down and perform mathematical calculations, when not two miles astern was an enemy vessel intent on capturing or destroying them.

Francis was soon back on deck next to him, struggling with his sextant on the sloping deck. He evidently managed to get an accurate measurement at last because he scuttled off below once more, presumably to perform his calculations.

A quick look at his watch and Fury saw it was nearly two o'clock. The sun would have set in four hours, which would allow them to slip past their adversary unseen in the dark and continue their journey to the north. Hopefully by that time they would not have ventured too far into the Bay of Biscay, and so would not have too far to beat back out again.

He began to pace back and forth once more, deep in thought, so that he did not notice Francis coming back up on deck fifteen minutes later to take a fresh measurement, before diving back down below yet again to perform the calculations. It was Francis himself who interrupted him some time later.

'Excuse me sir.'

Fury looked up.

'Ah! Mr Francis. You have your results?'

'I do sir,' Francis replied, the look on his face telling Fury it was not good news. 'During the fifteen-minute period I took my measurements sir, she gained nearly a cable on us. According to my last sight she was just under two miles away.'

'Thank you Mr Francis,' Fury replied, trying to keep his voice steady and without emotion. Even with *Renard* sailing before the wind their pursuer was still gaining on them. It did not look good.

He had one quick glance over the taffrail as he turned away from Francis, and it was clear that she had gained on them. It was a long time since he had performed calculations, but he set his mind working feverishly now. If she was two miles away, gaining by a cable's length every fifteen minutes, then it would take – how long? – before she was up to them. Roughly four hours was the figure he came to. In four hours the sun would be starting to set, so that it would be a very close run thing indeed. And if she managed to shoot something away before then . . . It didn't bear thinking about.

'Mr Francis!'

'Sir?'

'Have the men go aloft with buckets of water and wet the sails.'

'Aye aye sir,' the boy replied, digesting the unusual order for a moment before turning away to organise the men.

Ten minutes later and in the absence of any

419

suitable pumps on board, buckets were being passed up by a chain of men stationed on rigging, before going to the topmen out on the yards to pour down over the fore course and main topsail.

Captain Young had tried the same trick on the *Fortitude* when chasing *Renard*, knowing that wet sails would catch the wind better than dry sails. Fury was sceptical about whether it would make any material difference to her speed, but it was bound to have a greater effect on *Renard* than it did on the 2,000-ton *Fortitude*. Besides, it kept the men busy and, judging by the grins and enthusiasm with which they went about the task, they were obviously enjoying the competition with the strange sail up to windward.

'Deck there!'

That was the masthead lookout once again.

'Deck here!' Fury shouted back.

'The strange sail has hoisted French colours sir!'

He stared across at her with his telescope to see that the tricolour was indeed now flying at her masthead in place of the British flag which had preceded it.

Fury remained there, staring back at the other ship thrashing along after them and losing track of time as she grew perceptibly nearer. He was about to turn away when he saw a puff of smoke appear from her bow, the wind whipping it away an instant later. A dull clap reached them after a second or two, carried across the water by the breeze. Where the shot fell he had no idea – he quickly scanned the sea but he could not find any plume of water.

'Mr Francis!' he called, 'Have the aft-most larboard six-pounder cleared away and try a couple of ranging shots.'

'Aye aye sir,' Francis replied eagerly, shouting to a group of ex-Fortitudes to man the gun.

The chances of reaching them from that distance were remote – Fury was well aware of that – but it would give the men something to occupy their time. He walked past the group of men casting off the breeching tackles of the aft-most gun and made his way to where the de Lisseys and Gourriers were still looking on at events with mounting worry. He was determined to put on a display of coolness and unconcern, so as to put the ladies at ease.

'Please forgive me for this small diversion,' he said, bowing low. 'It will delay our arrival in Portsmouth by no more than two days.'

'If we reach Portsmouth, Lieutenant!' de Lissey's wife said.

'Madame, there is absolutely no doubt about that, I assure you.'

'But are they not gaining on us? Are they not firing at us?'

This was Sophie's father addressing him, with an edge of panic in his voice.

'They are certainly gaining on us sir, you are correct. But they will not catch us before nightfall. As for the shot, it was merely a ranging shot, to check the distance. As you can see, I have my men doing the same thing at this very moment.'

He pointed aft to where the gun was now loaded and run out, the men standing back out of its recoil path with one man holding the lanyard. Midshipman Francis was on his way over to them at that very minute.

'Well, I trust the lieutenant completely, as should you Papa!'

Fury turned back to them just in time to see a look of disapproval on the face of Sophie, clearly aimed at her father. A second later and she turned to Fury, her mouth breaking into another warm smile which very nearly disrupted his composure as he attempted to smile back. He regained it just in time for Francis to demand his attention.

'Gun loaded and run out sir.'

'Very good, I will be across presently.' He turned back to both families for one last charade. 'It would please me greatly if I could have the pleasure of your company at dinner tonight.'

He looked at them all, the surprise showing on their faces at the dinner invitation amidst their current plight. Still, not to be outdone, de Lissey recovered himself sufficiently.

'We shall be honoured, Lieutenant.'

Sophie's father followed suit. 'As shall we, sir.'

'Excellent! Shall we arrange a time later when we are not quite so busy?'

'As you wish, Lieutenant.'

'For now, I regret that my duty tears me away once more, so if you will forgive me.'

Fury made his bow, his gaze lingering upon Sophie a little longer than was customary, before he made his way over to the gun where the men were waiting.

'Who aimed it?' he demanded brusquely.

'I did sir,' Francis replied nervously.

Fury looked along the barrel of the gun, in the line of which he could see the bow of the strange ship rising and falling with each wave in the distance. Noting the elevation was at maximum, he stepped away with a grudging 'Very well' and gave the order to fire when ready. The man chosen to fire it waited for the uproll before jerking the lanyard, the gun barking out and leaping back against its breeching rope.

Fury and several of the men immediately peered over the hammock nettings to search for the fall of the shot. No one among the group of men crowding along the bulwark spotted it, Fury guiltily realising that he should have ordered someone to keep a lookout with a glass.

'Reload and try again lads,' he ordered, pulling his telescope out of his pocket and putting it to his eye to adjust it to the correct focus.

It took the men only seconds to reload the little six-pounder and haul on the tackles to run it out of the gun port once again, during which time Fury noted another distant clap which told of another shot from the bow chaser of their pursuer. Again, there was no evidence of where the shot fell.

'Ready sir!' Francis announced.

Fury whipped his glass to his eye once more and brought up the strange sail through the lens.

'Fire when ready,' he ordered.

There was another small pause before the gun barked out while the man holding the lanyard waited for the uproll. A moment later Fury saw a tiny spout of water rise up, about a cable's length short and somewhat to the right of the ship. He turned to the gun crew.

'Secure the gun. She's too far off and out of our current arc of fire.'

The men looked slightly disconsolate as they secured the tackles housing the gun, but Fury had no choice. It was pointless wasting shot when the vessel was clearly out of reach, even if it did keep up the men's morale. With the guns unable to bear, and with their pursuer gaining on them, he knew he would have to change course, even if it would mean delaying their arrival in England still further.

He turned to the helmsman, ready to try his second line of defence.

'Bear away four points to starboard.'

Renard was currently heading immediately before the wind to the eastward on what Fury had assumed was her best point of sailing, even though it meant the enemy ship was on a converging course. By turning southward and bringing the

424

wind on their starboard quarter they would be running directly away from their pursuer, but they would also be sailing further away from their destination. The frustration that Fury could feel was tangible.

'Brace the yards round there!'

Fury watched in silence as the men hauled on the braces until the yards were trimmed round in response to the new course.

'Mr Francis!' he called. 'I think we'll loose the main course and the fore topsail.'

With the wind now on their quarter they could afford to set the main course and fore topsail, as they would no longer be taking the wind directly out of the other sails.

'Aye aye sir,' Francis replied, shouting the orders which sent the men to their stations for making sail.

Even with a small crew, unfamiliar with each other and with the ship, the sails were set in admirable time. *Renard* thrust her bow into the short waves even more willingly as she heeled further over with the increased pressure aloft.

One glance showed that their pursuer had altered course to match, and was now directly astern, probably just over a mile and a half distant. Fury wished *Renard* had a gun mounted at her stern, so he could at least continue to fire upon her. His watch told him only an hour had passed since he had last looked, meaning there were still three hours to go before nightfall would save them.

Over the next half an hour Fury remained at the taffrail looking back at their pursuer. It soon became clear that she was still head reaching upon them, so he felt obliged to try something else.

'Mr Francis!' he called, turning his back on the taffrail and the enemy.

'Sir?'

'I want all the shot we can lay our hands upon brought up from below, wrapped in the men's hammocks and placed on the starboard side. When that is done I want every man over on the starboard side also.'

'Starboard side – aye aye sir,' Francis replied, and hurried off.

With the increased canvas aloft the ship was naturally heeling more to leeward, so by shifting as much weight as possible over to the other side to lessen the heel, the rudder would get more of a grip in the water, increasing the ship's speed. A desperate measure, perhaps, but at the moment Fury was willing to try anything.

Soon the men were busy bringing up shot from below and securing them in the rolled up hammocks, before placing them in the scuppers along the starboard bulwark. His passengers were looking on in astonishment at the proceedings, especially after the last shot had been brought up and the men all moved over to the starboard side of *Renard*, leaving them the only people on the larboard side.

At that moment the sound of another gun reached them, now closer, and as Fury whipped round he spotted a fountain of water directly astern of them about thirty yards away. Almost immediately another bang drifted down to them, followed by another ball, Fury seeing it fully this time as it ricocheted across two or three wave caps and plunged into the sea the same distance away as the first.

He immediately turned on his heel and strode forward to where his passengers were standing, now over on the starboard side with the rest of the crew. He bowed quickly to them.

'Your Grace, messieurs, miladies. I deeply regret this necessity, but for your own safety it would be best if you went below for the time being.'

'Are we in danger here?' the eldest son asked, somewhat foolishly in Fury's opinion.

'They are attempting to damage our rigging. If they succeed, there is a chance of injury by falling blocks or spars. You will be perfectly safe below, I assure you.'

Fury was most relieved that de Lissey took charge at this point.

'Come along!' he insisted to his family, discouraging any further questions from being flung Fury's way. 'The lieutenant has enough problems without having to worry about us.'

He gently took hold of his wife's arm and led her along the canting deck to the main hatchway, followed obediently by his sons. Gourrier led

Sophie behind them, Sophie sparing the time to glance back and flash him a smile as they went.

Fury watched them go below with some relief and then turned his attention back to the ship astern, which was keeping up a steady fire now with her two bow chase guns. Nine-pounders, perhaps?

He suddenly remembered the admiral's despatches which were still sitting down in his cabin, locked in the desk drawer along with the current signal book. He hurried down to the cabin, thankful that he had remembered them before it was too late. If they were captured and the enemy got their hands on those, then Fury would wish he had been killed because Their Lordships at the Admiralty would see to it that he never found employment again.

He fumbled in his pocket for the large iron key and bent down to unlock the top drawer of the desk. The lock was stiff and he braced himself to turn the key when there was a loud crash and splintering sound close at hand, followed quickly by a dull thud. Fury looked up in time to see a cannonball hit the deck and roll around as the ship pitched.

He could see the forward bulkhead, forming the partition between his cabin and the rest of the deck, had signs of splintering in one area where the spent ball must have hit it after smashing its way through *Renard*'s stern timbers. The noise of the rolling ball was beginning to annoy him, so he scrambled around the cabin after it, finally managing to pick it up – a nine-pound ball, as he had guessed. He walked over to the hole in the stern and pushed it through, hearing the small splash as it hit the water, before calmly turning back to the desk.

His second attempt at opening the drawer was interrupted by the cabin door being flung open, and he looked up to see Midshipman Francis standing there, a look of worry on his face.

'It is customary to knock, Mr Francis,' Fury said wryly.

'My apologies sir,' Francis stammered, 'I heard the ball hit our stern and thought—'

'Yes, yes, I know what you thought,' Fury replied testily. 'Well as you can see I'm fine, so if you will excuse me . . .'

'Of course sir.'

Francis closed the door quietly as he left and Fury lifted the canvas sack containing the admiral's despatches out of the drawer. He carefully opened the sack and checked its contents – including the lead weight placed at the bottom which would ensure the bag sunk immediately if thrown over-board – before reaching into the desk drawer and pulling out the signal books and journals, placing them carefully within the sack also. Happy that nothing had been forgotten, he securely tied the top of the bag and took it with him back up on deck.

When he arrived he threw it down by one of the

larboard six-pounders and moved to the taffrail. The enemy vessel was now no more than a mile astern, and the two bow chase guns were barking out alternately as fast as they could be reloaded. At this extreme range most of the shot was falling slightly short, with some, aided by ricochets from the wave tops, crashing into *Renard*'s stern, each one causing Fury to flinch slightly at the impact. He estimated that five or six had so far hit their stern, with all but one failing to penetrate *Renard*'s timbers and every one so far luckily avoiding any damage to the rudder. All had also avoided hitting the brig's pinnace, which was towing astern. The one which had smashed its way into the cabin while Fury had been at the desk had presumably been fired on the limit of the enemy's uproll, or else maybe had been fired with a greater powder charge than the others.

Gradually, as the next hour wore on and the sun began to sink painfully slowly over to the west, their pursuer crept nearer so that her bow chase guns were well within range, each shot flying high but miraculously avoiding any essential rigging as they passed *Renard*. Looking aloft, Fury could see one or two shot holes in the main and fore topsails, holes which would slow them down still further.

It was at this time that Fury made the decision which he had been avoiding for as long as he could, and he called Midshipman Francis over to inform him.

'Mr Francis, we will cast the guns over the side if you please, larboard side first.'

Francis looked only slightly surprised at the order. He touched his hat in acknowledgement, and with a quick 'Aye aye sir', went to inform the men.

It was tough work for the men for the next half-hour as they struggled with handspikes and crowbars to loose the cannon from their carriages and heave them over the side, quickly followed by the carriages. The increase in speed of *Renard* was perceptible, even without a cast of the log – unsurprising since they were now about ten tons lighter.

For the fifteen minutes following the last gun going over the side, Fury looked back from the taffrail at the enemy ship and discovered with satisfaction that their pursuer had made little ground on them during that time.

He remained there looking at the ship three quarters of a mile astern, with the sky overhead lighting up in a brilliant soft pink as the sun began to set. By Fury's reckoning it took a whole thirty minutes from the time the bottom rim of the sun touched the line of the horizon to the time it finally disappeared – not without one final peek – below the curvature of the earth.

His watch showed that it wanted ten minutes until six o'clock, and the sky was now a darker blue with the first of the stars beginning to appear through the cloud.

'Mr Francis! Call the masthead lookouts down and have six lookouts stationed around the deck, if you please.'

As his orders were relayed and obeyed, Fury could feel the confidence surging within him once more as the visible horizon shrank with the ever-growing darkness. In command of one's own ship, night was usually a time when the confidence seeped from the body like water through a sieve, and all the doubts which lay hidden from the daylight seemed to grow and grip at the throat. Tonight was different, however. Tonight the darkness was a welcome saviour from the certain death or capture thrashing along behind them.

The question of what to do once it did turn completely black – whether to remain on their present course or turn north or west – began to occupy his mind. The captain of the other ship, knowing they were British, would no doubt be expecting them to turn north as soon as darkness had fallen, to resume their course for England. At least that was what Fury would be thinking if the positions were reversed. The thing to do then would be to continue on their southerly heading, but every minute on this course was taking them further from England, and he was loath for that to happen.

Suddenly an idea occurred to him. He took a couple of minutes to bring the idea into sharper focus and turn it over in his head for obvious flaws or drawbacks but, finding none, he made his decision.

'Mr Francis!' he called, as a tearing sound aloft told of another shot hole being made in one of their sails.

'Yes sir?' Francis replied, appearing out of the ever growing gloom as the sky continued to darken.

'Go below and make sure there is not a light showing anywhere in the ship. Then have three powder casks brought up on deck, along with a length of slow match, flint, steel and a lantern. Understand?'

He doubted very much whether the young lad would understand, but Francis answered in the affirmative nevertheless. One more shot crashed into the stern, narrowly missing the rudder pintles as Francis turned to make his way below as ordered.

The outline of the other ship was growing blurred now as the final stages of darkness closed in. Francis was soon back up on deck reporting not a single lamp was lit anywhere in the ship, and with him he had the slow match, flint, steel and a lantern. Twelve seamen soon followed, carefully manhandling the powder casks on to the deck.

'Excellent!' Fury exclaimed, as Francis held the items in front of him. 'I want the pinnace brought alongside and those casks secured between two thwarts in it.'

Francis snapped an order to the men keeping the casks securely held on the deck, and soon lines and tackles were being readied. It was a challenging task to lower barrels full of gunpowder down into a boat secured alongside, while *Renard* was bowling along under all the sail she could carry, but it was eventually done with no mishap.

The dusk was sufficiently upon them to ensure none of it was visible to their pursuer, and by the time they were down in the boat, it was completely dark. Fury looked down into the boat as Perrin and Gooseman finished the job of securing the barrels between two of the thwarts amidships, with the bungholes uppermost. One look astern showed nothing but blackness, the other vessel completely swallowed up in the gloom.

'Up you come now!' he called down to them. They nodded in acknowledgement and began clambering back up *Renard*'s side as Fury turned inboard to organise the next part of his plan. He caught sight of Clark, and a quick shout brought him over. At Fury's request he handed over his knife. Fury knelt down and cut the slow match at what he estimated to be a length of ten inches, which should give them twenty minutes. Standing up again, he took the flint, steel and lantern off Francis, and began a careful descent down the side of *Renard*. He reached the boat and huddled down by the powder casks, placing his items on one of the thwarts.

Firstly he prized open the bung from the middle cask, took a length of slow match and stuck one end down into the barrel, making sure it was adequately buried within the powder. Satisfied, he took the lantern and made his way to the stern sheets of the boat, along with the flint and steel. It took only a moment to secure the lantern at the stern, and a quick fumble with flint and steel produced a spark sufficient to light it. Happy, he hurried back to the powder casks and lit the slow match, waiting only long enough to ensure it was well alight, before climbing quickly back up *Renard*'s side and on to the deck, where Francis was waiting.

'Very well, Mr Francis, have the boat cast off and pay out the line over the stern.'

'Aye aye sir.'

The line securing the pinnace to the side of *Renard* was loosed and the men walked with it to the taffrail, constantly paying it out as they went. Fury stood with them and watched as the distance between them and the boat increased, until finally it disappeared in the darkness, with only the light from the lantern betraying its location.

'That's the last of the line, sir.'

'Very well, release it,' Fury ordered.

The line dropped into the sea and disappeared. Another shot sounded in the distance, the fall of which was unseen as Fury turned to the men.

'To your stations lads!' he hissed fiercely, trying to make himself heard without his voice carrying far. 'Mr Francis, I want every order given and obeyed in silence. See to it that the men are informed, and then stand ready to convey my orders. We shall be coming round shortly to head north.'

'Aye aye sir,' Francis acknowledged, moving silently away into the gloom as he went along the brig's deck to inform all the men stationed ready at main or foremast of the need for silence.

Fury looked at his watch by the soft light of the binnacle; a little over five minutes had passed, meaning they still had nearly fifteen minutes before the flame would reach the gunpowder.

'Up with your helm,' he ordered quietly to the helmsman, when he was sure all was ready. 'Bring her to a northerly heading.'

The tiller was put over by the helmsman, and the brig's bow began to come round further away from the wind. Fury moved forward until he could distinguish the slight uniformed frame of Francis standing near the foremast.

'Brace the yards round there!' he hissed.

Francis acknowledged and turned to pass the order on to the men by the foremast, a task which proved unnecessary as they had all heard it themselves. Men were now clapping on to the braces of both fore and main and hauling to bring the yards creaking slowly round in response to *Renard*'s turn.

Fury kept an eye on the compass card as the brig's bow turned eastward and kept on swinging, until at last the wind was on the larboard beam. She was heeling over more now with the wind abeam as she plunged forward through the choppy waters of the Bay of Biscay, heading north at last. The helmsman straightened the tiller to right the rudder and settle her on course.

A short while later and the yards were braced round satisfactorily, allowing Fury to take a stroll over to the binnacle and see from the faint light of the lantern there that they were now heading slightly west of north. That was good. Any amount of westing they could make now would save them time later when it came to beating out of the bay towards the entrance to the English Channel.

Two more shots echoed out of the darkness somewhere in the distance, but no sound or other evidence of the fall of shot reached them. He could still see a tiny light, already far astern of them, which showed the location of the boat.

Francis was coming over to him now as the sound of another shot – surprisingly distant – reached them.

'Everything's drawing well sir,' he reported, referring to *Renard*'s current spread of canvas.

Fury grunted his approval. He started towards the binnacle to check his watch, but was stopped in his tracks as an explosion erupted in the distance. The dark sky astern lit up in brilliant white for a fraction of a second, before everything went black again. Fury blinked in quick succession to rid his vision of the momentary flashes of colour.

'It looks like it worked, sir,' Francis offered, the relief in his voice evident.

Fury's original intention had been to distract their pursuer with the explosion, allowing *Renard* to slip away in the confusion. He had considered the possibility of the illumination from the blast revealing their position, but had discarded it; the light from the explosion would be so brief and so intense that the chances of one of the enemy crew looking in their direction and spotting them at the exact moment the boat went up were minimal. More likely they would be focused on the single lantern attached to the stern of the pinnace, hopefully steering a course straight for it.

Fury would have liked to find out what damage, if any, the enemy ship had suffered as a result of the detonation. It would all depend on how close she was to the boat when it blew, but of course there was no way of knowing that.

'You may dismiss the watch below Mr Francis, and see that the men get something to eat and a tot.'

Fury did not hear Francis' reply of 'Aye aye sir', as the mention of food had suddenly reminded him of his dinner invitation to his passengers. The invitation had been made primarily as an act of cool confidence in front of the ladies at a time when it looked in all probability like they would be captured. Now, not for the first time, he silently cursed himself for his loose tongue as he tried to think of a way of retreating from the engagement. He would gain little pleasure from Sophie's company, surrounded as they would be by others, all demanding his attention.

He racked his brain hard to find an honourable way out of the engagement, but could think of nothing. Finally, with a sigh, he accepted his obligation and turned to Clark, standing nearby.

'Clark!'

'Sir?'

'Do any of the men know how to cook?'

'Cook, sir?' Clark replied, startled.

'Yes, cook.'

'Don't rightly know sir.'

'Well enquire amongst them, and if there aren't any, pick the two with the most potential.'

Clark saluted and hurried off, still with a puzzled look on his face. Fury could not blame him; a mere half an hour ago they had been in danger of capture, and now here he was trying to organise a dinner party. In ten minutes Clark was back, with Perrin and McSherry following behind, somewhat reluctantly it appeared to Fury.

'They're both convicted poachers sir,' Clark explained. 'If they can catch 'em, they must know how to cook 'em.'

'Thank you Clark,' Fury replied, turning to the two men. 'Poachers eh?'

'No sir,' Perrin protested. 'I worn't guilty sir.'

'No? Then how did you get convicted?'

'They caught me with the birds on me, sir, and I just happened to be carrying a gun.'

'Innocent eh?' Fury stifled a grin. 'Well, never

mind about that. I shall be entertaining our passengers in my cabin, so we shall need some food. What do we have on board?'

'Salt beef and pork sir,' McSherry answered. 'Pease. A little ship's biscuit, and maybe a morsel of cheese stowed away.'

'Drink?'

'Water sir.'

'Water? You want me to serve water at a dinner party?'

'We ain't got nothing else, sir.'

Fury let out a large sigh – this was going to be a complete disaster. 'Very well. Put some beef and pork in to boil, enough for seven people, along with some pease. Get whatever cheese you can find and serve it with the biscuit once we have finished our meal.'

'And the drink, sir?' Perrin prompted.

'We don't have a choice do we? Unless you can turn water into wine.'

'Not tried it sir. How is it done?'

Fury looked at him sharply to see if he was being mocked, but Perrin's face was a picture of innocence. 'Never mind. Just get the water.'

The two of them saluted and left Fury alone to think about what else needed organising. He caught sight of Francis by the tiller, surreptitiously trying to listen to what was being said.

'Mr Francis!'

'Sir?'

'Have our passengers brought up from below,

and have five extra chairs placed around the desk in my cabin. Is there a tablecloth on board?'

'A tablecloth sir? Haven't seen one, I don't think.'

'Very well, we'll have to manage without. With no other officers available to stand a watch, I'm afraid I cannot spare you to join us for dinner Mr Francis. You have my apologies.'

Francis didn't look overly disappointed. 'I understand, sir.'

'Carry on.'

Fury paced the deck in the darkness as the *Renard* thrashed her way along to the north, and it wasn't long before his peace and quiet was interrupted by the arrival back on deck of his passengers.

'We have escaped?' de Lissey asked, rather stupidly in Fury's opinion.

'Yes, Your Grace.'

'Excellent! Well done Lieutenant.'

'Dinner will hopefully be served soon. In the meantime I think a little fresh air would be desirable, if that is agreeable to everybody.'

He received nods in response, and so they settled down to wait on deck in the darkness while the food was prepared. Fury had hoped to get the chance to speak with Sophie, but she was already deep in conversation with de Lissey's wife over by the main shrouds. Instead he had to content himself with making small talk with de Lissey and Gourrier. Both men had much in common, each

having had to live in hiding because of their aristocratic background, but Fury could not relate to
either, and so he remained in silence mostly and
listened, while contriving to sneak the occasional
glance over towards Sophie.

Finally, to Fury's relief, the flow of talk was interrupted by Francis.

'I believe the food is nearly ready, sir.'

'Excellent.' Fury turned to his companions and
raised his voice so the ladies across the other side
of the deck could hear him. 'Shall we make our way
down to the cabin? Dinner will be served shortly.'

He led them down the ladder and aft to his
cabin, where his desk had been cleared and seven
chairs were now arranged at intervals around it.
The guests would have no legroom, and the size
of the desk meant that it would be very cramped,
but it was the best Fury could do. They each
picked a chair at random and, at Fury's behest,
seated themselves. Perrin and McSherry soon
entered carrying a combination of cutlery and
crockery, and this was distributed amongst them.
De Lissey got to his feet.

'If you will excuse me for a moment, Lieutenant,
I have forgotten something.'

He hurried out of the cabin, while the conversation ebbed and flowed around the table.
McSherry came in carrying a wine bottle, and
Fury's heart lifted. They had found some! He
made his way to Fury and stooped down to
whisper in his ear.

'Shall I pour the drinks sir?'

'You found some wine then?' Fury grinned back at him, being careful not to let his voice be heard over the din of conversation around the table.

'No sir,' McSherry whispered. 'It's water. We found the empty bottle 'tween decks and thought it would look better using it to serve the water. Add a touch of class, if you like, sir.'

Fury's heart sank. Not only would they be drinking water, but his guests would also have their hopes raised first by the sight of the wine bottle. It must have been left over from their first day at Toulon, when Gooseman and the other idlers had managed to get at the liquor while Fury was visiting Admiral Hood on board the *Victory*.

'Oh, very well,' he replied, bracing himself for the inevitable humiliation. McSherry snatched up Fury's cup and straightened himself as far as the low deck beams would allow. De Lissey walked in at that moment carrying three bottles.

'My apologies, Lieutenant, for my lack of manners,' he stated. 'As you have so kindly provided the food, it is only fitting that I should provide the wine. Lord Hood kindly gifted me these and I would be grateful if you would accept them instead of using your own stock.'

McSherry was hovering with the bottle half tilted over the cup, and Fury quickly seized the cup back from his hand.

'With pleasure, sir.' He half turned to McSherry, standing motionless. 'Get that bottle out of here!'

McSherry hurried out of the cabin with the wine bottle of water, while de Lissey placed his three bottles on the table. He barely had time to seat himself before Perrin entered carrying platefuls of boiled meat with generous side portions of pease. Fury looked at his guests with an apologetic smile as the plates were passed around, but his guests seemed pleased enough.

'Have one of those wine bottles opened, if you please Perrin.'

Fury's guests were already beginning to tackle their boiled beef and pork as Perrin disappeared with one of the bottles. It was lucky that the meat had not been too long in the casks, so that it could be eaten with relatively little chewing, enabling the conversation to continue unabated. The cups were filled with wine while they ate and the alcohol helped Fury's nerves, so that he almost began to enjoy himself. He could not help glancing frequently over at Sophie across the table to the right, catching her eye on more than one occasion and smiling through mouthfuls of pease.

De Lissey and Gourrier were evidently continuing their conversation from up on deck in quick French, but the rest of the table seemed content to eat in silence. Fury's plateful was finished by the time he heard his name mentioned.

'Eh? I'm sorry?'

'I was asking, Lieutenant,' Sophie repeated, 'what your plans are when we reach England.'

Fury looked around the table but the other guests seemed oblivious to Sophie's question.

'I must deliver Lord Hood's despatches to the Admiralty in London, then I shall go home to visit my mother.'

'When will you rejoin your ship?'

'I have been discharged from my ship, so I shall have to apply for another post.' He took a mouthful of wine as McSherry and Perrin entered the cabin again carrying trays of ship's biscuit with a small amount of cheese.

'So you will be visiting Portsmouth regularly?' Sophie asked, as the biscuit and cheese was passed around the table and the cups were topped up with wine.

'Yes, I would think so. I would be honoured to give you a tour of the town, should you be available when I visit.'

'That is most kind of you, thank you, Lieutenant.'

They smiled at each other, and Fury was so engrossed that he was only aware of his name being mentioned after it was repeated a second time. He looked across at de Lissey.

'I'm sorry, Your Grace?'

'The Comte and I,' de Lissey repeated, indicating Sophie's father next to him whose red face betrayed his enjoyment of the wine, 'were discussing how long we think it will take to defeat the Republican tyrants currently in power and restore the Bourbons to their true position.'

Fury reluctantly turned his attention away from

Sophie and tried to focus his mind on the question. His belief was that it may take ten years, possibly even longer judging by the Republican display of soldiering and siege warfare that he had witnessed in Toulon, and his honesty seemed to shock de Lissey and Gourrier. He gave his reasoning and listened to their views, and the discussion soon concentrated on the best strategy to be adopted to win the war in the shortest possible time. In the end they accepted his view that Europe did not have a land army to compete with the Republican army at present, and so the only way to force them into surrender would be through naval blockade, essentially strangling their economy and starving them out.

He looked around the table to see that the rest of the passengers were listening in on his explanation intently, and he became suddenly worried that the dinner party had degenerated into a council of war. The cheese was long gone, but Fury noticed the biscuit had hardly been touched. The last wine bottle was empty and Fury's head was telling him that he had drunk too much. De Lissey's wife tried to stifle a yawn, but it was noticed by her husband.

'Come dear, it is late. I think it is time we turned in.' De Lissey pushed his chair back and got slightly unsteadily to his feet, holding his hand out to Fury. 'I must thank you, Lieutenant, for your hospitality. When we reach England I hope you will allow me to return the compliment.'

Fury rose and shook his hand, and the rest of his guests followed suit, saying their farewells as they filed out of the cabin. He would have liked to talk more with Sophie, but she was ushered out by her father, leaving Fury alone with Perrin and McSherry. They began to clear the table and Fury suddenly realised how tired he was himself; the day's tension had taken a lot out of him.

It was twenty minutes by the time everything was cleared and he had the cabin to himself at last. As he climbed into his cot, he reflected with satisfaction that the dinner had not been the complete disaster he had anticipated, but nevertheless he had learnt his lesson: he would issue no more idiotic invitations during moments of danger in an attempt to impress. He would guard his tongue in future.

CHAPTER 23

The trade winds, blowing steadily across the Atlantic from the west, ensured that *Renard* spent a whole day beating out of the Bay of Biscay before finally being able to lay a course of north and thrash along with the wind abeam towards the entrance to the English Channel.

They weathered Ushant, at the westernmost tip of northern France, two days later, the grey low-lying rock and breaking surf showing faint through the light mist that hung like a blanket over everything.

A course of east-north-east then brought them through the mouth of the Channel with the wind on their larboard quarter, until at last the lookout reported land on their larboard bow just after two bells in the afternoon watch.

The shout brought everyone up on deck in a flash. The men, Fury included, looked on in eager anticipation at England once again, while the de Lisseys and Gourriers looked on in curiosity at what was to be their new home.

Midshipman Francis came scrambling down the

larboard fore shrouds from aloft, where Fury had sent him when the initial sighting had been made. There was an excited grin on his face as he came to a halt in front of Fury and touched his hat before making his report.

'It's the Isle of Wight sir, definitely. I can see the Eddystone lighthouse on the point.'

Fury felt a slight pang of nostalgia well up within him as Francis made his report. The Isle of Wight had been his last sight of England as the *Amazon* had made her way out of Spithead on her way to India, and that had been over two years ago, when he was no more than a boy. Now here he was returning in command of his own vessel – albeit temporarily – with his mother no more than forty miles away from Portsmouth.

'Very good Mr Francis,' said Fury at last in response to his report. 'Call all hands – we shall shorten sail soon.'

'Aye aye sir,' replied Francis eagerly, turning away to bellow 'All hands! All hands!'. The crew of *Renard*, already all on deck, hurried to their stations amidst a buzz of excited chatter.

'Silence!' roared Fury. 'This is still a king's ship!'

The noise died away immediately as the men recalled themselves back to their duty with no little effort. Fury regretted the severity of his outburst at once, realising that it was more down to his frustration at the uncertainty of his own future, now that their arrival back home was guaranteed.

He made an effort to calm himself and walked over to de Lissey, staring at the low smudge of grey which represented his first sight of England. His wife and two sons were standing next to him, following his gaze while clutching on to the hammock nettings to support themselves against the little brig's sharper pitching as she met the shorter, steeper waves of the English Channel, so very different after the long Atlantic swell they had been used to.

'The Isle of Wight, Your Grace. You will be able to see the Eddystone lighthouse soon.'

The interruption startled de Lissey from his reverie. In a moment of curious insight, Fury guessed that, although de Lissey's eyes had been on the south coast of England, his mind had been in his own homeland, thinking of places that he might never see again.

'Indeed?' de Lissey replied, recovering himself from his thoughts admirably.

'Yes. Portsmouth is just beyond – we should be at anchor by nightfall, all being well, so that you may leave at first light in the morning.'

Fury snatched a glance at Sophie, still staring at the distant land. She seemed to sense him, and she looked at him and gave him a smile. He turned to her father.

'I shall take you and Sophie ashore tomorrow also. I shall need to travel to London, but I will arrange lodgings for you before I leave. I have a small amount of money, which should be suffi-cient for you until you find your feet.'

'We could not possibly accept your money, Lieutenant.'

'It is merely a loan, sir,' Fury assured him. 'You can pay me back once you are settled.'

There was a pause as Gourrier considered the offer, before finally relenting. 'Very well, Lieutenant. But it is just a loan. I shall repay you with interest.'

Fury nodded in agreement. 'Of course.' He bowed and moved away to find some solitude as *Renard* slowly made her way up Channel.

Standing at the fore chains in silence, his mind wandered back to his childhood in Swampton. He did not notice the men rushing about the deck to their allotted stations, nor did he notice the sound and movement of *Renard* under his feet. He was oblivious, engrossed in memories of home and childhood, sunshine and rolling fields. Another life.

It was only when Midshipman Francis gently touched his arm thirty minutes later, to inform him they were ready to come about, that Fury shook off the memories and turned his attention to the task of bringing them safely through St Helen's road to their anchorage at Spithead.

The next day broke cold and misty, so misty in fact that the shore was hardly visible from the upper deck of *Renard* as she swung gently to her anchor at Spithead.

Fury had been awake for most of the night, unable to sleep with the knowledge that not one mile away was Portsmouth, and beyond that the rest of England, a sight he had not seen for over two years.

He was fully dressed by the time the first rays of light from the rising sun began to permeate the low cloud cover overhead. He had also had his morning shave – a task necessary almost every day now – by the dim light of the lantern hanging in his cabin, so that the man stepping on to *Renard*'s deck a short time later looked every inch an officer in His Britannic Majesty's Navy.

Shortly after breakfast at eight o'clock de Lissey came on deck to report himself and his family ready for departure. Sophie and her father were also already on deck, waiting.

'Mr Francis, have the longboat hoisted out at once, if you please,' Fury ordered, stepping down to his cabin to retrieve the despatches from Admiral Hood which it was now his duty to deliver to the Admiralty as soon as possible.

As he regained the deck he was pleased to see that Francis had had the forethought to have a chair rigged up to a tackle at the main yardarm, for the ladies to use for their descent into the boat alongside. That procedure was completed eventually, but only after much squealing on the part of de Lissey's wife.

'Mr Francis, you will remain here in command until I return, unless you receive any orders to the contrary.' Fury was feeling quite emotional as he completed the formalities, standing in front of the entry port prior to going down the little brig's side.

'Aye aye sir.'

Those were the last words he heard as he descended *Renard*'s shallow side, transferred himself to the boat, and made his way to the stern sheets – despatches still in hand – to take the tiller.

'Shove off! Give way all!' he called, sending the boat away from the brig's side and surging forward over the sheltered waters of Spithead towards the jetty at Portsmouth.

It was a little over fifteen minutes before Fury put the tiller over to swing the boat round as she neared the stone quay, the men raising their oars at a curt command from Fury and laying them in the bottom of the boat.

Fury was up and on to the stone quay in an instant, the joy of being back on English soil once again lost as he turned immediately to help out the ladies with their small amount of baggage.

'You may return to the ship now,' he told the men in the longboat, once he and the passengers were safely ashore.

He stood there watching for a short time to make sure that the boat was in fact returning to *Renard* – he had a small enough opinion of the men's ability to resist temptation in the guise of ale or women without an officer present to remind them of their duty. Satisfied, he turned to help de Lissey and his family with their belongings.

As usual, their arrival had already attracted the

attention of several peddlers looking for trade, so it was no difficult task to choose the soberest looking man among them and have him take their small baggage to the George Inn, with Fury leading the way along the cobbled streets. He stopped outside the door of the George and turned to de Lissey.

'This will be a comfortable enough inn for you until you get your affairs in order, Your Grace,' he said. 'For me, I regret that I will have to take my leave of you now. I have despatches from Lord Hood which need to be delivered to the Admiralty at once.'

De Lissey held out his hand and Fury shook it.

'I must offer my sincere thanks, Lieutenant, for ensuring the safety of myself and my family. If ever I am in a position to repay the debt, I trust you will not hesitate to let me know.'

Fury bowed stiffly.

'You are most kind, Your Grace. I have enjoyed your company greatly,' he lied.

He turned to the duchess and kissed her out-stretched hand, followed by a curt nod to each of their sons.

That job done, he led Sophie and her father through the streets to a small lodging house, which was the same one used by himself upon his arrival in Portsmouth prior to joining the *Amazon*. From what he could remember it was a small establishment, with very basic furnishings, but it was clean and well run, and, more importantly, it was cheap.

He hammered on the door, and when it opened he recognised the wizened features of the elderly housekeeper, even after more than two years.

'Good morning.' He indicated Sophie and her father, standing quietly behind him. 'This family require lodgings for a week. Do you have room?'

'We have one room, with a bed.' She paused and looked behind Fury at the Gourriers, as if checking them up and down. 'I suppose I could have another bed put in there, but it will cost extra.'

'How much, all told?'

'Ten shillings per night, including the extra bed. And they'll get a hearty breakfast each morning.'

'Very well.' Fury fumbled in his pocket and brought out his money, counting out enough for one week's lodging, and handing it over to the eager hands of the housekeeper. He turned to Sophie's father. 'I have paid for seven nights accommodation for you and Sophie. I will be back from London by then, at which time we can arrange something more permanent.'

Gourrier clasped Fury's hand and shook it vigorously, reiterating his thanks and his intention to repay Fury as soon as he had found work. Fury managed to extricate himself finally, and turned to Sophie.

'You will return soon?' she asked him.

'Yes,' he reassured her. 'As soon as my business in London is complete.' He took hold of her hand and they looked at one another in silence for a few seconds. Finally, he bowed and kissed her hand – her trembling hand, he noted – before straightening up and forcing a smile. Then he turned his back and walked away, trying hard to refocus on his duty.

His next stop took him to the gates of the dockyard where he was given the address of the port admiral, to whom he would need to report initially before beginning his travels to London.

The house was a large building three storeys in height, overlooking the anchorage with a white-washed front. The footman who answered the door in response to his knock showed him into a side room only after a careful study of his uniform. Fury placed the despatches on the table and made himself comfortable in a large leather chair.

It was probably the most relaxed he had been since he was packed off to sea by his mother and uncle. So much so that when the footman returned after twenty minutes to announce that the admiral was ready to see him, it was with reluctance that Fury rose, picked up the despatches, and followed him up the sweeping staircase.

Rear Admiral Benbow was an elderly man with thinning silvery hair and a paunch around his midriff which bespoke of having been too long ashore with rich food and little exercise. Nevertheless he looked a cheerful man, sitting in front of a roaring fire with his cheeks beginning to turn red from the heat. He rose to greet Fury, beckoning him to a chair opposite his own in front of the hearth so that almost immediately Fury began to feel uncomfortably hot around his collar.

'You are the commander of that little brig that came in yesterday, I take it,' Benbow began.

'Yes sir,' Fury replied, 'Lord Hood placed me in temporary command of her to carry his despatches to the Admiralty. She is a former prize.'

'Despatches eh?' Benbow mused. 'I suppose you want to take the post-chaise?'

Any despatches which needed to be sent by a port admiral to the Admiralty in London could be delivered by a special post-chaise under the charge of the admiral.

'If I could sir – they are quite urgent.'

Benbow reached to the small table next to his chair and rang a bell which was sitting there.

'What is this news that is so urgent?' Benbow asked while they waited for the footman.

Fury's reply was interrupted by the opening of the door and the arrival of the footman in question. Fury took the opportunity to study the room more closely, the ornate gilded decorations adorning the walls and the numerous oil canvases representing naval engagements. There was a dog in the corner, sleeping soundly, saliva dripping from the side of its mouth on to the wood panelled floor as it snoozed.

He heard the door click shut and realised that the admiral had given the instructions to the footman without him hearing it. Benbow was looking at him once again.

'Now, where were we Lieutenant? Ah yes, the latest news!'

'Lord Hood found it necessary to evacuate Toulon on 17 December, sir.'

'Good God!' exclaimed Benbow.

'A proportion of the French fleet was taken or destroyed by Captain Sir Sydney Smith on the evening of the withdrawal, and the fleet retired to Hierres Bay to the east. Admiral Hood informed the fleet before I left that he proposes to attack Corsica next. More news than that I cannot tell you sir.'

'I see. That is bad news indeed! No doubt John Bull will have much to say about it,' Benbow replied, having regained his composure after the news. 'The post-chaise will be ready in twenty minutes. Is there anything you need before then?'

'Thank you, no. Although . . .'

'Yes?'

'*Renard* – the brig I came in with – is anchored still in the roads. Lord Hood had agreed to buy her into the service . . .'

'I'll have her looked over by the adjudicator and we will agree a price for her. Anything more than that is out of my hands until I receive orders from the Admiralty.'

Fury thanked him once again and stood to take his leave. Benbow condescended to shake him by the hand and show him to the door, after which Fury had several minutes to wait while the coachman and postilion finished harnessing the horses of the post-chaise, now standing outside the front door in the street.

The horses were great black beasts, much bigger than he had seen before, neighing and scraping the cobbles with their hooves while the steam from their nostrils showed how cold it was.

'Ready sir,' said the coachman at last, with a touch of his cap.

Fury opened the door and climbed inside where the smell of worn leather accosted him. The sound of a whip soon reached his ears, followed quickly by the voice of the coachman shouting 'Up, up there!', encouraging the horses to break into a canter.

Fury had forgotten just how bumpy and uncomfortable it was to ride in a carriage, but he was reminded soon enough as they passed along the uneven roads through Portsmouth. Presently they were through town and out into the country on to the London road, where over 150 miles of countryside awaited them, broken only by toll roads here and there and small villages.

At least the ride was smoother now, reflected Fury, as he settled down and watched the countryside roll past through the window, determined to enjoy the journey no matter what the future might hold for him.

It was nearly twenty-four hours later before the carriage finally made its way through the outskirts of London and turned into Whitehall. They had gone through countless villages, and had changed horses at Petersfield and Cobham along the way. They had even stopped at an inn on the outskirts of Godalming, where Fury had ravenously devoured a sixpenny ordinary, before lying down in one of the rooms. Two years of being at sea had given Fury the ability to snatch a moment's sleep at any opportunity, so that when the coachman had come in to inform him they were ready to continue, he was sound asleep. That seemed like days ago now, and Fury stifled a yawn as the carriage continued up Whitehall and came to a standstill outside a very palatial building set back from the road behind a large wall.

This was Fury's first visit to the Admiralty, and he was struck by its imposing grandeur. The building, all in white stone, formed three sides of a square with the courtyard in the middle. A stone screen at the front overlooking the road, with a large archway in the middle, admitted entry to the courtyard beyond.

As he stepped down out of the carriage, the foul smell which had assaulted his senses upon first arriving in London now became sharper. Peddlers and hucksters of every kind were along the road trying to sell their wares, some of them no more than small boys, ugly and filthy. Fury felt a pang of sympathy for them, and realised just how lucky he was.

'The Admiralty sir,' the coachman confirmed.

Still tightly clutching the despatches, he waited till the street was clear and hurried across, pausing outside to let a couple decked out in fine clothes pass along the pavement, strolling along as if they had not a care in the world.

He looked up at the archway before walking through, the two pillars on each side both having some kind of winged unicorn statues on top. The courtyard itself was awash with activity, a continual procession of arrivals and departures accentuating the importance of the establishment. In many ways, the future of England rested on the decisions made within these walls. At the far end of the courtyard through the hurrying multitudes lay the main entrance, four tall stone pillars in front with a large engraved anchor at the top.

Fury felt the weight of history as he walked past the hurrying messengers and through the entrance into the hallway beyond. There was a large fire burning fiercely in the fireplace to his left, the crackling of the wood and embers audible even over the bustle of officers within the hall. The flames helped to supplement the weak light from the glass lantern hanging from the ceiling, the overall effect being to cast moving shadows along the oak-panelled walls on either side.

Two high leather-backed black chairs either side of the fireplace were occupied by officers, both engrossed in reading newspapers, while at the small side table beyond stood what Fury supposed to be a messenger, also studying a copy of the latest newspaper, the *Morning Chronicle*.

The porters, whose job it was to greet new

visitors and enquire of them their business, spied his uniform – a lowly lieutenant – and made no move in his direction. Years of employment at the Admiralty Office had obviously instilled in them a disdain of junior officers – lieutenants in particular – over whom they had found with gratification they could wield some little power.

Fury strode purposefully toward the nearest porter for the unpleasant task of trying to gain an interview with the First Lord.

'Excuse me, but I have urgent despatches for the First Lord, from Lord Hood.'

He addressed the request to a small ferret of a man with steel-rimmed spectacles, balanced so far down his nose Fury was amazed they didn't fall off.

'Very well. I shall see that he gets them at once,' he replied, looking up at Fury over the top of his spectacles, his hand outstretched.

'I must deliver these despatches personally. Now if you would be so kind as to enquire if the First Lord can spare me a few moments of his time, I would be greatly obliged.'

'The First Lord is a very busy man and has no time for people without appointments, especially lieutenants,' the man replied, still with his hand outstretched. 'I shall pass them to him, have no fear.'

'These despatches were entrusted to me by Lord Hood. I was ordered to ensure they reach the First Lord personally, which is precisely what I intend to do. Now if you cannot help me, kindly find me someone who can!'

The beginning of Fury's sentence was pitched a little above normal volume, and by the time he reached the end he was only a little short of shouting in his best quarterdeck voice.

'Is there a problem, Jeffrey?'

The voice – coming from behind Fury – made him turn. He came face to face with another gentleman wearing spectacles, his thinning brown hair showing flecks of grey which betrayed his otherwise youthful appearance. The change in the porter – Jeffrey – was startling.

'No problem Mr Barrow, sir. This gentleman was asking to see the First Lord, and I was explaining that he could not do so without an appointment.'

The obvious deference with which Jeffrey uttered the sentence made Fury look even harder at the newcomer, who was presumably a man of some importance.

'That is ordinarily correct, Lieutenant,' Barrow confirmed, looking at Fury. 'May I ask what your business with the First Lord is?'

The politeness of the question was in stark contrast to Jeffrey's manner.

'I have lately returned from the Mediterranean fleet, with despatches from Lord Hood. I was specifically ordered by His Lordship to deliver these personally to the First Lord.'

Fury tapped the bag holding the despatches

lightly with his hand, as if to add further weight to his argument.

'I see,' replied Barrow. 'In that case I am sure an interview can be arranged.'

He shot a glance at Jeffrey which displayed his displeasure more than any words could have, before turning to Fury once again.

'May I ask your name, Lieutenant?'

'Lieutenant Fury, sir,' Fury replied, bowing stiffly just low enough for politeness.

'If you would be so kind as to wait in there, Lieutenant, I will inform His Lordship of your presence.'

Barrow pointed to a room on the left of the hallway through which Fury could already see a multitude of officers within, the steady buzz of conversation floating across the hall over the crackling of the large roaring fire. Fury bowed once again, a movement which was copied by Barrow, before he strode down the hallway towards the entrance, past the fire and into the waiting room.

It was obvious as soon as he entered that he would have to stand. One quick glance told him there were at least two post captains in the room having to stand themselves, such was the crowd. They were deep in conversation with each other, no doubt to avoid the necessity of having to converse with any of the more junior officers crowded within.

Fury's entrance attracted not the least flicker of

interest from anyone, so he contented himself with finding a corner of unoccupied floor space, and waited patiently. His ears picked up fragments of several different conversations while he waited.

It must have been twenty minutes or so before a loud voice echoed over the din.

'Lieutenant Fury!'

His summons, so soon after his arrival into the waiting room, prompted one or two inquisitive glances as he crossed to the door, the officers no doubt wondering who he was to get seen before they did.

Fury followed silently as the porter led him along the hall to the staircase at the far end, sweeping up and to the right. The carpet felt thick underfoot as they ascended the stairs, pausing momentarily halfway up to let an officer pass – a messenger judging by the package he was carrying and the speed with which he flew down past them.

Another corridor stretched away at the top of the stairs which they continued down, the silence here in stark contrast to the noise and bustle below. The porter stopped outside a closed door on the left, so suddenly that Fury almost ran into the back of him. He knocked quietly and opened the door, beckoning Fury after him.

Fury followed him halfway into the room before laying eyes for the first time on a gentleman he assumed must be the First Lord, the Earl of Chatham, sitting behind his desk amidst a mass of paperwork. The porter announced Fury before quietly slipping out, leaving the two of them alone together.

As the First Lord looked up at him, Fury was surprised to see how young he was. Perhaps not young, he corrected himself, but at least younger than the decrepit old admiral he had been imagining. His head still showed a full crop of hair, although silvery and thinning towards the front, with thick bushy black eyebrows over deep-set, hawk-like eyes.

'Come in man, come in,' he waved testily, beckoning Fury further into the office. 'Take a seat.'

Fury obliged with a muttered 'Thank you, My Lord' and placed the despatches on his lap.

'Now Lieutenant, I understand you bring despatches from Admiral Hood.'

'Aye My Lord,' Fury replied, handing over the despatches to the outstretched hand of Chatham.

'Now pray, Lieutenant, why would you not let my porters deliver these?'

The tone of his voice was suddenly stern but Fury answered back immediately, confident he had fulfilled his orders to the letter.

'Lord Hood implicitly ordered me to deliver the despatches to you in person, My Lord.'

A small pause ensued before Chatham's features softened slightly.

'Quite right Lieutenant, quite right.' Another small pause. 'I shall read through the despatches later. For the time being sir, you can give me a verbal account of the situation in the Mediterranean.'

'Aye sir,' Fury replied, pausing to sort his thoughts into some kind of order. 'On the 17th Lord Hood judged it expedient to evacuate the fleet from Toulon. The besieging force of Republicans had been steadily growing and early on the 17th managed to take Fort Mulgrave, and subsequently l'Eguillette and Balaguier, covering the western shore. It was at that point Lord Hood ordered the evacuation of the troops, along with as many of the French fleet as could be safely brought out. Several thousand of the populace were also given protection by the fleet. Captain Sir Sydney Smith was employed in the task of burning the remainder of the French fleet still within the harbour. As far as my memory serves me only twelve French vessels survived the attempt, although the majority are in no way seaworthy.'

The Earl Of Chatham took the news with the stoicism of a true diplomat, merely nodding his head as Fury made his report.

'I had been expecting this for some time,' he muttered. 'Do you know what Lord Hood's plans are now?'

'His Lordship held a briefing with the captains of the fleet and informed them of his plans to use the fleet in the reduction of Corsica.'

'I see.'

The room was silent for a few moments while Chatham digested the news, before he raised his head.

'Very well. Thank you Mr Fury, you have been most helpful. That will be all, I think.'

Fury paused before uttering his next sentence – it was not wise to raise unimportant matters with the First Lord of the Admiralty, but he knew his chances of a speedy reappointment may lie in the Earl of Chatham's hands.

'Excuse me My Lord, if I may . . . ?'

'Well, what is it?' Chatham asked.

'I was given temporary command of a prize brig to deliver His Lordship's despatches, which is currently anchored in Spithead. Lord Hood thought it best to terminate my current posting on board *Fortitude*. I am therefore currently on half pay and I would be glad of another appointment as soon as possible, My Lord.'

Chatham looked at him in silence, causing Fury to shift nervously in his chair. Nevertheless he returned Chatham's gaze unflinchingly, waiting for the response which could decide his future. Finally it came.

'Very well, I'll be sure to bear your name in mind Mr Fury. Leave a contact address with one of the porters before you go.'

'Aye My Lord, and thank you.'

He got to his feet and put his hat back on, touching the peak to the First Lord before turning on his heel and leaving the room.

It took only a moment to make his way back down the silent upper corridor, now completely deserted, before descending the stairs and approaching the nearest porter he could find. He was relieved to see that it was not the same man he had dealt with earlier, so the task of leaving an address for him – he gave his mother's – passed away peacefully.

The coachman had pulled the carriage into the Admiralty courtyard, so that it was only a matter of three steps before he was standing with the door open shouting up to the driver to begin heading back to Portsmouth, thankful that he had been allowed the use of the port admiral's post-chaise for the return leg.

The journey back was much the same, the coach stopping overnight in exactly the same village as on the way there. He had one night's stay in Portsmouth at the Angel – he was not sure why he avoided the George Inn, but he did – during which time he called in to see Sophie and her father. Gourrier had not been successful in finding any work thus far, and so Fury had had to reach into his cash reserves once again to ensure they had enough for a further week's accommodation.

Fury only had an hour before his coach left for Swampton, but he was determined to spend some time alone with Sophie before he went. Since arriving back in England and arranging lodgings for Sophie and her father, he had been struck by the extent of his responsibilities to her. He had been so intent on bringing her out of danger that he had not considered just how much she would have to rely on him to survive, at least in the short term. The weight of responsibility was almost tangible. That said, his feelings for her had, if anything, intensified since he had first met her, and so he entered into the task willingly.

They went for a short walk through the town and along the waterfront, in spite of the bitter coldness which was exacerbated by the wind blowing in from the exposed anchorage.

'How long will you be gone?' She turned to look at him, her cheeks red from the chill wind. Fury had been pointing out the different ships at anchor in the harbour, and the sudden change of subject took him by surprise.

'A week at least. I cannot very well see my mother after more than two years and then leave her again after a day or so.'

'And then you will return to Portsmouth?'

'Yes.' Although the Earl of Chatham had promised to send details of his next appointment to his mother's address, Fury wanted to return and visit one of Portsmouth's prize agents sooner rather than later so that his claim for prize money would not be forgotten. 'Hopefully your father will have some success in finding work before then.'

'I'm sure one of us will.' She paused. 'I hope we will not be a burden to you.'

He looked at her worried face and his heart warmed to her. 'Of course not, you never have to worry on that score.' He grasped her hand and squeezed it as if to reassure her further, and he received a smile in response. 'Come on, let us get you back to your father. My coach will be leaving shortly.'

They turned away from the harbour and headed back into the town towards Sophie's lodgings, arm in arm.

'Will you tell your mother about me?' Sophie asked, after a short period of silence.

Fury had been debating that very question on his journey back from London, and had still not decided what to do. It was nothing to do with embarrassment, but his mother had always struggled to earn enough to put food on the table for Fury and his brother, and he wasn't sure how she would react if he told her he was now supporting Sophie and her father.

'Yes, I think so,' he lied, eager not to offend or worry her further.

They lapsed into another comfortable silence, each savouring the other's company for these last few minutes. They reached Sophie's lodgings and Fury left her at the front door, kissing her hand and promising to return soon. She had a tear in her eye as he turned away, and it took all his willpower to carry on walking without looking back.

It did not take long to reach the Angel, where his belongings were already packed, leaving only the paying of the bill to attend to before leaving for the coach.

His home of Swampton was in Hampshire, and was a mere forty miles from Portsmouth to the north. Even after such a long absence Fury knew every inch of it. He was surprised at the nostalgia welling up within him as he stared at the countryside with the carriage rolling along, the frost finally disappearing under the pale weak sun to reveal the harsh greens and browns of an English winter landscape. Over two and a half years away, and he was finally going back to Swampton, back home.

AUTHOR'S NOTE

Any keen students of naval history who have read about Fury's adventures at Toulon may have spotted inaccuracies in the events described. I offer my apologies for this. I have endeavoured to describe events as accurately as possible, but in certain cases artistic licence had to intervene.

For example, General O'Hara was not so lucky as to have men with the quickness of thought of Fury and Clark nearby, so that when he was shot during the attack on the Republican batteries at the end of November 1793, he was powerless to prevent his own capture.

I also had to bring forward the requisition of troops from the Grand Master of Malta for my own purposes. If I had adhered to the correct dates, then Fury would not have been around to take part in the gunboat battle with the Republican masked batteries, one of which, incidentally, was commanded by Bonaparte himself, at that time only a colonel of artillery.

Finally, I have to offer my apologies to Captain Hare, who commanded the boat which picked up Fury and Lieutenant Gore after they had successfully steered the fire ship into the inner basin. He was in fact on board the fire ship with Lieutenant Gore, risking their lives steering the blazing vessel into a position to reek maximum carnage, and although both men were badly burned, they were brought off safely.

Other events were, for the most part, as described. From my point of view, it was fortunate that the absence of HMS *Fortitude* from Toulon, occasioned by the damage she suffered during the attack on a Mortello tower in Corsica, allowed Fury the freedom to involve himself in many of the adventures surrounding the defence of that city. It also provided a realistic opportunity for him to return to England in temporary command of his own ship. It is now up to Their Lordships at the Admiralty to decide where his next adventures take him.